Creede of Old Montana

**Center Point
Large Print**

**This Large Print Book carries the
Seal of Approval of N.A.V.H.**

Creede of Old Montana

Stephen Bly

CENTER POINT PUBLISHING
THORNDIKE, MAINE

This Center Point Large Print edition
is published in the year 2009
by arrangement with the author.

First edition, October 2009

Cover photograph courtesy of
Missouri River Outfitters
Fort Benton, Montana 1-866-282-3295

The text of this Large Print edition is unabridged.
Printed in the United States of America.
Set in 16-point Times New Roman type.

ISBN: 978-1-60285-575-5

Library of Congress Cataloging-in-Publication Data

Bly, Stephen A., 1944–
   Creede of old Montana / Stephen Bly. — 1st ed.
     p. cm.
   ISBN 978-1-60285-575-5 (lib. bdg. : alk. paper)
   1. Large type books. I. Title.
   PS3552.L93C74 2009
    813'.54—dc22
   2009018870

Creede of Old Montana

CHAPTER ONE

No one knew how Avery John Creede got the scar on his face.

No one except Avery and the one who did it. He never talked about it. Most who knew him figured the other person was dead. Not the type of scar that makes you wince and turn your head, and never covered by a beard, it hung high on his cheekbone like a badge of honor.

But a person had to stand up to Creede and look him in the eye to see the scar. For the past six weeks on the trail north from Shiprock, no one had been that close.

July hot and August dry, the September heat that reflected off the brick wall left Avery with a stale feel, like a sweat drenched cotton shirt, long dried. He studied the wide river from the tiny, two-step balcony of his second-story room at the Grand Hotel. Although he could not see it now, he knew he was positioned under the arched 1881 stone façade, high at the building's peak. Like a pontiff overlooking an empty plaza, he surveyed the near deserted street below.

A lady with a famine-thin waist and a bleached yellow dress spun a parasol over her shoulder as she sauntered past the cottonwoods toward the riverbank. Like bait skimming across a still mountain lake, Avery figured she trolled for some man to set the hook.

His heavy bootheels nailed the polished oak flooring as he re-entered the cramped room past the brass bed posts to a white porcelain basin on a stand and a worn wooden side chair. He splashed tepid water on his shaved face, then glanced up at the mirror. The leather-tough forced smile and near empty brown eyes looked more like a Venetian mask than a retired cavalry veteran way past forty.

His black, beaver-felt cowboy hat, still damp with sweat from the long ride, wafted the aroma of a wet goat. He shoved it down to his ears. With oft repeated precision, he strapped on his holster. He yanked out the Colt revolver, reset the cylinder on the empty chamber and shoved it back down.

As if giving a lecture on gentlemanly attire, he rolled the sleeves on his dusty white shirt down, one direful fold at a time, then buttoned them. He never took his gaze off the dark brown eyes that stared back at him from the mirror. Shirt now fastened at the neck, he tugged the black silk tie around his collar. Rough calloused fingers completed the four-in-hand knot that he memorized as a child.

Oppressive Montana air crowded the room, like a mountain cabin after six weeks of snow in January. Avery closed the door behind him as he entered the hall, but didn't bother locking it. He wasn't sure if that was out of foolishness or apathy. Yet, years of conflict led him down the empty stairs at a cautious pace, one hand on the slick oak rail, the other on the hard walnut grip of his .44 revolver.

Wednesday died about 1 p.m. in Ft. Benton, Montana Territory. Resurrection wasn't expected for another two hours. The clock above the lifeless stove in the lobby ticked out of habit, but the pendulum winced as if the work wasn't worth its full effort.

Propped open with river rocks the size of cannon balls, the double front doors of the hotel invited a breeze that hadn't arrived yet. A wide nosed man with an uneven black beard studied the solitaire spread on the clerk's counter. He waved a seven of clubs at Avery.

"You sure you ain't never been to Purgatory?"

"I think I'd remember if I had." Avery didn't look at the man as he ambled toward the door.

"That's in Colorado, you know."

"Yeah, so I've heard." Avery parked in the doorway and surveyed the wide street.

"Maybe it was Butte . . . you ever been to Butte?"

"Many times."

"I bet it was Butte. You shot that crooked Faro dealer at the Copper Slipper, right?"

"Nope."

"He deserved killin', if you ask me."

The late afternoon sun beaconed off the big window of the Choteau County Bank as he stepped out into the empty street. The sound of the bank's heavy door slam precipitated a chorus of barking dogs.

Avery hesitated as if waiting for phantom traffic. He thought he saw shadows flicker in the narrow alley next to the bank.

"Where you goin'?" the man shouted from the hotel.

"Sailing," Avery grumbled.

Like a bit player in a melodrama, the man appeared in the doorway. "Sailin'? There ain't enough water in the old Missouri this time of the year for a big canoe, much less a . . ."

Avery's glare chopped the tail off the man's sentence.

"Eh . . . I was jist askin' 'cause you said three men would show up lookin' for you and I wanted to know where to tell them to look."

"Tell 'em to wait here."

"But if you don't come back, where shall I tell them you went?"

"Purgatory."

Avery Creede turned south toward the river. The woman in the yellow dress perched on a short wooden bench. She spun the parasol at a slow turn, like an easy target in a shooting gallery.

Avery glanced over his shoulder at the buildings behind him. The hotel door was open, as was the door at the Judith Basin Mercantile and the Rotten Gambler Saloon. Only the bank door remained closed, but now, curtains covered the afternoon's glaring light.

He tugged out his pocket watch by the gold chain and tapped on the glass as if to speed it up. Even squinting his creased eyes, he couldn't read the bank hours on the sign by the door, but noticed the window curtains sway from movement inside.

He turned back to the lady who began to saunter east. At the cottonwoods, he was cut off by the chirping protest of a female killdeer. The black stripe hung like a necklace above her white tummy, but it was the olive-brown wing that demanded his attention. Flailed out as if broken, she drummed the dirt like an Arapahoe war chant.

He allowed a smile to crease his tough tanned face as he searched the weeds for the cherished nest.

"That's a fine acting job, Mamma. But what are you doing with a nest this time of the year?"

Avery plopped down on the newly vacated bench. He massaged his chapped lips as he gazed at the slow moving, muddy water of the Missouri River. His thoughts drifted from three men he hoped to see . . . to one woman he figured he never would.

At his right, the killdeer continued her protest.

"Oh, my," the lady in yellow called out from the trail to the east. "Oh, dear," she repeated.

Avery sprang to his feet, but paused at the tone. He figured it was not a "help, there's a snake" urgency, but more like "Henry, take the garbage out and bury it right now."

Another, "Oh, my" and a loud squawk from the killdeer divided his attention.

He stared at the bird. "Diversion? Both of you are diversions." He spun back to town and stomped toward the bank.

"Could someone help me, please?" the lady shouted.

His right hand on his holstered revolver, he studied the front of the bank. In the alley shade between it and the mercantile, four long legged, solid colored Montana horses stood saddled and waiting.

The bank door banged open and a short man with a tattered campaign hat ran out, worn leather saddlebags draped over his arm. A Winchester 1873 saddle ring carbine waved in front of him.

Avery drew his gun and cocked the hammer with one motion. "Throw down!" he yelled.

"Like Hades, I will!" Jogging toward the alley, the man tried to shoulder the carbine one-handed. Before he had it any higher than the hitching post, 200 grains of lead from Avery's smoking revolver slammed into the man's thigh and crumpled the screaming bandit to the dirt. Saddlebags and carbine crashed beside him.

The shot from the second man out of the building came so close to Avery's hat that it sounded like a bumblebee on the chase. His return fire caught the robber in the right shoulder and spun him around. He tumbled face down in the bank doorway.

A bloodied teller stepped over the man and sprinted into the street. "The third one ran out the back door. He's gettin' away!"

Avery trotted to the narrow alley. His loud shout and a shot fired into the dirt in front of them, caused all four horses to panic. They backed and stumbled their way into the alley. When the dust cleared, a third bandit lay battered in the dirt. He clutched a dangling arm.

Now Wednesday in Ft. Benton resurrected. Three dozen people swarmed into the street. The first to greet him was the bank teller. "Mister, I don't know who you are, but thanks. They cleaned out my till." He wiped blood from his forehead. "I tried to stop them, but they was mighty convincin'."

"Get yourself to a doctor." Avery handed the man his bandanna.

The teller glanced back at the wounded men. "I think them three need the doc more than me."

A thin man with a silver badge on his black vest scooted through the crowd. "What happened?"

"You the sheriff?" Avery asked.

"Deputy."

"They tried to rob the bank."

"They did rob the bank," the teller reported. "What they couldn't do is get by this man. He shot two of them and run three horses over the third."

"Four horses," Avery corrected.

The teller's eyes narrowed. "Were there four of them?"

Avery pointed back toward the river. "Three bank robbers and a woman with a yellow parasol. She was the lookout."

The deputy waved for others to assist him with the injured men. "I guess we'll haul them to jail and have the doc patch them up there."

"You should have seen him," the teller told the crowd. "He stood up to them without a flinch at their bullets and shot them down. I've never seen anythin' like it."

Avery drew the toe of his boot across the dirt. "I happened to be the first one they saw when they came out of the bank."

The teller stared at the deputy. "No other man in this town would have done it."

The deputy threw back his shoulders. "I'll need you to explain this to the sheriff when he gets back from Judith Basin. Where you stayin'?"

Avery pointed at the two story brick building. "At the hotel."

"How long you goin' to be in town?"

"Depends."

"On what?"

"On Dawson, Pete and Tight."

"Who?"

"I'm waitin' for some friends to show up."

Most of the crowd followed the deputy toward the injured outlaws.

The teller winced as he rubbed the bloodied lump on his forehead. "Mister, I'm Harvey Grass. You didn't tell me your name."

"Creede."

"Just like the town in Colorado?"

"Yeah, only we're nothin' alike."

"Eh, yeah . . . well, Mr. Creede, after I get things settled down and close the bank, I'd like to buy you a drink."

"Make mine coffee."

"You a Temperance Man?" the teller pressed.

"Nope. It's just that I get quiet and introverted when I drink. I'm told that I'm not my talkative, friendly self."

The hotel clerk stood out on the front porch of the hotel when he returned. He picked at his beard as if expecting to find something. "Do you have any idea who you just went up against?"

"No."

"That was part of the Rinkman gang."

"Never heard of them."

"They hide out down on the Missouri Breaks in eastern Montana. They robbed the Northern Pacific at Gold Creek and the bank at Granite on the same day. I heard someone died in that one."

"Well, they didn't rob the bank at Ft. Benton, Montana, today." Avery studied the Missouri River from the hotel porch.

"Are you a federal marshal?"

"No." He spotted the Killdeer, but not the woman in yellow.

The clerk loosened his tie and unbuttoned his white shirt collar. "But you have been a lawman, right?"

"Nope."

"Then why did you do it? It's not even your money in the bank. You told me you hadn't been to town in five years and didn't know anyone. So, why risk your life going up against the likes of them?"

"I was mad."

"At whom?"

"The lady dressed in yellow thought she could divert me with a 'help, help.' "

"That made you mad?"

"Yeah, women have a way of doin' that to me."

CHAPTER TWO

Avery had never seen apple pie so green. The first bite slowed his appetite. The second killed it.

Harvey Grass napkined crust from his beard. "You with Custer?"

"I was part of the 7th at the Little Big Horn." Avery sipped the boiling hot coffee like it was lemonade. "But I was with Captain Reno."

The bank clerk tapped on his pie as if trying to crack a boiled egg. "Is it true that Reno pulled back and deserted Custer?"

"Harvey, you're mighty close to getting your faced mashed to look like that stale pie. Captain Reno did what he had to do to give us a fighting chance. That's more than Custer's men got. It would be to your advantage not to bring up the subject again."

"But, I thought . . ."

When Avery glared he noticed Harvey's throat lumped as if he was trying to chew a hunk of raw meat.

He coughed into his hand. "So, you are here to meet some fellow soldiers from that battle?"

"Retired soldiers." Avery licked his fork, then laid it on the plate.

Harvey carved out another bite. "Why meet at Ft. Benton?"

"We stumbled onto each other here five years ago. We had a good time at the 2-Dot Café and decided we'd meet again this summer."

"The 2-Dot Café? Didn't it burn down . . ."

"About five years ago? Yeah, I said we had a good time." The coffee steamed Avery's face and masked the bitter pie taste.

"What brought you all to Ft. Benton five years ago? I mean, if you don't mind me askin'."

"Pete Cutler and Tight Sheldon were pushin' longhorns up from Texas. Dawson Wickers was on the move after gettin' run out of Helena."

"Why did he get run out of Helena?"

"I didn't ask."

"Did you know Mrs. Sisk makes the best pie in town?" Harvey smacked his lips. "But, how about you, Mr. Creede, why did you come to Ft. Benton five years ago?"

"Remind me to try some of hers sometime." Avery shoved his plate to the middle of the table. "I came here five years ago looking for a lady."

"This is Mrs. Sisk's pie." Harvey picked his teeth with his fingernail. "Did you find the lady?"

"I'm still tryin' to figure that out."

"But it's been five years. Say, are you goin' to finish your pie?"

"Some things take time, Harvey."

"The pie or figurin' out the woman?"

18

Avery waved his coffee cup toward the bank clerk. "Help yourself."

Harvey Grass was scraping the plate when he looked up and shouted, "Hey, Doc, over here."

A man about Avery's age with short gray hair strolled toward them. "I heard I need to look at your head."

"It's just a lump, Doc, about like the one I got at the New Year's Eve Party." He wiped his beard with a linen napkin. "Here's the man you want to meet. He's responsible for your sudden increase in business."

The man tugged his tie loose, sat down, and reached across. "Dr. Robert Haksawe . . . but I'd rather you just called me Doc."

"I reckon so with a name like that. I'm Avery John Creede."

"From Deer Lodge?"

"I've been through there a time or two."

"So I heard."

The bank clerk leaned closer. "What did you hear, Doc?"

"Just rumors, Harvey. Wild rumors. Hold still and let me take a look at your head."

Avery tugged his tie down. "How are the three in jail?"

"If they don't swell up, they'll probably live. They're mad enough to make you the subject of every curse known in Montana."

"It wouldn't be the first time." Avery surveyed

two men in tight shirts who sauntered into the café. "Did they mention the woman in yellow?"

"Woman?" Doc wiped Harvey's forehead with an alcohol rag.

Avery studied the physician's clean fingernails, but avoided a glance down at his own. "A woman wearin' a yellow dress worked with them."

"I didn't hear about any woman." When the doc scratched the back of his neck, Avery noticed blood stains on his shirt sleeve. "But they implied they didn't plan on being in jail long. Sounded as if they counted on others to get them out."

"And when that happens, they will try to kill me, of course." As two men who entered earlier argued with the waiter, Avery slipped his hand to his gun.

Doc faked a grin. "They did allude to that idea several times. Fortunes of righteousness, I suppose."

"I reckon so. Hope it doesn't slow me down from doing right next time. Harvey, thanks for the coffee and pie. Let the doc take good care of you. A concussion is not a scratch."

"Where you goin'?" Harvey pressed.

"To the hotel. Maybe it cooled down enough that I can take a nap. I've been sleepin' on the ground for a week and I'm feelin' two or three years behind on my rest."

"You and your pals don't plan on burnin' down another buildin' with your jubilation, do ya?"

"I'm hoping for a decent piece of beefsteak and lots of good natured lies. But there's no telling what else will happen. I'm the quiet, bashful one of the bunch."

Whatever excitement the attempted bank robbery injected into Wednesday wore off by the time Avery sauntered across town. Other than a stage-coach parked at the livery behind the hotel, the street looked as deserted as before. A few people milled inside the shops that lined the street, each with door propped open, still in hopes of enticing a semblance of a breeze.

"Say, mister, we're havin' a sale on rings today. You interested in buying a ring?"

The short, bald man stood erect in the door-way of the City of Paris Jewelry Shop. His white shirt seeped with perspiration around his tight collar. His mustache was neatly trimmed.

"You just happen to have a sale today?"

"We have a sale every day. It's just a way to attract business."

"I like an honest man."

"Well, you found yourself the best jewelry shop in Montana." The man shoved out his hand. "I'm honest Abe . . ."

Avery hesitated.

21

"Oh, not that Honest Abe. I'm Abraham Hermann."

"Call me Avery, but I'm honestly not looking to buy any jewelry. City of Paris, you call it. Does the jewelry come from Paris?"

"Some comes from Holland. I doubt if any comes from Paris. I've never been there. Have you?"

Avery watched an old man on a swayback roan plod down the middle of the street. "Twice."

"Did you enjoy it?"

"That's what they tell me."

"Eh, yes, well, if you have the time, let me show you the new shipment I got in from my brother in St. Louis. My family has a big store there, and I . . ."

"You run a one man operation in Ft. Benton? What did you do to get banished to some remote river town in Montana Territory?"

Abraham Hermann glanced down at his polished black boots. "You are a very perceptive man. I married outside the faith. It was difficult for my family to accept."

Avery studied the man's narrow eyes. "Abe, was it worth it?"

"That was twenty-one years ago and I thank the Almighty for my wife every day that I breathe. It might have been the best decision of my life. I've got no regrets."

A grin crept across Avery's wide lips and locked in place like an eagle's talons latching onto a salmon. "I like that, living with no regrets. That's what we all want. Now, what are you going to try to sell me that I don't need?" He strolled deep into the store alongside Abe Hermann.

The jeweler surveyed his large glass display case. "What do I have the best chance of success with?"

Avery shoved his hat back and studied the shop. Every square inch of the narrow building crammed with merchandise. Racks of rings. Turquoise necklaces. Conchos for saddles and spurs. China vases. Jeweled eggs. Oval broaches. Silk scarves, ties and sparkling brass spittoons. He held his fist to his mouth and cleared his throat. "Eh, how about a woman's ring?"

"Wife?"

"No."

"Girlfriend?"

"Not anymore." Avery stared back out the open doorway at the empty street. For a second it was Ft. Collins in the spring. "I don't know if I'll ever see her again, but if I do, I want a ring that tells her she was truly missed."

"Oh . . . well, yes . . ." Abe tapped on the rounded glass display. "I have some nice ones. Did you have a price range? $2? $5? $10?"

Avery pulled out a gold coin and tossed it on the counter. It spun until it collapsed on the glass like a dizzy child. "I'll spend up to $20. But I've got one requirement."

Abe Hermann plucked up the coin and studied it. "What's that?"

"If I ever find her and she tosses the ring back at me, you'll let me return it and refund my money."

The jeweler rubbed his narrow chin. "You're serious, aren't you?"

"Yep."

"I can't imagine any woman rejecting one of our $20 rings."

"You don't know this woman."

"I don't know you, either, but I like the way you think." He held out his hand. "It's a deal."

Avery shook hands with him, then pondered the case. "Which one do you suggest?"

Mr. Hermann spread a deep-purple velvet swatch on top the counter. He removed a polished cherrywood tray from the case and spaced out five rings. "I would suggest one of these. My favorite is this one." He placed a bright gold ring with several diamonds in Avery's hand. "For the money, it's a very good buy. Just between you and me, it's probably the best value in the store."

Avery plucked them up one at a time, then rubbed his chin. "Which of these five is your wife's favorite?"

Abe glanced at the back door as if expecting her to enter. "My wife?"

24

"When that wonderful wife of yours looks at this case, which one does she say, 'Oh, Abraham, that is such a beautiful ring'?"

"Well, she likes this one with the narrow band that has rubies and diamonds."

"I'll take that one."

"It's not the best bargain. You try to sell it, one with all diamonds would be more valuable. That's my expert advice."

"And your wife, she is an expert about a woman's heart. Besides, if the lady refuses, I'll bring it back for your refund. I'll take the one with rubies and diamonds."

"Noelle will be delighted. She is a better salesperson than I am, even when she's not in the shop."

"Noelle is a beautiful name."

"Yes, and she is even more beautiful than her name. She went to Paris once as a child. Would you like it in a small cardboard box, or a purple velvet sack with silk drawstring for $1 more?"

When Avery closed his eyes he felt her body pressed close to his, but when he opened them, there was only a diamond-ruby ring, and a grinning Abe Hermann. "The box is more practical, since I have no idea when or if I'll ever see her again."

The jeweler leaned across the counter and lowered his voice. "Noelle much prefers the velvet sack."

A roar exploded across Avery's face like a racehorse breaking out after a starter's signal. "That's the first time I've laughed that deep in five years. You're right. Noelle is quite the sales lady. Stick it in the velvet sack."

The little velvet bag dangled by a lavender silk drawstring around Avery's middle finger. As he reached the hotel, voices cascaded out of the lobby where recent arrivals jostled for rooms.

Two salesmen, a bow-backed man in tattered boots, and a lady shadowed by a large floppy hat occupied the clerk. Avery meandered past, then hiked the stairs. At the first landing, he glanced around to see if anyone watched him.

None did.

When he reached the entrance to his room, he couldn't help stare at the velvet pouch and grin like Lewis Carroll's cat at his impulsive purchase. Visions of a black haired lady with wide easy smile danced in his mind. He shoved the door open.

The blonde woman inside wore a yellow dress and pointed a brass and rosewood pocket pistol at his midsection.

"You took a long enough time getting here."

He spun the velvet pouch. "I knew you'd wait."

Her thin lips tightened, blue eyes narrowed. "You don't even know who I am. You didn't know I'd be here."

26

Avery's right hand rested on the walnut grip of his revolver as he stepped forward. "You're the outside man for the three would-be bank robbers."

She pointed the pistol at his head. "Stay right there and keep your hands in front. Who are you?"

He took another pace toward her. "If I was anyone of importance, you wouldn't have to ask."

"I'll shoot you." She eased back two steps.

"What would that accomplish? You shoot me and you'll be tossed in jail with your pals. Only you'd be hung. They'll just serve a couple years in prison." Avery stalked her.

She backed into the balcony doorway. "I might hang, if they could catch me. But one thing for sure, you'd be dead before me."

He inched forward while dangling the velvet bag. "That's a good point."

She brushed blonde bangs from her blue eyes. When she squinted, wrinkles flared. "You're going to the jail with me and get the deputy to let them go."

"You think I can intimidate the deputy?"

"An angry squirrel could bully him." She pointed the pistol toward the door. "Now, go on."

"What about this?" He swung the velvet bag like a pendulum.

"What is that?"

He swung it back and forth like a New Orleans magician. "It's a ruby and diamond ring. I don't suppose you want to trade that pocket pistol for it?"

"Why don't I just take the ring and keep the gun?" She reached out her free hand.

The velvet brushed her fingertips then tumbled to the worn carpet. She stooped to scoop it up.

Avery twisted her wrist, then plucked the gun from her hand. With his knee he shoved her shoulders. She tumbled onto the tiny balcony, landing on her rear. He slammed the door and locked it from the inside.

The room echoed with the hammer of her closed fist. "Let me in!"

"Just relax. I'll go get the deputy. You'll soon be with your pals."

Her curses rattled the glass pane.

"You don't want to attract attention."

"Why not?"

He leaned close to the peeling paint on the off-white balcony door. "I told everyone in town to look for a lady in yellow, that you were one of the bank robbers. I intimated that you'd be packin' a gun and be ready to use it."

"How did you know that about me?"

"Some women are easy to read. Now, listen, keep your head down and be still. Half the people are totin' guns and lookin' for you. When folks are nervous, it's tough to tell a blessing from a curse. If you holler at them, they might panic and shoot you. You'd be an easy target on that balcony."

"Why would they shoot me?"

Avery scooped up the velvet bag and crammed it in his pocket. "You and the boys tried to take money out of the bank. That wasn't just bank money, it was their money. They take that personal. Of course, some of them will just shoot you for the reward."

The woman's voice quieted. "What reward?"

"Every bank robber has a reward. Just sit still and enjoy the fresh air. Prisons can be rather dank smelling."

Her voice quivered. "I didn't even get to see the ring."

"If you stay real still, I'll let you look at the ring when you're in jail."

"You promise?"

"You got my word on it." Avery headed for the door.

"Men are liars," she called out.

"Maybe you should form a gang of female bank robbers."

"Women are worse."

CHAPTER THREE

When Avery reached the street, a shoe bounced off his shoulder. He yanked out his gun as he caught the second shoe with his left hand.

The woman in the yellow dress glared from the balcony. "I hate you."

"I hear that fairly often." He holstered his gun and scooped up the other shoe. The black lace-up boots had been polished recently, but now were covered with dust. Avery noticed slight holes in the leather soles.

She leaned over the railing, revealing more than prudence should allow. "Give those back to me."

Avery wiped them on his pants leg. "You threw them away."

"I want them back."

"I'll give them to you when I return with the deputy."

"So help me, I'll kill you."

"You're not the first woman to tell me that either."

Avery toted the woman's shoes into the sheriff's office. A big man in a black vest perched behind the desk, a double barreled shotgun draped across his lap.

Harvey Grass reclined on a bench against the wall. He jumped up when Avery entered. The twelve foot square unpainted room smelled of grime and sweat.

Avery turned to the big man. "You the sheriff?"

"He's the mayor," Harvey explained. "Mayor, this is the man who stopped those bank robbers."

"M. J. Leitner," the man bellowed. "Most everyone calls me Mayor."

"Avery John Creede. Most everyone avoids me, if they can. Where's the deputy?"

Leitner tugged at his tie like a man who wanted to be somewhere else. "He had to go up to the Judith River country. We got word the sheriff's been shot and in a tight fix. Deputy Easley took a couple men with him and headed north. That leaves me, a haberdasher, to guard the prisoners. A sad situation, isn't it?"

Avery glanced down the narrow hallway leading to the jail cells.

"Them shoes is a little small for you, ain't they?" Harvey chided.

"I've got the lady who was helping these boys rob the bank locked up on my hotel room balcony. I figured the deputy would want to arrest her and have the whole gang."

The oak chair squeaked as the mayor leaned back. "I'm sure he would, if he were here."

Harvey folded his hands behind his head. "I

don't reckon we've ever had a whole gang in jail before, have we, Mayor?"

"I'm not sure we'll have the whole gang, even when the woman is brought in. Seven of them robbed the train near Gold Creek. That's what makes me nervous sitting here, wondering about the others."

Avery glanced at the empty pinewood gun rack on the wall. Fine dust hung in the air, as if too tired to settle. "Don't you have any other officers?"

"I'm afraid not." Leitner scratched his balding forehead. "Our two part-time deputies went with the posse."

"Maybe Harvey will watch the prisoners and you can go arrest her," Avery suggested. He drew his boot across the grit on the bare wooden floor.

The mayor shoved the shotgun on the desk. "I sell dry goods, not apprehend criminals. I have no idea how to arrest anyone." His neck flared as red as his wide nose.

To Avery, it felt like Deer Lodge all over again. He rubbed his chin as if determining whether he needed a shave. "You don't have any other lawmen in the area? A federal marshal? Railroad guards? Visiting sheriff?"

The mayor threw back his shoulders as though addressing an important campaign rally. "It's a difficult time to find men committed to public service."

Harvey jumped up. "Especially when the public keeps takin' potshots at 'em. Maybe you ought to pay 'em more, Mayor. I make better wages at the bank and I only get shot at once or twice a year."

The mayor looked straight at Avery. "Perhaps you could go back and reason the woman into surrendering."

"Right at this moment, reason is the last thing on her mind. I figure it might take two men to hogtie her and haul her over here."

The mayor slammed the desk. "Splendid idea. You and Harvey go and apprehend this woman."

Harvey rubbed the deep-purple lump on his forehead. "I've had my share of scuffles for one day. I don't want no woman bouncing a chair off my forehead."

When one of the prisoners in the back room hacked out a cough, Mayor Leitner lowered his voice. "I could deputize you two for temporary duty. Then you could take care of this matter."

"I'm not interested in the job." Avery dropped the woman's shoes on the bench. "I just want to take a nap and wait for some friends."

Mayor Leitner marched around to the front of the desk. "You won't get much of a nap with some wild woman locked on your balcony. What if I deputize you and Harvey, you bring this woman to jail, then turn in your badges."

"Do we get paid?" Harvey asked. "I could use

a few extra dollars this week, what with the shindig out at Kern's Corner this Saturday."

"Of course. The standard deputy pay is $3 a day and meals."

"A full day's pay for ten minutes work?" Harvey pressed.

The mayor pulled out a white handkerchief and wiped his forehead. "Yes, of course."

"I ain't ever been a deputy." Harvey threw his shoulders back. "What do you think, Mr. Creede?"

Avery rubbed the scar on his cheekbone. "Six dollars a day for each of us, plus meals."

Leitner flailed his hands as if trying to chase bees. "Not even the sheriff makes that kind of money. You're trying to gouge the City of Ft. Benton when we're in a bind."

"I don't want the job. I don't want the money. I'm tryin' to get the City of Ft. Benton to provide law and order. You can save money by doing it yourself. If you don't want to pay the $6, then I'll have no choice but to turn her loose, give her back her gun and tell her the only one watchin' the prisoners is a penny countin' mayor."

M. J. Leitner plucked up the shotgun. "You wouldn't do that."

"I'm not interested in doin' other people's jobs. But never underestimate a man who needs a nap. I like a quiet life."

"I reckon you abandoned the quiet life when you faced down them bank robbers," Harvey mumbled.

"You might be right. I may have to sleep with one eye on my door, but I won't have to babysit the whole city. Leitner, watch for a yellow haired lady with a yellow dress and in her stockin' feet. She'll have a sneak gun and a knife. Keep her in front of you at all times. Chances are, she'll make you use that shotgun." He tipped his hat at the bank clerk. "Harvey, take care of yourself."

"Wait . . . wait. Six dollars a day and meals it is." The mayor pulled two badges out of the drawer. "You'll just be deputies until she is jailed, correct?"

"I assure you, I don't want to remain a deputy one moment later."

Leitner held up his right hand. "Do you two swear to uphold the laws of the City of Ft. Benton, those of the Montana Territory and the United States of America, so help you God? Good. Here's the badges."

"But I didn't get to say, 'yes'," Harvey complained.

"It was a silent assent. I knew you wanted to."

"Do I need a gun?" Harvey asked.

Avery waved at the back wall. "Just grab that rope hangin' on the peg. I'll need you to sit on her while I truss her."

Harvey Grass rubbed his beard. "I ain't never sat on a woman before . . . at least not when I was sober."

"You ever brand a wild yearlin' in the brush?"

"Yes, sir. I grew up in west Texas."

"This will be the same thing, only we won't have a hot brandin' iron."

Avery's strides were longer than those of Harvey Grass and the bank clerk trotted to keep up.

"Are we in a hurry?"

"I'm long overdue for my nap."

Harvey peered down a side street. "I wonder if Miss Fontenot is still in town."

"Who?"

"Oliole Fontenot from down Cantrell way. She's a lady photographer. And I do mean a fine lady. She slipped into town last week to take pictures. I'd like to have one of me wearin' this deputy's badge. It would impress my mother."

"Harvey, you're a brave man. I saw that this afternoon. Why don't you quit the bank and become a deputy?"

"Did you ever see an old deputy with lots of grandkids?"

Avery led them across the street. "No, I don't think so."

"Neither have I, but I know lots of old bank clerks with big families."

"A good point."

Grass waved at the hotel. "Say, you flyin' a flag from your room?"

"What flag?"

"Look at the balcony railin'. Looks like a white flag. Or is it yellow?"

Avery trotted to the front steps of the Grand Hotel. "I surmise that's remnants of her dress. She must have sliced up her clothes and made a rope, then let herself down. She's one determined female, that's for sure."

"I thought she was wearin' a yellow dress?"

"Yep."

"Then what's that white part of the rope?"

Avery pulled the torn garment toward him. "Her petticoat."

Harvey looked up and down the street. "Then what's she wearin' now?"

"A blush, I reckon."

They still gawked at the homemade rope when the hotel clerk marched out. "Mr. Creede, I really must protest. This is a first class hotel. The manager has instructed me to issue you a warning about mistreatment of women in your room."

"A first class hotel wouldn't tell a woman with a loaded gun what room I'm staying in."

"She said she had news for you from a friend. So, I figured . . ."

"You were wrong."

"Nonetheless, if this happens again, you will

have to find other accommodations." The clerk's eye twitched like an amateur poker player who thought he held the winning hand.

"Are you the one who is going to toss me out of my room, or is that the manager's job?"

"Eh . . . that's for the sheriff or the deputies."

"We're the only deputies in town." Harvey beamed as he pointed to his silver badge.

"Yes, well . . . I'd appreciate it if you removed the torn dress." The hotel clerk spun and stormed back inside.

Avery handed his badge to Harvey. "Take this back to the mayor. Tell him we didn't need to be sworn in after all. She's gone and that's fine with me."

"But we ain't been paid."

"You can negotiate with the Mayor. I'll agree to whatever you decide."

Harvey shoved the badge back at him. "We can't quit now. We swore we'd be deputies until she was in jail."

"I said I'd be a deputy for ten minutes . . and the ten minutes is up."

"Can't we remain deputies until I get my picture took?"

"You keep the badges. Go get your picture, then turn them in. Tell the mayor to be on the lookout for a yellow haired lady, because she'll try to get those men out of jail."

"A yellow haired lady with no dress. Sort of

like that old tale about Lady Contriva, isn't it?" The bank clerk's grin revealed crooked, but clean white teeth.

"I think it was Lady Godiva, but Contriva fits this situation."

"You know, if we were to stay deputies for one whole day, I could do rounds tonight. I always wondered what it would be like to stroll into the Golden Horseshoe with a badge on my vest."

"You do whatever you like." Avery jerked on the dress rope, but it held tight. "I'm retiring right now."

Avery tossed the wadded up dress in the corner of his room and tugged off his tie. He sat on the bed, then shoved off his scuffed black leather boots. His gray socks felt thin, but clean. They didn't sag, but they were soaked with sweat.

He locked the door to the hall, but left the balcony doors open. He positioned the pillow at the foot of the bed, so he could lie down and keep an eye on both entrances.

A dark haired lady clung to his neck as they huddled in the alley shadows. Her thin body pressed against him felt more yielding than her tone. "I have to go to New York. I don't know why you won't come with me." Her voice was pitched high, but not irritating.

He relished the long embrace. "You know how I feel about cities."

"Avery, people change. Just because you had bad experiences as a boy, doesn't mean it would still be the same."

"Traveling two days on the stage and six more days and nights by train to attend a wedding of someone I don't know, and be surrounded by people who can't tell a beehive from a bake oven, is not my idea of time well spent. She's not even your relative."

"I can't miss Evelina Renalt's wedding. My mother would never forgive me."

"Your mother passed away last year."

"She would want me to go."

"You said you haven't seen Evelina in eight years."

She kept her warm arms wrapped around Avery's neck. "That's not the point."

"What is the point?"

"One must never refuse a Renalt invitation."

"Is that some Code of the East?"

She pulled away. "Are you mocking me?"

Avery drew her back into his arms. He nuzzled her black hair until his lips feathered her ear. "I'm missing you already," he whispered. "You are the most wonderful thing that has ever happened to me. I don't want to turn you loose even for three hours, let along three weeks. Please stay with me. I need you. All the battles in the past seem neutralized by your presence." Her soft, pink lips brushed against his rough, chapped ones.

This time, it was her voice that dropped to a soft whisper. "Do you mean that?"

"Yes, I mean it. In fact . . ." He let out a deep sigh, then looked straight into her eyes. "I need you with me so bad, that if there's no other way . . . I'll go to New York."

"That's sweet." She clutched him tight. He could feel every part of her body.

"I mean it."

"I know you do, Avery. Why didn't you tell me all of this when I was with you? Why did you wait until now? Until the middle of a dream?"

A knock on a door turned both of their heads.

Avery sat up. His shirt collar was damp and the dark haired lady gone. He yanked his revolver out of the holster.

"Yeah?"

"Mr. Creede?"

"Yeah?"

"Frederick Scully. I'm the owner of the Choteau County Bank. Can we talk?"

Avery jammed his gun into the holster, then swung open the door. A tall, thin man with dark mustache and gray wool suit strolled in and surveyed the room.

"Look, I was just doin' my job as a concerned citizen." Avery tried to stretch the crook out of his neck. "I don't need a reward."

Scully folded his arms then rocked back on the heels of his well polished, black boots. "I should say not."

A horse fly buzzed at the open balcony door. Avery unfastened his damp collar. "What do you mean?"

Scully tugged a folded paper from his coat pocket. "The bank robbers took $3,640 from the bank this afternoon. When I finished re-depositing the funds, there was $3,140 in those saddlebags."

"You mean the crooks had time to stuff some of the money in their pockets?"

"I've been at the jail and searched them all. They don't have the money and they certainly didn't have enough time to hide any."

"So why did you come see me?"

"They said to ask you what happened to the rest of the money."

Avery glared at the man. "Are you accusing me?"

"Mr. Creede, the sheriff and the judge can do the accusing. I'm just reporting to you that money is missing. It would be in your best interest not to leave town until this matter is solved."

"Scully, those three in jail will say and do anything to get even with me for standing them down. It's a wonder they didn't claim I shot

President Garfield and inflicted the black plague on Europe."

"I'm a banker, not a gunfighter." Scully parked himself in the doorway. "All I know is that $500 is missing and unaccounted for. I intend to recover my funds."

Avery stormed at the banker until Scully backed out into the hallway. "Understand this . . . I didn't take your money. I don't know who did. For all I know, you are skimming the funds. I will come and go as I please. And I will try to refrain from stopping any others that choose to rob your bank."

The banker's face flushed. "You can't intimidate me."

"You were intimidated the minute you heard one man stood down an entire gang of bank thieves. You were panic-stricken when you walked in the door of my room and demoralized when you crawled out. If I pulled my gun right now, you'd lose your dinner all over the dusty burgundy carpet. Good day, Mr. Scully."

Avery slammed the door, then stalked across the room. He paused by the cloudy mirror and examined the face with scar. "Well, Creede, what a pleasant fellow you are. Why did you jump all over him? It was the dream, wasn't it? You were mad at yourself and Scully appeared to take the blows. You can survive without her . . . but not very well."

He traced the scar, then leaned so close his suntanned nose touched the mirror. "And what are you doing in Ft. Benton, Montana? You don't even want to be here. But then, you don't really want to be anywhere."

Still in stocking feet, he shoved on his hat, strapped on his revolver, then pulled the lone wooden chair out on the balcony. A slight, late afternoon breeze drifted up the Missouri River. He turned the chair toward the lithesome wind, then plopped down, his feet perched on the railing.

Hat tugged low in the front, Creede closed his eyes. His mind wandered to Denver, Lake City, Ft. Collins . . . and a long, dry trail through Wyoming.

The sun set behind the hotel. Most of the street lamps had been lit. The lingering daylight serenaded like an overture before the play began. The streets below filled up with cowboys and horses. A rap at his hotel door brought Avery to his feet.

Both legs had fallen asleep propped up on the balcony railing and were wooden, lifeless. He braced himself on the chair and hobbled back into the stuffy room.

There was another knock, a softer one.

His feet reached the painful tingling stage. He called out from the footboard of the bed. "Yeah?"

44

The voice was male, yet tentative. "Can I talk with you?"

"Who are you?"

"Could you open the door?"

One hand on the wooden grip of his revolver, he unlatched the lock and cracked the door an inch.

In the hall stood a young man about sixteen or seventeen, sporting thick brown hair and wearing nothing more than the bottoms of some off-white, long handle underwear.

Avery glanced up and down. "You got the right room, son?"

"He's got the right room," a lady growled as she stepped around in front of the boy. She pointed a snub-nosed revolver at him.

"You?" Avery groaned. "Can't I get rid of you?"

"Get back in the room." She motioned with the barrel of the gun and both of the men retreated. She kicked the door closed so hard that it rattled the mirror above the wash basin.

"I see you found some clothes," Avery said.

"Those are my clothes," the young man protested.

"I figured that. A rough cotton shirt and ducking trousers don't do much for you."

"You ruined my dress," she complained.

"You're the one that sliced it up."

"You forced me to do it."

"What did he force you to do?" the kid said.

Avery turned to the woman. "What's this all about?"

"You're going to the jail and get them out right now, or I shoot this boy," the woman said.

"Why? Who is he? I don't know this kid."

"Yes, you do," she insisted.

Avery studied the pale skin, thin body, shaggy hair. "How'd you get involved with her, son?"

"She lied to me."

"That's not hard to believe."

She shoved the gun in the young man's bare ribs. "The boy says you are his uncle."

"He's mistaken. I don't have a relative within two-thousand miles. And my nephew was about six years old last time I saw him and lives in . . ." Avery recognized something in the boy's crooked grin. His hand slipped off the grip of his holstered revolver. "Ace?"

The boy's eyes widened. "No one calls me Ace but my Uncle Avery."

"Ace?" Avery stammered again. "What are you doin' all grown up?"

"I'm almost seventeen, Uncle Avery."

"Enough of this," the woman interrupted, "you do what I say or I'll . . ."

"Hush," Avery barked. "This is my sister's boy. Ace, you're supposed to be in Ohio. What are you doin' in Montana?"

"Looking for you."

The woman in man's clothing ground her teeth. "I'm not kidding, I'll shoot the boy."

Avery eased between the woman and the boy. "Where's your mother?"

The boy hesitated. "She died last spring."

A cramp hit his right side. Avery John Creede struggled to catch his breath. The pain wouldn't let go. "Rebekah's dead?"

"I wrote to you in May."

"Do you two understand I'm about to shoot you?" the woman hollered.

Tears puddled in Avery's eyes. "I didn't get the letter. What happened?"

"Doctor Hutchinson said it was pneumonia."

"Where's your stepfather?"

"Who cares? He ran off a couple years ago."

"Why didn't she write and tell me that Robert left her?"

"I don't think she was too proud of it. Hard for mom to admit she should have never married the guy."

"I tried to tell her."

The woman shoved the gun in Avery's back. "And I'm telling you to do what I say."

Avery ignored the sharp jab and draped his arm across the boy's shoulder. The boy stood about four inches shorter. "How in the world did you find me?"

"A lady in Denver said you'd be in Ft. Benton this week to meet some friends."

47

"I'm going to shoot the boy," the blonde woman insisted.

Avery glanced over his shoulder. "You aren't going to shoot anyone. Be quiet for a minute." He turned back to the boy. "What lady?"

"A black haired woman who has a smile that makes a man's heart beat fast."

"She was in Denver?"

"I went into every hotel in Ft. Collins asking if they had a Avery John Creede staying there. She overheard the conversation and told me she knew you."

"I suppose she was on her way to New York."

"She mentioned going to San Francisco."

"San Francisco? No, no . . . she's going to a wedding in New York."

"Enough of this!" The woman in ducking trousers jumped between them. "I'm going to shoot this boy if you don't help me."

"I haven't seen young Avery Creede Emerson in ten years."

"Well, take a final look, because he won't be here long." She aimed the gun at the boy's head.

Avery raised his hands as though to surrender, then stomped on her toe, and caught the gun as it dropped. Midst her hollers and curses, he shoved her face first on the bed, then sat on her backside like a chair.

"Ace, I still can't believe you're standing here in Montana."

Avery Creede Emerson rubbed his bare arm as if he were cold. "I can't believe I'm standing here in my longjohns."

CHAPTER FOUR

"Uncle Avery, are you the sheriff here?"

"Just a temporary deputy. As soon as I get this fine example of feminine loveliness locked in the jail, I'm retiring."

"Can I stay with you?"

"I insist. But it might take a little while for this to sink in. I lost my sis . . . gained my nephew . . . this is quite a day."

"It's a lousy day, if you ask me," the woman whined.

"Ace, hand me that curtain sash."

Avery pulled the woman's hands behind her and lashed them together.

"You have no idea the trouble you are in," the woman snarled. "It's not just those who are in jail. There are seven more riding this way and I'll make sure they let me drag you behind a horse for five miles before I shoot you."

"That gives me something to look forward to."

"You . . ."

"Look, lady, I'm going to give you an option. You can hike down to the jail either gagged or without a gag. But I don't want any yelling and cussing. What's it going to be?"

"Don't gag me. But you are a dead man."

"Ace, you stay here. I'll put her in jail and be right back with your clothes."

"You goin' to strip her, Uncle Avery?"

"You're not touching these clothes, you . . ."

Avery's hand slapped over her mouth as he pointed to the dresser. "Get me a clean bandanna."

Her voice lowered a bit. "I'll be quiet until you get me to the jail."

When they reached the bottom of the stairs, the hotel clerk met them at the front door. "Mr. Creede, this is your final warning. Guests are complaining about all the screaming coming from your room. The couple in the room next to you demanded to be moved."

"Get out of the doorway."

The man jumped aside. "I'm serious. We run a respectable establishment. I believe your kind would be better off at the Riverside Hotel."

"My kind? Just what kind is that?"

"I'll tell you what kind you are," the woman sneered. "You're a . . ."

One glance from Avery silenced her.

"You're a gunman . . . a shootist . . . and heaven knows what else," the clerk muttered.

"You are right about one of the three. I reckon heaven does know what I am. Probably even better than I know. And mister, I'm not leaving this hotel. In fact, I want to rent that room next to me. Put it in the name of Avery Emerson, my nephew."

"You're joking."

"Do I look like the kind of man who makes jokes?"

"Eh, no, sir."

Avery nudged the lady through the door.

The shadows were long, the air slightly cooled, and the sidewalks busy on the dusty street of Ft. Benton. Creede avoided the crowded, raised boardwalk and marched her down the middle of the street. Some pointed. Some mumbled. All stared.

A short lady in a gray dress and burgundy hat marched out to them.

"Mister, I don't know who you are, but you get that poor lady off the street right now."

"I'm the temporary deputy and I'm taking her to jail. You won't have to look at her long."

"You're not taking her to jail like that."

"He is a mean and vicious man," the blonde lady growled.

"Don't worry, dear, I'm the president of the W.C.T.U. and we will not stand for this."

"This 'dear' is part of a gang who robbed the bank today, and she tried several times to kill me."

51

"That's no business of mine. But no woman on earth should be humiliated by being forced to wear vulgar trousers and a flannel shirt. I insist you get her off the street and buy her a nice dress."

"And shoes," the blonde added.

"You don't care what she's done as long as she's properly dressed?"

"It is below any woman's dignity to be forced to dress like a man."

"She ripped her last dress to shreds."

"I've had some old dresses that were better off as rags, too." She grabbed the blonde's arm and lead her toward The Emporium. "They have some nice ready-made dresses on the back wall. I'm sure you can find something you like. I think a yellow or a pale blue would look best on you."

The Emporium carried everything from shovels to shoes, from sluice boxes to silver flatware. Some customers trailed after them as Avery marched the bound woman toward the back of the store.

A tall, thin, bald clerk scurried after them. "Are you the one who stopped the bank robbers?"

"Yeah. And this is one of the gang. But I was told by the fine women of this town that she should be allowed to wear a dress to jail. Do you have a place where she could change?"

"In the back room," he motioned.

"Grab a dress," Avery ordered.

"I can't select a dress with my hands trussed behind my back."

Avery tugged the curtain sash off her arms.

She sorted through the dresses and shoes. "You know, I could just run out that door. I don't think you're the kind of man who would shoot a woman in the back in front of all these people."

"You're right. I couldn't shoot you in the back. But I could shoot both legs out from under you."

"You would, wouldn't you?"

"Without hesitation."

"I can't believe anyone as mean as you has lived this long."

"It's a mystery to me, too. Now get in there and put a dress on."

"Which should I choose? The lavender or the blue?"

"I don't care."

"I just can't decide."

"Wear the blue," he shouted.

Everyone in the store turned to stare at them.

"Oh, do you like me in blue?"

"Lady, I don't like you at all, but the blue matches your eyes."

"My eyes? So you have noticed my features."

"I've looked at more of you than I ever wanted to, and I hope that after today I will never have to look at you again. Is that clear enough?"

She pulled the blue dress off the peg. "This might take a minute."

"I'm sure it will. Just don't get shot."

"Shot?"

"If you try to escape out the back door, I will shoot you."

"But you can only be in one place. How can you guard the back door and this one at the same time? I have a fifty percent chance of escaping."

"And a fifty percent chance of being shot."

"I know, I know . . . in both legs." She disappeared into the back room.

Twelve and a half minutes later she emerged, wearing the blue dress and black, lace-up shoes. "How does it look?"

"You don't care what I think."

"You're right. I bundled your nephew's clothes." She handed him a package wrapped in brown paper, tied with thick, rough string.

He took the package and pulled his gun. "Give me the scissors."

"What?"

"I want the scissors you cut that string with. You are packing them so you can stab me. Give them to me."

Several customers clustered near them.

"I think you are . . ."

"You want me to search for them?"

"Yeah!" a boy about twelve called out.

She turned her back to the crowd, reached under the full dress, and pulled a pair of scissors from her garter. She shoved them at Avery, sharp end first. "You know, I am going to be the happiest woman on earth when you are dead."

"You'll have lots of company. Put your hands behind your back."

"If I promise not to try to escape, may I keep my hands free?"

Avery glanced at the crowd, then tucked the package under his arm. "Go on. Let's get this over with."

The store crowd followed them to the front door, but by the time they reached the street, few paid them much attention. The sun had now disappeared behind the hotel, but the twilight prolonged the day. Most of the stores had turned on their lanterns and their dim glow softened the early evening.

With his right hand resting on the grip of his holstered revolver, Avery marched beside the woman. "Lady, I can't figure you out. Even if you got away with the bank robbery, you'd have to light out for Texas, or live out in the Breaks, always looking over your shoulder. There are better ways to live."

"Look, shoot me in both legs but I don't intend

to listen to moralistic tirades and sermons about how to live my life."

"How old were you when your mother died?"

"Why did you say that?"

"You didn't answer me."

Her shoulders slumped. "I was eight. Is it that obvious?"

"You remind me of someone I used to know. Were you raised by your dad or someone else?"

"My father took off the day my mother died and never came back. I was raised by my older brothers."

"Are your brothers part of this gang?"

"One is. Two were killed. The fourth one lives down on the Yellowstone somewhere . . . I think. Now you know everything about me."

"I know very little about you. I don't even know your name."

"Everyone calls me Sunny. But you are the mystery to me."

"I'm Avery Creede."

"I don't care what your name is. I can't figure you out. You risk your life to stop a bank robbery, but at the time you weren't a deputy or anything. Why would you do that?"

"Maybe my life does not hold as much value to me as you expect."

"That's good, because I don't think you're going to keep it long."

• • •

The front door of the sheriff's office was propped open with a round river rock. The shuttered windows gave the room a dark, stale feel.

"Mayor?" Avery called out.

"Maybe no one's home."

"Mayor, Creede here. Are you in the back?"

"Not exactly what you were thinking, is it?" she prodded.

"Sit down in that chair."

"What chair? I can't see anything."

He led her to the shadowy desk. "That chair."

While she plopped down, Avery struck a sulfur match on the side of the desk and lit the kerosene lantern. The features of the room danced in the shadows.

"I told you, no one is home."

Both of them turned when a groan filtered from the jail cells.

"Sounds like your pals are still back there. Let's give them a visit. They will be so happy to see you."

Sunny led the way. Avery carried the lantern in his left hand, his gun in his right. The iron doors on the right and left cells stood open. Avery cocked the hammer on his Colt revolver. He eased up to the rear right cell.

"Don't shoot me," a voice cracked. "I told you all I know."

"Mayor? What are you doing in there?"

"Creede? You're alive? Did you see them?"

"Who?"

"Six armed men."

Sunny chewed on her lip, then stared at the floor. "I told you they'd come for us."

"Mayor, what happened?"

"They plowed through the door and got the drop on us. They yanked the others out of jail."

"Are you hurt?"

"I think my skull is busted."

"Where's Harvey? Is he here?"

Mayor Leitner nodded toward the corner of the cell. "They killed him."

"They killed Harvey? But, why?"

"He wouldn't tell them where she was."

"I warned you they'd come . . ."

Creede jammed the gun against Sunny's temple. "Don't tempt me. You have no idea how close you are to getting shot."

"And you have no idea how little your threat means now," she murmured.

The groan from the mayor riveted their gaze.

"We've got to get you to the doc. Are there other keys?"

"The bottom drawer on the right in the office has a false back. Some extras should be stowed there unless the sheriff carried them with him."

Avery marched her out to the office at gunpoint and retrieved the extra keys.

"Your only chance is to turn me loose. If

they catch up with you holding me prisoner, they'll kill you," she said.

He shoved the barrel of the revolver in her ribs. "Get in that first cell. They aren't coming back. They abandoned you to face the murder charge."

"They will come for me. I guarantee that."

He clanged the cell door closed and locked it. "Lady, there is one thing . . ."

"I told you my name is Sunny."

"No one is named Sunny. Is that what your mother called you?"

"She called me Faustina."

"Eh . . . I reckon I'll call you Sunny. There is a flaw in your theory about those outlaws who rode in. If you were confident they would spring your pals, then why were you in a hurry to do it yourself? You could have just sat in the shadows and waited for them to bust out your pals. I saw the look in your eyes when you saw your pals had been sprung. You didn't look all that happy at their release."

"You have no idea what you are talking about."

"That's true enough. But you didn't tell me I was wrong, either."

Avery swooped in and helped the mayor to his feet. "Sit on the bunk for a second and get your breath." He tied a bandanna around Leitner's bloody forehead. Then he knelt down beside the slain bank clerk and temporary deputy.

"Harvey, you were a friend. In less than eight hours you survived a bank robbery and were shot at close range wearing a deputy badge. Life isn't fair, but heaven will be. And I'm hopin' you're there now. I'm sorry you got into this mess. I'm sorry I got into this." Avery pulled off his own deputy badge and tossed it on the bunk next to the mayor. "I'm not wearing the badge now, but I'll track them down. You can count on that."

"You can't quit now."

Elbows on knees, head in hands, Avery sighed. "Mayor, I told you I'd take this job until that lady was in jail. Well, she's behind bars, so I resign."

"This is all your fault."

"What is my fault?"

"If you'd have let them rob the bank, and get away, none of this would have happened. I wouldn't have been in the jail. I wouldn't have gotten my skull crushed, and Harvey would still be alive."

"You're blaming me for Harvey's death?"

"I'm just saying you can't walk away until this matter is cleared up."

"Just watch me." Avery Creede stomped out into the sheriff's office. Mayor Leitner shuffled behind.

"Who's going to guard me?" Sunny shouted. "They'll kill me."

Avery glanced back. "Who will kill you?"

"You can't leave me here," she wailed.

"It's out of my hands. I resigned." He turned to the mayor. "You stay here. I'll find the doc and send him over."

"I'm not staying here. They'll kill me."

"Why would they come back to the jail?"

"When they can't find her in your hotel room, I assume they'll be back."

"My hotel room?" Avery boomed. "I thought you said Harvey didn't say anything."

"He didn't. I wasn't so brave."

"You sent them over to ambush me?"

"I was trying to stay alive. Anyway, you are here, so they failed on that account."

"Ace! You sent an outlaw gang to my room and my kid nephew is there!"

"Your nephew? You didn't say anything . . ."

"Take me with you, Creede," Sunny screamed. "Please, if they got to your nephew, it will be too late. I know where their hideouts are. I'll take you there. Please."

Avery trotted back into the jail and opened the iron door. He grabbed her arm and jerked her out of the cell.

"That hurts."

"Not as much as a 200 grain bullet."

They reached the street at a trot.

"Slow down!"

"Lady, I don't care if I drag you, I'm not slowing down."

She scampered beside him. "Will you really go after the whole gang if they harmed your nephew?"

"You can bank on it. Will you really show me their hideout?"

"Yes, I will."

The clerk stopped them at the bottom of the stairs of the stuffy lobby. He packed a short barrel shotgun and shoved a brown paper at Avery John Creede.

"Get out of my way," Avery said.

"Mr. Creede, this is your eviction notice. We want you out of the building within the hour."

Avery shoved him aside.

"This last episode is unacceptable. You will be responsible for damages."

Creede took two stairs at a time, his revolver in his right hand.

"I can't keep up," she protested.

He released her hand and sprinted to his room. The door was busted open.

"Ace?"

The mirror was shattered, the contents of his saddlebags strewn across the wooden floor. He stomped over to the tiny balcony and spun back around as she appeared at the door. "They took him."

"That's not good."

"Do they think they're going to trade him for you?"

"I don't think they will do that. They want me dead, too."

Avery slumped down in the green velvet chair and rubbed his forehead. "They aren't getting Ace. I will not let this happen." Avery leaped up and waved his fist at the ceiling. "Did you hear me, God? I will not let this happen!"

CHAPTER FIVE

The menacing check of a Winchester lever brought Creede out of his depression, but it was too late to raise his gun. The fat man in a tight gray suit pointed an 1873 carbine at his head.

Creede raised his hands in disgusted resignation. "Who are you?"

"I'm the hotel manager and you are leaving right now. And take your woman with you." The bulge in the man's cheeks had a red, almost rouge glow.

Sunny folded her arms around her midsection, then tilted her head. "I am not his woman."

The hotel manager pointed his carbine at her as if she were a delinquent student in a classroom. "Whatever you call yourself, and whatever your occupation, moral or immoral . . . you are leaving with him."

She grabbed the kerosene lantern and marched

over to the man. "Are you calling me a soiled dove?"

Sweat puddled on his round face. "You might be the Queen of Romania, but I do know you're leaving."

"Mister, you might want to watch your words," Avery cautioned. "If she tosses that lantern out into the hall, your hotel will burn to the ground."

"My word, she wouldn't . . ." The color in his cheeks paled.

"She would." Avery lowered his hands and relaxed his shoulders. "You don't want to get her stirred up."

"Stirred or unstirred, I want both of you out of my hotel right now." The warble in the voice betrayed the bravado of the words.

Sunny circled the man as if inspecting a pumpkin. "You can't throw him out. He's Avery John Creede."

"I don't care if he's Stuart Brannon, you are both . . . did you say Creede?" He had to stiffen his knees to keep them from buckling. "As in that ruckus in Virginia City?"

Avery rubbed his scar. "That wasn't my fault."

"You shot seven men?" Each word coughed out like a cat with a furball.

"Eight if you count the one in the outhouse." He winked at Sunny.

Her arms dropped to her side. "You shot a man in an outhouse?"

"He was tryin' to hide."

"It doesn't matter." The rotund man stood straight and pushed his chest out even with his stomach. "You have left me no choice but to throw you out."

Avery stomped over to the man, each crack of his bootheel on the hard wooden floor making the manager flinch. "Mister, you couldn't throw out the dishwater. Put the gun down before you get hurt."

The man staggered back, but kept the carbine pointed at Creede. "I'm warning you. You and this . . . this . . ."

"I believe you called her the Queen of Romania."

"Both you and the queen, get out of my room right now."

"I paid until next Saturday. I'm not leaving." Avery stood no more than a foot in front of the man.

The man took another step back. His eyes glanced out into the hallway as if looking for help. "If you think I won't shoot, you are mistaken. Now get your duffle, this woman, and the lad next door and get out of my hotel."

"Lad next door?" Avery repeated.

"The clerk said you wanted to rent the room next door and foolishly did so while you were gone. Now, put some duckings on the boy and get out of my hotel."

Avery grabbed the muzzle of the barrel and shoved it up. The shot blasted through the hammered copper ceiling and the report sent shock waves that slapped his ears.

He jerked the carbine from the hotel manager's hand and tossed it to Sunny. She aimed it at the hotel manager.

By the time Avery made it to the hall, Avery Creede Emerson, still in longjohns, stood in front of the adjoining room, rubbing his eyes.

"Did you shoot someone, Uncle Avery?"

"Ace! Where have you been?"

Sunny and the hotel manager followed him out to the hallway. "Give me back my gun," he whined.

"I was so dadgum tired from the stage ride that I fell asleep. The hotel clerk said you rented this room for me."

Sunny poked the carbine into the manager's ribs. "You need to go upstairs and see if you shot anyone." Then she turned to Ace. "Your uncle thought you were kidnapped or dead."

"Shot anyone? I didn't . . ." the manager stammered.

"You pulled the trigger," she said.

Ace examined Sunny from shoes to smirk. "You look better in a dress."

"I'm glad I pass your personal inspection."

"I didn't mean . . ." Ace blushed.

Her narrow eyes riveted on his. "It's obvious

what a sixteen-year-old boy means."

He stared down at his bare toes. "Why aren't you in jail?"

Avery pointed at Sunny. "There was trouble at the jail. The gang of outlaws broke in, killed a deputy and roughed up the mayor, then took off with the prisoners. Looks like they came over here. Didn't you hear anything in my room?"

The manager glanced up the stairs, then loosened his tie. "Oh, my, if anyone was injured up there."

When Ace rubbed his eyes, he curled up little balls of dirt. "I must have been asleep. The gunshot woke me up." Ace stared at the carbine in Sunny's hands. "Is she going to shoot him? I've never seen anyone get shot."

"I hope not." Avery shoved the muzzle of the carbine toward the floor. "I'm glad to see you alive. I had visions of losing all my relatives in one day."

The hotel manager sprinted up the stairs.

Sunny turned the gun toward the two of them. "Did you notice that I'm now holding the gun?" Her light brown eyebrows peaked.

Avery stepped between Ace and the gun. "You can't shoot me."

"Oh, yeah?"

He lectured her as if she were a naughty dog. "Who would protect you from your friends? Or do you think they've left town?"

Sunny lowered the carbine. Her narrow shoulders slumped. "They won't leave without making sure I get what I deserve."

Ace's hands now covered himself as if he were naked. "Do you have my clothes?"

Avery rubbed the back of his neck. "I left them at the jail."

"At the jail?" Ace stomped down the hallway. "What am I going to wear?"

Avery stepped closer to her. "Why are you so sure your pals have turned on you?"

Ace spun around and hollered, "Uncle Avery, dadgumit, I need to get dressed."

"Go find something in my room."

"I think it's a matter of pride." She gazed over the mahogany railing at the lobby below. "They swore they'd kill us if we left the gang. Now they intend to keep their word."

"You think they'll kill those in jail?"

"They will have to. None of the gang can escape."

"So they will be coming after you next?"

Ace scooted between them. "I want to know what I should wear."

Sunny shoved the carbine against the boy's temple. "Get in there and get some of your uncle's clothes on right now. And don't come out until you are dressed."

"Eh, yes, ma'am." Ace disappeared into the room and slammed the door.

She handed the carbine to Creede, but he refused to take it. "Look, it's a long story. But the truth of the matter is, we needed the money from that bank to pull away from Rinkman and the others. They are crazy down there in the Missouri River Breaks. It's like a kingdom with an evil, inhuman king. The three you righteously jailed are probably all dead by now."

"That's why you were so frantic to get them out."

"I just don't want to die. Not now. Not this way."

"That's the first time you've made any sense. I'll try to keep them from killing you. But you're still a part of that bank robbery gang. You have to face charges."

"With the others gone, who's going to implicate me?" She pushed the blue dress off her shoulder and batted her eyes . . . "Judge, this mean man, Avery John Creede, was infuriated because I rebuffed his advances. That's why he's saying these horrible things about me. I was just an innocent girl on an afternoon stroll along the river."

Avery shoved his hat back. "Yeah, and I suppose you'll whimper that you are really attracted to the strong, judicial type?"

"Oh, yes, that is true. I am."

"At the moment, all I'm concerned with is keeping me and Ace out of harm's way."

"And all I want is to get as far away from here as fast as I can."

"The stage doesn't leave until morning."

"And there isn't a boat scheduled until Saturday."

"Have you got money to pay for a stage ticket?"

"If I did, we wouldn't have needed to rob a bank."

"How far do you want to go?"

Sunny batted her long eyelashes. "How far would you like to go?"

Creede stared at her wide eyes.

"That's a joke. I'd like to get to Denver. I've got a friend named April Hastings who has a place in the mountains west of town. I could hide out there."

"April's burnt down. You didn't want to go there anyway."

"Where do you think I should go?"

"I hear Purgatory is nice this time of year."

Ace popped out of the hotel room and brushed off the sleeves of his oversized suit coat. "How does this look?"

Sunny never took her eyes off Avery. "Now you're the one joking, right?"

Ace tugged at his brown wool trousers. "That bad, huh?"

Her glance was quick, like the last toss in a game of darts. "I was talking to your uncle. You look like a little kid wearing a man's outfit."

The pitch of his voice faltered. "I'm sixteen."

"It will do until we retrieve your other clothes," Avery said.

Ace jammed his hands in his trouser pockets. "Are we going there now?"

"I can't go out on the street." Sunny stared down the steep staircase. "It's dark, and they will be waiting in the shadows."

"Ace and I will go. You wait here."

"If they can't find me in town, they'll come back to the hotel."

Avery nodded at the open door. "Then wait in Ace's room. We'll pick up his clothes at the jail, then return."

Her voice was barely above a whisper. "How do I know you'll come back?"

"Because I said I would."

"I'm hungry," she announced.

"We'll bring you something to eat."

"I don't eat fish."

"You'll be lucky to get bread and water."

"You really know how to spoil a girl, don't you?"

"I don't know a thing about how to treat a woman."

"That's obvious. If you bring back beef, include a nice red wine."

Creede rolled his eyes.

"Never mind the wine. But be careful. They won't hesitate to shoot you in the back."

"You seem very concerned about my safety."

"Only until I get on the stage in the morning."

"But you said you didn't have any money."

She dangled a velvet bag in front of her. "I could sell this ring."

Avery lunged forward. "Give me that."

Sunny jerked it back. "Isn't that just like a man? Give me a ring and then demand I return it."

"Why did you give her a ring, Uncle Avery?"

"I didn't give it to her. She stole it."

"Why do you have a woman's ring, anyway?" Ace quizzed.

"It's a long story. Give it back."

"Will you loan me the stage fare?"

"Will you promise to never return?"

"Yes, and I'll promise that if I see you on the street in Denver, I will completely ignore you."

"Good. I've got plenty experience in being ignored."

Sunny rubbed the velvet pouch as if it were a kitten. "I'd like to meet her someday."

"Who?"

"The woman who doesn't deserve this."

"You don't know what you're talkin' about."

She reached over and patted his arm. "This time, I do."

Ace scratched behind his ear. "Well, I don't know what you two are talking about."

Avery plucked up the velvet bag and shoved

the carbine in her hand. "Stay in the room with the light off, and the gun aimed at the door. Just don't shoot us when we come back."

"You trust me by myself?"

"I'm hoping you run off."

"And I'm hoping you stay alive."

"At least until you are on the stage?"

"That would be nice. By the way, I don't like asparagus, just in case it's on the bill of fare. And don't forget dessert. I haven't eaten all day."

"Do you like Mrs. Sisk's famous pie?"

She licked her thin, pale lips. "Pie sounds real good."

Avery tugged the front of his hat down. "With any luck, they won't have any left."

When they reached the lobby, the manager and the clerk conferred at the front desk.

"Mr. Creede . . ."

"Don't aggravate me again."

"I've spoken with the mayor and he assured me you are on city business. But you must see my position. People are leaving the hotel. Mr. and Mrs. MacGregor in Room 302 have just checked out."

"I trust they weren't injured."

"No, but their mirror was shattered."

"And their nerves, no doubt. You shouldn't tote a gun around the hotel like that. However, I did think about us leaving."

The fat man's eyes sparkled. "That would be splendid."

Avery peered back up the stairway. "But then, for your sake, I decided to stay."

"Why?"

"Some men seem to be intent on killing me. I believe they are still in town. If they can't find me, they might come back to my room. Now, if I leave, and you rent it to someone else . . ."

"Good heavens, they might pop in and kill the wrong man."

"That wouldn't be good for business, would it? So I'll just keep the room and save you the grief. Where did you see the mayor?" Avery sauntered toward the front door, still propped open with a river rock.

"He was on his way home from Dr. Haksawe's. He was severely injured, you know. The doc gave him some medicine and told him to go get some rest."

The thin clerk stepped up beside the manager. "Are you still looking for three friends to join you, Mr. Creede?"

The manager raised his hands as if in surrender . . . or praise. "Are they like you? Perhaps they could stay elsewhere."

Avery Creede stepped out into the Ft. Benton night. "I reckon they will stay wherever they want."

● ● ●

Compared to the heat of the day, the evening air had a hint of coolness and humidity off the Missouri River. Avery tugged his tie loose and unbuttoned his shirt collar.

Ace matched him stride for stride. "Uncle Avery, is your life always like this?"

Avery's arm circled his nephew's shoulder. "No, most days it's not this peaceful."

They crossed the street in front of the Emporium and ambled down the boardwalk in front of the closed City of Paris jewelry store.

"Ace, I'm glad to have you out here with me, now that your mamma's with the Lord. But you need to know, if there's trouble in any town, it finds me out. It's always been that way. You might live a longer life back East."

"I reckon I'll take my chances out here. Will you teach me how to be a gunman like you?"

Avery paused to watch two men ride down the middle of the street. He didn't move or speak until they turned the corner. "No, but I'll teach you how to defend yourself."

"That's what I meant. Maybe I should buy myself a revolver and holster."

"I've got an extra, but there's no reason to wear one unless you know how to use it. Most men who get shot out West are packing a gun they can't handle with any accuracy. That's like trying to ride a wild bronc the first time you ever saddle a horse. It's a guaranteed disaster."

Ace stopped and gazed through the window of the café.

"Don't do that. Get over here," Avery called from the darkness of the alley.

With eyes wide like a raccoon caught in a chicken house, Ace scooted into the shadows. "What did I do wrong? I was just checking out the food."

"Never park in front of a lit window at night. You cast a dark silhouette and make an easy target for someone across the street."

Ace gazed out at the dark, but starlit night. "Easy target? Who would want to shoot at me?"

"If you go around claimin' to be the nephew of Avery Creede, you'll get shot at."

They continued to plod down the boardwalk.

"Why do people want to shoot you?" This time, Ace's voice drifted into a whisper.

Avery felt his face tighten as he grinned. "They're jealous of the scar on my face, I surmise."

"I've been meaning to ask you . . ."

"Don't."

"Man, woman or beast?"

"Yeah."

"Yeah, what?"

"It was caused by a man, woman or beast." Avery nodded at the next open door. "Are you hungry, too?"

"Yes, sir."

Avery pulled out three one-dollar coins and dropped them in his nephew's hands. "Go buy us three meals. Take them over to the hotel. I'll meet up with you and Sunny in your room. Leave my room empty in case those hombres come back."

Ace rattled the coins until Avery clamped his hand tight.

"Where are you headed?" Ace asked.

"I'm going to the jail to make sure someone took care of Harvey and to pick up your clothes. I'll be back in a few minutes. Let no one in until I get there."

"What do you want to eat?" Ace shoved the coins into his coat pocket.

"Get me whatever has beef in it and is quick."

"I heard you mention pie. Shall I get us some?"

"Under no circumstance."

Avery slowed his pace as he approached the darkened jail. He set his boots down soft on the raised wooden boardwalk as he held his Colt revolver. The heavy wooden door swung open slowly as he stepped inside.

He crouched down in the corner of the dark office and waited. He could hear the rattle of a freight wagon on the street and shouts or curses from down the block, but the room was silent.

He pulled a cartridge from his bullet belt and tossed it across the room.

Still no movement or sound.

He stood and scooted toward the desk, fumbled with the upper right drawer and pulled out some sulfur stick matches. The kerosene lantern needed the wick trimmed but he lit it anyway. It emitted a dull, dim glow. Avery set it on the desk and looked around the room.

He retrieved his cartridge and the bundle of clothes perched on the bench against the wall. As he carried the lantern back to the desk, a shadowy flash of plaid clothing down the runway between the cells caught his eye.

"Harvey, did they leave you back here?"

Avery shoved the package of clothing onto the desk, then plodded to the cells. He froze when he spotted a body sprawled on the dirty wooden floor of the first cell. Yanking his gun out of the holster, he spun around with the lantern and inspected the other cells.

His voice was weak, as if he were listening to someone else. "What are you guys doing back in jail?"

He held the lantern higher and spotted head wounds in each of the men.

"They shot you just like she said. But why did they bring you back here? What's the purpose in that?"

He spun back around as the front door rattled.

A startled man who wore a badge and toted a short barrel shotgun blustered through.

"Creede! What are you doing here?"

"Deputy Easley? I'm glad to see you back." Avery shoved his revolver into the brown leather holster.

The deputy shuffled to the cells. "You didn't answer my question."

"Is the sheriff okay?" Avery quizzed.

"I just left him at the doc's. I'm not sure he'll make it, but at least I got him home." Easley pointed to the men on the floor. "What's going on back there? What are they doing on the floor?"

"That's what I'm trying to figure out. I came for Ace's clothes . . . and . . ."

"Who?"

"My nephew."

"Blazes, Creede, these men are dead." The deputy shoved the shotgun in Creede's side. "Pull off your gun belt. Did you think you could just walk into the jail and shoot the prisoners?"

"Put the gun down, Easley. Others in the gang came and busted these guys out when the mayor was here."

"And you rounded them up, stuck them back in their cells and shot them?"

"Why on earth would I do that?"

" 'Cause you don't want them talkin' to the judge." He jammed the muzzle of the shotgun hard into Avery's ribs. "Maybe you know more than you're admittin'."

Creede backed away. "Easley, a lot has happened since this mornin'."

The deputy motioned toward the empty fourth cell. "Get in there."

"Don't shove that in my ribs again."

The growl in Avery's voice caused the deputy to back up. Avery marched away from the cell.

Easley's voice started to falter. "You heard me. Get in the cell."

Creede held the lantern up between their faces. "Go talk to the mayor. He knows what's going on."

"He doesn't know nothin' right now. I was just over there. The doc gave him some laudanum and he's out like a bear in December."

"Look, I'm on your side in this. I've been filling in while you and the sheriff were gone."

"Yeah, I bet you have. Get in the cell until we get this figured out."

Avery shoved the lantern into the deputy's hand. "I'm going over to the hotel. I'll be there all night and tomorrow morning. Check with the mayor when he comes to. You'll find out."

"And what if the mayor don't come to? How do I know you didn't cold-cock him too?"

"Then you can come to the hotel and try to arrest me. But you'd better bring help, because you can't do it by yourself."

"I said, get in that cell," Easley shouted as if trying to scare off a grizzly bear.

"I said I won't go." Avery hiked past the deputy and strolled toward the office. Even in the flickering light, he could see the bundle with Ace's clothes perched on the edge of the desk. He saw the front door standing half open. And the lights from the saloon across the street.

Then he saw nothing at all.

CHAPTER SIX

Creede woke up in the dark, slumped against someone's shoulder. The back of his head pounded. He sat up and gulped in rank air. "This smells like . . ."

"It is, Uncle Avery," a voice murmured. "You're in a two-holer behind the jail."

He peered in the direction of Ace's voice, but couldn't see him. "What am I doing here?"

"The kid saved you from being lynched."

Creede rubbed his throbbing head but couldn't see her either. "Sunny! What are you doing here?"

"We pulled you out of jail." Her voice filtered down from someplace higher. "The drunks got mean and hauled out a rope."

"They are scouring the streets for you now," Ace reported.

His right leg pinned underneath him, Avery struggled to find a more comfortable position. "Who is?"

Ace shushed him, then whispered, "Deputy Easley and his makeshift posse."

Avery unfastened the top button of his shirt and massaged his neck. "I'm guessin' Easley cold-cocked me. But that doesn't explain why I'm hiding in an outhouse."

"A lot happened while you were sleeping." Sunny's voice was a lot closer to his ear this time.

"Where's my gun?"

With Ace's shoulder pressed against his, Avery figured they were both sitting on the dirt floor.

"In the sheriff's office, I reckon. Uncle Avery, I've got your backup gun. Do you want it?"

Creede felt the cold walnut grip pressed in his hand. "Not until my head clears a little. Fill me in on what I missed."

Ace's voice lowered an octave in midsentence. "As near as we can tell, Deputy Easley believes you murdered the three in the jail because you were part of the gang and didn't want them to reveal that."

The outhouse door eased open to the starlit sky. Sunny stuck her head out and sucked in a breath of air, then closed it. "They say you took the $5,000 that's missing from the bank sacks."

His elbow on his raised knee, Avery cradled his forehead in his hand. "$5,000? Frederick Scully of the Choteau County Bank told me it was only $500 that was missing."

"There seems to be a revision," she quipped.

"So Easley tossed me in jail and then stirred up a bogus lynchin' mob? Why didn't he just hang me while I was unconscious?"

"I suppose he wanted a horde to take you from his control so he could feign incorruptibility," she said.

"Don't you just love the big words she uses?" Ace replied.

"I've heard her vocabulary on several occasions. Don't repeat any word which you don't know the meaning." Avery shoved his boot against the door and opened it a crack. Balmy night air rushed in. "How did you two get involved?"

"We were hunkered in the hotel room waitin' for you," Ace explained. "Eating cold supper and you know . . ."

"Yeah, I know . . . you were hunkerin' . . ."

"Did you know Miss Sunny used to be an actress?" Ace announced.

"Used to be? I watched her performance down by the river this morning." Avery patted the back of his aching head. "Go on . . . what did you do besides hunker in the dark?"

"We watched the door until we heard the ruckus outside in the street."

"A crowd formed," she added. "We knew you must somehow be part of it."

"I ate your pie, Uncle Avery."

"That pie would make any crowd angry." Avery pulled his foot back and let the door close. "Was Easley the one stirring things up?"

"At first," she said. "But it seemed to be Scully, the bank owner, that was most insistent. He claimed that you killed Harvey to silence him, too."

"So the drunks in the saloons came out to see some excitement?"

"That's about it." Ace heaved a big sigh. "You know what? The pie wasn't all that good, Uncle Avery."

"Did you see any of the Rinkman gang?"

Sunny stepped to the door for another gasp of fresh air. "No, but they had to be there somewhere."

"So, how did you two get me out of jail?"

"My son and I approached the deputy and asked to speak to him in private about a very delicate matter involving Mr. Avery John Creede."

"Your son? He's big enough to be your . . ."

"She made me slump."

"How did you get by the Rinkman gang?"

"She wore a bonnet and shawl."

Creede sat straight up and tried to work a cramp out of his back. "I'm afraid to ask. Just what was the delicate matter?"

"Sunny claimed that you had taken immoral advantage of her years ago when she was fifteen, and I was your illegitimate son. She wanted to identify you so she could file a charge."

"What a horrible story. You've been around town all day . . . how did he fall for that?"

"Deputy Easley hadn't seen me." Sunny's voice turned husky. "Besides, I can be very persuasive."

"Wooowee, Uncle Avery, you should have seen the way she dressed under that shawl. You could almost see her . . ."

"I don't want to hear about it. I don't want to see it."

Ace chuckled. "Well, the deputy didn't mind it a bit."

"It was nothing too revealing, I assure you," she added. "Once we were both inside the sheriff's office, it didn't take much to persuade the deputy to get trussed up and tossed in a cell."

"Which one of you did the persuading?" Avery asked.

Sunny stepped back from the door and let it close. "I think it was when Ace shoved the muzzle of the .44 revolver into his mouth and

85

cocked the hammer. The deputy seemed quite accommodating after that."

He could make out his nephew's shadowy silhouette. "You did that?"

"I just kept thinkin' 'what would Uncle Avery do?' "

"I've never done that in my life."

"Well, it worked."

"And then this kid nephew of yours tossed you over his shoulder and toted you out the back-door and into the outhouse. Then he snuck back into the jail and we waltzed out the front door as if nothing had happened."

Ace struggled to his feet. "The crowd just sat around waiting for the deputy. When he didn't show, they finally burst in. By then we were in here."

Avery took Ace's outstretched hand. "And the only one who can explain this is the mayor."

"We hear he's passed out on laudanum," Sunny said.

When his knees started to buckle, Avery braced himself against the outhouse door. "He'll come to sooner or later."

Sunny grabbed his arm to steady him. "Later might be too late."

"So, what's your plan?"

"I figure I should sneak out and get us some horses, while you and Sunny stay here. It's time to light a shuck, Uncle Avery."

"I don't run. I never have. I'm not startin' now."

"That's all noble and good, but this might be a judicious time to consider it," Sunny said.

Avery pulled himself away from her grip, then stretched the kinks from his neck. "I don't run. It's not negotiable."

"And I don't like being lynched," she snapped.

"You should leave now. Ace and I will take care of this."

"Don't give me that. I broke you out of jail. I've got enemies that want to kill me out there. And the three that were murdered were friends of mine. I'm not going anywhere."

"What do you think we ought to do, Uncle Avery?"

"We've got to get out of this outhouse before we are fumed. You two will have to sneak over to the mayor's house and drag him back here. I'm too woozy to be of any use for a while."

Ace pushed the door open and glanced up and down the alley. "But the mayor's passed out. Even if we get him here, what good will that do?"

"We'll wake him up. Bring him to the back door of the jail. I'll meet you there."

Ace coughed, then cleared his throat. "You going to sneak back into the jail?"

"It's the last place they will look."

Enough light filtered to reveal Ace still wearing Avery's oversized suit. "What happens if we can't get the mayor? What if the crowd finds us out?"

"Grab the closest horse and get out of town."

"Oh, so it's okay for us to run away?" Sunny mocked. "It's just the noble and brave Avery John Creede who's allowed to stay and fight."

"There's nothing wrong with a strategic retreat. But the Lord didn't give me that ability."

She shoved the door wide open. "Are you blaming your disagreeable personality on the Almighty?"

"I blame God for nothing, but I will give him credit for my blessings."

"What blessings?"

"The two of you."

"Easley must have really clobbered you in the head. It's been a long time since any man thought of me as a blessing."

Ace stepped out in the alley. "Do you want this gun?"

"You take it. I'll find mine in the jail."

Sunny followed Ace outside. "Do you think this plan will work?"

Avery stepped out behind her. "Do you?"

"You haven't got one chance in a thousand."

"Good." Avery stretched his arms straight out, then brushed off the sleeves of his jacket. "I've had worse odds."

A drift of cool and fresh air in the alley behind the jail refreshed Avery. Stars still littered the Montana sky, but the night that surrounded them had turned from soot black to charcoal gray. From what he could tell, only a few lights lit Main Street. Most of the distant noise emanated from the direction of the saloons.

Avery squatted outside the rear door of the jail. Rough-cut pine scraped the calluses of his hands. He eased the door ajar and slipped inside. In the darkness, he paused long enough to study the silence. He crept between the cells into the office out front. He felt his way along to the desk, retrieved the sulfur matches and struck one.

The smoke curled and stunk as shadows flickered across the room. He retrieved his holster and gun. A sharp pain flashed through his skull as he shoved on his hat, so he tossed it back on the desk next to the bundle of Ace's clothes. Another match revealed there were no longer any bodies in the jail cells. He retreated into the cell closest to the back. He left the jail cell door swung open about a foot.

After checking the chambers of his revolver, Avery blew out the match. He slid to the floor, his back against the wall in the cell's corner.

He tried to comb back his hair with his fingers, but dried blood matted it.

Though his head still throbbed, Avery fought

to stay awake. He forced himself to think about Dawson, Pete and Tight. He pondered where his cavalry pals might be and what kept them from the reunion. He thought about his sister, Rebekah, how her sweet, believing nature was both her strength and her weakness. He tried to remember why he didn't go see her at Christmas. He knew he had a reason at the time, but like all the previous reasons, it too had fled. He thought about Ace . . . almost grown, but still a kid. He tried to let it sink in that he was now in charge of raising the boy, but that only made his head throb more.

He thought about Sunny, how she spent most of the day trying to kill him, and most of the night trying to keep him alive. He wondered how the day would have turned out, if he had just strolled with her along the river and ignored the ruckus at the bank. His mind wandered to Deputy Easley whom he didn't know at all. Something didn't feel right, like he was in a play in the theater and everyone had a script but him. He pondered Harvey's brief friendship and his untimely death. Avery felt an increasing responsibility to bring Harvey's killers to justice.

But Avery John Creede refused to think about a woman with thick black hair that cascaded like a wavy waterfall halfway down her back. He blocked out of his mind the way her whole body yielded to him with every soft kiss. And he banished the notion of the exhilaration he experienced in her presence. While not thinking about the woman with black hair, he discovered the velvet pouch with the ruby and diamond ring still tucked in his coat pocket.

The creak of the rear door snapped him back to the darkened jail cell. He pointed the revolver and waited. The morning daylight now contrasted the alleyway with the jail's interior. The silhouette was familiar.

"Uncle Avery? You in here?"

Creede struggled to his feet. "Yep. You got him?"

"Yes."

Avery stole near the back door. "Did you have any trouble?"

Ace laced his fingers together and cracked his knuckles. "His wife was sound asleep in the chair next to his bed with a blue bottle of laudanum in her lap. She must have taken a nip or two herself."

"Is he awake?"

"Nope."

Avery slipped his gun back into the holster. "How did you get him here?"

Ace peeked inside the back of the jail. "We rolled him up in a carpet and propped him on top of a wheelbarrow."

"And no one stopped you?"

"No one said anything."

Avery helped tote the mayor into the jail cell. They laid him, still rolled in the carpet, on the bed. They shoved the wheelbarrow across the alley, then closed the back door and returned to the cell. Enough daylight oozed through the front window to allow them to find their way around.

"Where's Sunny?" Avery asked.

"She went to the hotel to gather up our gear. Are these my clothes?"

"That's them." Avery returned to the cell with the mayor. "That gang could be waiting at the hotel."

Ace unwrapped the bundle and took off Avery's coat and shirt. "She said she could sneak in without them knowin' it."

Avery paced up and down the hallway between the cells. "I didn't want her to do that. Why didn't she do like she was told and come back here?"

Ace pulled up his ducking trousers and buttoned his long sleeve flannel shirt. "She don't seem the type to do what she's told."

Avery peered out the front window at the early dawn. "Now we'll have to rescue her."

"She's one strong willed woman." Ace yanked on his boots.

Avery marched back to the jail cells. "She's a stubborn and foolish woman."

"She used the same two words about you." Ace strapped on the holster.

"Let's unwrap the mayor and see if we can rouse him."

Bootheels slamming on the sidewalk caused them both to duck down at the back of the cell and yank out their revolvers.

"Keep your gun hidden until we see how this plays," Avery whispered. "Follow my lead."

The door banged open. Deputy Easley and another man blustered into the office.

Avery strained to hear every word.

"Get us some coffee boilin'."

"Do you reckon they left town?"

"If we can't find them after four hours, they are gone."

"I'd feel better if we had hung him."

Avery peered over the bed but couldn't see anything.

"Runnin' off ain't a bad thing. It proves he's guilty, don't it?"

"He's not guilty, but folks are going to think that way."

"Where are the matches? Are you sure we'll get $100 each for this?"

"In the top righthand drawer. We'll make a whole lot more, once I'm sheriff. I told you, me and Rinkman have a plan."

Drawers slammed. "Here they are, over on the bench. How can you be sure about becoming sheriff? The sheriff might recover. He ain't dead, yet."

Avery could hear the kindling crackle.

"You ever know of anyone gut shot twice recovering?"

"I didn't know he took two bullets."

"He did. I should know."

"Why didn't you just let him die up at Judith Basin?"

"A heroic rescue looks good when a man is runnin' for sheriff."

"How about a lynchin'?"

"Sometimes it just can't be helped. Don't have to worry about it now."

"Hey, Easley, are you puttin' carpet in the cells now?"

Avery signaled for Ace to lie flat on the floor.

"What?"

"Looks like a roll of carpet back in cell # 4."

His eyes squinted almost tight, Avery watched the man approach.

"Shoot, Easley, you got two more dead men in this cell!"

The deputy sprinted to the cell. "That's him . . . that's Creede!"

"Rinkman must have plugged him."

"Well, I'm goin' to make sure he's dead," Easley growled.

Gun drawn, the deputy squatted next to Creede and groped at his neck for a pulse. Avery's left hand yanked on the deputy's tie, his right shoved the barrel of the revolver deep into his neck. "Tell your pal to drop his gun."

"Drop the gun," Easley yelled.

"What?" the man in the hall wheezed.

"You heard me."

"Move aside and I'll plug him."

"Elias, I'm a dead man if you try that. Do what he says."

The gun crashed on the hard wood floor. Ace scampered to retrieve it.

Avery shoved Easley and Elias into cell # 3.

"You can't get away with this," the deputy threatened.

"That's a dumb line. You read that in a dime novel? You were caught trying to bushwhack me. You have accused me of murder, when you admit I didn't do it. I'm not trying to get away with anything. You two will spend a long time in jail or a short time at the end of a rope."

Easley paced inside the cell. "You can't prove anything. It's our word against yours. And there's a lynch mob that won't believe a word you say."

"In that case, we might as well shoot them both. Right, Uncle Avery?"

"If neither of them want to confess, I reckon they force us to that."

"Can I shoot them? I need the practice."

"Practice?" Elias said. "What kind of kid are you raisin', Creede?"

"He's got a lot to learn, but he's makin' good progress. Start out with the short one and see how you do. I'll keep Easley covered."

Ace rubbed his smooth chin. "Should I shoot him in the gut or the head?"

"Wait . . . this is crazy," Elias protested. "I'm not going to get myself shot for a lousy $100. This was all Easley's idea."

The deputy slammed his fist into the man's jaw. Both men tumbled to the floor. They exchanged several blows, then Easley yanked a knife out of his boot. Avery fired a shot through the ceiling.

"Drop the knife," he shouted, and shoved the cell door open.

As the report of the .44 faded, the knife dropped. The front door of the sheriff's office was flung open and a half-dozen men poured in.

Easley waved his arms. "That's Creede, boys, shoot him. He's a dangerous man."

Ace leveled his gun at the crowd and Avery aimed at Easley. The crowd hushed.

"Shoot him," Easley shouted again.

An unshaven man wearing a bowler rocked back on his heels. "They got the drop on us."

"Shoot him anyway."

Avery grabbed Easley by the collar of his shirt and pushed him out in the hallway. "This is a good time to find out who your friends are. Anyone of you draws his gun, the deputy dies.

It's the deputy who is in league with the Rinkman gang. He's the one you need to jail."

"If you draw your guns at once, he can't shoot all of you."

"I ain't worried about him shootin' all of us," the bearded man said. "I'm just worried about him shootin' me."

"I reckon we can just wait and see how this hand plays out," another man offered.

"You boys know me. He's just making this up to save his skin. He's nothin' but a gunman from the Breaks and he's trying to rob us blind," Easley ranted. "You can't believe a word he says."

"Then believe me . . ." a muffled voice from cell # 4 rumbled.

"It's a talkin' carpet," one of the men mumbled.

Another man stepped closer to the cells. "You got one of them Arabian talkin' carpets?"

A third man trailed behind. "Arabian flyin' carpet," he corrected.

"It flies, too?"

"I'm Mayor Leitner, get me out of this rug and keep Easley behind bars."

CHAPTER SEVEN

The hotel clerk's thick lips curled at the edges, as if suppressing a smile. "Mr. Creede, all our rooms are taken."

Avery drummed the wood floor as he paced in front of the reception desk. "What do you mean? I have two rooms rented in this hotel and you know it."

The clerk adjusted his tie, then clinched his hands together. "Your blonde lady friend checked you out. She said you were leaving town."

Avery waved his black felt hat. "I paid for those rooms."

"Please, lower your voice," the man said. "I reimbursed her for the days you didn't use. She has the receipt."

The stench of spending half the night on the floor of the outhouse hovered about Avery's clothes. He used his hat to fan himself. "You know for a fact I am waiting for three friends. Why would I leave?"

The man rocked forward on his toes, but was still six inches shorter than Creede. "I assumed you changed your mind."

Avery reached across the counter and grabbed the man by the tie. "I didn't change my mind. I want my rooms. And I want a hot bath." Hushed voices of hotel guests descending the staircase caused him to loosen his grip.

The clerk pulled away from the counter. "That's quite impossible. I told you, those rooms are rented to others now."

Two ladies in silk dresses with hats to match strolled toward the desk, sniffed with upturned, narrow noses, then retreated toward the open front door of the hotel.

Avery stalked the lobby like a hungry wolf. "Where's my gear?"

"She took it."

"Took it?" Avery gazed out the front window at the two ladies who promenaded toward the river. Framed by cottonwood trees, the scene had the feel of a peaceful gallery painting. He turned back to the clerk. "Took it where?"

"That's not my concern. She drove a buggy up, loaded your belongings, and drove off."

Avery kneaded his temples in hopes his mind would clear. "She left in a buggy?"

"I believe it was Mr. Markson's buggy from the livery, but I'm not sure. All one-horse, black buggies look alike."

The blazing sun warmed the back of his neck as Avery stomped out into the street. He kicked dirt as he lumbered in the direction of the raised sidewalk on the north side of Main Street.

Sweaty toes rubbed against his thin wool socks.

A short man shot out of a store doorway as if jabbed with a hot poker. "Mr. Creede . . . Mr. Creede, may I have a word with you?"

"Abe, I really don't have time to shop."

"No, no, I'm not trying to sell you anything. I was wondering if you heard about why the bank is closed today? I need to cash some notes."

"Maybe it's because Harvey was killed yesterday." He glanced back at the imposing red brick bank building. "You heard about that, didn't you?"

"Oh, yes, everyone in town knows what happened at the jail. In fact, at first, some said that you were the one responsible for the shootings. I knew that couldn't be. I am a very good judge of character. I told my Noelle, 'Mr. Creede would never do that.' But Mr. Scully runs the bank by himself when Harvey has a day off, and he wasn't there this morning. Several of the other merchants in town searched for him, but he seems to be missing. I thought perhaps you knew something."

"The bank owner is missing?"

"I don't know . . . but no one knows where he is."

"Well, I'm looking for somebody, too. So, I'll keep an eye open for him." Avery ambled down the street to the east.

Abe Hermann scurried along the raised boardwalk to keep Avery's pace. "It is a real inconvenience not having the bank open."

"You have lots of funds tied up in the bank?"

Abe hopped off the sidewalk, leaned close to Avery, took a deep breath and fanned his face with his hand. "I only use it for daily cash and check exchange. Mr. Scully never gained my confidence. My family didn't build a jewelry business by trusting others with our funds. But some of the store owners . . ."

"The Gentile businessmen?"

Hermann grinned and revealed pearl white teeth. "Yes, they have more confidence in the bank. They are quite worried."

"The mayor is doing better. Perhaps you should talk to him. I've resigned my short tenure as deputy." Avery suddenly stopped and put a hand on the man's shoulder. "But, you can do something for me. I've got to ride out and see if I can track Harvey's murderers. I'm expecting three friends to come to town looking for me. Can you keep an eye out for them and tell them I'll be back in a day or two?"

"Certainly. Who should I look for?"

"Dawson Wickers, Pete Cutler, and Tight Sheldon."

"I presume they will pack guns on their hips. What do they look like?"

"Me . . . only shorter."

"Mr. Creede, when you come back to town,

Noelle and I would like to invite you to our house for supper some evening. I told her all about you."

"I'd like that. I'd also like to see Ft. Benton when it is peaceful and quiet."

"Except for the Fourth of July, this town is quite sedate. The biggest problem we had for weeks was dogs barking at night. That is, until . . . eh . . ."

"Until I came to town? Yeah, I get that a lot."

A bald man with a black visor scurried out to them. "Excuse me, are you the Avery John Creede that seems to be stirring up the town?"

"I'm Avery Creede, and mister, Ft. Benton has not begun to see what I can stir up when I get mad."

The man backed away. "Eh, are you mad now?"

Avery held his thumb and forefinger within a quarter inch of each other. "I'm that close." He studied the man's attire. "You a Faro dealer, or what?"

"Oh, no . . . no . . . no," Abe Hermann grinned. "This is Bryan DelRoy, one of our telegraph operators."

DelRoy waved tan pieces of paper. "I have two telegrams for you."

"There's a telegraph office in Ft. Benton? But you don't even have a railroad."

"Yes, but we believe we'll have one by next summer."

Abe Hermann shrugged. "At least some people think we will get a railroad. That's what every town in Montana hopes."

DelRoy threw his shoulders back. "We put in the telegraph line ourselves, as an encouragement to lay the tracks this way. I taught myself Morse Code."

Avery held one message in each hand. "Wait, this one is not for me. It's addressed to some lady . . . Mary Jane Butler."

The man pushed his gold wire frame glasses higher on his nose. "I assumed she was with you. Is that incorrect?"

"I never heard of Mary Jane Butler."

"My mistake." The man plucked the telegram from his hand. "Would you like to respond to your message?"

Avery unfolded the telegram and turned to the full light of the sun. Abe Hermann moved closer. "Perhaps it's from one of your friends who is late."

"No, it's from . . ."

"A lady?" Abe pressed.

"Eh, yeah . . ."

"The lady you bought the ring for?"

"Eh, yeah."

"And she is coming to see you?"

Avery stared at the words on the page. *"Avery, dear, we must talk. I simply can't go to New York without you. I'll be in Ft. Benton in three days. Wait for me, please. Carla.*"

The jeweler cleared his throat. "Well, is she coming to see you?"

"Yeah."

"Splendid. The two of you are invited to our house for supper. I look forward to seeing the ring on her finger. What is her name? I'll keep an eye out for her."

Avery folded the telegraph and slipped it into his shirt pocket. "Carla Loganaire."

"As in the Loganaires of Chicago?"

"Eh, yeah."

Ace led two saddled horses straight at him as he approached the livery stable. "Uncle Avery, guess what? The livery guy rented out his buggy early this morning to a yellow haired gal with a blue dress." Ace handed him the reins to the buckskin horse.

Avery adjusted the saddle and yanked the cinch tight. "Sounds like Sunny."

Ace circled to the left side of the black and white paint. "I think so, but she used a different name."

Avery swung up into the saddle. "Faustina?"

"That's a horrible name." Ace stabbed at the stirrup with his left boot but missed. "Why would anyone name their child Faustina?"

"I don't know why anyone would name a son Avery Creede Emerson." Avery leaned forward and patted the horse's neck. "What name did she use?"

"Mary Jane Cutler." This time Ace's boot found the stirrup and he yanked himself up into the saddle.

Avery spun his horse three times to the right. "You mean, Butler, don't you? Mary Jane Butler?"

The paint started to pitch, but Ace slapped his rump. The horse settled down. "No, he showed me the ledger she signed. It's Mary Jane Cutler."

Avery spun his horse three times to the left. "Wait a minute . . . there was a telegram for Mary Jane Butler . . . and now you are telling me there is a Mary Jane Cutler? I can't believe a small town like this has two women with such similar names."

Ace kicked the horse's flanks to catch up with his uncle. "What I'm saying is that Miss Sunny signed her name, Mary Jane Cutler. Where are we going?"

"To the Emporium to get you a hat and pick up some grub. So her real name is Cutler? Just like Pete? The telegraph operator must not know as much Morse Code as he thinks."

"Who's Pete?" Ace ran his fingers through his curly hair. "I don't like hats, Uncle Avery."

"I don't care. You're wearing one. Pete Cutler is one of the three friends that I came to Ft. Benton to meet."

"You think Miss Sunny might be related? Hats make me look like a kid."

Avery rode up to the hitching rail in front of the Emporium. "You are a kid."

Ace stopped next to him. "So, where are we going?"

"We're going to find the yellow haired gal named Sunny. I don't have any idea if this gal has a connection to Pete. She could just be stealin' the name. And then we are goin' to find the ones that killed Harvey Grass."

Ace slid to the ground next to his uncle. "I never heard of someone pretending to be someone they aren't."

Avery looped the reins over the hitching post and headed for the Emporium. "Remind me to tell you about Tap and Pepper Andrews some time."

"Who?"

"Never mind. We'll find her. And we'll find who killed Harvey."

"That's a whole gang. It doesn't seem like a fair fight."

Avery's lips almost curled into a smile. "I reckon if you stay out of it, the odds will be about even."

Ace hiked up the stairs. "I'm confused."

"Confused is a mild word. It's sort of a peaceful condition compared to where I stand. You know those dreams you have when you think you are falling?"

"Like falling through the black of night and there's nothing you can do about it? Yeah, I get those."

"That's what my life's like." Avery held the door. "Only my eyes are open."

Ace strolled into the crowded Emporium. "I reckon it will settle down sooner or later."

"Nothing in my life has ever settled down." The door banged shut behind him.

When they saddled up, Ace sported a dark gray, beaver felt hat with wide brim and rounded crown. He pushed it to the back of his head. "I think my hat will fall off."

"If it does, I'll tie it down with a purdy pink ribbon."

"You would, wouldn't you?"

"Trust me."

"Are we going after Miss Sunny now?"

"Yeah, we need to find her first . . . then go after the others. What direction did the livery-man say she was headed?"

Ace aimed the paint southwest. "She told him she was going to Great Falls."

"There's nothing there but a couple of houses." Avery turned the buckskin east. "She's headed back to the Missouri River Breaks."

"How do you know that?"

Avery kicked the horse and trotted south.

"It's the opposite direction from Great Falls."

Ace rode parallel until the trail narrowed. "So we're headed down river? Why would she go back? I heard Miss Sunny say she wanted to get away from there."

"She also said her name was Faustina. I'm not sure what to believe."

"I like Miss Sunny. Do you like her? She told me you hated her."

"She's been a nuisance."

"That's not always bad. Mamma said churnin' butter was a nuisance, but it surely tasted sweet on fresh biscuits. Maybe you just need to wait for the fresh biscuits."

"Am I getting a lecture from my kid nephew?"

"Do you need one?"

"Now you're sounding like your mother."

"That's the nicest thing anyone ever said to me."

Avery stared at Ace, then both began to laugh. "Come on, Avery Creede Emerson. We've got a yellow haired gal to find."

"Why are we going south?"

Avery waved at the weathered twelve-foot pole with green glass insulator on the side. "The telegraph office must be down this street."

"You goin' to send a telegram?"

"Nope. I'm going to pick one up and deliver it."

• • •

Well past noon, they rode east out of Ft. Benton. Dust fogged around the horse's hooves, but didn't drift higher. The movement created the only breeze. The road was narrow and rutted, but they rode side by side.

"Uncle Avery, read me that telegram again."

Avery handed it to him.

Ace looped his reins over the saddlehorn and leaned back. " 'Sis . . . if you get to Ft. Benton before me, wait. I have to sweep through the Breaks one more time. Find my friends Avery, Dawson and Tight and tell them I'll be late. Peter.' All this time, Miss Sunny was your pal's sister."

"So it seems."

Ace handed back the telegram. "But she tried to kill me several times."

Avery kicked his horse to a canter. "No, she threatened to kill you. That's a lot different. Hundreds of people have threatened to kill me, but only a couple of dozen have actually tried."

After an hour in the saddle, Avery and Ace slipped to the ground and walked the horses.

"Uncle Avery, we've ridden for miles and not seen one sign of Miss Sunny. Are you sure she's headin' down river?"

"I'm positive."

Avery pointed to the soft yellow soil sporting

an occasional sage and scattered buffalo grass. "That's why."

Ace squatted down next to the parallel ruts that veered south. "Buggy tracks?"

"They lead to those granite hills. The tracks are so fresh the wind hasn't filled them in yet."

"What wind?"

Avery pulled himself back into the saddle. "That's my point."

"Why would someone drive a buggy off the road?" Ace jabbed his left foot at the stirrup and missed.

"To keep out of sight."

Ace stabbed the stirrup with his second attempt. "Do you think Miss Sunny is hiding from us?"

Avery surveyed the horizon. "Maybe."

"Why would your pal's sister want to hide from us?"

"She doesn't know that I'm a friend of Pete's. We don't even know if she is Pete's sister."

"I don't think Miss Sunny would lie to us."

"How did she jump you and get your clothes?"

"Eh, she lied to me. But she wasn't wearin' anything but her underwear. You got to believe a lady in her underwear."

"There are a few things your mamma didn't teach you." Avery pulled out his gun, checked the chambers, then shoved it back into the holster.

"If we find Miss Sunny, will there be shooting?"

"I don't think so. But there might be shouting."

"Something puzzles me. Miss Sunny . . . or Miss Mary Jane . . . or whoever she is . . . took off to get our things at the hotel and meet us at the jail. Now, I can see her getting scared and run off . . . or maybe if she had a sinful heart, stole something and left town. But I looked at your belongings in the hotel, and . . ."

"They aren't worth stealing."

"Yeah . . . and you have your gun and I have the other."

"I was ponderin' the same thing. If she stole something of value around town, why bother packin' off with my duffle?"

"I'm thinkin' maybe she got scared and ran. If that was the case, she wouldn't be headed down river, but away from trouble."

Avery glanced over at Ace's big brown eyes. "So you're thinkin' maybe we're going the wrong direction?"

"That thought has been swimmin' in my mind."

"I like the way you think things out, Ace."

A dimpled grin broke across the sixteen-year-old's face. "You do?"

"Yep. And your logic makes good sense."

Ace sat straight up in the saddle. "It does?"

"Yep." Avery reined up.

Ace parked next to his uncle. "Do you mean we're turning around and looking for her on the road to Great Falls?"

"Nope." Avery reached over and tugged the front brim of Ace's hat. "You have one fatal flaw in your logic, young Mr. Emerson."

"What's that?"

Avery stood in the stirrups, drew his Colt and aimed it at the giant granite boulders to the south. "What do you see over there?"

"The buggy! You were right."

"Amazing, isn't it?" Avery plopped back down in the saddle. "I'm going to swing around and come up from the west. When I wave my hat, follow those buggy tracks to the boulders. Keep your gun drawn and laying in your lap, and don't shoot anyone unless you feel your life is threatened."

"You know what I was thinkin'?"

"That you wish you were at home back East?"

"Oh, no. I was just thinkin' that I've only been with you for twenty-four hours and already I've had more excitement than in my entire life."

"You're young."

"Yeah, I was thinkin' that, too. How did you survive to be so old?"

A wide grin broke across Avery's face. "Prayer."

"Do you pray a lot? Mamma was a praying woman."

Avery dropped his head and rubbed the back of his neck. "Yes, she was. Just like her mamma before her. I'm never embarrassed to admit I pray, but it's not my prayers that keep me alive." He looked up at the blue clear Montana sky. "It's His prayers that keep me alive."

"Jesus? You think He's praying for you?"

" 'Who is he that condemneth? It is Christ that died, yea rather, that is risen again, who is even at the right hand of God, who also maketh intercession for us.' I reckon He's praying for me, and it's those prayers that keep me alive."

"Now you do sound like mamma."

"That's the nicest thing anyone's said about me. Let's hope He's praying for us both right now."

Avery rode his horse down toward the river and dropped so low, he could no longer see the granite boulders. As soon as they came back into view, he waved his hat at Ace and plodded his horse toward the parked buggy. The driving horse rigged to the buggy stood with one hind hoof off the ground, as if asleep.

The tap of horseshoes on the rock surface startled the horse. He took two steps, stopped, and stared as both riders approached.

"Can you see anything, Uncle Avery?"

"No one over here."

They rode up to the black leather buggy.

"There's your gear in back."

"That means it's the right rig."

"Maybe she's hiding in those rocks."

"I don't think so," Avery's revolver stayed in his lap, his finger on the trigger. "If she didn't want to see us, she'd shoot us. If she did want to see us, she'd be headed this way. It doesn't make any sense for her to be in the rocks." He slipped down out of the saddle and circled the parked buggy.

"Can you read her tracks?"

"Not on granite rock. Ride around the outside of these boulders. See if there's a trail. There are some sand pockets in this granite. Maybe we'll spot a footprint or a clue. I don't understand why anyone would walk away from a buggy . . . unless she had another buggy with a fresh horse waiting."

Ace turned south. "Where are you going?"

"I'm going to climb up in those rocks."

"I thought you said she won't be up there."

"I said, it doesn't make any sense to be up there. But not much of this makes sense anyway."

Avery pulled himself up on the shed sized boulder next to the buggy. Then he stared at the crevices below him.

Ace spun back in the saddle. "Should I fire a shot if I find something?"

Avery John Creede pulled off his hat and

rubbed his sweaty forehead. "No need for that." His voice lowered as he nodded toward the fissure. "I just found something."

Ace slipped down out of the saddle. "Is she hurt?"

"He." Avery climbed down to investigate a crumpled body.

"He?"

"Yep." Avery squatted between the rocks and felt for a pulse. "He's not feeling any pain. He's dead."

CHAPTER EIGHT

Ace scampered hand over foot across the boulders. "Who is it?"

Creede tried to turn the body over. "Scully."

"The bank manager?"

"Yep, shot several times." He surveyed the rocks above the boulders.

Ace hunkered down on his heels. "What was he doing with Miss Sunny's buggy?"

"I don't have any idea." Avery struggled to lift the dead man to his shoulders.

"Do you think Miss Sunny did this?"

"I'd like to think not. But then, I didn't figure she'd run off and leave us at the jail, either. Grab his feet."

"Ain't life a mystery sometimes?"

Avery staggered up out of the rocks.

"What are we going to do with him?"

"I'm ponderin' that. I'm just not going to leave him out here for buzzard bait."

They stumbled as they toted Scully down off the boulders. They shoved him on the passenger side of the buggy.

Ace brushed off his hands on his britches. "Do you think she's still around? It seems strange she'd go off and leave the buggy. Why would she do that?"

Avery stared in the direction of the river. "Because she headed somewhere the buggy couldn't go."

When Ace rubbed his square jaw, he left a streak of dirt. "Like down some narrow trail?"

"Into the Missouri River Breaks, I reckon."

"On foot?"

"Or horseback."

"Where'd she get a horse?"

"Maybe from Scully."

"You think she charaded us into thinkin' she didn't want to go back to the Breaks?"

Avery hiked around the black driving horse to check the buggy's rigging. "Sounds sort of like Br'er Rabbit beggin' not to be tossed in the briar patch."

"Mamma read me those stories."

"I figured."

"How come we put Scully in the buggy?"

"You've got to take him back to town."

"Me? You aren't going?"

"I'm headed into the Breaks. Tell the mayor I'm tryin' to pick up the trail of those who killed Scully and Harvey."

Ace tied his horse to the buggy. "You want me to just wait around town until you return?"

Avery pulled a $10 half-eagle out of his pocket and dropped it in his nephew's hand. "Spend the night in town, then leave at daybreak and catch up with me. I'll be traveling slow, trying to read the sign. I expect you'll find me by noon."

"I don't track very well, Uncle Avery."

"I'll be headed down the trail to the southeast. Just head for the river. I'll jam a .44 caliber brass case in the dirt when I leave the trail. Look for another to the right or left and follow that direction."

"What if I can't find you?"

"If you haven't caught up to me by tomorrow afternoon, go back to Ft. Benton and wait. I've got to be back there in three days to meet a lady. Remember?"

Ace swung up into the buggy and plucked up the lead lines. "Should I round up some help in Ft. Benton?"

"No. I don't know who to trust." Avery shoved Scully's body away from the edge of the black leather seat. "And don't let anyone follow you back. If you can't shake them, just wander back to town and wait."

Ace circled the wagon west, then pulled up. "Do you ever take a vacation?"

"A what?"

"I got a pal named Grover and his dad works for the county bridge department. Every summer he gets a one week vacation. They go over to the Atlantic Ocean and camp out on the beach and fish off a pier for cod. Do you ever take a week off?"

"You've been with me two days and you want a vacation?"

"No, sir. It just seems to me that if this is the way you live all the time, you'd get run down sooner or later."

"Yeah, you're right about that part. I can't remember when I wasn't tired."

"Maybe you can catch up on some sleep Sunday after church. We are goin' to church on Sunday? I made Mamma a pledge before she died."

The sweet, trusting face of his sister flashed across Avery's mind. "I'll do everything to see that you keep your pledge."

Creede waited until the buggy disappeared over the western horizon before he pointed his buckskin horse southeast. He let the horse plod along at a slow walk as he studied the dusty narrow trail. The hills ahead of them were barren of trees. Scattered sage and bunchgrass littered the landscape. Occasional granite outcroppings looked more like they had been arranged, than some natural, random formation. The hot September sun reflected a dull, flat gold against a pale blue, almost transparent sky.

No towns. No houses. No cattle. No horses. No people.

Just the steady clop of his horse's hooves and ringing in his ears, ever present since his days in the cavalry. A fog of powdery dust left no print distinct enough to read. The shadows lengthened. The sun hovered above the western horizon.

Avery stopped for a swig from his canteen. He swiped a bandanna over his forehead and the back of his neck, slid out of the saddle, then studied the trail. The horse stared at him like a soldier awaiting a command.

"Well, Junior, young Ace has a point. My life never slows down. No vacation. No day off. No lazy afternoon fishing. No listenin' to the band play in the park. Never a Sunday afternoon nap. Not since Ft. Lincoln. Not since the Little Big Horn. Not for ten years." He slapped the flies away that buzzed around the buckskin's big brown eyes. "Maybe because there's no one to do those things with . . . until now."

●●●

When they crested the rise, he spied the wide, dark brown, winding course of the Missouri River in the distance. He yanked the cinch tighter, then relaced the latigo. Settling back on the slick, hot leather of the saddle, Creede surveyed the long, narrow trail.

He leaned forward and patted the horse's neck. "Whoever is ahead of us will stop for the night along the river. I reckon they'll look for a clean patch of water. So will we, boy, so will we."

No trees framed the river, but narrow sand beaches lined each side, littered with driftwood, bleached bones, and river rock campfire rings. Creede turned off before he reached the sand. He stepped down from the saddle, shoved an empty brass casing into the dirt, then planted another one two feet to the northeast.

He rode parallel to the Missouri until twilight squint caused him to pull up, mark the trail, and ride down to the river. As Junior drank at the water's edge, Avery washed his hands, neck and face, then scrutinized the mud. Old hard prints of deer, bear and cougar were scattered next to the river, but no sign of horses or humans. In the last flicker of twilight, he surveyed a sandbar about one hundred feet out in the river. Several large driftwood logs formed a makeshift barricade. Green bushes had sprouted up along the long, narrow island.

Creede yanked himself back into the saddle, then spurred the horse out into the river. "Don't know how deep it is, boy, but that sandbar looks like a peaceful place to camp. Maybe I'll surprise myself and get a quiet night's rest."

The shallow water provided no hindrance, but the spongy mud caused Junior to sink down to the stirrups. Avery tucked his feet up to the D-buckle to keep his boots dry. Halfway across, the river bottom firmed up and he stopped Junior for a break. Night settled in and he could no longer see the sandbar, nor the brush or driftwood ahead of him. A full range of stars blinked to life in the coal black, moonless sky. The air above the river felt calm, even balmy and smelled moist, like the time, as kids, he and his sister sailed on a tiny boat across Chesapeake Bay on a Sunday night after church.

The only sound was the gurgle of water lapping around Junior's legs.

And the check of a lever action rifle.

Avery stood in his stirrups, his revolver drawn, when hot, punching pain sliced across his left arm just below the shoulder. At that same moment, he heard the explosive report of the gun.

He dropped to the saddle, kicked the horse's flanks and charged in the direction of the sandbar. Two rapid shots from his revolver quieted the assailant. The fire blasting out of the gun lit the night like fireworks on New Year's Eve.

"You got to jump it, boy," he growled as he spurred the buckskin. Hot blood pulsed down his arm and puddled at his cuff. He clamped his knees tight, leaned forward in anticipation of the leap.

His hat . . . his head . . . his neck . . . his chest . . . his duckings . . . his boots . . . his entire body flew forward into the darkness of the night.

But the saddle and the horse didn't budge.

His hat tumbled off and he closed his eyes, even though it was pitch dark.

Whatever he crashed into was not as hard as the driftwood logs.

Nor as gritty as the sand.

Nor as thorny as the brush.

It was yielding.

And wet.

And wiggling like a five-foot snake . . . or a woman.

"Get off me, you son of a . . ."

"Sunny?" he choked.

"Who are you?"

He struggled to his feet. His left arm throbbed so much he could hear his heart beat. "Avery."

The Winchester lever checked in the darkness.

"Sure, and I'm . . ."

He ducked down. "You're Mary Jane Cutler and you already shot me once."

Her voice mellowed. "I shot over the top of

you, and how do you know my real name?"

"I stood in the stirrups, and you hit my arm." Avery took another step back and felt water swirl around his boots. "Your brother Pete is a friend of mine."

"How bad are you wounded? Why didn't you tell me yesterday that you knew my brother?"

"I don't think the bullet stuck. Yesterday, I didn't know who you were." He yanked his bandanna out of his pocket and hunkered down to dip it in the river.

"Are you one of Pete's army pals?"

"Yeah. We were with Captain Reno at the Little Big Horn."

"Where are you, Creede? I can't see you."

"I'm trying to tie a bandanna around my arm."

"Let me tie it. I didn't know I was firing at some ex-cavalry hero who was going to stand up and take a bullet. Put out your hand."

He swatted darkness until he felt her arm, then clutched her wrist.

Her hips brushed against his, and she tugged the bandanna from his hand. "What's that sticky stuff?"

"Blood."

"Is this the right place?"

"A little higher."

"Avery, I'm sorry. I thought it was the others chasing me. I was scared."

He pulled the bandage a little higher. He

smelled lilac perfume, but could make out only a faint silhouette. Both of them whispered in the quietness of the sandbar.

"Did you come to rescue me?"

"I came to find you. I didn't know if you needed rescuing or not. You took off without telling us where you were headed and I believe you have our belongings."

"Did you think I'd just run off and leave you and Ace? Where is your nephew?"

"He took the buggy and Scully's body back to Ft. Benton. Did you kill Frederick Scully?"

"Do you think I did?"

"What I think doesn't matter. Did you shoot him?"

"Mr. Creede, what you think about me does matter. Do you think I killed him?"

Avery discovered that if he pushed his right hand against the bandanna his wounded arm felt better. "No, Miss Cutler, I don't think you killed him."

"Thank you, Mr. Creede. But people really do call me Sunny, not Mary Jane."

His right hand in front of him in the dark, he led her to a driftwood log. "Let me sit here and catch my breath and you tell me what happened at Ft. Benton. You left me and Ace at the jail with the mayor opiumed up and asleep in a rolled up carpet."

"I assume he came to in time to back you up."

"Just barely. But when we went to the hotel, the clerk said you checked us out and rode off in a buggy."

"Of course I did . . ."

"Shhh," he cautioned. "Did you hear something?"

"Maybe it was your horse. Anyway, I got the buggy to try to get you out of town. I wasn't sure the mayor thing would work."

"And I suppose you took a wrong turn?"

"Why do always think the worst of me?"

"Maybe it's because you helped rob a bank, threatened my life, my nephew's life, shot me, and called me names I have never heard before from a woman's lips."

"I'm telling you the truth. I got the buggy to help get you out of town. When I swung around the alley behind the bank, Scully blocked my way, then hopped in the buggy with a gun in my face. He made me drive out to those boulders. Said he had business with Rinkman . . . and I would be his insurance."

"Insurance?"

"He had the mistaken idea that I was on Rinkman's side and he wouldn't want to see me harmed. He looked crazy enough to kill me, so I did what I was told. While we waited, he blabbed out the plan."

"What plan?"

"Scully was just a riverboat gambler and Rinkman set him up in the bank business. It had to do with some sort of stock certificates. Rinkman was suppose to come to town, rob the bank when Scully was the only one present . . . and steal money and certificates."

"But you and your part of the gang ruined the plan?"

"So it seems. At first, Scully thought Rinkman got the days wrong. Then he figured they were trying to cheat him. Anyway, Rinkman showed up, took everything out of the bank, and left while all the attention was on the three that were killed in the jail."

"Scully was cleaned out but didn't get robbed? That would be hard to explain."

"He's not a complete dummy. After the first attempted robbery, he signed all the stock certificates over to Mr. & Mrs. Frederick Scully. He's not married, but he said it looked more official."

"So he shows up with you at the boulders demanding the certificates or he'll shoot you."

"Yes, and Rinkman said 'shoot her and save us the trouble.' "

"I suppose Scully panicked?"

"He spun the buggy, I leaped out, and they shot him dead."

"He must have been shot a dozen times."

"That's the way they work. They want everyone in on each murder so they are all guilty."

"Nice guys. But there is one puzzling thing. Why didn't they kill you?"

"I convinced them that I was the only one who could walk into Deadwood and cash those stock certificates."

"Mrs. Frederick Scully? They believed that?"

"They believed me enough to not shoot me. They trussed my hands and jammed me on a saddle horse and brought me down to the river."

"Where are they now?"

"Down river a few miles. They will be looking for me, but maybe not until daylight. They know by now I have a carbine."

Avery plopped down closer to her. "Are you sure you don't hear something?"

"You're too jumpy. Do you want to hear my story?"

"Yeah, so how is it they let you steal a gun?"

"Getting a gun is easy. Men close their eyes when they kiss. I traipsed off to the river to do a lady's thing, and just slipped into the river. I thought I could cross it. I swam out halfway, but my wet clothes weighted me down. I was just about to promise God the moon when a horse swam by."

Avery pressed his right hand harder against the bloody bandanna. "A horse in the middle of the river?"

"Kind of like a miracle, don't you think? I grabbed his tail and let him pull me along. We

127

made it this far, and were both exhausted. When I caught sight of him against the starry sky, I realized he's not a horse, but a moose."

"You held on to a moose's tail? A moose tail is just a little stub."

"I wasn't choosy at the time. I thought maybe the Indians bobbed the tail."

"A moose? Out here in the Breaks? I can't believe that."

"He's still here. Poor guy. He was so worn out he just fell over in the sand and sucked air."

"I've got to see this."

"You got any matches?"

Creede lead Junior behind the driftwood barricade and tied him off to a snag. He fumbled in the leather pouch and yanked out a match. With a strong blast of sulfur, the match flared.

He got a glimpse of Sunny's stringy hair. "You're soaking wet."

"And you are a bloody mess."

Then darkness snuffed the match.

"Give me your hand," she demanded.

"Careful, it hurts."

"The other hand." They walked slow, her fingers laced in his. "Can you can hear him gasp for breath?" she said.

"Sounds like a baby."

"What do you know about babies?"

Creede paused. "Shhh!"

A muffled infant cry broke the silence.

He dropped her hand and yanked out his gun.

"Don't shoot . . ." The voice was low, scared and young.

Avery squatted down. "Who are you?"

"Charles Smith."

"How old are you?"

"I am Charles HighEagle Smith and I am eleven years old."

"Who's with you?"

"My mother and my little brother."

In the flickering light of another match, a buckskin clad, dark skinned boy appeared next to a lady with long black hair. A baby tucked into a cradleboard straddled her lap.

"Blackfeet?" Avery asked.

"Flathead," the boy answered.

"You're a long way from home."

"I was at the Catholic Indian school in Wyoming. When my father was killed, my mother and brother came to bring me home. They don't speak English very well. We thought it would be safe on this island. It is very dangerous to be on shore. There are evil men who live there."

Avery stood and lit another match. "Tell your mother not to be scared of us. We'll rest up until morning and then leave."

The boy hunkered back down in the brush.

"Mother is not afraid. When she was a young girl she had a dream about a Moose Woman saving her."

"Moose Woman? Oh, no . . . not me."

Avery laughed. "But you made someone's dream come true."

"I'm not going through life being known as the Moose Woman."

There were muffled words.

"Mother says be quiet. There is someone coming in the river."

"Up river?" Creede whispered.

"No," Charles HighEagle Smith replied, "in a boat, down river."

Guns in hand, Avery and Sunny waited at the upper end of the sandbar. A lively discussion tumbled out of the small boat, but not in English.

Sunny checked the lever on her carbine. Avery lit another match and used it to light a dry stick. Three men cowered beside a small, round bull-boat.

"Chinamen," Sunny blurted out.

"You can shoot us but we will not surrender our gold." One man held a leather pouch over the water. "We would rather pour it in the river than let you steal it again."

"Whoa, boys," Avery said. "We don't want your gold."

"You don't?"

"Like you, we just want a night's rest. You are welcome to camp here too."

The man in a long black shirt spoke to the others, then turned back. "We will go to the other end of the island."

"Well, you can't do that. There's a moose at the far end and an Indian woman and her two children. Me, my horse and the Moose Woman are camped against the driftwoods. But you can stay right here. No one will bother you."

"The Moose Woman?" the Chinese spokesman said.

Sunny's fist slammed into Avery's stomach. He buckled to weaken the blow.

CHAPTER NINE

The campfire crackled. The fat sizzled. The morning air filled with the get-up-and-get-going aroma of sweet meat.

Sunny slept on top of Avery's bedroll.

Squatting next to the fire, he watched the first tawny light of the sun peek over the eastern horizon. His lower back ached from sitting all night in the sand. He had leaned against a driftwood log, carbine in his lap, trying to stay awake and watch for intruders.

None came.

But sleep did. In spite of the sore back, he felt rested.

Junior stood half-awake, concealed from the shore behind a few large green bushes.

The muddy water of the Missouri circled the little sandbar, but made very little sound. Avery figured he was due for a quiet, peaceful morning.

"I'm not asleep."

He looked over at Sunny. "Good mornin'."

"I'm laying here with my eyes closed and not moving, but I thought you should know that I'm not asleep."

"Thank you for telling me that."

"You're welcome."

"Why did you think I wanted to know?"

"I was afraid you might do or say something embarrassing."

"Like what?"

"Like mumbled, 'She's the most beautiful woman I've ever seen' . . . or something like that."

"The thought never crossed my mind."

"It didn't?" Her reply was a definite pout.

"Your brand new dress has more mud than the Missouri. Your face and hands are dirty. Your hair is stringy and plastered against your head and you sleep with your mouth wide open. Trust me, the thought of calling you the most beautiful woman never crossed my mind."

She kept her eyes closed. "You don't have to beat around the bush with me, Creede. Why don't you just blurt out what you really think? Under all those minor temporary blemishes, you'll have to admit I'm a paragon of perfection."

"You're just babbling in your sleep."

"If you are through extolling my virtues, I think I'll open my eyes. Is anyone else watching me?"

Creede glanced up and down the sandbar. "Nope."

She blinked open her left eye and craned her head around to see him. "Look who's calling the kettle black."

"Yeah, but I look this rough all the time. I've seen you scrubbed up."

"So, you have looked me over."

He stabbed the frying meat with his knife and flipped it over. "Where is all of this leading?"

"Are you angry?"

"Why do you say that?"

"You always look mad and I'm not opening my other eye until you smile."

Avery rubbed his forehead. "You give me a headache."

"I bet you say that to all the girls."

"You're right about that." He forced a grin.

"Is that the best you can do?"

"I'm afraid so."

"Okay, but you need to work on smiling and not being so angry all the time."

He stabbed his knife in the sand. "I'm not angry."

Sunny sat up and stretched her arms. "I was exhausted. I think I conked right out after I read Pete's telegram."

"You had a busy day."

She stood and brushed down her blue dress. "Is there any part of the river that has clean water?"

"There's a little eddy near the west end that's not too bad. That's where I cleaned up."

"What? Is that your clean self?"

"I'm afraid so."

Sunny surveyed the sandbar. "Where is everyone?"

"The Chinese left a couple of hours before daylight. Mamma and the two little warriors headed out about an hour ago. They told me to say thanks to the Moose Wo . . ."

"Don't you dare use that term, Creede."

"Talk about angry looking."

"You have never seen wrath until you've seen mine." She glanced at his saddle and gear bag. "I don't suppose you have some soap."

"In that tobacco tin on top of my saddle."

"You actually carry soap?"

"Yeah, after all, cleanliness is next to grumpiness."

Her wide grin interrupted the smudges on her cheeks. "You surprise me, Creede. With work, you could be halfway sociable."

"Why would I want to?"

"I know, you like being petulant." She wiggled her bare toes in the sand. "Did my moose leave, too?"

"Eh . . . I reckon you can say he sorta stayed around."

"What do you mean 'sorta'?"

Avery pointed his knife at the deep-purple meat frying in the pan. "Part of him is here."

Sunny's face turned white. "You killed my moose?"

"I didn't harm him. The Chinese said he wouldn't survive the night, so they carved him up before daylight. They took the horns, innards and organs, then split most of the meat between themselves and the Indians. I took a couple of choice chops."

Sunny tossed the soap tin into the sand and burst into tears. "They had no right to kill my moose. Why didn't you stop them?"

"It was a done deal before I knew what they were doing."

"He was my moose," she bellowed.

"You can't keep a moose like a dog. What did you intend to do with him?"

Her sobs were beyond control. She threw her arms around Creede's neck. Tears soaked his shirt. "You men never understand." She pulled back, snatched up the soap tin and stomped to the west end of the sandbar.

Hair combed. Face and hands washed. Dress dried out. Sunny sat on the saddle near the campfire. "I'm not going to eat that meat."

"That's fine. I'm hungry enough to eat it all."

"You can't eat mine."

"But you said . . ."

She grabbed a chop off the plate. "I'm going to bury it. My moose should have a proper burial."

"It's not a he. It's a dadgum hunk of meat."

She gouged a trench in the sand with her bare toes, then tossed the meat into it. She squatted down and covered it up with sand. She stepped over the brush, broke off a green twig, then planted it on the burial site.

Sunny stood, bowed her head and closed her eyes. "He was a good moose, Lord, and I think he deserves to go to moose heaven. Amen."

She turned back to Avery. "There . . . that's better."

"You're crazy."

"For saying a prayer over a dead moose?"

"For having a funeral for a medium rare steak."

"You don't have any sensitivity."

"You're wrong. I was deeply touched by your

attachment to the moose. You inspired me to pray as well."

"I did?"

He looked down at the meat in his tin plate. "Yep. 'Dear Lord, bless the food I am about to eat.' " Avery ducked the flying shoe.

She sat silent while he ate. He motioned toward the skillet. "You have anything against eggs? Or are you going bury them too, then hold services?"

She scraped the scrambled eggs into a tin plate and grabbed a fork. "The eggs didn't save my life."

"They might. No telling when we get our next meal." Avery pointed down river. "Now, tell me about life in the Breaks. Everyone I talk to is afraid to go or afraid to leave."

"Salt and pepper?"

"What's salt and pepper?"

"I can't eat these eggs naked."

He handed her a small metal tin with holes in the top.

"It's like a little kingdom of its own." She peered at the tin. "Salt or pepper?"

"Both, I think. Who's down in the Breaks?"

"Mostly cattle rustlers. They don't steal big herds . . . just six to ten at a time. They'll graze them for several months while they have time to rebrand them . . . then a couple times a year, just like the big ranches . . . they'll run a thousand head down to Wyoming . . . and sell them to the army or the railroad." She shook seasoning on the eggs.

"And this guy Rinkman makes all the money?"

"It's green. What did you say was in this?"

"Something Wanda made for me. Go on . . ."

"Rinkman's got a bookkeeper and everything. A man gets paid in proportion to how many he's brought in. Rinkman takes twenty percent and the individual gets the rest." She shoved a big bite of seasoned eggs in her mouth.

"Quite a going business."

"Whoa . . ." Sunny fanned her mouth with her hand. "Rinkman does the same thing with stolen goods. He's got several big warehouses. He keeps a tight inventory and sells in bulk, mostly across the line in Canada. Again, each man's paid for what he's brought in. Who is Wanda and why did she try to kill you with this seasoning?"

"It's a long story and she did stab me once."

"Is that where you got the scar on your face?"

"No. Now, go on."

"The boys only get paid a couple times a year. No one complains. Rinkman's got several stores down there. The boys get to buy on credit." She took another bite. "These aren't too bad once your mouth numbs. Some of them have built houses and have their families with them." She grabbed his coffee cup and took a swig. "It's a nice enough community."

Avery took the tin and unscrewed the lid. "How many people live at Rinkman's place?" He sniffed the tin. "This didn't used to be green."

"I'd guess over four hundred, including women and children. Since everyone is wanted for some crime or another, they don't let law-men come snoop around. It would take a raid by a thousand cavalry men to clean it out. And then there'd be a lot of dead soldiers." She took another bite. "This stuff is too spicy to spoil."

"At least your eggs aren't naked. But why are you connected with them? Other than your line about pretending to be Mrs. Scully?"

She scraped on the empty tin plate, then stared into the campfire embers. "It's not something I like to talk about. Here's the short version. I spent five years as an unsuccessful actress in Denver."

He stuck his fingers in the spices, then licked them. "Unsuccessful?" he managed to choke out.

"I was starving to death, but I convinced Pete I was doing quite well so he wouldn't worry. Anyway, Rinkman showed up at the theater one night. He spent money hand-over-fist and fed me a line about this town up on the Missouri River Breaks that needs a theater. He wanted to hire me to come up and act and direct. Said there were others who would like to learn what I know. Hey, I like this stuff. Are you going to tell me who Wanda is?"

"Nope."

"I was living in an eight-by-eight room above an Oriental butcher shop. I was impressed with the five double eagles he tucked in my hand. So I bought some nice clothes, and a few second-hand scripts and rode in his buggy until Montana . . . then I straddled a mule down Pleasant Valley."

"That's what he calls the place?" He jammed the lid back on the tin. "Maybe I should throw this out."

Sunny snatched it out of his hand. "No, I like it."

"And your acting job in Pleasant Valley?"

A long pause caused Avery to look away.

She took a deep breath. "Rinkman's got one of the fanciest cat houses outside of San Francisco. Oak staircases, velvet wallpaper, crystal chandeliers. And a big stage. He wanted me to direct the girls in some plays that he wrote, and then at the end . . . well, the girls do their business." She looked over at the black iron skillet. "May I have more eggs?"

With one hand he cracked two more eggs into the pan. "I presume he wanted you to, eh, participate with them?"

"I told him what I thought . . . where to shove that scheme of his . . . and went to get the mule to

140

ride out of there. But one of the girls pulled me aside and informed me that no one leaves Pleasant Valley. It doesn't matter how far you run, some of the gang will show up and kill you."

Avery chopped and stirred the eggs with his knife. "You didn't direct the soiled doves, did you?"

"No, but I convinced them I was a good enough actress to help them rob banks."

"Did they believe you?" He stirred the eggs again then held the skillet over for her inspection.

She nodded. "After we dropped down and robbed the bank at Rawlins, Wyoming, they believed me. But they wouldn't let me out of their sight. When we got back to the Breaks, Pete was there."

"Why?" He scraped the eggs into her plate, then licked the knife blade.

"He came looking for me. One of my friends in Denver told him where I was headed." Sunny sprinkled green seasoning on her eggs.

Avery poured himself another cup of coffee. "He's not an outlaw. Why didn't they shoot him?"

"He was driving eight head of Texas beef that he said he stole down in Johnson County."

"And they believed him?"

"Yep." She shoved another forkful of eggs

into her mouth. "Whoa . . . whoa . . . whoa!"
Tears ran down the corners of her eyes. "But
before the two of us had a chance to speak much
in private, Rinkman sent Pete and some others
to rob the government warehouse at Ft. Laramie.
That's the way he did it with new guys. You had
to go prove yourself on the day you came to
the Breaks. Meanwhile, he did tell me to try to
get to Ft. Benton. Said he had some friends
there that would help."

"Me, Tight and Dawson, I suppose. But Pete
couldn't rob that warehouse. He's on a first
name basis with everyone at Ft. Laramie." The
coffee scalded the roof of his mouth.

"Rinkman didn't know that. About five days
later, part of the gang straggled back to the
Breaks. They said Pete's horse went loco and
pitched him into the river and he drowned."

"Is Pete still doing that old trick? He and that
horse of his are the real actors."

"I knew Pete didn't get bucked off." She
motioned for his coffee cup. "But the others
went to Ft. Laramie. They were ambushed. The
soldiers had been tipped off about the raid."

"Pete?"

"I think that's what Rinkman believes, but
those that rode down there insist Pete died in
the river. Half of them were shot at Ft. Laramie."
She took a big swig of coffee.

Avery waited for her reaction. "Maybe one of

the wounded men will tell all of this to the army?" He studied her mouth. "Didn't that coffee scald you?"

She stared at the cup. "I couldn't even feel it. Anyway, there are no wounded men in Rinkman's band. If you can't mount your horse, your own pals will plug you."

"I don't reckon Rinkman takes defeat well."

"He ranted and shouted and wanted to kill all five of them. But three of the survivors were the ones with me on the bank job. I convinced him robbing banks was more profitable than government warehouses." Sunny dove back into the remaining eggs.

"He went for that?"

"I suppose he thought he could kill us later if he needed to. They told him we were headed down to the railroad again. Said we would rob the freight office in Pine Bluffs." She pointed her fork at the plate. "These are the best eggs I've ever eaten."

"You were hungry. Why did you come west instead of going south to Wyoming?"

"We thought we had a few days lead. The boys were set on going to Mexico after the robbery. I was going as far as Arizona. It could have worked if I was a better actress. I couldn't believe anyone could be so heartless as to not help a woman in distress." She scraped her fork across her plate.

"Why didn't you just run off when the three got thrown in jail?"

"I didn't have a penny and they saved my hide down in the Breaks by letting me be part of their gang. Besides that, I was mad." Sunny sucked on the fork like a lollypop.

"At who?"

"You, of course." She yanked the fork out and waved it at him. "I wasn't about to let any man ignore me like that."

"I suppose when they get up this morning and see that you are gone, they will come looking for you."

"They know I went into the river. I'm hoping they think I drowned, which I would have if my dearly departed moose hadn't swam along." She glanced at her empty plate.

"You want more eggs?"

She held up her plate and licked it. "No."

"Did you even consider that moose was Divine providence?"

"Are you going to preach at me now?"

"Do you need it?"

"Probably."

"It will have to wait."

"Why?"

Creede lowered his voice. "Would you recognize Rinkman's men if you saw them?"

"I know most of them."

Avery held his finger to his lips. "Peek through

the brush and tell me about those two on horse-back at the water's edge."

She shoved her plate to the sand, then moved the leaves. "That's Hawk and Sal," she whispered.

"Sunny, we see the smoke from your fire. We know you are over there," one shouted.

"Who was you talkin' to?" the other man yelled. "Do you have someone over there?"

Sunny unbuttoned the back of her dress, and stepped out. "I was just cussing these buttons. I can't get my dress fastened."

"Rinkman's mighty angry that you run off like that."

"Run off? I went for a swim to clean up and the current swept me away."

"Swept you upstream?"

"It was a strong current."

"We got to kill you or take you back to Rinkman. Which will it be?"

"I'm thinking. I'll tell you one thing, I'm not going back until my dress is buttoned. Hawk, would you come over here and help me?"

"Yes, ma'am, I can do that."

"We can both do that," Sol piped up.

Hawk drew his gun and shoved it at his partner. "She said me, not you. I don't need no help with a woman's dress."

CHAPTER TEN

Sunny threw her arms around Avery's neck and slammed her lips into his.

His arms circled her thin waist. Her lips felt lithe. Warm. With just a hint of reserve. "Is he buyin' this?" he mumbled without pulling back.

Her arms pressed tight against the back of his neck. The lips-to-lips pressure didn't slacken. "I don't know. My eyes are closed."

Avery opened his eyes, only inches from hers. "No, they aren't."

"Well, they were for a minute," she whispered. "You wearing Hawk's coat and hat. I think we might sucker him."

"You seem to be enjoyin' this."

"Shut up and kiss me."

"Hey, Hawk! You ain't supposed to be doin' that! Rinkman wants us to shoot her, not love her up. Did you hear me?"

Without turning his head, Avery reached back and waved him off.

"If you aim to break the rules, by god, I'm goin' to break 'em too!"

Avery could hear the horse splash into the water. Sunny tugged him down behind the driftwood. By the time Sol splashed his way around the logs, Avery crouched behind the bushes, his gun drawn.

"Who in blazes are you and what happened to Hawk?" Sol shouted.

The other outlaw lay in the sand, unconscious, with tied hands and feet.

"I'm Avery John Creede and your pal ran his head into the barrel of my gun. Keep your hand away from your holster and get down off your horse."

Sol's thick black mustache hung like a pair of whipped dog tails. "You tricked me wearin' his hat and coat."

"I think lust chumped you over here. There's a lesson in that but somehow I reckon it's wasted on the two of you." Avery yanked the gun from Sol's holster. "Keep your hands up."

The outlaw stared down at his partner. "What are you goin' to do with us?"

His gun jammed in Sol's back, Avery shoved him toward the river's edge. "Shoot you, drown you . . . or take you to jail. I can't decide."

Sunny folded her arms across her chest. "I'm in favor of something slow and painful."

Avery shoved Sol's revolver into her hand. "Keep this aimed at him while I tie him. If he flinches, shoot him."

"Wait!" Sol stuck his arms up like a first grader wanting permission to go out and use the privy. "Ain't you goin' to cold-cock me first?"

"You like pain?" Avery tugged the braided leather rope off the saddle.

The wrinkles on Sol's face put creases in the layer of dirt and grime. "You got to have the decency to cold-cock me. If Rinkman thinks I was captured without a struggle, he's likely to shoot me. Have mercy and bust my skull. That way I can say I was ambushed, but put up quite a struggle. A little blood wouldn't hurt either. Kinda smear it on my knuckles. That always looks good."

Avery stepped back. "Are you kiddin' me?"

With the quickness and velocity of a mother killing a snake with a hoe, Sunny slammed the barrel of the revolver into the back of the outlaw's head. He crumpled to the sand. Blood trickled across the dirty brown hair.

"You seemed hesitant," she said. "Besides, I owed it to Sol. He was the worst one about keeping his hands to himself."

"I just never met a man who wanted his skull busted."

"Choosing the lesser of two evils." Sunny handed Sol's gun back to Avery. "And when it comes to the wrath of Jed Rinkman, any choice is better."

"Jed?" Avery shoved the extra gun in his belt. "I thought maybe he didn't have a first name."

"No one calls him that but the girls."

Avery stooped in the sand and yanked the

rope tight around Sol's hands and feet. "I heard about a Jed Baker down in El Paso who went loco one night and knifed every gal in the . . . eh, cantina. But he wasn't smart enough to come up here and rule the Breaks. At least, I don't think he was." He stood up and glanced down river.

Sunny swept back her shoulder length blonde hair. "What are we going to do with them?"

Avery squatted next to the smoldering embers of the cookfire, and poured the last of the coffee over them. "One time, when I was with General Crook down in Arizona, we sent a couple of our Yavapai scouts up river to locate a camp of an Apache called Long Jim. A few hours later this raft comes floatin' downstream with both scouts scalped and lookin' like pincushions, there were so many arrows in them."

"I imagine it was a deterrent to the troops. You want to scalp these two and put them on a raft?"

"Nope. It was a great deterrent to the soldiers and scouts, but not to General Cook. He led us after them on a gallop. By nightfall, Long Jim was dead and the others on the run back to Mexico."

"I think Rinkman would take it personal, too."

Avery put the saddle on his horse and tugged the cinch tight. "We'll have to get these two back to Ft. Benton. We'll accuse them of killing

149

Harvey and the prisoners. Even if they didn't pull the trigger, they were there. Maybe they'll implicate Rinkman."

Sunny packed the dishes to the water's edge and rinsed them off. "If he hears about it, he'll come back to town to kill them."

"Maybe the best way to stop him is to lure him out of the Breaks."

She marched straight at Avery. "Speaking of lure, don't look toward the bank. Here comes another of Rinkman's men."

Avery fought the urge to turn around. "Which one?"

"Can't tell, he's too far away." She threw her arms around his neck. "Kiss me."

"How many times you think this charade will work?" He pressed his chapped lips against hers.

"Maybe one more time."

"Are you sure someone's over there?"

"You don't think I'm so desperate to kiss you that I'd make this up, do you?" She pressed her lips tighter against his.

Avery closed his eyes. His arms circled her waist and he felt them tug her closer. "You seem awful anxious to do the kissin'."

She began to sway back and forth. "It's for your own safety. He's at the water's edge."

Avery blinked his eyes open. "What's he doing now?"

Sunny kept her lips smashed against his. "Staring."

"Hey, you two . . . I hate to interrupt . . . but I need to talk to Uncle Avery."

Avery spun around. "Ace?"

The sixteen-year-old tipped his hat. "Howdy, Miss Sunny. I'm mighty glad you're safe and sound. You are safe, aren't you? I take it you two are gettin' along better now."

Sunny brushed her bangs out of her eyes. "Hello, Avery Creede Emerson."

"Look, we were just . . ." Avery stammered.

Ace rested his hand on the horse's rump and leaned back. "I know what you were doing."

Avery brushed his calloused hand across his lips. "It wasn't what you thought."

"Of course it was." Ace's grin hung from ear to ear. "I'm not nearly as naïve as you think I am."

"We've got two of Rinkman's men cold-cocked and tied." Avery motioned toward the driftwood. "We thought you were another, so it was all just a diversion."

"Didn't look like a diversion." Ace pushed his hat back. "No, sir . . . it looked like you two enjoyed it."

"It was a pleasant diversion," Sunny called out. "And it worked. We thought we'd try it again."

Ace sat back down in the saddle. "You two

151

sound like ten-year-olds with their hands caught in the cookie jar."

"Are you giving me a lecture?" Avery blustered.

"Do you need one?"

"No. Come over here. Help me pack these two Missouri Breaks outlaws."

By the time Ace reached the sandbar, Avery wore his own coat and hat.

"You really did have two of Rinkman's men." Ace grinned. "I surmise you'll teach me all these tricks."

Sunny poked her finger into Ace's stomach. "I've got a feeling you don't need any lessons."

Ace tipped his hat. "No, ma'am. I don't reckon I do." He squatted down next to the bodies. "What are we going to do with them?"

"Take them back to Ft. Benton and toss them in jail. Is the sheriff recovering from those bullet wounds?"

"Talk is, he might not pull through. I visited with the mayor last night when I brought Scully's body in. He said he hired an old friend from down near Billings to serve as temporary sheriff."

Avery rolled his blanket tight, then tied it behind the saddle. "What's his name?"

"Kind of a foreign sounding name. Madera or Mandara, somethin' like that."

Avery paused. "Captain Mandara?"

"You know him?"

"He's the best man the army ever drummed out of the corps." Avery jammed the dishes back into the burlap grub sack.

"He got kicked out?"

"He saved his men from the wrong decision of some idiot general."

"And they didn't like that?"

"He disobeyed orders. 'Course I would have done the same thing. Where did you say he lives now?"

"South of the Yellowstone, at Cantrell. East of Billings a ways."

"First, Tap Andrews moves up. Now, Mandara is in Montana. That's a good thing. This territory might make statehood yet."

Sunny sat on a driftwood log to pull on her stockings. "I know his wife."

"His wife died," Avery said. "Left him with all those kids."

"No, he remarried." She shoved her foot into her shoe, then bent to tie it. "Her name is Isabel Leon. But when I knew her, we called her The Marquesa. Talk about one fiery Puerto Rican actress."

Ace handed Sunny her other shoe. "The mayor said Mandara won't be up for a couple of days."

Avery checked the bits and cinches of both outlaws' horses. "Who's watching the prisoner?"

"Some volunteers, but I don't think anyone

wants the job. The talk is if Rinkman comes back to town, all of those on both sides of the iron bars will be shot dead."

"We'll bring them two more to watch. I don't reckon that will make me popular."

Ace reached for his coat pocket. "The telegraph operator said you were the most popular man in town already. You got two more telegrams."

"Who's looking for me now?"

"The top one is from a man named Tight. It was addressed to you, Pete and Dawson. He's laid up in a Colorado hotel near a hot springs, suffering from consumption. He said Doc Holliday gives you his howdy and claims you still owe him five dollars."

"Doc's still alive?" Avery pulled his revolver, pushed the cylinder out and checked the chambers. "Sounds like we need to head down to Colorado."

Sunny stepped between the men. "I need to go down to the Breaks and find Pete."

"Yeah, that's what I mean." Avery shoved the gun back into his holster. "After we take these two back to town and I meet with . . . eh . . ."

"Your precious Carla Loganaire. Yes, I know that. I don't have any lines in that scene, so I'll stay off the stage. My brother's risking his life to find me in the Breaks. I figure I should do the same."

"Can't you just wait a day or two? I really need to see her, but I don't want you to go down there alone."

"There isn't any rush for that," Ace piped up. "The other telegram. It's from your darlin' Carla. Said she might be a few days late because her Uncle David insists she be in Cheyenne to meet some Englishmen who are interested in buying his Platte River Ranch."

Avery opened the telegram. "A few days? What is a few days?"

"I could explain that to you," Sunny added, "but I don't think your heart wants to listen. But I do need a horse, that carbine, and Hawk's bullet belt."

Avery yanked his hat off and rubbed the bump on the back of his head. "A few days . . . if she thinks . . ." He stuck his face in hers. "I offered that lady my heart on a platter, but she can't make up her mind if she wants it."

Sunny turned away and mumbled something.

"What?" Avery pressed.

"Nothing. Some women are fools." She sucked in a deep breath. "I have to go find Pete."

Avery watched her eyes that refused to look at his. "Yeah, and I need to find Pete, too. Ace, take these two back to Ft. Benton and see that they get locked up."

Ace kicked sand over the remnants of the fire. "Maybe I ought to rent a hack and make this a

155

regular route. You could just pile the bodies along the trail like cordwood. You want me to come back out tomorrow and look for you?"

Avery stooped down and grabbed Hawk's shoulders. "Stay in town until Captain Mandara shows up. We'll find Pete, then come back."

"How long do you reckon it will take you?"

Sunny grinned. "A few days."

"Are you sure you don't need some help?" Ace said.

"I reckon the Lord will have to be our chaperone," Avery replied.

"I meant, help loadin' those two outlaws."

Avery motioned for Ace to lift Hawk's feet. He flung Hawk belly down over the saddle like a sack of onions. "Tell Mandara everything that's been going on down here."

Ace reached down for Sol's feet. "Even the kissin' part?"

Avery and Sunny rode along the canyon rim single file until the sun hung high overhead.

"It's too hot to wear this hat and coat," she complained. "Besides, I don't think we'll fool anyone into thinking I'm Hawk."

Avery wiped the sweat off his face. "All we need to do is look like a couple of men from a distance."

"Men don't wear blue dresses and ride sidesaddle."

"From the bottom of the canyon we're just a couple of miniature silhouettes. It might fool them."

She halted her horse. "From that distance they couldn't recognize me if I was buck naked."

"What?"

"You heard me, Avery John Creede."

He shoved his bandanna into his back pocket and plodded Junior along the canyon rim. "You said that to make me blush."

"You blush easy. I could bat my eyes and make your face turn red. You haven't been around women very much, have you?" She pulled off the heavy, wide brimmed, dark, beaver felt hat and tugged on the coat sleeve.

"More than I wanted to, that's for sure."

"There's a long story there," she said. "But right now, I'm taking off this hat and coat. They stink, and they make me perspire. I don't like to sweat."

"That's all you're taking off."

"That really got you stirred up." She laid the coat and hat across the pommel of the saddle. She shook her hair loose and stretched out her arms. "You see, Mr. Creede, I can let my hair down and no one is going to shoot me. Besides, we haven't seen anyone all morning." She cupped her hands around her mouth and shouted, "Hey, down there on the river . . . here I am, shoot me!" She stood in the stirrup. "Someone down there is smoking a pipe or some . . ."

The palm of Avery's hand caught her in the small of the back and shoved her out of the saddle. He dove to the ground next to her and mashed her head to the dirt.

The heavy lead bullets buzzed like a swarm of bumblebees. Both horses dashed away from the canyon rim.

"Of all the dumb . . ."

Sunny forced her head out of the dirt. "But I didn't see anyone. Did you see anyone down there?"

Avery tugged at her to crawl back away from the rim. "No, I didn't. That worried me all morning. There had to be someone looking for Hawk and Sol. That's why we rode this high line."

She drug herself through the dirt. "You've been worried all morning and you didn't tell me?"

He sat up behind an olive-green sagebrush. "Which of Rinkman's gang has a .50 caliber Sharps rifle?"

"That's almost a mile away." She sat up next to him. "Can they shoot that far?"

"You didn't answer me." Avery stood and offered her his hand.

"I didn't pay attention to gun sizes."

Avery stalked the horses. "Someone knows we're up here. If they are looking for us, they'll be up here in a few minutes. If they are chasing us off . . . we need to stay away from the edge and they won't bother us."

Sunny turned her back, hiked up the front of her dress, and wiped her face on the inside hem. "Pete had a buffalo gun."

"A trapdoor or a Sharps?"

She dropped her dress and turned around. "How should I know? One of the girls at Pleasant Valley said the new guy had a buffalo gun. She thought it was a strange gun for an outlaw to pack."

Avery grabbed Junior by the reins, then rubbed his nose. "Pete's a good shot."

"My brother would not shoot at me." She marched up to the dark brown horse and scooped up the dragging reins.

Avery led his horse east, parallel to the canyon rim. "What if he thought it was Hawk and Sol?"

"He knows what I look like. I don't think that bullet would have hit me. Do you think that bullet would have hit me? What if he was warning us?"

"What if someone else has Pete's gun?"

"I don't suppose you want to just ride on and ignore them?"

"We're going down after them."

"Charge and never retreat?"

Avery stopped near some granite boulders.

"We came down here to find Pete. We can't find him up here. Hold these reins."

"What are you going to do?"

"Give the shooter something to occupy his fingers. We'll go down over here through these boulders. It should give us some cover half the way down."

Avery hiked west, pulled out his knife, then knelt down next to a small sage brush. He hacked away until it was chopped off at the ground. Then he cut another smaller one. Within minutes he had them lashed together. Hawk's coat circled the big one, his hat was tied down to the smaller one.

"The 'sage man' doesn't look a thing like Hawk," she called out.

"I only need to fool him for a couple minutes. Stay over there . . . we'll have to walk the horses off the rim."

On his hands and knees, Avery pulled the sage man to the canyon rim.

"They can't see him back there."

"That's my point. Are you ready to head off the rim?"

"Not until you lead the way."

Avery stood up and peered over the canyon.

"Get down, you fool!"

Avery dropped to his belly and shoved the sage man to the edge where he stood. As he scampered toward Sunny, a bullet speared through Hawk's ducking coat. The rifle report filtered across the canyon.

"He shot Mr. Sage."

"Yeah, but Sage didn't fall over dead. He'll have to shoot him again. Come on." He tugged Junior off the rim into the boulders.

Sunny stumbled as she led the brown horse after him. "Do you think this diverted him?"

Avery slumped down as he skidded on loose granite gravel. "We'll know that in about sixty seconds."

CHAPTER ELEVEN

In the blazing sun of a Montana September, Avery and Sunny led their horses off the rim of the canyon. They plodded through the boulders and down toward the Missouri River. The air heated up as they descended. Sweat rolled off Avery's leathery tanned face. They paused behind the last large boulder. He pulled off his black hat and swiped his forehead on his shirt sleeve.

"From here we'll be in the open."

Another rifle report shattered the hot canyon air.

Sunny pulled the canteen off the saddle horn, pulled the cork, and wiped it on her dress. "Is he still shooting at Mr. Sage?" She took a deep gulp, then handed it to Avery.

"I reckon." He took a deep gulp, swished his mouth, then spit. "But I can't figure why. A good shot with a long range rifle would have plugged the charade. He's shooting like a man who's taking target practice. I'm beginning to think that first shot at us was just luck."

"That eliminates my brother as the shooter." She shook dry weeds and dirt from the hem of her dress. "What do we do now? How do we get to the river?"

"I'm thinkin' of chargin' right at him. You stay in back of me." He hung the canteen back over the saddle horn.

"Avery John Creede, you have an obsession with running into bullets. How did you ever live so long?"

He deliberated on the river. "By always doing the smart thing."

"What's smart about riding straight at a 50 caliber bullet?"

"I didn't say straight." He shoved his hat back on. "We need to zig and zag."

"And that guarantees not being shot?"

He kept his eyes on the river. "It's very hard to get a long range gun trained on a close moving target. They are great for shooting a standing buffalo or a sage man at a thousand yards, but . . ."

Sunny leaned back on the boulders. "But not

162

a bunny bouncing around in the garden?"

"Yeah, that's it." He glanced at her smudged face. "Of course there are other reasons not to use a Sharps on a rabbit."

"Oh?"

"Bunny-bits comes to mind. A big bullet makes small targets explode." He yanked the cinch tight on her horse. "Make sure you keep me between you and the shooter."

She smiled. "How chivalrous. And if he shoots you dead, what would you suggest I do?"

"Head back for the rocks."

"What? Give him an easy target to explode? No, Mr. Creede, I will charge right at him." She pulled Hawk's revolver from the saddle bag and pointed it at the river. "I shall shoot him between the eyes and say, 'Take that, you wretched cur. You have taken the life of my love. Now I send you to the eternal lake of fire.'"

Avery tried to read her blue eyes. "You'll say what?"

"Obviously you've never seen me in 'Deadwood Dan and the Greasy Hill Gang.' I played Amanda. Actually it was one of my . . ."

He cocked his head. "This isn't a play. Those are real bullets."

"Mr. Creede, if I stop and consider what I'm doing, this whole thing becomes a nightmare from the moment I first met you. I'm better off pretending to be in an ill-attended play. I've worked smaller crowds. After all, the 'whole world . . .' "

"I always wondered," he interrupted, "if the whole world is a stage, where does the audience sit?"

Sunny clapped her hands. "Yes, I love it. Avery's got a witty retort."

"I'll try not to let it happen again." He yanked the cinch on Junior and swung up in the saddle. "Are you ready?"

"I just have one question. If we ride right at him or them and don't get killed, what do we do then?"

"We . . . we subdue him and we, eh . . . find out why he's shooting at us."

She mounted the horse. "This is amazing. Avery John Creede charges into battles with little thought about whether he wins or loses. It's the battle, isn't it? Life isn't worth living if there's not a dangerous enemy to face."

"You don't understand what my life is like."

Sunny threw up her hands. "No, I don't. I certainly hope your darlin' Carla Loganaire understands it, because you'll drive any wife crazy."

Avery felt his neck heat. "Maybe you should wait back here in the rocks."

"Okay."

"What?"

"You are the all wise warrior. I shall obey your every command."

"I never thought you'd . . ."

She waved him off. "Run along now and have fun. Be nice and don't get dirty."

"You're mocking me," he snapped.

"Of course I am. There is only one way you are going to keep me safe. You'd better gallop between me and the shooter." She kicked the brown horse and bolted toward the river.

Avery caught up with her by twenty yards. He forced them to the left. He heard the report, saw the smoke from the rifle, but couldn't tell from where. The dry alluvial soil fogged as they thundered toward the river. Another shot shattered through the canyon. Avery turned right. The gunman stood and pointed the long-barreled rifle at them.

Creede fired two quick shots. The man ducked behind the rocks. With Junior still at a gallop, he swung out of the saddle and hit the ground running. Out of control and unable to slow down, Avery leaped a sage, just as the gunman stood again.

Avery's right foot buckled under him. He slammed face down in the dirt. His gun bounced out of this hand. He struggled to his knees and the gunman pointed the big caliber rifle at his head.

This time the gun blast was muted, more distant than Creede expected.

No blackness.

No blood.

No ripping wound.

No choirs of angels.

Just a scream, the crash of a Sharps rifle into the rocks, and a thud.

Avery scooped up his revolver and turned back to see Sunny on horseback, gaping down the barrel of Hawk's revolver.

"You shot him."

"It seemed like the right thing to do."

"I had him but, I, eh . . . I . . . tripped."

"So I noticed."

"Twisted my ankle in that hole."

She slipped to the dirt and hiked toward Avery.

He hobbled over to the downed gunman. "That was a good shot. Not too many can shoot straight from a galloping horse."

"Why are men surprised that women can shoot straight?"

Avery stooped over the face-down man whose dark duckings were slicked with grime. The gunman's shirt had been white at one time, but now looked like a back alley after a flood. He felt for a pulse. "For most men a shot like that takes a lot of practice."

"Why would you assume I haven't prac- ticed?"

Avery glanced up. "He's dead."

Sunny walked back toward the horses. "I'm sorry for that. I've never worked without a script before. I wasn't sure what was expected of me. But when a famous gunman like Avery John Creede trips in a bunny hole, I thought it my duty to preserve his life for womankind."

"Womankind?"

"Oh, yes. Some day there will be no more brave, gallant, pig-headed and suicidal heroes left."

Avery picked up the long rifle. "This is Pete's gun. I'd like to know how this guy got it, but you eliminated any possibility of interrogation."

She stopped and took several deep breaths. "Are you saying I shouldn't have shot him?"

"No, I'm rather glad not to be shot with a .50 caliber bullet. Twice is enough."

"You were shot twice?"

"Twice by a big bullet. Once out on the Dakota plains. And once at Ft. Grant when my drunken commanding officer fell off the front porch with a musket in his hands."

"Are you sure that's Pete's gun?"

"I was with him down in Cheyenne when he carved these three notches in the buttstock."

"Were you with him when he shot those Lakota Sioux renegades from over two thousand yards?"

"Eh . . . yeah, well . . . I was with him when he carved those notches," Avery repeated.

"Are you implying that's not what happened?"

"That's between you and Pete. I'm stayin' out of this. Where did you learn to shoot a revolver?"

"Are you changing the subject, Creede?"

"Yes, ma'am."

"I'll tell you where I learned to shoot straight, if you'll tell me why Pete carved those three marks."

"Some things are best unsaid."

"Okay." She stormed back to the downed man. "Let me look at him. Maybe I can recognize who he is."

Creede grabbed the man's shoulder and turned him over. The bearded man's brown eyes were still open. Blood dripped from his half open mouth. "Have you ever seen him?"

"Never."

"We don't even know if he's one of Rinkman's gang." Avery closed the man's eyelids.

She held her hand over her mouth and took a couple more deep breaths. "He's not one of Rinkman's."

"How do you know that for sure?"

Sunny bent over and rested her hands on her knees. "He never sends them out alone. He doesn't trust them. He won't even send the same two out together very often."

"Don't know why anyone would want to stay with him in the first place."

"Because they're absolute failures in life." Her

168

cough was shallow. Sweat beaded on her fore-head. "They have never had anything, never done anything, never been anything . . . all of a sudden they are part of a powerful gang. I know that sounds stupid. The gals that work the houses down in the Breaks are the same way. They like it down there. Say it's better than being in Lead or Butte. I think I'm going to be sick."

"It's a clean wound, you shot him through the neck and he drowned in his own blood."

Sunny ran over to the tallest sage and heaved several times.

Avery searched the saddle burlap gear bag tied to the back of the man's horse. He struggled to lift the man to his shoulder, toted him off the rock, and lay him in the sand beside the river. He knelt down and searched his pockets.

"You looking for money?"

"I'm trying to find out who he is. You okay?" He stood and offered her his bandanna and realized there was no clean corner.

"No thanks, I'm better now."

"Wet it and wrap it around your neck. It will help. Trust me. You might go down to the river and wash your face to cool you down. I've been through the same thing with new recruits in the army. It's okay."

"It's not okay." Sunny trudged down to the river while he lashed the man to the saddle.

Avery studied hoofprints in the sand when she returned, his wet and somewhat cleaner bandanna around her neck.

"You're right. This is better. Sorry about that. Most all my shooting has been in the theater. Twice a night, for weeks, I'd pull the trigger, usually to defend my honor. But the men always got up . . ."

"After the applause?"

"After the curtain. Some nights there wasn't enough of an audience to applaud. It just dawned on me that I've killed a man."

"We were defending ourselves."

"He could be some woman's husband."

"I reckon so, but some things can't be helped. He hadn't had a bath in a year, I can tell you that. I think a wife would make him wash."

"But he was some mother's son. There was a day when she held him in her arms and thought he was the most beautiful baby she'd ever seen."

"Is this another one of your plays?"

"How many men have you killed?"

"Haven't counted."

"Don't you have any remorse?"

"A man can't serve in the army and have remorse. It will not only endanger your own life during the next battle, it will endanger your comrades fighting alongside you."

"But doesn't it permanently scar you? You know, on the inside."

Avery rubbed his chin and fought the urge to put his arm around her. "I've got to leave that kind of judgment to the Lord or it will eat away at me."

"But what if a person didn't believe in the Lord?" She clutched his arm. "Then how would they bear the burden?"

He brushed the wet, blonde bangs off her forehead. "Are you saying you don't believe in God?"

"I'm just saying, how does a non-believer deal with the guilt of killing someone?"

"How does Rinkman deal with it?"

"His heart is so hard, it doesn't bother him at all."

Avery slipped his arm around her shoulder. "Do you know why it doesn't bother him? Because he doesn't believe he will ever be accountable for his actions. So, the one who doesn't believe in God has no worry at all. The fact that you have remorse proves that somewhere in that sweet heart of yours, you believe the Lord is watching."

"Why did you say that?"

"Because it's true. If you believe you will be accountable, then you believe . . ."

"No, the part about me having a sweet heart."

"I said that?"

"Yes, you did, Avery John Creede."

"Well, I just meant that if you'd stop pretending everything is a play, and . . . well . . . I think you could become a nice lady."

She pulled away. "Become a nice lady? What am I now?"

Avery kicked the dirt. "That's not what I meant. I think, well, you know . . . I mean, I reckon you are trying hard to be something you aren't. And . . ." He took a deep breath and puffed it out. "Ever' once in a while . . . it seems to me . . . I get a glimpse at the real Mary Jane Cutler . . . and . . . well . . . I like what I see."

"Do you have a tough time speaking with all women, or is it just me?"

"I reckon I can talk to you better than others. I know you better than most."

"We've only known each other three days."

"Yeah, that's what I meant." He stepped away and concentrated on the river. "I think you believe in God, but are maybe angry at Him because you think He let you down somehow. So you've decided you're not going to speak to Him."

"Why do you say that?"

"Is it true?"

"What does it matter to you?"

" 'Cause I've been there. It's a rotten place to be."

She gazed out at the slow moving, brown

colored water. "So now you are at a good place where you can shoot people and not have it affect you at all?"

"No, I just try to do whatever the right thing is. In this part of the country, dealing with people like Rinkman . . . that might include shooting. I can find peace with the situation if I'm convinced I did the right thing." He shut his eyes. "Sunny, I'm sorry you had to shoot that man. I do know how that changes a person."

She leaned her shoulder against his and murmured something.

"What?"

"You can call me Mary Jane, if you like. Sunny is my stage name." She spun around and marched back toward the body. "Are we taking him back to Ft. Benton?"

Avery followed her. "No, we'll bury him. I think we should figure out where he got this gun. So we'll need to follow his trail as far as we can. This proves that Pete is in the Breaks. And if he gave up his rifle, then he probably needs our help."

Avery used the wide driftwood stick to shovel brown sand on top of the body.

Sunny sat on a rock, elbows on her knees, chin propped in her hands. "That's a shallow grave."

"The best I could do without a shovel. I'll cover it with rocks."

She leaned back and looked up at the late afternoon sky. "You know what I'm thinking?"

"That being a less-than-successful actress in Denver wasn't all that bad?"

"Hah! Shows how little you know."

"What were you thinkin'?"

"That this would be a very good time for us to get to know each other better."

"How do you propose we do that?"

"You tell me what those notches mean on my brother's gun, and I'll tell you how I learned to shoot straight."

"I don't think you want to . . ."

"Of course I do. Have you ever seen Mr. Cody's show?"

He rolled a huge boulder over the grave. "The Wild West play? No, I haven't."

"I did, and I was amazed."

"At the acts?" Avery tossed some cantaloupe sized rocks on the gravesite.

"At how big the audience was. I've never played before a crowd like that. So I went looking for a job. Mr. Cody was very encouraging. He said he had just the role for me. He wanted me to get a nice tan, put on a long black wig, wear a beaded buckskin dress, and shoot the wick off a lit candle next to some Indians. I told him I couldn't shoot well. He told me to come back when I had learned."

"So you lined up candles and practiced?"

"No, but I found a guy in Denver who would give me shooting lesson in return for . . ."

He pulled his hat off. "Do I want to hear this?"

"In return for free theater tickets. I must have practiced for close to a year."

"Then you went back to see Mr. Cody?"

"I went to see his show again and planned to audition. But, I never did. He had just hired Annie Oakley. So I have an unused talent."

"It was needed today."

"That's my story. Your turn."

"I never agreed to this sharing stories thing."

"Of course you did. There was silent agreement when you refused to stop me from telling mine."

"Silent agreement?"

"Yes, now what do those notches on Pete's gun mean?"

"I don't think I should . . ."

Sunny slammed her fist into Creede's stomach, then grabbed her hand and shook it. "Tell me now, or I'll bust my other knuckles on you."

CHAPTER TWELVE

Avery moseyed to the river's edge, then stooped to wash his hands. "I'm going to give you the short version. Many years ago, when we were young bucks stationed at Ft. Russell, we went into Cheyenne with a couple of days off. Naturally, we intended to have a good time."

"Naturally."

"Well, Pete was shootin' snooker and I played poker at the Chicago Café."

"In Cheyenne?"

"Yeah, it was a cheap joint on west Lincoln Street. I think they specialized in cheating drunken soldiers. It burned down a few years ago, which is a benefit to the town, no doubt. Anyway, this Englishman dressed in a white linen suit and highly polished, black loafers wandered in. Don't know why he bummed around that side of town. He was lousy at poker. He kept losing all evening. Around midnight, I won a big pot and he couldn't cover the bet. So he wrote out two passes to the Wyoming Club, one for me and one for Pete."

"THE Wyoming Club?" Sunny blurted out. "The one where all the rich men gamble, drink and . . . eh, play?"

"That's the one." Avery wiped his wet hands on

his ducking trousers. "This was our one chance to see what was inside, so Pete and I headed that way. The guards out front threatened to shoot us, but one glance at the passes, and we were ushered inside by an old guy dressed in black top hat and tails."

"Is it as fancy as they say?"

Avery strolled back to the waiting horses. "Beyond belief."

"The décor or the women?"

"Both. Mahogany paneled rooms, crystal chandeliers, thick green carpet . . . uniformed waiters, big leather chairs. I've never seen anything like it. They have way too much money. And the women . . . they were like . . ."

"Don't describe the women. I get the picture. I suppose you're going to tell me these notches represent Pete's . . . eh, victories that night?"

"Yes, ma'am. That's exactly what they mean. I told you I didn't want to tell you this. We were young soldiers at the time. It's not an era in my life I am particularly proud of. Every time we went out against the Sioux, we knew there was a chance we wouldn't come back. We wanted to make sure we didn't waste any opportunities."

"Is that what you call them?" She scribbled in the dirt with her finger. "How many notches did you carve on your gunstock that night, Avery John Creede?"

"None."

"Oh?"

"I don't want to sound too virtuous. The Lord hadn't grabbed my heart and soul yet, and I did plenty of things I now regret. But on that occasion, I spent most of the night in jail." Avery tightened the cinches on both horses.

"Jail?"

"For busting the jaw of the Faro dealer at the Wyoming Club. He took a look at us and judged us as two easy marks. He cheated me and I didn't take that well. I told him to cut it out or I'd bust his nose. He said that fisticuffs were not permitted at the Wyoming Club."

"But you busted his nose anyway?"

"And his jaw."

"How many Cheyenne lawmen did it take to apprehend you?"

"Just one."

"Tap Andrews?"

"No, that was way before his time. Pappy arrested me. He just walked into the club, looked down at the Faro dealer and said, 'The man's a crook and no doubt deserved it, but I got to take you in, son.' "

"And you gave up without a protest?"

"Pappy had a way about him. Kind of like your dad taking you out to the woodshed. You didn't like it, but you knew he was right. He turned me loose the next morning and said to stay out of Cheyenne for a month. It was some years after that when I got arrested by Tap. That wasn't too bad. The two of us set up all night playing cards. Did you say you knew Tap?"

"I know Pepper," Sunny said. "We have some mutual friends. Why did Tap Andrews arrest you?"

"Nope." Avery stepped up on the stirrup and threw his leg over the horse. "Just one story at a time. And I've finished mine."

Sunny grabbed the saddle horn and swung herself up. "I don't believe you."

He watched her eyes. "What I said about Pete?"

"He told me they were for victories in the Indian wars. I know my brother. I don't believe you for a minute, Mr. Creede."

He kicked Junior's flanks and trotted ahead. "Good."

She raced to catch up. "What do you mean, good?" she hollered. "That whole story you told me was a lie, wasn't it?"

"Nope. But I was hopin' you wouldn't believe it."

They rode east along the river. Avery led the dead gunman's horse; Sunny plodded behind. Clouds drifted over as the sun set behind them. For the first time in several days, the air cooled.

Sunny trotted up beside him. "It might rain."

"I was just ponderin' that. I'd like to find us some shelter."

"There's a miner's deserted cabin along here somewhere. We used it on our way into Ft. Benton. It marks the beginning of Rinkman's domain."

"How far ahead?"

"I'm not sure, but it's tucked away from the river and is half dug out into the hill. It's not much, but it will keep the rain out and it doesn't have fleas."

"That's more than I can say for a few hotels I've bunked in. Let's hope we can find it before this thing breaks loose."

The rain hit hard before dark. Lightning melted the colors into white or black. Every clap of thunder pushed the horses into a gallop. The storm skipped the sprinkle stage and the heavy clouds opened up like bathtub water tossed out a second story room. Sunny draped Avery's coat over her head, a soggy, heavy umbrella.

Avery swung around beside her. "I'd gladly stop if I could find us any protection. We need to find that shack soon."

"It's up there."

He could barely see her point north. Lightning flash reflected off the rising cliffs. "I can't see anything."

"Either can I, but I can smell it." Sunny stuck her nose out from under his coat. "Smoke."

"I can't smell anything but wet horsehair."

"Trust me. It's up there."

"If there's smoke, then someone beat us to it."

"Maybe they'll share."

"And if they don't?"

"I'll shoot them all. I want to get out of the rain."

"Are you sure you smell something?"

"I am positive."

Avery turned Junior north from the river and they wound their way through boulders and brush. He could feel the incline of the canyon wall, but couldn't see more than a few feet in front of them. The sporadic lightning provided a temporary beacon, but it rolled on down river and ceased. Avery's soaking wet ducking trousers chafed at his legs. Water squished between his toes. Within a quarter of a mile the rain stopped. Stars began to peek between the clouds. The wind cooled down even more.

Avery's coat was now wrapped around Sunny's shoulders. "I'm freezing."

He peered into the darkness. "Where is this cabin you smell?"

She turned her nose up. "I don't smell it anymore."

"You mean we're off the trail? When did you lose the scent?"

"The minute I took your coat off my head."

Avery mashed the water from his shirt sleeves. "You were smelling my coat?"

"It is quite smoky, you know."

"Then we don't have any idea where the miner's shack is. We might as well stop and try to build a fire."

"Or we could see what that flickering light is up there on the slope of the mountain."

"What flickering light?"

"Amazing. The great Avery Creede can't smell and can't see. Look up there . . . see that flickering light?"

Avery squinted. "Maybe you're just looking at a twinkling star."

She prodded her horse forward. "Mr. Creede, you may sit here and freeze your backside, but I'm going to that cabin."

Avery trotted ahead of her. "I'll lead."

"Lead where? You can't even see it."

"I'm not having a woman lead me in the dark."

"You'd rather ride off in the wrong direction than have a woman know more than you?"

"I'd rather ride in the wrong direction, rather than have a special lady get herself hurt riding into an ambush."

"Then you do believe me that there's a cabin up there."

"Yeah, I believe you."

"What convinced you I was right? The sincerity of my voice?"

"Nope. It was that flickering light up there."

"You see it?"

"Yeah, but it's dim."

"Can we hurry?"

"No."

"I told you I'm freezing."

"Which is at least one step better than being dead."

Avery slipped to the ground and led the horses toward the light. The clouds had all sailed east as they approached the cabin in the moonlight. He stopped well short of the cabin. "You stay behind these rocks. I'm going to check what's happening inside."

"What if someone on the porch shoots you?"

"Ride up there and kill them all, and enjoy the fireplace inside."

Sunny sat straight up in the saddle and waved the revolver in front of her. "Yes, I believe I will."

"I'm not going to start anything. I just want to size it up."

"Could you do it quickly? I believe my entire body has turned blue."

"Hmmm."

"What do you mean, 'hmmm'?"

"Reminds me of a gal I knew in Lake City, Colorado. Stay here."

Avery jammed his wet hat over the saddle horn and handed Sunny the reins. He pulled his gun and plodded up the hillside. Every second or third step he stopped to survey the landscape.

Silver smoke curled out of a stovepipe at the right side of the door. On the left, a ripped canvas curtain shaded the night from a glassless window. He leaned against the rough cedar, board and bat cabin and listened.

"You go check on the horses."

"I ain't goin' out there in the rain."

"It stopped rainin'."

"Why do I have to go?"

"You lost."

"You cheated."

"I was just teachin' you a lesson."

"Yeah, maybe I should teach you a lesson about knives."

"If you two will shut up, I'll go check the horses."

Avery trained his revolver on the door and hunkered in the shadows, but the door didn't open.

"Deal me another hand, only this time don't cheat."

"Same bet?"

"Are you sure Rinkman will give us a bonus?"

"Positive."

"Okay, same bet, but if you cheat me this time, I'll slice you thinner than roast beef at a widow's boarding house."

As Avery focused on the door, his leg started to cramp. He stretched it out in front of him. His soaked shirt hung heavy on his shoulders and he gritted his teeth to keep them from chattering.

The first shot blasted out from the rocks near Sunny and the horses and shattered the cornerpost of the cabin behind him. Avery spun around. Gunfire flashed from a revolver as someone returned shots at the boulders.

Avery blasted at the shadowy figure and heard a scream. Another shot from the rocks slammed into the front door. The flickering light disappeared from inside the cabin.

"Blackie, what's going on out there?"

"They shot me!" a voice behind Avery screamed.

"Who shot you?"

"I can't see 'em."

"Is it Rinkman?"

"I don't know . . . I'm bleedin' . . . help me get in the cabin."

"Hey, Mr. Rinkman, we got him, just like you wanted. We was just waiting out the storm. We didn't kill him yet. We was savin' that for you. You hear me?"

Avery ducked low against the building and crawled in the mud to the small porch.

The blast of a .50 caliber Sharps rattled his eardrums and splintered the front door.

"Alright, we surrender. We're comin' out with our hands up."

The men staggered out the front door, hands

held high, but still held their revolvers.

"You go right. I'll go left," one of them mumbled.

"Drop those guns right now," Avery shouted.

"Who in the blazes . . ."

Avery's shot splintered the porch post. Both guns banged on the wooden porch. "Don't shoot us, mister. We don't even know who you are."

"What's goin' on over there?" the wounded man shouted. "I'm bleedin' to death, I tell you."

"He's got a gun on us, Blackie. We cain't do nothin'."

Avery retrieved the revolvers.

"You ain't one of Rinkman's?"

The other man glanced into the shadows of the moonlit porch. "Who are you?"

"The angel of death. And tonight, it's your turn, boys."

"Doesn't anyone care that I'm bleedin'?"

"Blackie, shut up. We're face to face with the grim reaper here."

"Who's out in them rocks with a big bore rifle?" the other asked.

"The angel of light," Creede said.

"Tell him not to shoot us."

"Her. Didn't you boys know the angel of light was a woman?"

"Mister, you ain't makin' any sense." The man to his right yanked a knife from his boot. Moonlight glistened on the blade as Avery slammed the barrel of his gun into the back of the man's head. Just as the one collapsed on the porch, the other lunged at Avery and slammed him back into the cabin wall.

"What are you doin'?" the wounded man hollered. "I need help, now."

Avery caught a fist in the chin that staggered him to his knees. He dropped all three guns and dove at the man trying to scoop them up. A boot battered his kidney, but he managed to grab the man's legs. Both tumbled into the mud. A knee slammed against his chin and he felt blood trickle from the corner of his mouth.

He rolled the man to his back and pounded a fist into his jaw, another into the temple and a third square into the man's nose. Blood sprayed across the man's face. He collapsed beneath Avery.

"Burns, what's happening? What's going on?"

Avery staggered to his feet and grabbed up his gun. He hobbled over to the wounded man.

"You got to help me. I'm bleedin' to death. Did Rinkman send you?"

Avery squatted down and shoved a bandanna at him. "Hold this against the wound."

"It's soakin' wet."

"And it's dirty, too, but you don't have a lot of options. I've never met Rinkman." He folded the bandanna and pressed it against the man's shoulder. "Hold this."

"If you ain't from Rinkman, what are you doin' down here in the Breaks?"

Avery wiped his bloody lips across his shirt-sleeve. "Lookin' for a couple men."

"Who?"

"The one who killed a deputy in Ft. Benton."

The man turned his head and spat out blood. "You a lawman?"

"No, just a friend of Harvey's."

"I don't know who killed him. All three of us were with Rinkman when we busted into the jail, but the deputy was already dead. Those in jail said someone kicked open the door, shot him, and left them behind bars."

"Did you shoot the three in jail?"

"Rinkman and Morris did that down at the river. There was nothin' we could do. When Rinkman goes off crazy like that, there's no one who can stop him. I'm innocent of their deaths."

"We'll let the judge in Ft. Benton decide."

The man propped himself up on his elbow. "You taking me to jail?"

"If you don't die on me first."

"You might as well shoot me now. Once Rinkman finds out we're in jail, he'll come shoot us too."

"I don't need to waste a bullet. Maybe you'll get lucky and bleed to death."

The man held the bandanna tight. "You said you were lookin' for two men. Who else?"

"A friend named Pete Cutler, you know him?"

"Did he tote a Sharps?"

"That's the one."

"Yeah, I know where he is." The man coughed a couple times. "I need a drink. You got any whiskey?"

"No."

"Will you turn me loose if I tell you where Pete is?"

"Why should I believe you?"

"Look, I'll probably bleed to death. It's a cinch I won't go back to Rinkman. Give me a chance to ride away. I didn't start this tonight. I was shot at from those bushes and just tried to protect myself."

"You aim to ride out of here wounded . . . and with no gun?"

"Yeah, no gun. Nothing but a horse and saddle. Mister, I'll just ride north. If I stay alive and make it through the Blackfeet into Canada, I'll never come back."

"And you'll take me to Pete first?"

"Yes, sir. Is it a deal?"

"Only if I find Pete alive."

The wounded man motioned to the back of the cabin. "The horses are behind the cabin near the back door."

"A dugout with a back door?"

"Just a tunnel into the mind shaft, then a ladder. My horse is the spotted one."

"And what about Pete?"

"He's roped and gagged and inside the cabin."

Avery stood up. "Pete's in there?"

"We were taking him back to Rinkman."

"Sunny. You can come up now, Pete's in the cabin."

"She's still alive? I thought Rinkman took care of her."

Avery trotted toward the brush. "Sunny, let's go untie Pete."

Avery held his gun as he approached the brush. Junior and the other two horses stood right where he left them. "Sunny?"

The moonlight made her yellow hair look white. She sprawled in the rocks, her face pale, her body twisted.

He shoved his gun in his holster and knelt at her side. He touched her cold, wet forehead. "Sunny! Mary Jane . . . it's me . . . Avery. Oh, darlin', darlin' . . . what happened? No . . . no . . . no . . ." He pulled back her wet hair, then searched for bloodstains or a wound. "Come on now . . . don't do this to me. You can't be hurt. You can't be . . ."

He struggled to lift her in his arms, then staggered as he stood. Her body hung limp. As he hiked out into the clearing, tears rolled down his leather tough cheeks. "What am I doing? Why did I let her come out here? I knew this could happen. You are a fool, Creede. You've always been a fool with women." Like Abraham offering Isaac, he held her up to the heavens. "Lord, I'm way too weak a pilgrim to go through this again."

CHAPTER THIRTEEN

Firelight shadows blinked to an off-beat rhythm against the thin cedar walls of the cabin. The air hung heavy, filled with grit and old sweat. Avery leaned against a beam, gun drawn. The blonde lady reclined on the hard wooden floor, wrapped in a dusty buffalo robe. Her face paled light pink from the heat.

Pete Cutler lightly fingered the bruises and cuts on his face. His left eye was almost swollen shut. "I can't believe that I was rescued by St. Avery again. He's got this special connection to the Lord, you know."

Sunny squinted at her brother. "St. Avery?"

Avery felt the rough cut wood claw at his back through the still damp shirt. "It's a nickname the boys gave me, to tease me, I reckon."

"No, it's true." Pete's buffalo robe slipped off his shoulders. "Anytime one of his friends got in a bad way and tossed up a prayer for deliverance, St. Avery showed up and rescued them."

Avery stared at the flames. "Not every time."

Pete shook his head. "No, not every time. That wasn't your fault, Avery."

"What wasn't his fault?" Sunny said.

"I should have got there sooner."

"Got where sooner?" Sunny asked.

Pete rubbed at the rope burns on his wrists. "Doc said it wouldn't have mattered."

"It mattered to me."

Sunny blew in her hands, then held them in front of the flames. "What mattered to you?"

"I don't want to talk about it." Avery shoved his gun back in his holster.

"You have been talking about it," Sunny remarked with some irritation.

Pete cleared this throat. "More important, what are you doing here, now?"

"Looking for you," Avery replied.

Sunny scrawled the initials MJC in the grime on the floor. "Are you changing the subject?"

"So you, Dawson and Tight waited in Ft. Benton. When I didn't show, you and Sis decided to come looking for me?"

Avery shrugged. "Something like that. Only Dawson and Tight haven't showed either."

"You shouldn't have brought her back down here."

"Pete, I reckon you know that no man can tell Mary Jane what to do."

"She lets you call her Mary Jane?"

Sunny tugged the buffalo robe back up around her shoulders. "If he's nice."

Pete gave his sister a hug. "I'm glad you came. I woke up all trussed up like a hog, with my face and ribs battered and St. Avery outside howling at the moon. What happened out there?"

"The boys put up a scrape," Avery said.

"I shot your Sharps from the back of a horse." Sunny rubbed her shoulder.

"That recoil will knock you to the ground."

"Yes, and I must have hit my head on the rocks. He thought I was dead."

Avery rubbed the corner of his eye and noticed blood on his finger. "I knew she was okay when she woke up and slapped me."

A slight grin broke across Pete's battered face. "You slapped him?"

She raised her chin. "A natural response when I get clobbered in the head and wake up to find some man's trying to carry me off."

"This kind of thing happen to you often?" Avery asked.

She stuck out her tongue. "There are some stories better left untold."

Pete nodded toward the gunmen. "You got two tied in the corner. Where are the other two?"

"The one that had your rifle is buried down next to the river. I reckon he took off on his own."

"And your gracious St. Avery let the one called Blackie take a horse and ride off."

Avery rubbed his fingers, so cold and calloused that he couldn't feel the touch. "Blackie took a bullet in his shoulder. He lost a lot of blood. Not much I could do for him, and he promised to lead me to you."

"But I was here in the cabin."

"I didn't know that. We headed up here to get out of the rain. We didn't know anyone was here."

"By chance we stumbled onto you," Sunny offered.

"No chance," Pete added. "St. Avery works by an inner voice."

"More like a kick in the pants," Avery said.

"So you let Blackie just ride away?" Pete said.

"Had to keep my word. He went without a gun. Said he would try to get to Canada. He was sure Rinkman would kill him if we went back to Pleasant Valley."

Pete gazed around the room. "We're a fine looking outfit. Sis has a limp shoulder and a knot the size of a walnut on her head. Your face looks like it ran into a fence post, and I can't find any place but my left big toe that doesn't ache like it's been run over by a train."

Sunny leaned her head on her brother's shoulder. "We'll look better after a good night's sleep and a chance to wash up in the morning."

Avery stood and shoved on his hat. "We've got to go right now."

"Go? I'm still cold and damp," Sunny complained.

"We've got to get out of the cabin. Sunny, pack up our gear. Pete, help me bring the horses around."

Pete struggled to his feet. "Are you saying the Lord just kicked you in the seat of the pants, again?"

"I just remembered that these two in the cabin called out to Rinkman as if they expected him to show up. He's headed this way. He wants you for betraying him and Sunny to waltz into Deadwood and cash those certificates."

"Where are we headed?" Pete asked.

"Back to Ft. Benton."

"He'll come after us."

"Yeah, that's what I'm countin' on."

The nippy Montana morning wind was at their backs, as crimson light filtered across the night sky. Pete lead the way. Sunny followed with the old buffalo robe over her head. Avery came third, leading the two horses with roped and bound gunmen. They were tied down like a heavy pack on a miner's mule . . . feet on one side, head on the other.

"Are we going to chase the river all the way back to town?" Pete asked.

Avery kicked his left foot out of the stirrup to relieve a cramp. "Yep."

"Wouldn't the rim be a little safer?" Sunny quizzed.

"Nope."

Sunny twisted toward Avery. "All the way out here you said the rim of the canyon was safer than being down here."

"That's because we were alone then."

Pete halted his horse and squinted at the rim. "I don't seem 'em. White or red?"

"Red."

"Blood or Blackfoot?"

"Blackfoot."

"Hunting party or war party?"

"With the Blackfoot, it doesn't matter."

"How many?"

"At least six."

"Are they going to come down?"

"Yep."

"I still don't see 'em."

"You will."

"Are we going to shoot first?"

"I hope not. Come back and take these lead ropes. I'll ride point for a while."

Sunny scanned the early morning horizon. "Should I be worried?"

"Just keep that buffalo robe over your head and scream on cue."

"What do you mean, scream on cue."

Avery never pulled his eyes off the canyon rim. "You're an actress. You'll know when it's time for your line."

"You know how I don't like working without a script."

As they reached the rocks, six Indians rode out and formed a semicircle across the trail: three bareback, three on saddles. All carried repeating rifles across their laps. All wore buckskin trousers. None wore shirts. Two had their dark black hair cropped short. One boasted an eagle feather tucked behind his ear.

"The one with a feather is riding Blackie's horse," Avery observed.

"Are you sure?" Pete said.

"Oh, yeah."

"Where's Blackie?" Sunny said.

"Don't think about it."

The one with the feather rode straight at them.

Avery motioned for the other two to wait as he trotted ahead to meet him. Junior's nose twitched inches away from the Indian's horse when the two men stopped.

"You had a fight?" The Indian pointed at Avery's face.

"Yeah."

"Who won?"

"We did. The losers are back there." He motioned toward the two outlaws strapped to the horses.

"Are they dead?"

"Nope."

The Indian hollered something to the five behind him, then turned back. "We want their horses."

Avery shook his head. "We need them. Don't have any extra. Five horses, five people."

"We will buy them. We have gold."

Avery inched his hand to his holstered revolver. "Just like you bought that horse from Blackie?"

The Indian jolted straight up. "It was a present. I gave him a gift. He gave me one."

"What did you give him?"

"His life. We let him walk away."

"And he gave you his horse?"

"His horse, his boots, his clothes. It was a fair trade. But we will pay you with gold." He waved a small leather pouch that hung around his neck on a buckskin string. "I have plenty of gold."

"I reckon that, too, was a gift."

"No, this man didn't want to bargain, so I killed him. You sell the horses to us?"

"I need them to carry those two bad men."

"We will buy the men, too."

"They aren't for sale."

"We could take them from you."

"Yes, but several of you would die first. Ask them which ones would like to die first."

"I will not ask them."

"There are better horses coming behind us."

Eagle Feather stood in the stirrups and peered down the trail. "I don't see them."

"You will."

He plopped back down in the saddle, then

turned to yelp a command. One of the Indians galloped up the slope toward the canyon rim.

Another called out in English, "Why does the woman hide under the buffalo robe?"

"She is very sick. She has very pale skin. Quite ugly," Avery droned. "Besides, she is crazy . . . loco."

"What does she do?" Eagle Feather asked.

"She screams whenever she's sees the sun. It's awful. Pull back her robe, Pete."

"Are you sure?" Pete said.

"Go ahead."

Pete yanked the robe back. Sunny let out a heartstopping series of shrieks. He threw the robe back over his sister's head.

The Indian's horse started to buck. He spun it around several times to get him settled down. The others hooted and howled.

Avery motioned back at Sunny. "If you want to buy someone, I'll gladly sell you the woman."

Eagle Feather shook his head. "I already have one that screams in the night. I do not need one that screams in the day."

Avery rubbed his chin. "Then I'm afraid I am stuck with her."

A couple of the Indians shouted and waved at the canyon rim where a lone Indian raised his carbine numerous times.

Eagle Feather nodded. "You are right, there are more coming."

"Six men?" Avery asked.

"Twelve."

"That means more horses."

"Will they sell them to us?"

"I don't think so."

"We will have to take them."

"Be careful. They are bad men. They will not want to talk."

"We can win," Eagle Feather insisted.

"Six against twelve is not a good fight."

"You are wrong. It will be six against one . . . twelve times."

He signaled for the others to head up the canyon rim, then he leaned over, and spoke low. "Sell her to the Flathead . . . they will buy any woman."

Avery offered a polite smile. "I appreciate the advice."

"Perhaps I will see you again."

Avery tipped his hat. "Perhaps."

"What is your name?"

"Avery John Creede."

"I like that. Yes, I will see you again. I like that name very much." He turned his paint horse toward the canyon rim.

"And what is your name?"

The Indian grinned wide, revealing straight, white teeth. "My name is now Creede." He kicked his horse and galloped up the mountain.

• • •

Sunny tossed the buffalo robe back on the horse's rump. "I can't believe you offered to sell me.'"

"I knew they wouldn't want to buy you."

"How did you know that? How could you be sure?"

"Indians always want what you don't want to give up . . . and never want what you give away freely."

"Oh, is that a rule? A code?"

"More like a guideline," Pete chimed in.

"And if it didn't work, what then?"

"I reckon I'd just have to shoot them all."

"That's a wonderful plan."

Pete rode up next to him. "What I want to know is how you knew for sure there would be riders behind us?"

"It was a guess. We're leaving a muddy trail. Anyone could pick it up."

Pete got off his horse and stretched his legs with a groan. "Don't you worry about stirring up a fight between those two groups?"

"Which ones should I be worried about?"

"I'm not sure."

Sunny tried to rub her mud-caked blue dress. "I am not a sickly pale white."

"You are to the Indians."

"I can't believe a couple of screeches dissuaded them."

"You're very good at it."

201

"I learned that for a role in MacBeth."

"You played Lady MacBeth?"

"I played one of the witches, and if you say one word, I will slice you so thin there won't be enough of you left to sell to the Indians for dog food."

About noon, Pete signaled up the trail. "Someone's headed toward us."

"It's Ace," Sunny reported.

"He was supposed to wait in town for us," Avery chided.

"Who's Ace?" Pete asked.

"Avery's nephew."

"Where did you get a nephew?"

"From my sister."

"I didn't know you had any family. I never heard you talk about a nephew."

"I reckon there's a number of things you don't know about me."

Sunny rode next to her brother. "Do you know how Avery got that scar?"

"No, I don't," Pete snapped. "And never bring it up again."

"Hmm, Avery truly is a man of mystery."

"Everyone out west has a few things in his past that shouldn't be talked about," Pete replied.

Sunny raised her eyebrows. "He told me all about those notches on your rifle."

Pete swung round and glared at Avery. "You did?"

"Yeah, I told her about those three Apaches who tried to kill General Crook and kind of went crazy and you killed them all."

"Oh . . . yeah . . . well, you're right. It's something I just don't like to talk about," Pete murmured.

Ace galloped up to them. The mud on the trail had dried, but there was still little dust. "You've been busy. Howdy, Miss Sunny."

She nodded at the two gunmen strapped over their saddles. "This is only half of them. We buried one, and we think there's one running to Canada naked."

Ace's eyes grew big.

Avery rode up. "It's quite a story. Ace, this is a good pal of mine and Miss Sunny's brother, Pete Cutler."

"Yes, sir. Glad to meet you."

Pete leaned across the saddle and shook his hand. "You realize if you hang around this uncle of yours, your life will be in constant turmoil."

"Yes, sir, Mr. Cutler. I believe you're right."

"Call me Pete."

"Yes, sir, Mr. Cutler." Ace rode beside Avery. "Did you clean out the Missouri River Breaks?"

"I think we just stirred up a hornet's nest."

"We're ready to get back to town and clean up and relax," Sunny added.

"Things is hoppin' in Ft. Benton. Deputy Easley escaped."

"How did that happen?" Avery questioned.

"The sheriff said he and Easley had hidden a jail key inside the leg of one of the bunks, just in case they ever got locked up in their own jail. The mayor seemed happy that he's gone, and the sheriff's pulling through."

"Is Captain Mandara there yet?" Avery said.

"No, but Dawson Wickers showed up."

"Dawson's in Ft. Benton?" Pete replied.

"He was, but he left. Said he got word Tight was in jail in Bozeman, and he was riding down to get him out."

"Tight's at a hot springs in Colorado," Avery insisted.

"I tried to tell him that, but Dawson said he'd be back in a few days."

"A few days? We'll just ride down after him," Avery said.

"You can't do that. Your darlin' Carla is going to be here tomorrow," Ace remarked.

"Carla's around?" Pete asked.

Ace pushed back his hat. "She's going to be here tomorrow, but she sent you a present today."

"A present?" Sunny quizzed. "She sends presents ahead? Just like Queen Victoria, no doubt."

"Sort of a present," Ace added. "A Chinaman."

Avery spun Junior around to face his nephew. "What are you talking about?"

"This Chinese fella showed up with a note from your darlin' Carla, sayin' that she hired him to cook for you. She knows how much you like Chinese food, and there probably isn't a good place in all of Montana, so she sent you a cook."

"Well, isn't that nice," Sunny grumbled. "And to think some people have a tough time knowing what to buy. What's his name?"

"I think it's Chu-Ling, but I'm not sure," Ace said. "I rented us rooms at the hotel and put him in yours."

"That's absurd," Avery fumed. "Why didn't you tell him to find his own room?"

"He doesn't speak any English."

CHAPTER FOURTEEN

Steam from the bathwater hugged Avery's face and seemed to draw out layers of dirt, grime and sweat. He scrunched down in the brass tub, only his face above water. He rung out a wash cloth and draped it over his head. The cuts and bruises from the fight in the Breaks stung, then eased in the heat.

A voice from the other side of the curtain intruded.

"Do you need more water, Mr. Creede?"

Avery sat straight up. "Eh, no ma'am . . . Miss Molly."

"I have your clothes washed and pressed." The words rang clear, but the tone was a musical singsong.

"Already? Have I been in here that long?"

"You had shave and haircut first. Remember?"

He ran his fingers through his wet, dark brown hair. "You are a very good laundress." Avery heard a cupboard open.

"It is one of few jobs Chinese women allowed to do."

Still sitting in the tub, he grabbed a white towel and dried his hair. "Did you have a chance to talk to him?"

"Yes, we had nice visit. He good man. I think I will stitch sleeve in your coat."

"You don't need to do that. What did he tell you?"

"It is not need. It is desire. I want to sew your coat sleeve. Your lady friend, Miss Loganaire, hire him $100 a month, for three months, to be cook."

"So, she already paid the man?"

"Yes, salary to cover cost of food as well. His name is Chu-Ling. He was cook in San Francisco. He had to leave in a hurry, for reasons he not say, but his life in danger. You know they having anti-Chinese riots in some cities."

"I have heard that. Molly, I am sorry for such

injustices in this world. From what I can tell in the Bible, it's been that way for a long time." He stood and tied the towel around his waist. "I'm a drifting man. Why do I need a cook?" He clutched another clean towel and dried off his arms. "I'll straighten this out when Carla comes to town."

"Do you need talc, Mr. Creede? Chu-Ling anxious to cook for you."

"No talc. I'm white enough without it." He checked the closed curtain, then stepped out of the brass tub. "I don't see how that can work. I don't have a kitchen, or utensils, or dining room table. Tell him to wait a few days and I'll get this matter settled."

"Mr. Creede, I have proposal. I have place for Chu-Ling to cook . . . and he can stay in extra room out back next to wash-house. You eat at my table. I only ask that I enjoy his cooking too. I eat in the kitchen, of course."

Avery finished drying his feet. "You know, Molly, I don't believe my toes have been this clean in a year. Listen, I'll take you up on the offer. Tell him I will have several guests at each meal. He should plan on four or five. But, you will not eat in the kitchen. You will dine at the table with us or it's no deal."

"Thank you, Mr. Creede. I enjoy your kindness. It is not good time to be Chinese in the United States."

"You wish to go home?"

"I am home, Mr. Creede. This my land now. I only want to live in peace."

Avery strolled out into Main Street basking in his fresh cleanness. A young man wearing a long-sleeve white shirt, buttoned at the neck, trotted up beside him. "Hey, you look good all scrubbed up, Uncle Avery. There's only a few bruises showing, besides your scar. When are you going to tell me how . . ."

"Never." Avery felt his hat slip a little lower on his ears. He pushed it back. "Where's Pete and Miss Sunny?"

"At Baker & Brother Mercantile. Pete said he needed some supplies for his Sharps. Isn't this a beautiful day?"

"You have an awfully wide smile, Avery Creede Emerson. What's her name?"

"What?"

"I've seen that same smile on hundreds of army privates. It's the 'I-met-this-girl-and-she-makes-me-feel-good-from-the-inside-out' look. What's her name and where'd you meet her?"

"I can't believe you said that."

"You are avoiding my question."

Ace jammed his hands in his ducking pockets. "Her name is Tabitha, but her folks call her Tabby. Isn't that a great name?"

"Who are her folks?"

"You know them . . . Mayor and Mrs. Leitner."

"The mayor's daughter? How old is she?"

"She'll be sixteen on Christmas Eve. Isn't that a great day to have a birthday?"

"When did you meet her?"

"Two days and four hours ago. You told me when I brought the last one in, to go talk to the mayor. And Miss Tabby was sittin' on the front porch swing reading a novel that was over one inch thick. Can you imagine that? I've read novels that are one-half inch thick, but never one that wide. Isn't that something to find a girl who likes to read thick books?"

"She's left quite an impression on you."

"Not only that, I dream about her at night. But that's okay, because she said she dreams about me too. Do you think the Lord speaks to us in dreams? Miss Tabby says she thinks He does. Isn't that something to find a girl that thinks the Lord is speaking to her?"

"And just what do Mr. and Mrs. Mayor think about you hangin' around with your tongue lollyin' out?"

"Her mamma is the nicest lady. Reminds me of Aunt Martha. She calls me 'Young Master Emerson.' She can cook okra and make it actually taste good. Isn't that something?"

"And Mr. Mayor?"

"I think he tolerates me. Guess what, Uncle Avery? The mayor told Miss Tabby that men like

Creede and Emerson live by their courage and their guns, and never stay in one place very long. He called me a man . . . ain't that something?"

"Oh, it's somethin' alright."

"Do you think I need to shave before I go visit Miss Tabby? Should I put on a coat and tie? What do you think I need?"

"I think you need your mamma."

"What?"

Avery hiked toward the hotel. "Have you ever shaved before?"

"Yes, sir, I shaved on the fourth of July."

"That was a couple months ago. I think you can wait until Christmas."

"Maybe on Christmas Eve? Isn't that . . ."

"Yep, a wonderful day for a birthday."

"Do you have any advice, Uncle Avery? I mean, when I'm with Miss Tabby, what should I do? What should I say?"

Avery stopped to place his hands on Ace's shoulders. "There's only one thing you have to remember. You remember this, and you will do just great."

Ace's eyes widened. "What is it?"

Avery leaned until their noses almost touched. "Remember, your mamma is watching everything you do and say from right up there in heaven."

Ace pulled back. "That's all you are going to tell me?"

"Do you need more than that?"

He spread a crooked smile. "No, sir, I don't reckon I do."

Sunny tucked her left arm into Avery's, her right into her brother's. "Isn't this nice? I'm being escorted by two bruised and battered retired cavalry officers."

"I'm sure you're the envy of ever' gal in town," Avery said.

"Yes, and I'm going to enjoy a special supper prepared by Avery John Creede's personal chef."

Avery wiggled clean toes in clean socks. "I don't know if he can cook or not. But, it's a great adventure. I haven't understood one dadgum word he's told me."

"He does know your name," Pete piped up. "Did you hear what Chu-Ling calls him?"

"Oh, I hope it's something memorable," she said.

Pete patted her arm. "He tries to say Mister Creede, but the C gets lost and he runs the name together. Not only that, he doesn't do well with Ds either. So it just comes out Misteree."

"Oh, yes! I love it!" Sunny howled. "You are a man of mystery!"

"I don't think it's all that funny."

Sunny prodded him with her elbow. "Oh, Avery, you are such a poop!"

Pete pulled off his hat and fanned himself.

"You know, there were some officers who called him the same thing."

"Really?"

Pete burst out with a laugh. "It was a different word than poop, but it meant the same thing."

The threesome continued arm-in-arm down a narrow side street, then stopped in front of Molly's Laundry, Baths and Ironing.

Sunny surveyed the unpainted board and bat square building. "What a charming café. Most people would not know such a place is tucked away on a side street of Ft. Benton, Montana."

"I like the location," Avery said. "Maybe no one can find me back here."

"I say, Mr. Creede!" The shout filtered down the street like a plaintive cat at midnight.

Sunny glanced back. "Isn't that the mayor?"

They waited for the short man in the dark suit to catch up. "I say, Creede, you are a difficult man to find."

"Can't be too tough. It's a small town."

"Could I have a word with you . . . alone?"

"I don't think I want to hear secrets," Creede grumbled.

"Ah, more mysteries for Misteree." Sunny tugged at Pete's arm. "Come along, dear brother. We better get to the Café Molly before all the good tables are taken."

"Café what?" the mayor huffed. "There are no restaurants here on D Street."

"My, you would think a man holding political office would know his town better than that." Sunny nudged Pete to Molly's front door.

Avery and the mayor sauntered down the dirt street.

"Isn't that woman the one you arrested?"

"Yep, and she's also the one who saved my life. Now, what is this about?"

The mayor motioned for Creede to follow him down the street and past the buildings. "This is a rather delicate matter."

"Is this about Ace? Look, Leitner, the boy's mother died this spring, and he has no one left but me. I think you need to . . ."

"This is not about young Mr. Emerson."

"It's not?"

"He's a fine lad."

"He is?"

"I would think a scion of yours would have better discernment, though. I'm afraid Tabitha Ann is immature and spoiled. I don't for the life of me know what he sees in her. She is very much like her mother."

"He seems quite enamored."

"Yes, but that will wear off, I assure you. That's not what I need to talk to you about. Here's the situation, Creede. Captain Mandara cannot make it here until Monday. You heard about the ruckus down at Cantrell, didn't you?"

"No."

"Elephant trouble."

"What?"

"A circus came in on the train to Billings. They toured around to outlying towns to stir up customers and they hauled an elephant out to Cantrell for a novelty."

"How do you haul an elephant?"

"A baby elephant. According to the people I talked to, all was going well until Tap Andrews' daughter . . . you know, the dark skinned one . . ."

"Angelita?"

"Yes, she led the elephant around selling rides while the trainers got pickled in the saloon. But when she got to the Captain's place, the little elephant, overwhelmed no doubt with all those Mandara kids, went beserk and stampeded inside Mrs. Mandara's hotel. I understand he did extensive damage before he could be contained."

"Wait, are you telling me Captain Mandara can't be here because an elephant destroyed his hotel?"

"That's the jist of it. He'll get here early next week, once he makes some repairs and shovels out the . . ."

"I know the Mandaras and Andrews, but the only time I met Angelita was in the train depot at Cheyenne. She tried to sell me my own gun." Avery stopped in front of the empty corral next to the blacksmith shop. "What does this have to do with me?"

"Can I be blunt?"

"It would be a nice change."

"I need you to be sheriff until Mandara comes or I will have to kick you and your friends out of town."

"Wait a minute. Are you threatening me to be sheriff?"

"I have no choice. You told me when you arrived with the prisoners that Rinkman would be following you."

"Yeah, he will come after me . . . and will want to 'interrogate' those three associates of his."

"Yes, well . . . I sent them down to Deer Lodge."

"To the prison, without a trial?"

"They seemed anxious to confess to any crime that would get them out of Ft. Benton."

"I reckon they would."

"I need you to be here as a buffer between the Missouri River Breaks outlaws and the fine citizens of this town."

"I've already told you, I won't take the job."

"Then that leads me to the second choice. I will have to demand that you and your associates leave Ft. Benton before morning."

"Why would you do that?"

"In hopes that if Rinkman and gang come to Ft. Benton, and there is no one here he is looking for, he will pursue them elsewhere."

"And bypass the town?"

"Yes."

"Or he could just burn it to the ground out of anger."

"Why would he do that?"

"Because he's violent and unpredictable. Look, Leitner . . . if you think . . ."

"Mr. Creede, listen to me for a moment." The mayor tramped over to the empty corral and leaned on the top rail, his back to the street. "Look at this from my point of view. We are a supply town filled with merchants and clerks. This is not a cattle town like Dodge City. Or a mining town like Tombstone. It's a merchant town. These men didn't open the west, nor fight off savages to establish their place. They brought capital and supplies up the river. They purchased a lot, built a store, and want to make a living for their families. I want to do everything I can to insure them that right. Most every cowboy in the area is out gathering cattle, or pushing them up to the mines in Canada. Right now, the only men we have in town are too old, too young, or totally ill-equipped mentally and physically to go against a dozen armed men. My sheriff is recuperating. My deputy turned out to be a crook and broke out of jail. I have a wife and daughter and to keep safe. Just what options do I have?"

Avery leaned on the top corral rail beside him. "You can grab a gun and be a man."

"Should I, by myself, sit in the sheriff's office again, with a shotgun across my lap and try to repel Rinkman, who you admit is violent and unpredictable? That would insure my wife as a widow, and my daughter fatherless."

"Are you demanding that I leave town?"

"Begging would be a better word. Creede, do you have other suggestions for me?"

"Mayor, I do understand your situation. Let me tell you mine. I have been in more gun battles than I can remember. For seventeen years I was dressed in army blue. Since then, a month doesn't go by that I am not fighting for my life. I envy every one of these merchants. I can't even imagine how life like that would feel. I would be delighted to gather up my friends and ride out of here."

"Then you'll go?"

"I can't. Tomorrow or the next day, a very attractive lady from Chicago will arrive. She has given me a glimmer of hope that some day soon I can settle down to the very peaceful life you enjoy. It is my one opportunity to change. I have to wait in town to follow that possibility. If I don't, I will spend my life thinking, if only I had waited one more day. So, you see my position?"

The mayor wiped the dust off his forehead. "Then we are at a crossroads. Where does that leave us?"

"Well, I can't leave town . . . and I reckon Rinkman will come looking for me first." He sighed. "So, I'll take that job. But my goal is not to kill Rinkman or shoot up his gang. What I want to do is keep you, your family and all of us safe."

"I won't hide in the root celler. I sell hardware and farm implements. I've never had anyone shoot at me. And I've never shot a man. Give me a role that I can fulfill, and I'll do it. I'm not a coward, Mr. Creede. But I'm not a fool either."

"I appreciate your truthfulness. I've never had problems with an honest man. Can you find ten other men like you? I won't put them out in the open with a gun in their hand. I need some men who will stand with us."

"I think I can line that up. They won't be the kind that can help much in a fist fight, but they will follow orders. How about your associates? Will they stand with us?"

"I'll let them make that decision on their own."

"Fair enough." The mayor reached in his pocket and handed Creede the sheriff's badge. "When your lady friend arrives, we'll be honored to have you and her over for a meal."

"Thank you, Mayor, but I already promised we'd supper with Abe Hermann and his wife."

"Yes, quite . . . we'll feed your nephew some, no doubt. I believe he's dining with us tonight."

"Run him off anytime he gets in the way."

"Speaking of run off . . . this is a minor matter. But my wife's dog seems to have run away. You didn't see a rather chubby, short haired brown dog that answers to 'Chop-Chop'?"

"Nope."

"Well, he never gets too far from the wife. He'll show up. It's the least of my worries tonight. Thanks, Creede. Maybe Rinkman won't show up at all."

An hour later, Avery pushed himself away from Molly's small pine table. "I've got to admit, Chu-Ling knows how to cook. The spices and sauces were as good as anything I've ever had."

"Beats eatin' out of the saddle bag." Pete wiped his mouth on a flour sack towel.

"What kind of vegetable is this?" Sunny said. "It's wonderful."

"Bok choi," Molly said.

"It tastes sort of like a turnip cabbage."

"What I like is the meat. What is this?" Avery asked.

Molly said something to Chu-Ling. His answer was curt. "He said it is not proper to ask a recipe."

"I don't want a recipe. I just couldn't tell if it is beef, buffalo or elk. Tell him it's delicious. Whatever it is, he can serve it again, that's for sure."

Pete picked his teeth with his fingernail. "I can't believe you took the sheriff job."

"Just for a couple days. I've got to wait here

for Carla anyway. And I will have to confront Rinkman whether I wear a badge or not."

"I don't," Sunny said.

"I agree. Pete, you and Sunny should head down and see if you can find Dawson. Tell him Tight really is in Colorado. Besides, I don't think your sister should be here when Rinkman shows. Both of you are better off out of town."

"That's not why I'm leaving," Sunny remarked. "I have no intention of watching you and your darling Carla."

"I think you'd like her."

"I don't. In fact, I hate her already."

"She's a nice lady," Pete said.

"Then I know I'll despise her. We'll go find Dawson in the morning."

"You want us to take Ace along?" Pete asked.

"If he'll go, but I don't think you can peel him off the mayor's front porch."

"He's not quite as bashful with gals as his uncle," Sunny said.

"I'm not bashful."

"Oh? In that case how about you and me taking a long stroll by the river tonight?"

"I don't have time. I've got to figure out what to do if Rinkman shows."

"Aha, that proves my point." Sunny turned to Molly. "Ask Chu-Ling if he has a recipe to cure Creede's timidness with ladies."

Molly rattled off a long sentence.

Chu-Ling grinned and nodded his head, then began a lengthy discourse.

"He says he has several recipes that will help, but he needs yew bark and caribou antlers."

"Tell him I don't need that," Avery huffed. "But I do want to know what kind of meat I ate."

She spoke again to the cook, but he didn't respond.

Chu-Ling cleared the dishes off the table, paused and rubbed his smooth chin, then spoke to Molly.

She turned to them. "He said to tell Misteree that the meat is chops. Chinese chops."

CHAPTER FIFTEEN

Spice tonic water aroma mixed with early autumn as Avery plopped on the park bench. Rolling freight wagons rattled toward the dock. "How's your week been? I trust it was calmer than mine.

"Since we last chatted, I stopped a bank robbery, a nephew appeared, been beat up a half-dozen times, got shot at more than that, had to shoot a few men to save my life, got tossed in jail, thrown in an outhouse, had my skull cracked, been a deputy sheriff, got pitched off my horse, found a lady to dislike . . . but she's growin' on me . . . inherited a Chinese cook who can't speak English, and now eat meals of unknown origin and substance."

Avery leaned back. A slight breeze drifted lukewarm across his fresh shaven cheeks and loped along at pace with the wide river in front of him.

"Yep, it's been a typical week for me. I see you're still up to the same old tricks."

The small brown bird with white and black rings around its neck flapped a wing in the dirt at the base of the huge cottonwood tree.

"And I'm still no threat to you. I told you before you are way past the season for this sort of thing. But you'd do well not to hang around too close. What my life lacks in purpose, I make up for with crisis."

Avery brushed dust off his coat sleeve, then straightened his black tie. He pulled his watch out of his vest and tapped on the glass as if to hurry the minute hand. He slid it back into the pocket. He pondered down river at the horizon where the thirty yard wide, six foot deep Missouri River dropped over the curvature of the earth.

His calloused fingers drummed the smooth wooden bench. Long legs stretched out in front of him. Hat pushed to the back of his head, he dropped his chin to his chest and closed his eyes.

"Lord, I'm not one to bother you. But I've got some major decisions to make real soon, and I don't want to mess things up. I'd appreciate any

advice you had in this matter. Most times my life seems out of my control. I just take what you lead me to day by day, but now . . . "

"Mr. Creede . . . " Abraham Hermann stormed up from the street behind the bench.

Avery sat to attention. "Abe, how's the jewelry business?"

"I've looked all over for you. Are you busy? You looked like you were taking a nap."

"I was just visitin' with . . . eh, the Lord."

"Oh my, and it's not even the Sabbath. I trust you have no serious difficulties."

"I was prayin' for the peace of Jerusalem."

Hermann's narrow eyes widened. "You were?"

"Among other things. My mamma taught me always to pray for the peace of Jerusalem."

The jeweler's eyes twitched. "So did mine. Peace is a wonderful thing. My people have had so little of it."

"Nor have I. What can I do for you?"

"You are an eclectic man, Mr. Creede."

"If that means hard to predict and more diverse than I look, I reckon you're right. But I'm sure you didn't hike out to the river to discuss my idiosyncrasies."

"Quite. My Noelle, who is a gift of God to me no matter what my family says . . . has always cooked kosher meals for me. And she wanted to know if you and Miss Loganaire would be agreeable to dining on . . ."

"A Jewish meal will be fine. I expected nothing less."

"Thank you, Mr. Creede. I know it might seem odd for a man who marries outside of the faith to be concerned with dietary rules. But I will not tempt God beyond my one failure."

"I understand. Did you ever consider that perhaps you and I aren't all that different?"

The jeweler looked down at his dusty black shoes. "Up to a point, perhaps. I trust that is so."

Avery rubbed the corners of his eyes, surprised they were clean and not mud-caked. "You are looking for a Messiah. I have found one."

"That is the point of divergence, isn't it? Not many have put it to me so succinctly."

"I'm looking forward to our meal tonight."

"Will you give her the ring before you come to supper?"

"That is one of my other prayers." Avery settled his sights on the slow moving, murky river. "I suppose I'm naïve to think the steamboat might pull in on time."

"I can't remember it ever being punctual. She is coming by river?"

"That's what the last telegram said. There have been many delays and lots of changes."

Hermann shuffled toward town. "I must get back to the store. My Noelle wants to spend the afternoon cooking. She is very excited about this evening. We don't entertain guests too often."

Avery resumed his river watch. The nervous bird ceased her protest and scrunched down on one small mottled egg.

"You know, Mrs. Killdeer, I wonder if Abe knows how much I envy his life? A quiet routine. A loving wife. A peaceful future. Maybe this meeting with Carla is the first step to that."

He closed his eyes again and pitched back on the bench. He could almost feel her arms around his neck. He remembered how it was to waltz into that hotel in St. Louis, how every man turned to stare at the lady on his arm. He felt the surge of excitement when her long, thin fingers inter-twined with his. When he pursed his lips, he felt her soft teasing kiss that hinted of better things ahead.

"Hi, Mr. Creede. I thought we should talk, but if you need to rest, I understand. My grandfather says that older people do need their naps."

Avery leapt up and yanked off his hat. He tried to focus in on the blonde young lady in the red gingham dress.

"Not that you are old, or anything, heavens no. My grandfather is fifty-four, and I'm sure you aren't that old. At least, I don't think so. My friend Prissy's grandmother is only forty-two, but that's what happens when you live in the mountains one hundred miles from anyone. I told her that they should have moved to Virginia City and it would never have happened like that. Can you imagine being bored in Virginia City? Neither can I. Of course, I don't get bored in Ft. Benton. Some say it's a very dreary town but I find it quite sanguine. Isn't that a wonderful word? I have my own copy of Mr. Noah Webster's Dictionary and I read in it almost every night."

Avery gazed into the brightest blue eyes, the color of bachelor's-buttons. "I reckon it's over an inch thick."

"Why, yes it is. Have you read it?" Blonde curls bounced as she chatted.

"I've read parts of it, but never did finish it cover to cover. I don't know how it ends, but I've heard good reviews."

"Mr. Creede, you have a great sense of humor, just like . . . Oh, dear . . ." She held her hands together as if to pray. "I know we haven't formally met, but it's not proper for a lady to . . ."

"Miss Leitner, I presume?" He bowed at the waist.

She curtsied. "It's nice to meet you, Mr. Creede." She sashayed to the bench and swished down, skirt and petticoats spread past halfway across. "You may sit here, Mr. Creede."

"I think I'll stand . . . it will help me wake up from my old man's nap. Can I do something for you, Miss Leitner?"

"You may call me Tabitha."

"And you may call me, Mr. Creede. I presume you had a purpose for this visit."

"Yes, I do. As you know, Ave and I have been . . ."

"Ave? You mean Ace."

"Ace is the kind of name you give a dog. His name is Avery, and so I gave him the nickname Ave that rhymes with brave . . . isn't that so like him?"

"He's a good kid."

"Kid? I think of him as a very strong and courageous man. He says he is very much like his Uncle Avery. I read that if you want to know how a young man is going to turn out . . . get to know his father or grandfather. So . . ."

"You thought you'd come check me out?" Avery tugged the sleeves down on his suit coat.

"I trust you don't mind. If Ave and I are going to spend a lifetime together, I thought I should know what it would be like. You know, when he's older."

Avery tried to wipe the grin off his face. "Do you need to take down a few notes, or can you remember all of this?"

"No notebook. I have a very good memory."

"I was just being facetious."

"Oh?"

"It's in the thick book. It means I was teasing."

"Oh, you are like Ave. I'd like to ask you a

question. I trust you don't think it too forward. My mother says I ask things that are better left unsaid. But how can a young lady learn about the world if she isn't allowed to inquire? Just the other night I asked them a simple question and father choked on his meat. My mother turned bright red. Neither would speak to me for an hour. Is that any way to treat a daughter who is almost sixteen? I should say not. Would you like to hear what I asked them?"

"No."

Her wide smile melted.

"There are some things you should only ask your parents."

"Perhaps you are right. My friend Rebekah asked her mother how a woman knew for sure she was great with child, and the next day she was shoved on a train and sent to a girl's school in Connecticut. I haven't gotten a letter from her in over two years. Have you ever been to Connecticut, Mr. Creede?"

Avery pulled out his watch, tapped on the glass, then slipped it back into his pocket. "I was in New Haven one time to talk to folks about a new Winchester." He surveyed the empty river. "You had a question?"

"Oh, yes. Mr. Creede, why is it you have never married and had children?"

"That's what you came out here to ask me?"

"Yes. If Ave is like you, I want to know why

someone would go through his entire life all alone."

"I haven't gone through my entire life . . . at least, I don't think so."

"But you are childless and alone."

Avery sucked in a deep breath, then paced in front of the park bench. "I was in the army for years. That's not a good situation for a family. And since then, well . . . my line of work isn't very conducive to a wife and children. But I haven't ruled that out of the question. When the right lady comes along . . ."

"Is the right lady in the steamboat?"

"That's what I hope to find out."

"Ave told me about Miss Loganaire. I do hope to meet her. I've read about her in the newspapers. I think she and I are a lot alike. You know, beautiful, witty, charming, personable, with exquisite taste. Wouldn't it be incredible if Ave and I . . . eh . . . and . . . eh . . . you and Miss Loganaire would . . . eh . . . then that would make us all . . . eh . . . relatives."

"That would be astonishing. Something so stupendous should be approached with care and caution. Being such a student of thick books, I'm sure you agree that many a wonderful plan has been derailed by rash decisions."

"I hadn't thought of it that way." She stood and held out her gloved hand. "Very nice to visit with you, Mr. Creede. I must be going. Ave promised to rent a buggy and take me for a ride. I want to show him the Turnbull place on the Great Falls Road. It's for sale, you know."

"I didn't know that."

"And at quite a reasonable price. Of course there is some work to do. It hasn't been lived in for over a year, unless you call Toro Turnbull normal. The roof needs repair. The kitchen wall has all those gunshots blasted through it. The porch sags . . . and the privy . . . well, you know what happens to abandoned privies. But, I'm sure Ave can fix everything in no time. Do you do carpentry, Mr. Creede?"

"No."

"I'm surprised. Ave seemed to indicate you can do anything short of walking on water."

"Ace is a personable, optimistic and ambitious young man."

"Oh, yes, isn't he scrumptious?"

"You took the word right out of my mouth."

"Scrumptious . . . out of my mouth? You have a wonderful sense of humor. Perhaps I should have a notebook and write that down. Goodbye, Mr. Creede. Wish me luck."

"Goodbye, Miss Leitner. I wish you luck . . . and Ace protection."

"Protection? Don't be silly. There is no danger riding out to the Turnbull place."

Avery watched Tabitha Leitner march back to the boardwalk in front of the closed bank, head high, arms and hair swinging. He faced the river, then sauntered along the dried mud trail to the east.

"Miss Leitner," he muttered aloud. "The disturbing thing is you and Carla are a lot alike."

A tiny puff of smoke on the horizon snapped him to attention. He straightened his tie, brushed back his hair, reset his hat. He scurried to the boat dock and stood behind a half-dozen workers loitering next to several dozen one-hundred-and-twenty-pound sacks of wheat. First the smoke stacks appeared, then the rest of the stern-wheel steamboat chugged into view. He pulled the velvet sack from his pocket and peeked inside at the ring.

"Uncle Avery!"

A scrubbed up and spice tonic smelling Ace trotted toward him. "Did Miss Sunny and her brother leave yet?"

"They headed to Billings this morning. You didn't want to go with them, did you?"

"No, sir. Like I said, if there is going to be trouble here in Ft. Benton, then I reckon my role is to protect Miss Tabby."

"Why were you looking for Sunny and Pete?"

"Miss Sunny promised to teach me how to . . ." Ace's face flushed.

"Maybe I can teach you."

"Oh, no, it wasn't something that you . . ."

"Something I don't know anything about?"

"That ain't it. I need a woman . . ."

"Don't we all?"

"No, I mean, it's something only a woman can teach."

"You remember what I said about your mamma looking down?"

"Yes, sir. I'm not talkin' about something sinful, no sir. Miss Sunny promised to give me a few pointers on . . . eh . . . you know . . ."

"Kissing?"

"Yes, sir. That's it. I saw you and her do it so good, I figured I could use her help."

"I'm sure you'll figure it out on your own."

They both watched as the boat chugged close to the dock, then cut the engines and drifted closer.

"Isn't she beautiful?" Ace said.

"Nothin' quite like a big steamboat."

"No, I meant Miss Tabby. Ain't she somethin'?"

"Scrumptious."

"That's what I think. Say, Uncle Avery. I wondered if . . . eh, well . . ."

"How much do you need?"

"Two dollars."

"You're going to rent a $2 buggy?"

"I wanted a nice one, and this one comes with a buffalo robe and mink mittens."

"It's September. You won't need a buffalo robe."

"But what should I do if Miss Tabby gets chilled?"

"Scrunch up close together."

Ace flashed a dimpled grin. "That's a great idea. Maybe you know more about this than I give you credit for."

"Here's $2 anyway. Get her home before dark."

"We ain't scared of the dark, Uncle Avery."

"Then be scared of what happens in the dark."

Ace glanced back out at the river. "She is beautiful."

"Miss Leitner is a very pretty girl."

"I don't mean her." Ace pointed at the boat. "I mean your darlin' Carla. That's her, isn't it?"

A dark haired lady with shimmery green silk dress and plumed hat strolled down the gangplank. Tall, thin, shapely . . . Carla's presence made handsome women feel plain and caused brave men to stammer.

He envisioned the first time he saw her at the governor's mansion in Carson City. *Carla, I decided I didn't like you because of your arrogance and pride. But that was before the midnight stroll, honest confessions, and one incredible kiss.*

" 'Bye, Uncle Avery, see you tonight."

Avery nodded but bored in on the brown eyes, wide smile, perfect white straight teeth. He pulled off his hat. He hadn't recalled all the highlights in those dark eyes.

"Carla, you look . . . eh . . . scrumptious."

"What a delightful word, my Avery." Her arms circled his neck. Her soft, warm lips pressed to his. "Oh, I was so glad to see you here. I was afraid you would be off chasing your windmills and not have time to see me."

His arms circled her waist and held her tight against him, so full, she was not as thin as Sunny. "Windmills?"

"Don Quixote, dear Avery. I will buy you the book. You really should read more. There is a whole world waiting for you in novels."

"The world that I live in keeps me kinda busy."

"And I am going to help you get that world sorted out, so that you can spend more time in mine. I simply do not like myself as much when I'm away from you."

"I like the sounds of that."

"Did you bump your head on the door? It looks like you have a bruise on your forehead."

"I've had an adventure or two lately."

"Well, I'm going to take good care of you from now on. You are the only one on the face of the earth, besides Daddy, that knows all about me, and loves me anyway. You do still love me, don't you?"

"I reckon you know how I feel." He tugged at the velvet ring bag in his pocket.

She leaned close and kissed his ear. "I really, really missed you, sweet Avery." Carla stood back and brushed the shoulder of his coat. "And the first thing I will do to take care of you is get your suit cleaned."

"I just had it cleaned by the only laundress in town."

"Oh dear, I keep forgetting this is the frontier." She slipped her warm hand into his. "Please forgive me for being raised rich and spoiled. I know I must change. That's why I need you so much." Carla clutched him tight, then released her grip. "I'm sorry if I sound flighty. It was a long, tedious trip and I had no idea what kind of reception I'd get from you. You were rather upset with me when we parted."

"Disappointed rather than upset." Avery cleared his throat. "I have something I want to give you."

"And I have several things for you, too. But first, would you be a darling and see that my trunks get unloaded? I don't want them dropped."

Avery shoved the ring bag down. They strolled arm-in-arm to where the baggage was being unloaded. "I trust your trip up here was peaceful."

"It's a rather dirty little boat, not at all like the big ones on the Mississippi. But this is the West, what can I say? I refused to eat the food. The sanitary conditions were even worse than those in north Africa. And you know how bad . . . well, I've told you about them, haven't I? No, Carla . . . this is Avery . . . you don't have to talk that way. Sweet Avery, what I mean to say is, 'I'm hungry.' "

"We'll have a very good meal tonight. I've made supper arrangements. Some very good friends, the local jeweler and his wife, have invited us over for dinner."

"Oh, isn't that nice?" Carla dropped his arm. "But I'm afraid you'll have to cancel out. I have been dreaming of Chu-Ling preparing us one of his specialty Chinese dinners."

Avery frowned. "These are good friends, Abe and Noelle Hermann. We can have Chu-Ling cook tomorrow night."

"I'm sure they will understand. Besides, I invited others to join us for our Chinese feast. We'll rent the ballroom at the best hotel in town. There is a decent hotel?"

"Who did you invite?"

"A gentleman rancher. He owns an absolutely huge place here in Montana. He was on the boat all the way to the last stop. We sat on the deck and visited for several hours and it was absolutely delightful. Everything is so large out here. Would you believe he doesn't even know how many acres he has? I can't imagine how I would have tolerated that little boat without his company. You can see why I have to keep my invitation to him. He said he and some associates were coming to town tonight. I invited them to the best Chinese dinner outside San Francisco."

She stood on her tiptoes and surveyed the town from the dock. "Which is our hotel? I do hope it's something better than that two story brick one."

"I'm afraid that's the best in town."

She managed a smile. "I'm sure it's charming inside."

"It's clean."

"That's a start." She hugged him and kissed him on the cheek. "You can't imagine how wonderful it is to see you. I have some important things to talk to you about."

"What kind of things?"

"About our wonderful, glorious future. Father wants us to be in Chicago in two weeks. I told him of course we'd be there. But I insisted we would only stay three days, and then come back west because that's where we belong. I informed him under no circumstances would we go to New York. I told him you hated New York. He was quite pleased to know that. Daddy hates it too. Enough of that. We'll talk later. I simply must freshen up. There are my trunks. Can you get a porter to take them to the hotel?"

"No porters here. But I'll borrow a hand truck from the hotel and get them to your room."

"I trust we have adjoining rooms." She kissed his cheek again, her upper body pressed against him. "You are the most wonderful man on earth. Have I told you that lately?"

Her cheek felt velvet smooth against his, like the bag in his pocket. "I don't think so."

"Well, you are." She stepped back. "What are you wearing that pinched me?"

With reluctance, he released her. "My badge . . . I was appointed sheriff for a couple days."

"You, a sheriff? Oh, my Avery darling, haven't you done enough charity work in your lifetime? That's not a job for you."

"It's something I needed to do for some friends. It's only a couple of days."

"That's my Avery, never thinking of himself, just helping his friends. You are the inspiration this lady needs. She also needs a steamed bath and a clean dress. Would you make the arrangements for the hotel dining room?"

"Carla, I really can't bow out of our dinner commitment."

"But neither can I, darling Avery. My goodness, a Loganaire doesn't invite people to dinner and then cancel. Let's talk about it after we both clean up."

"I'm as clean as I get."

"Oh, yes, of course. That didn't come across right. My rustic, handsome Avery. You look wonderful. You could be on the cover of *Harper's Weekly*. You will be quite the scene in Chicago. Whatever you do, don't let LeArlene Knight show you her Civil War souvenirs."

"I'll remember that. Carla, let's get this straight. I will not disappoint my friends that are already preparing supper for us. Who is this rancher friend? I'll go to him and personally explain the situation and how it is all my fault. He will have no one to blame but me."

Carla pinched her narrow lips, then nodded. "This is why I need you. You are such a sweetie. You are probably right. Besides, Chu-Ling will need all day to prepare one of his meals. Tomorrow night will be just fine. Tonight we dine with your Hebrew associates."

"I'll go explain things to the Montana rancher. What's his name and where will he be staying?"

"I never ask a man where he lodges. But, he is quite an influential rancher. He owns most of eastern Montana. I'm sure he will be easy to find around town. His name is Mr. Rinkman."

CHAPTER SIXTEEN

Soft lips. Warm arms. Firm hands. Swaying hips.
  Not just a kiss.
But it was the kiss that dominated Avery's thoughts almost every night. The head-to-toe, mind-blurring, heart-pounding, "glad-I'm-me," mashed lips encounter . . . that set Carla

Loganaire apart from most every woman on the face of the earth.

At least, most every woman that Avery had ever known.

"That's dangerous," he told her.

"I hope so. I really have missed you."

Carla slipped her hand in his as they strolled along the path by the river. Her fingers felt good entwined in his. Not good, like a comfortable shoe, but exciting like a new shoe. Light from town gave them just enough reflection to find their way.

She held up her left hand. "Can you see the beautiful ring my cowboy gave me?"

"I'm afraid your other rings overshadow it."

"And my other rings are locked in Mr. Hermann's safe tonight. This is the only one I have on."

"I liked the ring."

"So did Noelle Hermann. They are a delightful couple. I'm glad that you insisted we eat with them."

"They are nice folks."

"You know, that kind of meal would not happen in Chicago. The Jewish people have their own part of town. We seldom mix."

"Noelle's a sweetheart, isn't she?"

They promenaded so slow, it was more of a dance than a walk.

"A French Catholic married to an American

Jew . . . only out west could they find accep-
tance. I was surprised at the theological discus-
sions you and Abraham had."

"We aren't afraid to challenge each other to
think about what we believe."

"I saw a different view of you tonight, dear
Avery."

"What view was that?"

"Avery John Creede, the politician. Firm, yet
gracious. Very diplomatic. You would make a
splendid United States Senator. And I know half
of those serving in the Senate right now. I can
hear the sergeant at arms announce in the
Senate chamber: 'The Honorable United States
Senator from Montana, Avery John Creede.' Don't
you think Senator Creede has a nice sound?"

"I would rather fall into quicksand than go to
Washington, D.C."

Carla burst out with single laugh. "An apt
description of politics."

"Besides, Montana is merely a territory and
I'm not sure I'm goin' to settle down here."

"It will be a state soon. Do you know Marcus
Daly?"

"I know he owns the Anaconda Mine in
Butte. But I've never met the man."

"Father is a friend of Mr. Hearst. I believe they
helped Mr. Daly purchase the mine. Last time he
was at our house, he indicated statehood was
imminent."

"Perhaps, but I will not run for public office."

The Missouri River lapped against the bank, with a gentle, sleepy sound, as if tired from a long day of work.

"I agree, dear Avery. Father always said the real source of power in the country were the men who run the businesses."

"That might be true in the East. Out here it takes courage and a steady aim."

"You know, my Avery, if you ever wanted a job in mining, I'm sure Father could . . ."

"Carla, I told you over and over, I don't need your father's money, nor his assistance in finding a job."

"I know. And you are right. But don't always speak with disdain of Father's money. Grandfather started the hardware business with nothing but a wagon load of goods he drove all the way from Boston. Father has worked long hours since age fourteen, to make it the success it is. It is honest, hard-earned money that you scorn."

"I don't scorn your father. I know he is an industrious man and that he loves you dearly. But it is important to me to know that I can take care of you on my own. You are way too charming and beautiful a lady to have your father need to buy you a husband."

Still clutched hand-in-hand, Avery felt his palm turn sweaty.

"Oh, you are a sweet talking man, Mr. Creede."

"Never has anyone told me that."

"Well, I told you that, and I'm a very good judge of character."

"Not always. You missed with your newfound rancher friend."

Even in the dark, he could see her eyes narrow. Her grip tightened.

"I still have a difficult time believing Mr. Rinkman is the treacherous man you accuse him to be."

"Carla, Rinkman is dangerous, violent, and unpredictable."

"But you've never met him."

"I've seen his work. I've never met Michelangelo, but I can tell a lot about him by studying what he has accomplished. Rinkman took his own men out of jail and shot them in the head. He killed Harvey. He rules a fiefdom with fear and oppression. Oh, I know Rinkman, alright."

He took a deep gulp, but the humid air tasted stale, used.

"But you admitted your knowledge of what goes on down in the Breaks is based on the testimony of your gunslinging pals, Pete and Sunny."

"Whom I have no reason to doubt."

"Have you ever been wrong in your assessment of people?"

"Women, yes, but never men."

"Do you intend to kill him?"

"I never plan to kill anyone. But I will protect myself by any means available."

"Will you arrest him?"

"Yes. Harvey was a friend of mine and I owe it to him. The judge can decide what is just."

"Why would Rinkman bother spending all that time with me and inviting me to his ranch?"

"He was recruiting you, Carla."

"I can't believe that."

A west drifting breeze sprung up and cooled the sweat on Avery's forehead.

"Darlin', I would get lost in Chicago. I would ask a man on the street corner directions and believe any old thing he told me. It is like a foreign world. I think maybe the West is foreign to you."

"You could be right. There are things I don't understand. But I know what it means when you call me darlin'."

She hugged him as if she clutched a life preserver and was about to drown. It was a desperate move that shouted "I need you." Her yielding lips whispered, "I want you." They held each other tight for several minutes.

Then he pulled away, his shoulders stiff. "Carla, is this something new, or are we just going down the same path again?"

"What do you mean, sweet Avery?"

"You know how I feel about you. Any fool can see that. And I believe you feel the same about me."

"You know that I do."

Avery pulled off his hat, took a deep sigh, then look intently at the shadowy river. "Everything will go along great until that turning point."

Carla whispered, as if she knew what he was about to say, but didn't want to hear it. "What turning point?"

"Some day . . . two weeks . . . or two months . . . or two years from now our stubborn prides will collide and there is no solution but to ride off in opposite directions."

"Like we did in Denver?"

"Denver, Prescott, San Francisco, Santa Fe."

"Santa Fe was different. Mother was dying. I had to go."

"You're right. But you didn't get that telegram until after the scene at Feliz Madres."

"And you think it's a cycle that we can't break?"

"I'm ponderin' that. I'm wonderin' if either of us has changed enough to weather that storm when it comes again."

"I certainly hope you haven't changed, dear Avery. It's that fearless enthusiasm of yours that's so enduring. You are the only person in my life that isn't following a script."

"What do you mean, a script?"

"When you grow up a rich little girl in Chicago, you only get to play with other rich little boys and girls. All of us have been coached by live-in teachers about what to say, how to act, and what to think. If we learn it well, it's like a play. I know every line such men will speak before they say it. It's as if I'm living one giant, life-long drama. All I do is walk through it, reading the lines." She poked him in the ribs. "Then Avery John Creede saunters onto the set."

"And I didn't know the script?"

"You didn't give a hoot if there was a script or not. You didn't know the rules. You shattered my well designed future."

"I've heard similar things. I don't reckon I fit into anyone's script. Sorry about that."

"No, it was a good thing. A wonderful thing. All of a sudden my future was not cast in bronze. There were choices to make, consequences to face. New possibilities littered the horizon. I loved it. Do you remember the first words you spoke to me?"

Avery thought of the sweet scent of her French perfume that first turned his head. "I remember I was very nervous. You were the most beautiful woman I'd ever seen."

"And you had very limited exposure to women. Do you remember the first words?" she prodded.

"I couldn't think of anything impressive to say. I think I mentioned your hat."

"I remember every word: 'Lady, that is the most absurd hat I have ever seen in my life. Why don't you go bury it in the back yard and put it out of its misery?' "

Even in the dark, Avery felt his face flush. "Did I say it that way?"

"Word for word."

"I've never been called suave. I suppose you were angry."

"I didn't know how to be. I was at a loss. No one taught me what to say when some drifting gunslinger insulted me. I just stared in disbelief."

"And I tried to apologize. Remember?"

"Oh, yes. You said in that deep, throat tingling voice of yours, 'Nothin' personal, ma'am. I reckon someone sold you a bill-of-goods with- out a mirror. Kinda like buyin' a horse unseen; it doesn't always work out for the best.' "

"Yeah, I reckon I said somethin' like that."

"And you blushed when you mumbled, 'Can I buy you some supper to make up for that insult?' "

"I was shocked that you said 'yes.' "

"I had to find out if you were a naïve cowboy, or the smoothest operator since Don Juan. Half-way into dinner, I had you pegged."

"Which was it, naïve or smooth?"

"Both." She stood on her tiptoes and kissed his lips.

He kissed her back, but kept his attention on the river.

"Avery, I think I've changed."

"And so have I. I've been givin' it a lot of thought the past few days. Well, ever since I got to Ft. Benton."

"Let me tell you about my changes first. I've been practicing these lines for days."

"You reading from the script?"

"Perhaps, but it's my script. I wrote it. And it comes from my heart."

"Well, beautiful lady, how have you changed?"

"I decided I don't have to live in the East. I will live wherever you want in the West, but a few things are important. I'm not ready to live in the wilderness. You have to realize that scares me. I can travel all over, but to live in an isolated ranch house with you out saving the world . . . would terrify me. I need neighbors who could hear me if I scream for help."

"That's reasonable."

"I'd really like to live in a city like Denver, but that's up to you. I would like to be close enough to a town that has a number of stores where I could shop. I could take the buggy to town on my own once in a while."

"You plan on learning to drive a rig?"

"Yes, because that's the second thing. We've

had this discussion before. I can agree to no full-time servants. But I would like to have someone come in once a week and help me clean. I've never cleaned a house in my life. I need some help, and I need to learn how."

"I don't have a problem with that."

"Also, I decided I don't need to attend every social event in Chicago, New York and Boston. But, I will need to go to Chicago a few times each year to check on Daddy."

"Of course. But that's a lot of switches in your life. I don't know if it's right for me to demand such things."

"You didn't demand them . . . I offered them. I think we both know there has to be some compromises."

"I reckon you're right. What changes did you have in mind for me?"

"Those are up to you."

"You didn't have any in mind?"

"Of course I did. But they are not mandates . . . merely guidelines."

A gunshot from the eastern edge of town silenced them.

"Is that normal?"

"Perhaps. Some of the boys get a little tight and like to celebrate."

"Do you need to check it out?"

He paused. "There wasn't a second shot, so it's not a gunfight. Just a celebration, no doubt.

But I better head that way. I'll walk you to the hotel, then check it out."

"Nonsense. You said yourself there was nothing to it. I want to see how my local sheriff handles such things. This might be the only time in my life I get to witness my Avery, the lawman and legendary gunman. After we settle down and you quit all this gun business, all I will have are the stories your wild cowboy pals like Pete and Sunny tell when they stop by to see us."

"You can walk with me a ways . . . but if I tell you to stay back in the shadows, you mind me."

"Woof!"

"What's that mean?"

"It's dog language for 'yes, master.' I can 'stay.' I can 'sit.' I can even roll over and play dead."

"Are you sayin' I'm treating you like a dog?"

"Dear Avery, I'm teasing."

"And I am not teasing. I want to keep you safe."

"I always feel safe when I am with you."

They stole through the dark, empty alley holding hands. A couple of blocks away a dog growled. The sound of a tinny piano drifted from across town. The smell of woodstove smoke choked the passageway as they broke out into the east end of Main Street.

"It seems quiet over here," Carla offered.

"I'll check with Garcia, the night man at the livery. Maybe he knows."

"I think I saw someone in the shadows by that hardware store. They were on the porch, but ducked between it and that other building."

"Wait here. I'll check it out."

"I most certainly will not. It's dark and scary. I'm going with you, Sheriff."

They crossed the empty street, then hiked up the wooden steps to the boardwalk of the hardware store. Avery drew his gun, then waved it toward the bench. "Sit," he whispered.

Carla sat.

He shuffled over to the narrow, two foot wide walkway between the buildings. "Okay, boys . . . this is the sheriff . . . come out where I can see you."

"Uncle Avery?"

A young man in suit and tie emerged, leading a blonde girl.

"What are you two doing here?"

Ace glanced over at the benched Carla. "I reckon the same thing you two are doing here."

"I heard a shot," Avery said.

"We were . . . eh . . . lookin' for Mrs. Leitner's dog."

"Chop-Chop disappeared several days ago," Tabitha said. "Mother has been beside herself with anxiety. That dog was a gift on the day my baby brother died. She thinks of him as part of the family. We need to find him before Mother starts wearing black."

Carla rose up beside Avery.

"Miss Leitner, this is Carla Loganaire. And this is my nephew, Avery Creede Emerson, whom I call Ace."

Tabitha curtsied. "Pleased to meet you, Miss Loganaire. You are older than I thought. Not that I can see well in the dark, but all we ever get around here are old newspapers and I was reading about your 25th birthday party at the Lake Michigan Pavilion where eight-hundred people showed up."

"That was three years ago."

"Like I said, all I ever have is old news. I was wondering one thing . . ."

"Oh?"

"Why haven't you ever got married?"

"Why haven't you?" Carla shot back.

"Oh . . . Oh . . . I really like her, Mr. Creede. I told you I would like her. I haven't got married yet because I hadn't found the right man. Until I met Ave . . . that's A – V – E and it rhymes with brave. Is that the same reason you haven't married . . . you needed to find the right man?"

Carla slipped her arm into Avery's. "Oh, I found the right man. Now I just have to talk him into making a commitment."

"Honest? Hey, that's no problem. If you need

any advice, I can tell you something that really works."

Avery shoved his gun in the holster and turned back toward the livery. "I came over here because I heard a gunshot, not to discuss relationships."

"Does he change the subject often?" Tabitha asked.

"All the time," Carla replied.

"Have you tried kissing?"

"Quite often."

Tabitha flipped her bangs back. "Wow, I guess older men are tougher to convince. How sad."

"Ace, did you hear that gunshot?"

"Yeah, when we got back from our ride up the river."

"We are not going to buy the Turnbull place," Tabitha announced.

"It was burnt to the ground," Ace added. "Anyway, we dropped off the buggy with Garcia. Miss Tabby was a little chilled, so we thought we'd set on the bench in front of her daddy's store and . . ."

"Look for a dog?" Carla pressed.

"We heard the shot from behind the livery but were sort of distracted until we saw you in the shadows coming this way. Naturally, we ducked in the alley, so I could protect Miss Leitner."

"I'll go see Garcia," Avery said. "You take Miss Tabitha home so you don't make Mrs. Leitner even more worried. It's late. I thought you were coming back by dark."

"We got to town by dark . . . it's just that . . ." Ace stammered.

"Explain that to the mayor and his wife."

Avery and Carla strolled toward the big unpainted barn that served as livery, feed store, and saddle shop. The wide front door stood open, to reveal a pitch dark building.

An aroma of horse sweat, new leather, and old manure greeted them.

"Garcia?" Avery called.

"I can't see anything," she said.

"Hold onto my coattail."

"Garcia?" Avery drew his gun. "He usually leaves a light on back in the office."

They shuffled a dozen more steps forward.

"Where's the office?" Carla asked.

"I think we're in it." Avery shoved his gun in the holster, tugged a sulfur match from his pocket, and struck it on the rough wood post in front of him. He lit a kerosene lamp perched on top of assorted papers, then surveyed the tiny office.

"Perhaps he went to dinner," she said.

"Maybe. But Ace said the shot came from out back."

Avery led them through the barn, past a dozen stalled horses to the corral behind the building.

"Garcia?"

"Oh, dear," Carla cried out, "over there by the gate."

They rushed to the man crumpled by the corral. Avery handed Carla the lantern and knelt down.

"Is he dead? I think I'm getting sick."

Avery tapped the man's cheek. "Garcia? Hold the light down here. I can't see any bullet wound."

"He's got blood all over his head. Avery, I know I'm getting sick."

"Take a deep breath, suck in the air. I think he's just been bushwhacked. Garcia?"

One eye blinked open. "Mr. Creede?"

Avery kept his hand on Garcia's shoulder. "Take it easy. You've been cold-cocked."

"There were ten of them on five horses."

"All riding double?"

"They said they wanted to buy five horses. They lied."

"Rinkman's men. The Blackfoot must have stolen five horses."

"How do you know that?" Carla asked.

"Because I told them to." Avery carried the liveryman inside the barn and laid him on the small cot in the office.

"Uncle Avery!"

Avery scooted to the front of the livery stable. Carla scurried behind.

Ace waved down the street. "The jail's on fire!"

"Rinkman's going to burn the whole town

down, just to find me. Go tell the mayor and others who aren't fighting the fire to meet me at the bank. Stay away from the jail. They intend to use it like bait."

"Where are you going?" Ace asked.

"To see if Rinkman is with them, or just sent his men ahead."

Ace loosened his tie. "You don't know what he looks like."

"I do," Carla said. "I'll go with you."

"You aren't feelin' well, and I won't jeopardize your future," Avery insisted.

"I feel better and you walking into gunfire jeopardizes my future. The least I can do is to point out your adversary."

Avery started for the middle of the street. "Stay," he ordered.

"Woof, woof."

"What does that mean?"

"No."

CHAPTER SEVENTEEN

When the half-keg of gun powder exploded, the ground shook. Windows rattled at the hardware store over a block away.

By the time Avery and Carla hurried within two-hundred feet of the sheriff's office, the building exploded into flames. Bystanders watched from a distance safe enough not to singe their eyebrows. Two crews of men operated hand-pumps to wet down adjacent structures.

Avery hung back in the shadows and observed the faces. Light from the fire made it seem closer to noon than midnight.

"Can you see Rinkman?" he asked.

Carla dug her fingers into his arm. "It's a big crowd. Perhaps if we moved out in the open."

A heavy cloud of acrid, black smoke made him cough. "No, if he's looking for me, I don't want to be an easy target."

"Why would he look for you? You've never met the man." Carla fanned the smoke away from her mouth with her hand.

"He's lost some men and a couple of hostages. I figure one of his boys spotted me in town, and he's waiting for me to show."

"What do you intend to do?"

"Find him before he finds me."

Something tapped his shoulder. Avery spun around, gun drawn.

A short man in a suit waved his hands. "Wait . . . Creede . . . it's me, Mayor Leitner. Young Mr. Emerson said you wanted to see me."

"Get together any men that aren't fighting the fire and block off both ends of Main Street. Make it so no one can get in or out, unless they are on foot."

"What if they dismantle the barricade?"

"Throw some lead their way. They'll scatter."

Carla tugged her hand out of his arm. "Did you just say 'throw some lead their way'? My, goodness . . . I thought that was only used in Mr. Buntline's cheap novels."

Avery ignored her. "Can you do that, Mayor?"

"We'll try. What are you going to do?"

"Find Rinkman."

"Where is he?"

"Someplace where he can watch everything, but not be seen."

One of the fire crews pushed their pump wagon back toward the river to refill the tank.

The mayor pointed down the street. "The bell tower of the Catholic church is a good place for that. At least, that's what Tabitha tells me. It was her favorite hiding place when she got angry with her mother."

"Where is your daughter now?"

"Ace is protecting her."

"Block the exits. I'll try to flush out Rinkman."

The mayor slipped through the shadows and scurried across the street.

Carla tried to slip her fingers into his. "I presume we are going to the church tower?"

He pushed her hand down. "Me, not you. You stay here."

"You need me to identify Rinkman."

"Not anymore . . . he'll be the one in the tower."

"Well, I'm not going to go back to the hotel. What can I do to help?"

Avery glanced around. "Stand in front of the church, so he can see you. Stare at the fire like everyone else. Wear your mildly distraught look."

"I have a mildly distraught look?"

"You have a minor, a mild and major distraught look."

"How will that help you?"

"It will keep him looking out front. Maybe I can sneak up from behind."

"A diversion. And should I flash an ankle at him?"

Avery shoved a cartridge into the last empty chamber of his revolver. "This is not a time for humor."

"Are you calling my ankles humorous?"

"I've never seen your ankles."

"That can be arranged," she cooed.

"Count to a hundred, then hike out and do what I told you. Whatever you do, don't look back up at the church tower. Don't turn around."

"Oh, this is exciting. Like being in a play."

Avery grabbed her shoulders. "Carla, this is not a play. It's real and it's dangerous. Count to one hundred, then move."

"In English or French?"

His frown leveled her smile.

"Don't look back at the church."

"Un, deux, trois, quatre, cinq . . ."

"Carla!"

"Shouldn't you be going, dear Avery, my hero . . . perhaps Russian is better . . . shayst . . . seeaym . . . DYEH-veht . . ."

Avery had to turn sideways to squeeze through the walkway between the church and the doctor's office. The back alley was not illuminated by the fire. He felt his way along the back of the church. He inched straight up a ladder nailed next to the back door. The dried cedar shingles popped beneath the weight of his boots as he scooted closer to the tower.

He pulled his gun as he advanced to the cupola.

More explosions ripped through the fire at the jail. Avery inspected the crowd below. Most had moved back to the safety of the boardwalk. Only Carla and a little dark headed boy stayed out in the street.

He heard muffled sounds from inside the tower. He squatted on the peak of the roof and searched for silhouettes.

Fire in front, darkness behind, Avery crept on his hands and knees nearer the bell tower. Each creak of the shingles signaled his presence, but no one appeared at the cupola railing. He caught his knee on a nail. When he tried to jerk it free, his trousers ripped.

Still, no movement in the bell tower.

He glanced down at Carla who squatted with

her arm around the little boy's shoulder. Avery leaned against the cupola railing and held his breath. He pulled the hammer back on his revolver.

Heat surged through his leg muscles as he pushed himself up.

"Throw down," he commanded.

A man jumped up in front of him waving his arms. "Don't shoot, Uncle Avery."

Avery's gun hand dropped. "Ace?"

"Hi, Mr. Creede." It was a cheery, young lady's voice.

"Miss Leitner? What are you doing up here?"

"My Ave is protecting me. Isn't he brave?"

"Where's your shirt?" Avery demanded.

Ace rubbed his bare chest. "Miss Tabby was cold, so I let her wear it."

"Just like my Ave to give me the shirt off his back. I just love wearing it. Did you ever notice how wonderful my Ave smells?"

Avery shoved his gun into his holster. "Get your shirt on, then take Miss Leitner home."

"But you said it could be dangerous at her house. I wanted to keep her safe."

"No one ever comes up here," she said.

"I did."

Tabitha pulled off his shirt. "Did you come looking for us?"

"I came looking for Rinkman."

"Maybe he's over there. There are two men

prowling around the corner of the bank roof."

"I can't see them."

"When the jail exploded, we spotted them."

"Ace, take Miss Leitner to her mother."

"That back ladder is steep, Uncle Avery."

"I'm sure Miss Leitner has experience with it."

"No, this is her first time to climb up here."

"That's not what her daddy says. Now, go on."

Ace pulled his shirt over his head. "You told me you'd never been up here."

"Oh, maybe once or twice. But they were just boys. I've never been up here with a man like you."

"Boys? What boys?"

"Oh, isn't my Ave cute when he's jealous?"

Avery scooted to the front of the church where a crowd gathered on the boardwalk. Carla still positioned herself in the street, back toward him.

"Carla," he whispered.

She continued to stare at the jail flames.

"Psst . . . Carla. Miss Loganaire."

The little boy next to her turned and peered at Avery.

"I need to talk to Miss Loganaire," he motioned.

The boy spun around and leaned his head against her hip.

Two women scurried behind Avery on the boardwalk.

"Excuse me, I need to ask you a favor."

"We never talk to strange men."

"I wouldn't trouble you if this weren't important . . . . I need to talk to that lady right out there and . . ."

"Mister, if you continue to harass us, we'll contact the sheriff."

He revealed his badge. "I am the sheriff . . . at least for now. Just hike out there, tap her on the shoulder and say, 'Miss Loganaire, the sheriff needs to talk to you for a moment back on the boardwalk.'"

The woman wearing gloves, clasped her hands. "Did you say Miss Loganaire? The Chicago Loganaires?"

"Yes. Could you do that for me?"

"Here in Ft. Benton? Did you hear that, Esther? A Loganaire woman right here in our town. I really must talk to her."

"I saw her mother once in San Francisco. Or maybe it was her grandmother. She wore a Parisian dress that would make the Queen jealous."

"She knows Queen Victoria, you know. They had tea at some castle and went to a horse auction. Can you imagine the Queen of England at a horse auction?"

"Ladies, would you just mention that I need to talk to her?"

Both women tightened the ribbons of their hats, then sashayed out to Carla.

Avery couldn't hear the conversation, but paced the boardwalk waiting for her to turn around. Finally, the two women shook Carla's hand and strolled down the dirt street away from Avery.

He threw up his hands and shouted above the noise of the crowd and the crackling blaze. "Carla!"

An old man with a cane shuffled up. "I've been married sixty-one years, and my wife pays me no mind at all. She talks me to sleep every night, and when I wake up in the morning, she's still talking. Yes, sir, you got your hands full."

"Dyeh-SEHT," he shouted.

She finally twirled toward him. "Oh, Avery . . . it's you."

"I've been trying to get your attention."

"I heard you call, but thought it might be Rinkman."

"Rinkman? I sound like Rinkman?"

"Well, those two ladies said a very suspicious man was trying to get me back in the shadows of the boardwalk. You were going to be in the church bell tower."

"Rinkman wasn't there."

"When you counted in Russian, I knew it was you. Ten is DYEH-seht. It really does matter how you pronounce it. What do we do now?"

"I've got to get on top of the bank roof. I think I spotted Rinkman."

"Do I stand out in the street again? I'm a little tired of this role. Can't I have a speaking part?"

"Guns may blaze and someone get shot. You should wait in your hotel room."

"Wait for what? Wait to see if you foolishly wasted your life? Avery John Creede, I want to witness what it is you are willing to risk your life for."

"It's hard to explain."

"Then let me sit in the shadows and watch."

"He's a little shorter than me, right?"

"All men in Montana are shorter than you. Except Stack Lowrey. You'll know Rinkman. He has blank green eyes."

"I'm not going to see his eyes in the dark."

"It's just as well."

"Stay back in the shadows."

"The whole town is in the shadows. Oh, Avery, can't we get this over with? This is not the way I envisioned we'd spend this evening."

Avery jogged along the boardwalk and into the walkway between the bank and the dry-goods store. The bank's back door was propped open with a brick. Avery slipped into the dark building. Light from the fire filtered through the front windows, revealing an outline of the staircase to the second floor. Gun drawn, he crept up the stairs and slipped into an office with news-papers scattered across the floor.

As he crept across the room, flames lit the sky several blocks away. He pushed open a window.

"It's the mayor's house," someone in the street shouted. "The mayor's house is on fire."

The extra flames lit the room and allowed him to see a ceiling ladder pulled down, and the evening sky above. He spotted a kerosene can, but ducked down in the corner when a shadow of a man loomed at the opening above him.

"The hotel?" a voice questioned.

"The mercantile, then the hotel, then this bank," another man replied.

The silhouette at the roof opening backed down the ladder. Avery waited for him to reach the doorway, then slammed the barrel of his revolver into his head. He crumpled forward, then somersaulted down the stairway.

Avery needed both hands to climb up the ceiling ladder to the top of bank. He peered across the roof. A man stared at the blaze at the mayor's house. Easing out on the roof, Avery drew his gun. He jammed it inside his coat to muffle the sound as he cocked the trigger.

click – click – CLICK

As if orchestrated, at the sound of the third click, an explosion from the mayor's house lit the night. The man spun around, gun drawn and pointed at Avery.

"Creede?" His mouth twisted, his eyes blank. "I thought you were in Mexico."

"Owens? I thought you were in Hades. When did you take the name Rinkman?"

"When I busted out of Yuma. It's my real name. What are you doing here?"

"I'm going to arrest you."

"Are you the one who's been sneaking down in the Breaks and picking off my men?"

"I didn't pick off anyone. I faced them straight up. You're the only one who ever shot men in the back."

"Ten years has made you dumb and careless. Tiny has you covered. You're dead."

Creede didn't take his eyes off Rinkman. "Tiny is unconscious at the bottom of the stairs."

"We are both too good a shot to have this standoff. I'll shoot you dead, and you'll shoot me dead."

"Put your gun down, and I'll arrest you. That way you can live until they hang you," Avery growled.

"I don't much like that plan. Let's both lay our guns down and finish what we started in Tucson, eleven years ago."

"We did finish it. You lost."

"Only because Juanita hit me in the back of the head with a spittoon."

"Put down your gun, Owens."

"The name's Rinkman. I've got a good thing

267

going down in the Breaks. It's worth fighting for. How about you, Creede? You got anything to live for? Because if you pull that trigger, we're both dead."

Rinkman stooped down, put his gun down and slid it to the side. "Now, you'll have to kill an unarmed man. I don't think you can do that, Creede. You couldn't do it in the army. You couldn't do that on the border. And I don't think you can do it now."

Avery aimed his gun at Rinkman's head. "What if you're wrong? What if I've changed?"

"Then I'll die knowing that the legendary Avery John Creede was afraid to face me straight up."

Avery released the hammer on his Colt. Rinkman's fist caught him under the chin. He dropped the gun and staggered back.

"You're pathetic, Creede. You live in a make believe world."

Avery tackled Rinkman at the knees. With his palm on the man's temple, he slammed his head into the roof of the bank. "You are the one who created a kingdom of fear and violence."

Rinkman's knee smashed into Avery's stomach. He rolled to his back gasping for breath. "A kingdom isn't built on meekness." His boot hammered at Avery's forehead.

On the third kick, Avery grabbed the boot and twisted it hard to the right. "The kingdom that lasts forever is." Rinkman cursed, then stumbled and tried to stand. Avery's left fist caught him in the stomach, the right smashed Rinkman's ear.

Rinkman staggered, but was propped up by the low, false façade at the front of the bank. He reached into his boot and pulled out a knife. "What you get is what you take. It's always been that way." Rinkman lunged.

Avery jumped back, but felt a hot pain. Warm blood oozed down his left arm. When Rinkman thrust again, Avery's elbow caught the gunman's nose. He lurched to the short wall, blood spraying down his face.

Creede rushed him. Rinkman leaped over the façade, and tumbled down into the street below.

Avery scooped up his revolver as he sprinted to the ladder. Taking two rungs at a time, he dropped to the second floor office, then ran down the steps and out the back door. He tried to wipe the blood from his mouth, but smeared it across his cheek and into his eye.

In front of the bank, a crowd formed around a screaming lady. "He killed my Athena!"

Avery pushed through the crowd. "Who killed Athena?"

"A man jumped off the bank roof onto my dog . . . he killed my sweet Athena," she wailed.

"Where did he go?" Avery shouted.

"Oh, look . . . she's moving. I think she's still alive . . ."

"Where did the man go?"

"Oh, thank you, Lord . . . you delivered my Athena from the perils of violent men like this one."

"Over here, Creede!" an angry voice shouted from the shadows.

"Avery, do something!"

Rinkman yanked Carla's arm behind her, his knife at her throat.

"So, you do know Miss Loganaire of Chicago. When she told me she was going to meet the bravest man in the West, I should have known it was you who lied to her. Throw your gun down, Creede, or Miss Loganaire will make it to heaven before you."

"Avery, he's hurting me."

"That's stupid, Rinkman. You can't make it out of this town. These people won't let you."

"You're a dreamer, Creede. Which one is going to stop me?"

Carla tried to pull away from Rinkman. "Avery, I'm serious. I want to go home. I don't want to be here."

"Turn her loose!"

"What if I just slice her throat a little at a time. That way we can all watch her bleed to death?" Rinkman rasped.

"I'm going to be sick," Carla said.

"What will it be, Creede?"

Carla doubled at the waist, coughed, then

vomited all over Rinkman's arm.

He jerked away from her and tried to shake his arm clean.

Avery rushed him. The flash of firelight reflected off the knife's blade as it flew from Rinkman's hand. He yanked right and felt the point rip through his coat and pierce his left shoulder. Before he could jerk the blade completely free, Rinkman tackled him. They rolled in the dirt street.

Avery clutched the knife to stiffen his fist and slammed his knuckles into Rinkman's face several times. He pinned his arms down with his knees and aimed the knife at Rinkman's chest.

Both men gasped for breath.

"You . . . can't win, Creede . . ." Rinkman huffed. "Look around."

Through eyes filled with dirt and blood, Avery caught a glimpse of eight mounted gunmen that circled them.

"I say the word and you're dead."

"Don't say the word too fast, Rinkman. When I die, I'll collapse on top of you. This knife will nail your heart to the ground. You know it's true. Have them throw down."

"You want us to shoot him, Mr. Rinkman?"

"Wait, boys."

The knife pricked through Rinkman's shirt and brought blood. "I'll die happy, knowing you are in Hades at last," Avery growled.

"Just say the word, Mr. Rinkman," one of the men called out.

"Ride out of here, boys."

"We aren't leaving you."

"I said turn and ride out of town before some timid citizen gets an ounce of bravery and shoots you in the back. Go on."

"We ain't going to let him kill you."

"Creede will not kill an unarmed man. Now go on, I'll be along later."

"Avery, I'm very sick," Carla said, pale and shaking. "Stop this right now and take me to my room."

CHAPTER EIGHTEEN

His left arm wrapped in a bloody bandanna, Avery searched the street in front of the bank for his hat. He stopped at the crunch of bootheels.

"Uncle Avery, where's Miss Carla?"

Avery dusted his found hat off on his pant-leg. "She's in her room at the hotel."

"I heard she got sick."

"An effective use of vomit."

"Sure wish I could have seen that!"

Avery and Ace strolled over to a streetlight. "By the looks of your bloody shirt, you were needed elsewhere."

Ace surveyed the roofline of the two story brick building. "Did Rinkman really jump off the top of the bank onto a dog?"

"Yep, about the time the mayor's house caught fire. Is everyone okay? Did he lose everything?"

"It wasn't his house."

The high pitched melody of a girl's voice floated across the dark street. "There's my hero."

A man in a dark suit scurried over with a young lady on his arm. "Miss Leitner, Mayor, did you trap the others?"

"No, they turned down the alley between the hardware store and McNutley's. They rode straight into the river, then swam their horses downstream."

"I didn't think that was wide enough to ride down."

"One of 'em got stuck."

Avery tried to tighten the bandanna wrapped around his left arm. "He got stuck?"

"Jammed between those two buildings with his legs pinned to the stirrups. Couldn't budge either way."

"What did you do with him?"

"He's still there. Where's Rinkman?"

"He's secure for a while."

"But the jail burned down."

"He's not in the jail."

"But . . . where . . ."

"Don't ask. Just trust me."

Tabitha Leitner clutched Ace's arm.

Avery waved at the square brick building. "I was up on the second story when the second explosion happened. I thought for sure it was your house. I'm glad to hear everything is okay."

The mayor patted Ace's shoulder. "We have young Mr. Emerson to thank. His quick thinking saved my house and my family. He is, indeed, a hero. My word, that's a lot of blood on your arm."

"I'll need the doc to sew it up. It stings like a dozen snake bites. What's this about Ace saving your house?"

"You should be proud of him. Mr. Emerson intercepted the Rinkman gang and told them that the Quibbs house was ours. They burned down the wrong place."

Avery glared at Ace, who stared down at his boots. "I don't expect that went over big with the Quibbs."

The mayor paced back and forth. "That's the point. I bought the Quibbs place next to us. My wife thought her mother might like to live there. But Mother Brewer didn't like it, which is a blessing. So, I was fixing it up for a rental. I was going to let Captain Mandara use it as a sheriff's house while he was in town. The point is, the house was vacant. It's a financial loss, but my family and my home are safe. That is quite a nephew you have."

Tabitha laid her head on his shoulder. "My Ave."

"Quick thinking, Ace."

"I just thought, what would Uncle Avery do?"

"Mayor, leave the barricades until morning. Keep some men posted. They can fire a warning shot if Rinkman's men return. My hunch is we won't see them again tonight."

Avery headed across the street. River breeze flooded into town and stung the cuts on his face.

The mayor jogged to keep up. "What are we going to do with Rinkman? They'll burn down every building until he's released."

"I'm going to send a telegram to Helena. I'll have the U.S. marshal meet me in Great Falls and take him back to the territorial jail. The quicker we get him out of here, the better."

"We?" The mayor spit the word out like a sour grape.

"Me and Ace will escort him."

"When?"

"Sometime before dawn. I've got to check on Miss Loganaire, roust the doc, and get a few things ready."

"How can I help?"

"Get me a wagon, two black horses and an empty pine coffin."

"Coffin? Who's dead?"

Avery hiked toward the hotel. "That's yet to be determined."

Ace laced his fingers with Miss Leitner's. "I'll walk Miss Tabby home."

"You'll come with me."

"But . . ."

"I am sure Miss Tabby is very safe with her daddy."

Close to 2:00 a.m., most lights still burned in Ft. Benton. The fires and confusion thrust crowds onto the streets. Avery and Ace trudged to the hotel, where the nightclerk waited at the front door. The lobby smelled of lilac and acrid smoke.

"Do you know, Mr. Creede, Ft. Benton used to be a quiet town, except when the cowboys came to town on a Saturday night."

Avery stared at the clerk's narrow, bloodshot eyes. "You mean, I brought all of this on?"

"I suppose it could be a coincidence. You aren't going to drip blood all over the new carpet, are you?"

Avery glanced down at his ripped coat. Dark red patches of blood made the gray wool stick to his arm. He turned to Ace. "I suppose my face looks about like my arm?"

"A little worse. You got dirt plastered in the blood."

Avery studied the bright red streaks in his nephew's face. "You don't look so good yourself."

"When I saw them light the dynamite, I had me and Miss Tabby dive over the fence into her backyard. It was the roses that ripped me up."

"And Miss Leitner was with you?"

"Yep, but she didn't get into the rosebushes. I was takin' her back, just like you said, but being cautious. We sorta took the long way home."

The clerk stepped between Ace and Avery. "Perhaps if you two continued this conversation in your room. We do have other guests. I would rather they wouldn't. . . ."

Avery grabbed the man's tie and yanked it toward him. "You know, the Grand Hotel has such splendid hospitality, always making their guests feel right at home. I'm going to recommend that all my friends stay right here."

"You wouldn't?" the clerk gasped.

"Yeah, I would. But whatever you do, don't let Dawson Wickers get near the woodstove." Avery released the man's tie.

The clerk struggled to stand straight. "Why is that?"

"Just pray it doesn't happen. Come on, Ace."

"Where we headed?"

"To the room. Change your clothes and clean up. I need to talk to Carla."

"Like that? You're about as purdy as a carcass in a butcher shop."

"Thank you. Maybe I'll stay in the hall."

"Them rosebushes ripped up my back. Is it all bloody?" Ace spun around.

"Looks like you were hit with a shotgun."

"No, foolin' . . . this is what it feels like?"

"I didn't say it felt like that. I said it looks like that."

"You been hit with a shotgun blast?"

"More times than I care to remember. I got a question for you, Avery Creede Emerson, and I want a straight answer. Your shirt is bloody, but it's not ripped. Can you tell me how that happened?"

"Eh, I reckon I didn't have my shirt on at the time I hit the roses."

"Did you have on your pants?"

"Uncle Avery!"

"You didn't answer me."

"Yep, I had on my pants. Miss Tabby just loves wearing my shirt."

"And what were you really doing at the house next door?"

Ace chewed his tongue, then rocked back on his heels. "Just tellin' her goodnight."

"Inside the house?"

"On the front porch swing. And these men rode up and hollered 'Which one is the mayor's house?' She jumps up and says, 'I'm the mayor's daughter, what can I do for you?' "

"Not exactly the smartest thing to say to the Rinkman gang."

"She's just a friendly girl."

"So I've noticed."

"Well, they shot out the front window. I grabbed her to run next door. Good thing it was dark. They tossed the dynamite in the window and the explosion knocked us over the fence. I fell in the roses. She fell in the pansies. Isn't that just like Miss Tabby, to fall into some sweet smellin' flowers?"

"And you got her daddy thinking you're a hero."

"Well, I did shove her off the porch when they started shooting. And got her safely out of the yard."

"Go try to wash up. Put on some clean clothes and stay there. I don't want you to leave the room. Do you understand that?"

"Yes, sir. You aren't going to tell her daddy and get Miss Tabby into trouble, are you?"

"I'm thinkin' about it."

"It was all my fault, Uncle Avery."

"Was it your idea to stop at the house next door?"

"No, sir."

"Your idea to pull off your shirt?"

"No, but I consented."

"Did you insist on kissing her and she didn't want to?"

"No, that wasn't it."

"Then, what is your fault?"

"I reckon it's my fault that I didn't show any self-control. The Lord promised we'd be able to handle the temptation what would come our way and I ain't been doin' very good."

"That's the first smart thing I've heard you say since you met Miss Leitner."

"It came to me as I lay on my back in the rose garden. I was layin' there in mortal pain and wonderin' why is it that me and Miss Tabby get interrupted ever' time we start to . . . well, you know."

"And what was your answer to that?"

"I didn't get an answer 'cause Miss Tabby ran over to see if I was alright and she started . . ."

"I'll be there in a few minutes."

"Are you goin' to practice self-control, Uncle Avery?"

Avery pinched his lips together and tasted blood and sweat.

"Lookin' like you do," Ace added, "I don't reckon you'll need it."

His knuckles felt raw as he rapped on the oak door. "Carla?" It swung open a few inches.

Her voice sounded flat. "I'm out on the balcony. I needed some fresh air."

"I need to go clean up. I just want to see if you are okay."

"I am alive, if that's what you mean. For a while this evening, I wasn't sure that would be the case."

"I apologize. I should have insisted you come back to the hotel."

"Are you going to come in or just stand in the hall?"

"I look bad."

"Avery, come here and look at the stars."

"What?"

"Come out on the balcony."

"Carla, really, I'm bloody. I'll be back in a few minutes . . ."

Heels clicked, then she swung the door completely open. She glanced at him and broke out in sobs.

"It's not as bad as it looks." He started to touch her shoulder, then pulled the bloody arm back. "The doc will sew me up. I've been hurt a whole lot worse."

"Avery, Avery, Avery . . . . I can't do this. This is a foreign land! I don't understand any of it. It's like living in Arabia. I don't know the language. I don't know what is expected of me. I don't know why you have to live this way."

"Carla, I just need to clean up."

"Please come out to the balcony with me, before I get sick again."

A whiff of sweet perfume rolled past him.

"Turn off the lamp so you don't have to look at me."

She took his dirty, bloody hand and led him across the room. "If I can't look at you now, how will I do it when you are hurt worse than this?"

The two of them filled the tiny balcony. She gasped deep breaths between sobs.

He fumbled for the right words. "Carla, I know it's been, well . . . sort of . . . a rough night on you."

"Rough night? I have seen more blood and violence in the past hour than my entire life combined. I was held at knife point and thought I would die a horrible, painful death. Then I had the delightful privilege of vomiting in front of an entire town. The man I want to marry was beaten, shot at, stabbed and looks like he's been run over by a train. This isn't a 'rough night.' It's a nightmare, and I'm still living it."

The only sound was a distant coyote yipping at the moon. Avery's voice softened. "Things will quiet down."

"When? I can't live this day again. I really can't."

"I've got to take Rinkman down to a U.S. marshal in Great Falls."

"Why you?"

"It's my job. I'll just be gone a couple days or so. When I get back, Captain Mandara will be sheriff, Rinkman will be in jail, and then we'll have some peace."

"Until when? When does the horror start all over again?"

"No more being sheriff. I promise you that."

"You mean there is someplace in the West that doesn't require Avery John Creede to put his life on the line?"

Avery's heart beat fast and hard through the pain in his left arm. "I reckon there's lots of them."

"Such as?"

"It's kind of late at night to be takin' a quiz."

"Name them."

"Well, there's Denver, and San Francisco, and . . ."

"And?"

"You can't judge my whole life by just one night."

"You mean this sort of thing has never happened before?"

"No, I didn't . . ."

"And you said you've been hurt worse."

"I was in the cavalry twenty years."

"I can't live like this. I want to be stronger, but I just can't do it. I don't have the mental strength for this. I've got to be honest."

"When I get back, we'll go down to Denver and think things through at one of those fine hotels."

"What about your army pals you were meeting?"

"Don't know which of the rest will show. But we'll have a nice supper at the hotel . . . talk about old times until dawn, then go our separate ways."

"What are you asking me to do, Avery? I will not stay here to watch you get killed and then have to spend the rest of my life in some upstate New York sanitarium."

"Wait until I get back from this trip. We need some time alone to figure this out."

"I told you this is not a comfortable environment for me. What am I supposed to do in Ft. Benton?"

"Visit with the Hermanns. Noelle would love the company. Help them rearrange the jewelry store so it looks like one of the fancy ones in New York."

A slight grin escaped. "I suppose I could do that . . . but I'm so scared."

"With me and Rinkman out of town, you'll be safe."

"That's not what I'm afraid of. I was so terrified tonight. It is as if some of my sweet dreams of my Avery were wrung out of my heart."

"Sweet dreams of me?"

"Remember the night you and I were out on Daddy's boat on Lake Michigan all alone?"

"With six crew members?"

She flipped her wrist. "Oh, they don't count.

Remember how we studied the stars that night? You held my hand and pointed to the constellations and told me the name of each?"

For the first time, the intense pain in Avery's arm eased. "You're right. It is a sweet memory."

"I want some more like that." Her voice was soft, unsure. "All I can think about now is that knife at my throat, and you all bloodied and beaten."

"But I won the fight . . . and I'm here with you . . . and these are the same stars."

"Oh, Avery darling, don't you ever yearn for a more peaceful life?"

Avery leaned over the railing and surveyed the street below. "Just about every day."

She slipped her arm in his.

He winced.

Carla pulled back. "Then let me take you to a place where we can have a peaceful life."

"Lake Michigan?"

"There are other places."

"I think we just had this conversation about Denver and San Francisco."

She placed her narrow finger on his rough, chapped lips. "Shhh . . . let me tell you another Carla Loganaire dream. Have you ever been to Monterey?"

"Mexico or California?"

"California. Just out of Monterey, along the cliffs overlooking the ocean are some beautiful, windswept cypress trees. Pleasant summers. Mild winters. The tradewinds flood your heart and soul with a lazy calm. Daddy bought some property from Leland Stanford. We could build a home. They will soon have a railroad into San Francisco. We could have a house in each place. Doesn't that sound wonderful?"

"Maybe I could hire on to be the gardener."

"Nonsense. Money doesn't come into this."

"It does for me. I need a job."

"You could grow avocadoes and almonds. Sounds idyllic, doesn't it?"

Avery tried to bend his stiffening neck. "I don't even know what an avocado is."

Her voice floated out like a lullaby. "And every evening we could sit on the veranda, sipping on hot chocolate and watching the sun go down on the Pacific Ocean."

"You thought of all of that standing on this balcony?"

She dropped her chin to her chest. "I've been thinking about it since I was ten years old."

"You have a head start on me. Can you give me a couple of days to ponder it?"

"I suppose that would be fair. Will you really consider it?"

"Yep, as long as the dream includes a contract on how I can pay your daddy back."

"Oh, Avery!"

"I need that option, Carla."

"I'm sure we can arrange that."

"When I get back, if that still sounds like a possibility, the three of us will go to San Francisco, rent a rig, and drive down and look it all over."

Her eyes widened. "The three of us?"

"I inherited my nephew, Ace. I'm afraid he comes with the deal now."

She pointed across town to the dying embers of Quibb's house. "I'm sure he could stay here with the mayor, just until we check things out."

"He is most definitely not staying with the mayor."

"Okay, Ace comes with us. My cousin has racehorses just south of San Francisco. Could Ace stay with them while we go to Monterey? I just want us to make that decision on our own."

"I think that might work." Avery took her hands and tugged her closer. "Will you wait for me?"

"Will you consider raising avocadoes and almonds?"

"Almonds I will consider, but I won't commit to anything I've never seen."

"You are serious, sweet Avery?"

"You've given me a dream I never had."

"Just like the first night I met you. You gave me a dream."

"Sheriff, is that you up there?"

Avery glanced down at the dark street and didn't recognize the shadowy figure.

"What do you want?" he called out.

"Tiny's getting away."

"Who's Tiny?"

"Rinkman's man who was stuck in the alley. He done shuck his boots and his duckings and is trying to pull free. It's quite a sight."

"I will wait four days for you to come back," Carla said. "Go on, do what you are meant to do. In fact, having a man try to escape in his long underwear might bring a smile to this gloomy night."

"It's even funnier than that, ma'am," the man shouted up. "Tiny ain't wearin' no underwear."

CHAPTER NINETEEN

The hotel lights provided a dim reflection off the windows in front of the bank. Ace studied his image. "I feel funny dressed like this."

Avery pulled on his long coat. "You look just fine in a silk hat and black coat."

"It's not natural."

"It is for an undertaker." Avery adjusted his top hat to a rakish tilt.

"Are we going to get him now?"

"Yep."

"Where is he?"

"In jail."

Ace's hat slipped low and rested on his ears. "The jail burned down."

"Not all of it." Avery pulled himself up in the wagon, then patted the seat next to him. "Come on, junior assistant undertaker, we have a customer to retrieve."

Thick, acrid smoke hung like fog around the charred remains of the sheriff's office and jail. The night air cooled as the sky hung a heavy coal black. Avery drove the wagon around to the alley and pulled up next to a tiny wooden structure.

"The outhouse?" Ace pushed his hat back. "The jail outhouse didn't burn down?"

"Amazing, isn't it?"

"You hid Rinkman in the outhouse?"

"We've had experience with it before."

"But what if someone found him?"

"Who's going to use an outhouse next to a smoldering fire? Besides, I nailed the door shut." Avery tied the lead lines to the hand brake and stepped to the ground.

Ace leapt down beside him. "He's going to need some airin' out."

"I'll let him get a couple deep breaths before we drop him into the coffin."

Rinkman was still unconscious when they

yanked him out of the privy and shoved him into the pine box. Avery drove slowly through town, past the hotel and out to the road toward Great Falls. Neither spoke until the lights of Ft. Benton receded. The sky turned a slight hint of charcoal gray. The stars' glow faded. The breeze rolled straight into their faces, nipping the cheeks, but failed to penetrate the heavy black coats.

Ace flapped the front of his coat, as if to cool off. "You reckon this will work?"

"I don't know."

"Won't they be watchin' all the roads out of town?"

"Maybe . . . but right now they think Rinkman's still in town. They could be ponderin' how to go in and rescue him. One thing I know about guys like Rinkman . . . they don't like competition. That means all the smarter ones in his gang have been chased off or shot. I don't know who makes decisions when he's not around."

"You sayin' they won't figure out what to do?"

"I'm hopin' they just stall long enough for us to get on down the trail."

The crossroad to the southeast was just a dim mark in the prairie dirt. Avery pulled the wagon over, handed the reins to his nephew, then stepped down.

"Did you see something?" Ace said.

Avery pulled his coiled rope out from under the wagon seat, then slapped and dusted the trail where they turned.

"What are you doin'?" Ace pressed.

"Don't want it to be too easy to track where we turned off the road."

"Turned off? You mean we aren't going to Great Falls?"

"Nope."

"But you told everyone we're headed there."

"Yep."

"Where are we going?"

Avery yanked a piece of paper from his pocket and handed it to Ace.

"A telegram? Who from?"

"Read it while I check the riggin' on the team."

" 'Wanted for cattle rustling: Curly Buck Clamer and King Snake DuPrix. If seen, notify me at once. U.S. Marshal Kib McCoy, Lewistown, M.T.' What do we have to do with a couple cattle rustlers?"

"Nothin', but it shows that there's a U.S. marshal in Lewistown. We'll take Rinkman there. This trail should cross the river and swing around to Lewistown and on to Billings."

Ace folded the telegram and handed it back. "But, that road will take us back into Rinkman territory. No one would be foolish enough to take that road."

"That's what I'm hopin' they think."

Avery climbed back into the wagon seat. "Scoot over, you're drivin'."

"I'm what? You never let me drive."

"This is the first time we've been in a wagon together. What do you mean I never let you drive? The doc gave me something to kill the pain while he sewed up my arm and it made me groggy. I'm going to take a nap. You up to it?"

"Yes, sir. I can do it."

"Wake me up if you see someone headed our way. Are wide awake?"

"Yep. I've got some ponderin' to do."

"About a lady?"

Ace nodded his top hat. "Yep."

"Well, so do I."

The axles squeaked. The wagon boards snapped and creaked. The stiff springs tossed the seat back and forth as the hooves of the two big horses clomped in the dirt. The rising sun warmed the black coats. The breeze, now at their back, died down to a wispy sigh.

Avery slept.

The tree looked out of place among the sage and bunch grass of the prairie. Like a fawn lost in a meadow, it stared at Avery as he approached. The gnarled trunk revealed its age. The branches twisted and turned and poked spiny fingers out and up, forming a circular shape like a lollipop.

No green leaves colored the branches. Instead every inch of the tree was draped with tiny white flowers.

As he eased closer, a cherry-sweet fragrance engulfed him like after-shave tonic in a barber's chair. He plucked one of the flowers. Five delicate white petals surrounded the bright pink core. At the center, long, erect stems of the pistil offered globs of yellow pollen skyward like a ritual sacrifice.

Avery surveyed the countryside.

No houses.

No road.

No fences.

No cows.

Nothing but the blossoming tree, himself . . . and a man wearing a long, white coat and wide brimmed straw hat.

"Is this your tree?" Avery asked him.

"It's a magnificent almond tree, isn't it?"

"I'm amazed that it grows out here on the prairie."

"It doesn't."

"But . . . here it is," Avery insisted.

"I dug it up, put it in a wagon and transplanted it."

"It's beautiful."

"It's dying."

"It is?" Avery looked closer.

The man pulled off his hat and wiped his

forehead with a white handerchief. "In two months it will be dead. You can't grow almonds out here. I knew that before I planted it."

"So, why did you do it?"

"She wanted me to."

"You went to all this work, knowing it would fail, just because a woman wanted you to? That doesn't seem reasonable."

The man pinched his lips together and shook his head. "You haven't seen her smile. Or felt her touch."

"Where is she?"

"Gone. But she'll be back before it's withered away . . . I think. Perhaps you should do something."

Avery looked around. "Me?"

"Yes, do something."

"What? But, it's your . . ."

The jab to his side was severe. "Uncle Avery, do something!"

Avery's top hat covered his eyes to block the morning sun. He laid slumped against the back of the wagon seat. He didn't twitch a muscle. "How many are there?"

"Three. They're ridin' straight at us, carbines across their laps."

"Fake it."

"Me?" Ace's voice changed to a high pitch.

"Tell 'em we're taking a body to Billings, and I'm drunk and passed out. If it's Rinkman's men they might recognize me, but they don't know you."

"Really?"

"Do it."

"You goin' to draw your gun?"

"It's in my hand already."

The wagon rumbled to a halt. With one eye barely slit open, Avery remained still and peered out from under his hat. The lead man he recognized as one of those on horseback at the bank.

"Mornin' fellas," Ace called out. "It's a fine day for a buryin'. Eh, that's our slogan."

"Ain't you a little young to be an undertaker?"

"Yes, sir, I'm just an apprentice."

"Is your pal dead?"

"He's my boss. Got drunker than a miner in the mother lode. Passed out and left all the work to me. Ain't that a trick?"

"Where'd you come from?" the man with a hole in his hat asked.

"Ft. Benton."

"You were there last night?"

"Yep. You should have seen it." Ace waved his hands. "Two fires at the same time and some kind of ruckus at the bank. I don't know what was goin' on. I was helpin' put out the fire at the mayor's house."

"You don't say?" the lead man replied. "What was the cause?"

"Some said it was old Ruckman. You know,

that big rancher fella from down in the Breaks. Me, I don't know nothin'. I mainly just dig holes and bury them."

"You mean, Rinkman? Did they catch him doin' it?"

"I heard that was the commotion at the bank. All I know is Ruckman was caught. That new sheriff hauled him out of town right away."

"He did?"

"That's the rumor."

"Where did they head off to?" the third man asked.

Ace paused and squinted into the sun. "I don't know if I should go telling you. For all I know you could be Ruckman's men."

"Rinkman. His name is Rinkman, and if we were his men, we'd have shot you already."

Ace scratched his forehead. "I reckon you're right about that. Well, listen, I heard this from Crazy Ed . . . you know how he stretches things . . . he said the sheriff was goin' all the way to the territorial capital in Helena."

"Helena?"

"That is, if you believe Crazy Ed. He also thinks President Lincoln wasn't really shot, but he just made that up so he could retire up on the Milk River. He claims that Mr. Lincoln lives up there raisin' goats to this day. Ain't that somethin'?"

"Have I seen you before?" hole-in-the-hat quizzed.

"Could be." Ace smiled. "I'm quite popular in Ft. Benton . . . at least with the young ladies, if you get my drift. You have a daughter?"

The lead man frowned. "When did that sheriff and Rinkman leave town?"

"Me and the boss was tryin' to recover this body and get him prepped for burial, so I don't know when they left. I just heard the mayor say he was glad to get them out of town."

"Who do you have in the box?"

"Two Thumbs Freeman. He's the one that was usually passed out on the bench in front of the Prairie Roller Saloon. A sad story."

The lead man waved his carbine at the coffin. "Maybe we ought to take a look."

"Yes, sir. You can do that. I'll pull the nails for ya. But, he's purdy rank."

"He couldn't have started to sour this soon."

"Well, you see . . ." Ace yanked off his top hat and ran his fingers through his hair. "Two Thumbs was in the privy behind the jail when the fire broke out . . . passed out. From time to time he sleeps back there. When the privy burned, he died in the fire. The outhouse collapsed, and he fell down . . . well, you can imagine the mess. I think that's why the boss got so drunk. Couldn't stand the smell any other way."

"Yeah, I can smell it. You undertakers will do anything for a buck."

"That reminds me." Ace jammed his hat back on. "Have you boys taken care of your final demise?"

"What?"

"We have an inexpensive insurance policy that will cover your funeral costs up to twenty-dollars. If you are interested . . ."

The man with a gray horse pointed his carbine at Ace. "Get out of here before we rid the world of a drunk and a smart-alec kid."

Ace grabbed the reins and slapped the rump of the lead horse. The wagon lurched forward. "You boys should plan for your future," he shouted.

The blast from the carbine plastered dirt onto the horses' legs. They bolted down the trail. It took two miles for Ace to bring them under control.

He pulled the rig over and parked. "How'd I do, Uncle Avery?"

"Great, but I thought you carried it on too long. What if they wanted to buy your buryin' insurance?"

"Hadn't thought of that."

"Where on earth did you get all of that spiel?"

"In a play called 'Mr. Blackman's Daughter.' I seen it in Platte City, Nebraska, on my way out here to find you. Mr. Blackman's an undertaker, and Roy, that's the hero, is tryin' to smuggle Mr. Blackman's daughter, Lilly, out of town in a coffin. He said he was hauling the town drunk. Ain't you seen that one?"

"I must have missed it, but I'm glad you didn't."

"Do you think it worked?"

"Until they hear that the temporary sheriff and a talkative kid left town in a wagon."

"I don't think many saw us leave."

"It might slow them down for a while."

Screams and curses from the coffin caused the horses to lurch.

"I think Rinkman's revived," Ace said.

"I don't suppose those particular words were used in 'Mr. Blackman's Daughter'?"

"No, sir, but it is a curious combination of profanity."

Avery drove the rest of the morning. With Rinkman gagged, they left the lid off the coffin unless someone passed them on the trail. With the sun straight up in the blanched blue sky, they pulled off the trail and parked in a draw that sported one dead cottonwood tree.

While Ace unhitched the team to let them graze, Avery propped Rinkman against the tree trunk.

"I'll pull that gag off your mouth, but if you start screamin' and cussin', I'll shove it back. Understand?"

Rinkman nodded.

The gunman took several deep breaths. "You two are dead men. You know that, don't you?"

"You missed your boys, Rinkman. While you were sleepin' in the coffin, they came by. I guess they didn't recognize the smell."

"You have no idea the vengeance I have planned for you."

"I've been thinking about that. I believe the best idea is to shoot you now."

"If I'm dead, they will destroy every building and every person in Ft. Benton."

"I don't think so."

"Those were my instructions," Rinkman blustered.

"But with you gone, who is going to make them do it? I got a feeling if they knew you were dead, there would be a big fight down in the Breaks to see who's the new boss."

"You have no idea of the loyalty of my men."

"Let's try an experiment. I'll hang you on this tree, and leave your body to dangle so they can find you here. I trust that will be before the buzzards pick you clean. Then we'll watch and see what happens. Of course, you'll be lookin' up from hell."

Rinkman spewed curses. The gag was shoved back in his mouth.

Ace moseyed over carrying a one gallon bucket. "You two havin' a theological discussion?"

"Yep, we were ponderin' eternity."

"Chu-Ling sent us some Chinese stew for Misteree. It ain't too bad cold. I wonder what's in it? Did you know that Miss Tabby's mamma's dog disappeared about the time . . ."

"Shh. We don't want to spoil Rinkman's appetite."

"We goin' to feed him?"

"If he keeps quiet."

They made it to Square Butte at sunset and filled the canteen at the springs. But they didn't camp until they reached the eastern tip of the Highwood Mountains where the rocky, treeless hills blended with the buckskin brown prairie. Supper consisted of leftover stale bread and fresh jerky of unknown origin.

With Rinkman chained to the wagon wheel, and Ace snoring near the dying embers of the campfire, Avery drug his bedroll next to the staked horses. He plopped down on top of the canvas, rolled up his coat for a pillow, and concentrated on the stars.

Lord, I'm tryin' to make plans for my life, but nothing ever happens according to plans. It's just one crisis after another. I talk to Carla as if I can break the cycle and do anything I want. But it doesn't happen that way. Before I make her promises, I got to know You'll let me keep those promises.

Of course, I'm not sure she can keep her promises either. I know she wants to. We're a lot alike in that way . . . both of us controlled by circumstances more than personal choices. She was born into her life. Never known anything else. Never had any say in the matter.

And, I reckon, I was born into mine. It's funny that way. Ever' once in a while our two worlds overlap. I don't know if that's enough . . . but oh, my . . . what a beautiful dream. A big, wonderful dream.

A soft crunch stirred him. A whinny jerked his hand to his holster. He opened one eye. A shadowy figure hovered near.

A carbine pointed at his chest.

"What . . ."

"I'm sorry, mister, but I need your horse. I'll ride him to Ft. Benton. You can find him at the livery. Go to the sheriff's office and he'll give you two dollars for the use of the horse. This is an emergency."

The voice was higher pitched than he expected. Urgent.

A woman's voice.

A familiar voice.

"Sunny?"

"Avery?"

"What's the matter? Where's Pete?"

He stood up and her arms clutched his neck.

He wrapped his around her waist.

She sobbed and held him tight.

His wounded arm throbbed, but Avery rocked her back and forth. "What's wrong, darlin'? Is Pete dead?"

Sunny continued to cry. "I haven't prayed to God since I was twelve years old. Tonight I just wanted to curl up and die, but I prayed and prayed. Walking across the prairie in the dark, I kept praying, 'Lord, bring my Avery to me. Jesus, I just can't make it without him.'" She whimpered and hugged him even tighter. "God answered my prayer, Avery. He answered my prayer."

CHAPTER TWENTY

Avery ran his calloused fingers through Sunny's matted hair. "Is Pete dead?"

"I don't know." She continued to sob, her head on his chest. "They beat him up bad and carried him off. It was awful. They held me down and I had to watch it all."

He felt the muscles in his neck tighten. "Who beat him up?"

Sunny wiped her eyes on his shirt. "Rinkman's men. It was all a trap, Avery. They sent the telegram and put Tight Sheldon's name on it. They thought you would be the one to come find him."

"How did they know about me and Tight?"

She rubbed her nose on the back of her hand. "I guess one of the clerks at the hotel is a friend of theirs. They wanted to capture you. They ambushed us on the other side of White Sulphur Springs."

Her heart pounded against his. "Pete put up a fight?"

"He bloodied up a couple, but there were six of them. They pistol-whipped him until he was unconscious." She sobbed again. "Maybe he's dead. But I think they wanted him alive to make some kind of deal with you. All they want is you, Avery John Creede. You seem to be the sacrificial offering. They figure if they get rid of you, their problems will be over."

He brushed a soft kiss across her ear. "You're okay now, darlin'. Somehow you got away."

She took his hand and put it on her bare arm. "Not until my dress got ripped and I bit him."

Avery lowered his hand to her waist and rocked her back and forth.

Her voice softened. "I've been walking, running, crying and praying all night. Oh, Avery . . . I've never been so happy to see anyone in my life."

"Do you need something to eat . . . or just some sleep?"

Sunny clutched his neck tighter. "I need you to hold me for the rest of my life."

Avery let out a deep sigh. His hand dropped to his side.

"Did you marry your Carla yet?"

"Nope."

"Have you made wedding plans?" It was more of a plea than a question.

His voice was low, like the rumble of a train, miles away. "No. We're just sort of in the ponderin' stage."

She leaned close and slipped her arms around his waist. "Is she here with you?"

"No, just Ace and the infamous Rinkman."

"You have Rinkman?" she blurted out.

"I arrested him in Ft. Benton."

"Without a fight?"

He glanced back at Ace, asleep next to the embers. "I'll fill you in, but first, tell me everything that happened to you. Would you like me to build up the fire?"

"Is that your bedroll?"

"Are you sleepy?"

"Let me just curl up in your arms," she whimpered.

Avery rubbed his temples.

"If I do something improper, you have permission to shoot me," Sunny added.

He laid back on the bedroll. She scrunched down beside him, then clutched his arm.

He winced.

"Are you hurt?"

"I took a knife in that arm."

She laid her hand on his cheek.

Avery groaned.

Sunny sat up. "Is there any part of you I can hold onto and not cause you pain?"

"My other arm is only partly hurt."

With a curtain of bright stars above them, she crawled over him, and cuddled up in the crook of his arm, her head pillowed on his shoulder. "This is exactly what I've been begging God for. I don't know if I've ever had Him answer my prayers before. Tell me what happened in town."

"And you tell me more about those prayers."

"Well, ain't this cozy? Howdy, Miss Sunny!"

Avery sat straight up to face the rising sun and a grinning nephew. He fumbled for his gun that wasn't in his holster.

Sunny sprawled on the bedroll. "Good morning, Ace." She dangled the revolver above her. "Are you looking for this, Avery John? It hurt my ribs, so I pulled it out last night."

Avery holstered the gun, then struggled to his feet. "Sunny . . . came in about midnight and we talked for hours."

Ace winked. "I know just what you mean. Me and Miss Tabby do the same dadgum thing."

"It's not like that." Avery pulled her up.

"Yes, we really did talk most of the night," Sunny said.

"You don't have to apologize to me."

"She's not apologizing," Avery said. "We tried to be quiet so we wouldn't wake you."

"Ain't that nice you were thinkin' of me? Did Uncle Avery tell you that him and Miss Carla was contemplating movin' to Monterey and raisin' almonds and avocadoes?"

"No, he didn't mention that."

"I didn't tell *him* that," Avery snapped. "How do you know what Carla and I talked about?"

"You mumble in your sleep."

She slipped her hand in Avery's. "Monterey, huh?"

Her fingers felt warm, comfortable, like a deerskin glove that's been worn all winter. He squeezed her hand. "That's just one of many things we discussed."

They hiked to the fire. Dried tears streaked Sunny's face. Her violet gingham dress had one sleeve ripped off. The high lace collar, now buttonless, dangled like an ill-tied scarf.

She marched straight to the man chained to the wagon wheel.

"Well, if it isn't the powerful Jed Rinkman. You're pathetic. You stink. I'm not sure why they kept you alive."

Rinkman's thick, dark black hair splayed in all directions. "You're all dead," he snarled.

"That's what you said yesterday," Avery mumbled. "Let's get some breakfast and coffee. We've got to go find Pete."

Ace waved toward the prisoner. "We ain't takin' him to the U.S. marshal?"

"Not yet."

"If my brother's dead, I get to shoot him." Sunny glared at Rinkman.

Avery pulled out his gun and handed it to her, grip first. "Go ahead. Shoot him now."

She checked the chambers. "I might need more bullets."

Avery pointed at his bullet belt.

"What are you doing?" Rinkman yelled. "For God's sake, Creede, you can't let her do that."

Avery scratched the stubble on his scar. "As far as I can tell, Rinkman, God wants you dead, too."

"Don't shoot him in the head or heart," Avery said. "He'll die too quick."

She aimed at the outlaw's boot. "I was thinkin' about shooting him once every five minutes or so. First his foot . . . then his knee . . . then his thigh . . . then his . . . ."

"Creede!" Rinkman screamed. "Get that gun away from her! She's crazy. She's always been crazy."

Avery tried to rub the pain out of his arm. "Sunny, it's up to you . . . but I think we might have a better chance at getting Pete if we keep him alive."

She handed him the gun. "I know. But it didn't

hurt to dream. And it was a lovely dream. Not as lovely as Monterey, but nice, nonetheless."

"You cannot even imagine the suffering you have brought upon yourself," Rinkman threatened. "You will wish you were dead."

"Give me back the gun," she retorted.

Rinkman's thick mustache sagged as he hissed. "I should have left you in Denver. You're a lousy actress, a lousy bank robber, and lousy at what a woman like you ought to be good at."

Avery tossed her a coiled rope.

She whipped Rinkman's face. Parallel trickles of blood streamed down his face, as he screamed and cursed. Her backhand blow gouged the same pattern on the other side.

She tossed the rope down and stalked away.

"You through?" Ace quizzed.

"I'm beyond tired. Rinkman's just not worth my effort. Besides, what are a few scratches? I'm sure the Lord has something much worse planned for him."

"Yes, ma'am." Ace jammed his hands into his front pockets. "The Bible says there's a lake of fire where the torment goes on day and night forever. Say, are you trustin' the Lord now, Miss Sunny?"

"I'm trying." She squatted next to Avery and waved her hands over the fire. "I'm really trying."

Ace hunkered down across from them. "My

mamma told me all about Jesus when I was six years old."

"My mamma up and died when I was twelve." She hugged herself. "It took me a long time to forgive her . . . and I guess I never forgave God . . . until last night."

The wagon loaded, Rinkman bound and gagged in the back, and the team harnessed, Avery offered his hand to Sunny.

"Will you allow me to sit in the middle?" she said.

Ace swung up on the far side of the wagon. "I don't care where I sit as long as I don't have to wear that top hat and black coat." He plopped down beside her. "What's the plan now?"

Avery pulled himself up and untied the lead lines. "We'd better go after Pete again."

"We goin' to trade 'em Rinkman?"

"If we have to." Avery whipped the lines and the wagon jolted forward. "I'd like to get Miss Mary Jane Cutler to Ft. Benton where's she safe."

"I'm not going."

Ace pulled out his revolver, checked the chambers, then shoved it back into his holster. "You reckon we could get a posse to ride with us into the Breaks?"

"No. They won't do that. Tight would go. Dawson would go. But they aren't here. It's you and me, Ace."

She shouted, "I told you, I will not go to Ft. Benton."

Avery laid his good arm across her shoulder. "I don't want you anywhere close to that gang. You don't need to go through that ever again. They've hurt you way too many times already. You can stay with Carla in Ft. Benton until . . ."

She pushed his arm away. "I absolutely will not do that."

Avery slapped the line. The team broke into a trot and the wagon rattled as he spoke louder. "This gets more complicated by the minute. I want to figure out how you, Pete, Ace, Carla and me can get out of Montana alive. We'll just walk away and let the locals handle the problems."

"That's not good enough for me anymore, Avery," she snapped.

"What are you talking about?"

"Suppose your plans work. We all get out of Montana. You, Ace and your darling Carla would ride off to Monterey. Me and Pete would go back to Denver. He'd get restless after he heals up. He'd hear about some old army buddy who needs him in Silver City or Bisbee and off he'd go. I'll be cleanin' rooms, or waitin' tables, or worse, in Denver . . . tryin' to pretend I'm an actress. I've already done that scene. I'm not goin' back. And all the while, I'd know that Rinkman was down in the Missouri River

Breaks. He and that gang of his would continue to kill, rob and rape. So that's not a good enough plan. I want a scheme to make sure Rinkman gets what he deserves, then I could go back to Denver in peace. Rinkman needs to pay for what he's done to me, for what he's done to hundreds of others. When I know that's happened, then maybe I could forget about Ft. Benton and the Missouri River Breaks. And in time, maybe I'd even learn to forget what was happening in Monterey."

Tears streamed down her face. Avery hesitated to put his arm back around her shoulder. "Don't move me to California too quick. I told you it was at the ponderin' stage."

Ace leaned forward. "Is there somethin' goin' on between you two that I don't know?"

Avery gazed at the reddish-brown prairie ahead of them. His face felt warmer than daylight could have caused. "I think that's what we're trying to figure out."

"In the meantime, I am not going back to Ft. Benton." Her voice was crisp, decisive. "Let's see if we can find Pete . . . and still have some justice for Rinkman. I think I've proved that I can shoot straight and take the pain. The worse thing that could happen to me is to die alongside Avery Creede. That might not be so bad."

Ace pulled off his wide brimmed cowboy hat. "Well, Uncle Avery, what's your take on this?"

After a long tense pause, Avery said, "We head straight at them."

"We're going back down there?"

Sunny patted Ace's knee. "Your uncle doesn't know any other way."

"Did you learn that from General Custer?" Ace stared at her hand.

Avery scowled. "I learned nothing from Lt. Colonel Custer."

Sunny pulled her hand back. "I take it that talking about Custer is off limits."

"Shoot, I don't even know how he got that scar. Do you know?"

"He won't tell me either."

"Are you two going to discuss my weaknesses all mornin'?"

Ace fiddled with his hat. "He's a little touchy, you know. And at times he's a hard man to figure."

"On the contrary, he's quite easy to figure," she replied. "There's right. There's wrong. There's the Avery way to do things. He doesn't change course. He doesn't bend in the wind. He defies whatever comes his way and meets it head on. He is predictable, Ace."

"This is a meaningless conversation," Avery boomed.

Ace ignored him. "Mamma called him bull-headed. She always said, 'Uncle Avery is as stubborn as an oak tree, but I love him and hope he never changes.' She figured we need oak trees."

Sunny folded her hands in her lap. "Are you going to be another oak tree?"

"No, ma'am." Ace jammed his hat back on. "Mamma said one oak tree in a person's life is all that they need."

"Your mamma was a wise woman."

"She also told me that an oak tree should never marry another oak tree."

Sunny giggled. "Yes, I could see how that could drive them both nuts."

Avery groaned.

Sunny patted him on the knee. "Oaks don't have much of a sense of humor." She turned to Ace. "Did your mamma mention who oaks should marry?"

"She said they should marry a willow. But I'm not sure what that meant. Maybe it refers to some gal tall and limber."

A dust devil whirled across the trail and no one spoke for several moments. It made Avery squint his eyes, and left a bitter taste on his lips. "You two done railin' on me?"

"We weren't talking about you. We were talking about Ace's mother. I wish I could have met her."

"I miss her sometimes, especially at night." Ace leaned forward, his elbows on his knees, face in his hands. "She had a way of making everything seem okay. Whenever Robert . . . that was my stepdaddy . . . treated us rough when he came home drunk, me and mamma would climb up in the attic for the night. She'd pull up the stairs and lock them. Then she'd sing me some hymns and tell me what she thought the Lord wanted us to do. Sometimes when things are tough, I just wish I could go up to the attic with mamma and lock the door. I suppose that sounds childish."

Sunny's voice lilted, like a lullaby. "No, it sounds like you had a wonderful mother."

Ace sat up straight. "She was wonderful, wasn't she, Uncle Avery?"

Avery wiped the corners of his eyes. "One of the finest women the Lord ever put on this earth."

"That's what everyone said at her funeral."

Sunny brushed fine red dust off her dress. "How did she die?"

Ace bit his lip, his voice shaky. "Pneumonia took her. She had a cough all winter long. Then she got to where she couldn't eat. I did the best I could to feed her, Miss Sunny. Honest, I did."

She hugged Ace. "I'm sure you did."

Avery rubbed the back of his neck, as if kneading stiff dough. "I didn't know she was in that shape. I should have gone home."

"Doc said no one could help. It wouldn't have mattered."

Sunny hugged Ace. "I know what it's like to want real bad to change things, but there wasn't anything you could do but just sit back and watch it all play out."

Ace wiped his eyes on his shirt sleeve. "I reckon that's what faith is all about . . . trustin' things is okay, even when they don't look that way."

"You angry with God for taking her away too soon?"

"I was purdy mad at God, but the preacher straightened me out."

"How did he do that?"

"Well, see, his wife was my school teacher. It wasn't a real big school, and if you were smart enough, they'd just skip you up a class. I never did go to the third grade or the sixth grade because they said I didn't need it. So the preacher said that was what happened to Mamma."

"She got promoted?"

"Yep. He said Mamma passed all the tests of life early, and the Lord let her skip the rest of life down here on earth. He said Mamma was advanced on to heaven early because there weren't any challenges for her left down here. Made some sense to me."

The cool breezed seemed to lift her shoulders and her chin. "I think it does, but it doesn't make losing her easy."

Ace tapped on the front railing of the wagon.

"Yeah, but now, you, me and Uncle Avery are still down here because we haven't passed all the tests yet."

Sunny tried to tuck her torn lace under her buttoned collar. "Using that analogy, I'm afraid I'm still in the first grade. I'm not sure I've passed anything."

His dusty face dimpled. "Shoot, Miss Sunny, I reckon you're one of the nicest ladies I ever met."

"Avery Creede Emerson, if you can remember back a couple of weeks, I took your clothes at gunpoint and threatened to shoot you and your uncle."

The wide grin dropped off his face. "Well, I . . . eh . . . I reckon we all have a wart or two. A man don't toss out a diamond just because it has a flaw."

"You know what I'm wishing, Avery John Creede?" she said.

"I've got a feelin' I'll never guess it."

"I'm wishing your nephew was ten years older."

Ace leaned back against the wagon seat. "Really? Mamma always said I was grown up, you know for my age and all."

Avery cleared his throat. "Well, I hate to interrupt this enlightenin' conversation, but we've got a strategic decision to make."

Sunny raised her thin, blonde eyebrows,

enlarging her blue eyes. "Are you asking our advice on tactics?"

"This is where the road branches. Either we go left, back to Ft. Benton, or . . ."

"I said I'm not going back there."

"Let me finish. We go back to Ft. Benton and cross the bridge. We have to cross the river somewhere. If we don't do that, we go right and try to find a place to drive or float this wagon across the Missouri River."

"Go right at the Breaks." She waved her arm straight ahead. "That's the Creede of Old Montana."

"You two have never tried to swim a team across and float a wagon."

"Have you, Uncle Avery?"

"A dozen times, but with a cavalry platoon to help me out."

"Seems to me an oak and two willows can get the job done. What do you say, Mr. Emerson?"

"I'm wishin' I was ten years older."

CHAPTER TWENTY-ONE

The sky looked worn out, like a blue rubber sheet stretched so thin that it almost appeared white. Even the daylight was dull, as if the sun longed for the short work-week of winter. There was no breeze, but it wasn't hot . . . nor was it cold. It was nothing.

The dust from the wagon wheels hovered like ground fog. Sunny slept on Ace's shoulder. He returned the slumber, his head propped on hers.

Avery took the time to review his life, plot his future and doze off a few times himself as the wagon rumbled along. By midafternoon, they banked the Missouri River.

"That looks kinda wide and deep, Uncle Avery. Do we cross it right here?"

"Nope. We've got to search for just the right spot."

"I'll go upstream. You and Miss Sunny check downstream."

Avery stood in the wagon and surveyed the river. "No reason to check upstream. See that creek? It pours into the Missouri straight ahead. All the silt it carries forms the bottom of the river right in front of us. So this is a sticky, muddy mess and a lousy place to cross."

Ace pointed west. "I said I'd look upstream."

Avery plopped back down in the seat. "That's a waste of time. The silt from this creek raises the creek bottom, and works as sort of an underwater dam. The water will be a little wider and a lot deeper. We need to look downstream. Just a mile or so down from this creek ought to be the best place to cross."

"You didn't know it was so scientific, did you, Ace?" Sunny said.

"Don't know much about science, but it sort of feels like upstream is the right place," Ace insisted.

Sunny patted his knee again. "Well, why don't you just take a look? We'll meet up with you later."

Ace shoved his wide brimmed hat back on his head. "Say, you ain't just tryin' to get me out of the wagon?"

She put her hand on his cheek. "Of course I am."

"In that case . . ." Ace jumped off. "I'll hike about a mile, then turn back if I don't find a good spot to cross."

"We'll wait for you downstream."

"How much time shall I spend lookin', Miss Sunny?" Ace called.

"A half-hour would be nice."

Avery drove the team across the rocky creek, then east along the Missouri. "Avery, have you ever been to Monterey?"

"Yep."

"Have you ever farmed almonds and avocadoes?"

"I've never seen an avocado."

"Have you ever farmed anything?"

"I helped my grandfather plant thirty-two acres of corn one year when I was twelve."

"Did you enjoy it?"

"I hated it."

Sunny stared down at her dusty lace-up shoes. "Then why are you considering being a farmer?"

"I haven't got that far. Right now I'm ponderin' bein' a husband."

"What have you decided?"

"No conclusion, but I'm warmin' up to the idea."

"So, you are thinking of marrying your darling Carla?"

"Don't rush me. Once I've settled on bein' a husband, then I have to contemplate bein' Carla's husband."

"So, you're thinkin' about whether she is the right one for you?"

"I'm wonderin' if I'm the right one for her. I'm wonderin' if I'm the right one for any woman. I tote a lot of baggage, Mary Jane Cutler."

"You know that you and Pete are the only ones I allow to call me by that name?"

"I like how it rolls off my tongue."

"So do I." She slipped her arm in his. "What sort of baggage do you tote, Mr. Creede?"

He yanked back on the lead lines, stopped the wagon, then motioned straight ahead. "There it is."

"What?"

"A good place to try to cross the river. You see how the bank slopes down right here . . . and over there just downstream a bit. It will be a diagonal crossing at best. Maybe we can get up out of the water over there."

Avery tied the lines to the handbrake. He pulled off his holster and gun, and hung them on the wagon seat, then tugged at his boot.

"What are you doing?"

"I've got to wade out there to see how deep the water is. Barefoot, I can tell whether there's sand, silt or rock at the bottom of the entrance to the river."

"Should I pull off my shoes and socks too?"

"No need yet."

"Are you goin' to wade out there with your britches on?"

"Yes, ma'am, I think it's appropriate."

"Would you do that with an army platoon?"

"No, ma'am . . . I'd make some private strip down to his longjohns."

"It seems to me, if you are going to swim out there a ways, it might be best not to soak your duckings."

"I'm not strippin' down . . ."

"How many pairs of pants do you own, Mr. Creede?"

"Just these and my suit trousers. I am not in the habit of . . ."

"If you move to Monterey," she interrupted, "you will need one of those fine striped bathing suits they advertise in *Harper's Catalogue*."

Avery pulled off his other boot. "I'd never wear one of those."

"Oh, you will if your darling Carla asks you to. In fact, that would be a nice wedding present. I'll buy you lovely purple and white striped matching bathing suits. A 'His & Hers' gift is always appropriate."

"I'd rather swim in my longjohns."

She clapped. "Exactly my point. Pretend your underwear is a bathing suit from Paris as you survey the river. I'll go back and open the box, so that we don't suffocate Rinkman, although that doesn't sound like too bad an idea."

She crawled into the back of the wagon as Avery slipped off his trousers, folded them neatly, then stacked them on the wagon seat.

He explored the swift moving, muddy water.

"Isn't that better?" she called out.

He scooted to the wagon. "You said you weren't going to look."

"I never said any such thing. Of course I'm going to watch you. You might get carried away by the current and I'll need to jump in and save you."

"You're the one getting carried away."

"Avery John Creede, you are way too self-conscious. Is this how you'll act with your wife?"

"You aren't my wife."

He paused for a reply. All he heard was the rush of the river. "I'm going out there. I'll be right back."

"If you don't come back," she called out. "May I shoot Rinkman?"

"Help yourself." He stuck his feet in the water. He was surprised how frigid it was. His toes curled under his feet.

"One more thing, Mr. Creede," Sunny hollered.

"Yeah?"

"What baggage?"

"Baggage?"

"When we stopped here, you hinted that you might carry too much baggage to be a husband . . . what baggage were you talking about?"

"We can talk about that later."

"But, if you get swept away in the current, that will nag at me. I want to know what baggage you tote."

"My feet are already freezing." He pushed deeper into the water.

"Could the baggage be that you are unsociable, bullheaded, judgmental, demanding, impatient, quick tempered, with a past of violence and danger?"

He stepped back out of the water. "That sort of covers it."

"I think a woman could live with that."

"You think she could?"

"I didn't say your darling Carla could . . . I said I think a woman could. Most any gal would know what she was getting with Avery John Creede. There's nothing deceptive about you."

"I could, you know, change a bit, I reckon."

"No, you can't. Oaks don't bend in the wind. They can never be willows . . . if they bend, they will break."

The mud near the riverbank squished between his toes. "Is it okay for oaks to get wet?"

"Of course." She waved her hand like a queen dismissing a wayward servant. "But you should take off that shirt."

"I am not taking off my shirt."

"You have only two shirts, correct? And the other one is your white shirt for your suit. Why get that one soaked?"

"I don't have on my long handled shirt. I'm not taking it off."

"That heavy cotton shirt will weigh a ton wet. It will rub your wounded arm raw."

"I told you, I am not . . ."

Sunny crawled down off the wagon. "This is absurd. I'm going to hide in the bushes. You pull off your shirt and swim out there and test the water. When you are back here with your shirt and britches on, holler at me, and I will come back. Now, go on. Pete needs our help."

She stomped behind the thick, six-foot high wall of brush that lined the river. "Okay, I'm hidden. Did you pull off your shirt yet?"

"This is embarrassing."

"Avery, spin around slow . . . do you see any human, in any direction, watching you?"

"No."

"Then pull off your shirt and go check the river!"

Avery stepped over to the wagon, slipped out of his long sleeve, heavy cotton shirt, then folded it with military precision and placed it on top of the ducking trousers. He studied his wounded arm and the old scars on his bare shoulders.

"Hey, what is goin' on here anyway?"

Avery threw his arms across his chest. Ace approached from the other side of the wagon.

"I'm going to swim out there and check the river for a place to cross."

"Yeah, sure . . . and where is Miss Sunny?"

"Here in the bushes," she called out.

"Are you dressed, or are you half-naked, too?"

Sunny marched straight out to Ace. "I am fully dressed, young man, and I do not appreciate those insinuations."

Ace stared down at his boots. "I was just teasin', Miss Sunny. I wasn't castin' doubts on your virtue."

"It was just the opposite. We were tryin' to be discreet," she snapped.

"No reason to be modest now," Avery sighed. "You two wait . . ."

"Oh, my word . . ."

"What's the . . ."

"Uncle Avery, you have more scars on your chest than a punkin in a briar patch."

"I don't call them scars."

"What do you call them?" Ace asked.

"Baggage." Avery turned to the river. "Take care of Miss Cutler. I'll be right back."

"There's no reason for you to get all wet," Ace insisted. "I found us a good place to cross upstream."

"I told you those places upstream are too deep and wide."

"Oh, it's deep and wide, alright, but it has an advantage that this place don't."

"What kind of advantage?"

Ace rocked back on his heels. "A ferry crossing."

"A ferry? Out here?" Avery pressed.

"A big old flat raft, a cable, a donkey-engine and a ferryman's shack on the other side. There's a bell to ring on this side."

"A ferry?"

"He seems to repeat himself a lot," Sunny said. "Put on your clothes, Avery, dear . . . let's take the ferry over the river."

Avery drove them back across the creek and up river along a deep rutted trail. "Did you get the ferryman's attention yet?"

Ace leaned over the edge of the wagon and spit in the sand. "Nope. I kept out of sight. I wanted to make sure it was safe. If you park behind this brush, we can sneak up there and spy it out."

Avery, Ace and Sunny crept through the brush until they spotted the landing, cable, and ferryman's shack on the other side.

"I still can't believe this. There's not enough business out here to warrant this crossing," Avery mumbled.

"Maybe it's an unsuccessful venture," Sunny offered.

Avery squinted, his voice low. "There's an old man sitting on the riverbank. Looks like he's fishing."

"Hope he's having luck," Ace whispered. "Might be how he gets by out here."

Avery motioned behind the bushes. "We'll need to put on the coats and top hats."

"Why do we need them out here?" Ace whined.

Avery led them back to the wagon. "We can't take chances."

"But there's just one old man."

"Old men can tell tales."

Sunny helped them pull on their long coats. "What do you want me to do?"

"There's some black bunting under the seat. Wrap it over your head and shoulders. You can pretend to be the grieving widow."

"I don't even want to pretend I'm Rinkman's widow. I'll be a . . . a sister, burying her wayward brother . . . or a cousin. Never his wife."

Costumes in place, Avery drove the wagon straight up to the dock. The old man stayed hunched down over his fishing pole.

Ace jumped down and rang the school bell mounted on a twelve foot high post. The peals shattered the stillness. The team lurched forward.

Avery stood up in the wagon. "Hey, mister!" he bellowed. "We want to take the ferry across!"

The old man didn't flinch. Didn't look up. Didn't holler back.

Avery pulled his gun and fired a shot straight up. The horses danced sideways. The old man tossed down his pole, then meandered to the edge of the landing. "Ferry is closed today," he shouted. "Only open on Monday and Friday. This is Wednesday . . . or maybe Thursday, but it's not Friday."

"We need to get across. We'll pay you extra."

"I told you we are closed today. Tomorrow I

can ferry you across . . . $2 for the wagon, .50 cents for each person."

"I'll give you $5 to pull us across right now."

The old man pulled off his tattered straw hat and waved it at them. "County only pays me for two days a week. I don't want to start up the engine. You'll just have to wait."

"This is an emergency," Avery hollered. "We have a man to bury, and he's turnin' ripe. We have to get him in the ground today."

"Bury him over there. He won't know the difference," the old man replied.

"We have his sister here. The family wants a burial on that side of the river."

"The ferry is closed today and the fish are bitin'. You'll have to wait."

"Will $10 tempt you?" Avery shouted.

He hesitated. "I reckon it would."

"Send the ferry over. I'll give you $10."

"I said it was temptin' . . . I didn't say I'd succumb to the temptation. Now if it were $20, I don't think I could resist."

"That's robbery," Avery replied.

Sunny peered out from under the black bunting. "Now we see how he stays in business."

"That's more money than I make on the funeral, but I'll pay it just to get this man in the ground. Send over the ferry," Avery shouted.

"Let me see the funds."

"He can't see anything from that distance," Ace said.

Sunny poked Avery in the ribs. "Hold it up, maybe it will placate him."

Avery held a gold double-eagle coin above his head.

"Turn it over," the man hollered. "I want to see the other side."

Avery turned the coin over. "This is the stupidest thing I've ever done."

"I doubt it," Sunny added.

Fifteen minutes later the donkey-engine built up enough steam to pull the flat, railless ferry across the river.

Avery drove the shy team out on the large raft. All three sat on the wagon as it inched it's way back across the fast moving river.

Sunny patted both of them on the knee. "Isn't this nice? A river cruise with two handsome men. If this broke loose, we could ride it all the way to St. Louis."

Avery tugged down the front of his hat. "Or until it tipped over two miles downstream."

"Sometimes, Mr. Creede, you have a very dull imagination."

"Thank you."

The liveryman stopped them a few feet from shore. His hand on the long clutch lever, he called out, "Toss that coin over here and I'll bring you on across."

Avery whipped out his gun. "I don't pay until the job is done."

"You are mighty quick with a gun for an undertaker."

"I wasn't always an undertaker."

"Put the gun away. I was just funnin' you about tossin' the coin."

Avery shoved his gun in the holster and the ferryman brought them to the dock. The team and wagon on the shore, Avery paid the liveryman.

"Open the gate," Ace called out. "We need to get this ol' boy in the ground."

"Can't open the gate until you get inspected."

"Inspect us?" Avery sputtered. "We've had enough of this extortion."

"I'm just the ferryman. Those boys are the inspectors."

Four men stalked out of the ferryman's shanty, each with a carbine at their shoulder pointed at Avery, Ace and Sunny.

CHAPTER TWENTY-TWO

The four armed men just stood there, as if waiting for a command from an unseen leader. Ace and Sunny glanced at Avery. The team of horses seemed to sense his action ahead of time. They were primed to race when Avery whipped the lead lines across their rumps. They bolted through the flimsy gate, then galloped down the road.

As gunshots blasted behind them, Avery shoved Sunny down below the wagon seat.

"They'll come after us!" Ace shouted, as he clung onto the side rail.

Wind lashed Avery's face as he kept his head tucked down so the top hat wouldn't fly off. "Yep. But we get to pick the place."

The lid rattled off Rinkman's pine box and Ace crawled into the back of the wagon.

Sunny struggled back up to the wagon seat and clutched Avery's arm. "They could have shot us dead right there at the ferry."

"But they didn't." He swerved off the roadway and drove west to the low hills.

"You took a big chance," she shouted above the rattle of the wagon. "You didn't know they would be so slow to shoot."

Avery tried to lick the bitter yellow dust off his lips. "I knew."

Ace shoved the struggling Rinkman back into the box, then climbed up to the wagon seat. "Looks like they are headed this way."

Sunny released his arm. "Avery John Creede, you can't possibly know when a man will shoot or not."

He whipped the team harder. "I read it in their

eyes. I've looked at many a man who wanted to kill me. I can tell the ones who will be quick to pull the trigger."

"Can you teach me how?" Ace called out.

"I'm hoping to teach you how to never need that." Avery glanced behind them. "How many?"

Ace craned his neck around. "Can't tell. I reckon all four. I don't think the ferryman will leave the river."

Dirt flew off the horses' hooves, choking the sunlight. The wagon seat slammed against Avery's backside at every bounce. Both horses showed signs of lather. "I think one of the gunmen will stay to watch the crossing. I say only three came after us."

"What's our plan?" Sunny asked.

Avery squinted at the whirling dirt. "To live 'til tomorrow. That's about as far as my plans ever stretch." He stormed the wagon into the first draw he could find, circling the team so that he could face the only entrance into the low hills.

He shoved his revolver at Sunny. "Hide behind those boulders on the north. Ace, you position yourself on that rim on the south. Both of you keep out of sight. Don't reveal your position, unless you have to. And keep your gun on whichever one is closest. If I get shot, your best defense is to shoot Rinkman."

"What are you going to do?" Sunny asked.

Avery tied the lead lines to the railing. "Visit."

With Ace and Sunny concealed, Avery pulled out the double barreled shotgun. He yanked Rinkman from the pine box. Leaving him gagged, he propped him up in the wagon seat. Standing behind the outlaw leader, he shoved the muzzle of the shotgun against the man's neck.

Avery heard the hoofbeats first, then spotted the dust spiral of three riders headed for the draw. They spread out over the seventy-five-yard-wide arroyo and stopped past pistol range.

"That's far enough, boys," he shouted. "I'm guessing you don't want me to use this shotgun on Rinkman."

"Mr. Rinkman? We didn't know they had you," the man in the middle called out.

"Well, we do, and I'm lookin' for an excuse to shoot him. You move two feet closer to me and he's dead. I reckon this double barrel shotgun will separate his head from his shoulders. What do you think?"

The man advanced, then spun his horse in a circle. "I don't think you'll live to sundown."

"Hey, that's Creede, the one we're lookin' for." The hatless man on the left inched his horse forward, then stopped.

"Where are your compadres?" the one on the right, with the dirty gray hat said. "There was two others in the wagon when you busted through the ferry gate."

335

Avery didn't take his eyes off the man in the middle. "They must have fallen out of the wagon."

"That's ridiculous. Where are they?" dirty-gray-hat asked.

"You can't see them? That should worry you. And the fact they have guns pointed at you should worry you even more."

The torn brown leather vested man replied, "You're all bluff, mister."

"There's one way to find out. Ride that horse closer."

The middle man waved his carbine over his head. "Circle him, boys."

"Did you notice how this hombre wants both of you to ride next to the rocks? If my pals are armed and hidin' out of sight, where do you think they are? You ride out there and you are both dead . . . and, of course, I plug Rinkman. That just leaves me and your pal here. Suppose he does shoot me. My two pals are out of sight and will cut him down. So, in your plan . . . all three of you die, Rinkman is decapitated, and maybe with luck, you gun me down. Doesn't sound too promising."

"You're all talk, mister," the red faced man in the middle shouted. "You don't have a chance and you know it."

"If you believed that, you would have rushed me the moment you rode into this canyon. But let me give you another plan; it's a plan where all of you, including your worthless boss, live. Somewhere in the Breaks you are holding Pete Cutler. I want him here, alive. Go get him and I'll trade you Rinkman for Pete."

"How do we know you won't kill the boss while we are gone?" dirty-gray-hat asked.

"If I wanted him dead, I would have done it by now."

"This is stupid . . . let's charge him," the one in the middle shouted.

"Easy for him to say. He doesn't have a gun pointed at him from behind the rocks. You two are dead."

"There isn't anyone holding a gun on you," the man fumed.

"Let's try an experiment. I'll signal my pals to shoot one of you to prove a point. Who wants to volunteer?"

Both men on the sides of the draw backed to the entrance.

Avery looked at the man in the middle. "Your partners are smarter than you. They know how to keep from being shot."

"I'm not afraid of you." He kicked the flanks of his horse and charged.

The sound of Avery's shotgun blast rattled the wagon.

Rinkman fell over on the seat.

Buckshot scattered in front of the rushing

horse. The dark brown gelding reared back in terror. The rider tumbled to the ground as the horse retreated in panic. His hoofs clipped the fallen rider above the right ear. He crumpled to the ground.

Avery stood in the wagon and waved the shotgun at the other two. "Boys, go get Pete and we'll make a trade."

"What about Clayton?"

"It seems to me Clayton wanted your boss dead. Why else would he press the case? And he didn't seem too concerned about your lives, either. I'll keep him here so he won't get you into more trouble."

"How do we know you'll be here when we come back?"

"Even if I'm not, you'll be alive. That's worth something."

"Mister, life was much simpler before you came to the Breaks."

"You mean you always had someone to tell you what to do?"

"I reckon so. Is Mr. Rinkman okay?"

"The report from the shotgun probably gave him a bad headache and his hearing won't be very good for a while, but he's okay."

Avery aimed the shotgun at the riders until they rode out of sight, then jumped off the wagon. "All right, you can come on out."

Ace hiked over to the downed gunman. "You

sure had them buffaloed." He knelt beside Clayton. "This one's out like a log in the forest. Did you know he would charge you?"

"Yep. I'm surprised he waited so long. But I didn't know the horse would kick him."

Ace pushed his hat back. A dirt line, like a tattoo, marked his forehead. "I'm mighty glad it didn't come to us having to shoot the side men. The dust cover hung up on your '73 carbine and I couldn't check the lever. It's jammed tight. Miss Sunny might have clipped the other one, but I'd've had to throw rocks at the guy on my side. What are we going to do with him?"

"Grab a rope and tie him up."

"It's going to seem like babysitting again. Are we really going to loaf here for two days and wait for them?"

"Nope. We've got to find some place better than this. Sunny's been down here, maybe she knows a decent place to hide. Maybe that miner's shack we found in the rainstorm, or something similar."

Ace glanced around. "Where is Miss Sunny?"

Avery stalked north. "Mary Jane?"

There was a muffled call.

"Sunny, where are you?" he yelled.

"Mr. Creede, would you please hurry?" Her voice maintained a controlled panic.

He scampered over several boulders and spied her sprawled out, face down in the dirt, the revolver flung several feet away.

"Are you hurt? What happened?" He knelt beside her and started to lift her.

"Don't move me!" she hollered.

"Did you break something? Did you get shot?"

"Would you please be quiet and let me explain?"

"Let me get you out of here first."

"I said, don't touch me. Not yet, anyway. I am not hurt."

"I don't understand . . ."

"Shut up, Creede, and just listen! I crawled over those rocks, and decided to stand up on that little one so I could peek at what was going on."

"But I told you to stay out of sight."

"Hand me my pistol," she said.

"What?"

"Give me that gun!" she shouted.

He handed her the revolver.

She pointed it at him. "Avery, do not interrupt me again. I am a frustrated woman and I will pull the trigger."

Avery leaned on the rock and folded his arms.

"I know you said not to peek, but I did anyway. When Rinkman's men rode up, I ducked back down and slipped off the rock. I am not hurt, just a little dirty and bruised, but as you can see, I couldn't have helped you if I wanted to."

He opened his mouth.

She cocked the hammer.

He held up his hands and leaned back.

"When I fell, my heel jammed in that snake hole. My leg is not broken or injured, but there is one very angry snake in that hole. He has been buzzing and fuming. Several times I've felt him strike against the heel of my shoe. If I pull my foot away from that hole, I will get snake bit. I couldn't reach my gun to shoot him, and I knew that would spoil your ploy, so I laid here in the dirt praying you'd survive."

"Snakes don't buzz; they rattle."

"That's what I meant. Now, figure out how to safely get me out of here without a rattlesnake bite."

"I'll unfasten your shoe and we'll leave it jammed in the hole. When you're at a safe distance, I'll shoot it."

"My shoe, or the snake?"

"We'll flip the shoe away with a stick and shoot the snake."

"Can you get my shoe off without either of us getting bit?"

"You have the gun. If the snake comes out, shoot him."

Avery scooted over to her feet. She shoved the gun back to him. The dry, yellow dirt fogged her shoes and dress. He tugged at the laces.

"Hurry," she called out.

"I don't expect you need any help," Ace called out from the rocks above.

Avery didn't glance up. "I'm just taking off her shoe."

"I can see that. You want me to wait at the wagon?"

"No," Avery huffed. "I want you to watch this. You might learn something."

"I already know how to take off a girl's . . . eh, shoe."

"There's a rattlesnake in that hole," Sunny explained. "Avery's trying to keep me from getting bit."

"A snake?"

Avery tugged at the laces. "Yeah, a big one that's been buzzing around in there."

"Snakes don't buzz, they . . ."

"Apparently, this one does." Avery held on to her foot with one hand, and the tall, lace up leather shoe with the other. With care, he lifted her foot out. "There you go."

Ace offered her his hand. She limped on one shoe across the boulders.

Avery retrieved a small sage stick. "You two ready for this snake to come out?"

"Be careful," Sunny spit back.

Avery cocked the hammer on his Colt. With his left hand on the stick, he shoved it down into the shoe and then flung it over the rocks.

A large, angry bee buzzed at him. He swatted

it away. When it made a return pass at him, Avery shot it.

"Whoa . . . that was one large bumblebee, Uncle Avery."

"I've never wasted a bullet on a bee before. Just a reaction."

"Forget the bee. Get the snake," Sunny yelled.

Avery peered back at the hole. "I don't see a snake."

"There's a big snake in there . . . shoot it."

Avery squatted down and stared. "The hole's empty."

"There is a snake in there and I expect you to kill it," she huffed.

He jammed the stick in the hole and wiggled it around. "I don't think so. I'd say it was just a large bumblebee."

"I didn't lay there in the dirt for a half-hour because of a bee. There was a snake in there. Maybe he dug a tunnel and buried himself."

"Miss Sunny, snakes ain't like worms." Ace grinned as if giving a science lesson to kids. "They don't dig in the dirt."

"They most certainly do. That's a snake hole, isn't it?"

Avery tossed the stick down. "Nope, it was dug by some other varmint. Snakes are like lousy relatives . . . they just move in and never leave."

"Maybe we could find the bee bits and you could mount it on a plaque," Ace suggested.

"How funny, but there is a big and very dangerous snake in these rocks somewhere. I for one don't intend to get bit by it."

"No doubt there is a snake somewhere in these rocks, but there wasn't a snake in that hole."

Ace moseyed over to her. "Here's your shoe, Miss Sunny."

"Was there a snake in it?"

"No, ma'am."

"Are there fang marks on the sole?"

"Nope."

"There was a snake in that hole . . . ," she mumbled as she tugged on her shoe and laced it up.

"Ace, go see if you can fetch Clayton's horse. Keep your gun handy, just in case those two we chased off are even dumber than they look. Then we need to load him up and find a safe place to wait out our two days."

Sunny chewed on her lower lip. "Give me your gun again."

Avery handed her the revolver. "Who you going to shoot?"

"I am going to do what you refused to do. I am going to kill that snake."

"But, Miss Sunny, there isn't . . ."

She twirled around and pointed the gun at Ace.

"Eh, go right ahead, ma'am."

Sunny marched around the boulder and over to the hole in the ground. She bent at the waist, held the gun about a foot above the hole.

BAM!

BAM!

BAM!

BAM!

"Did you get him, Miss Sunny?" Ace ventured.

She stomped back over to Avery and handed him his gun. "What do you think, Mr. Creede? Could any snake live through that assault?"

"No, ma'am, I'll have to agree with you. There is not a live snake left in that hole."

"Thank you for that observation."

"I reckon that you showed the snake world a thing or two," Ace added.

"It is nothing compared to what I have planned for either of you if you ever tell anyone about this."

CHAPTER TWENTY-THREE

Houses, like horses, each have their own personality. Maybe it's the roof-line, or where the windows are placed or the way the yard is maintained. But some houses seem friendly . . . some aloof . . . some hostile.

A house full of kids appears alive.

A deserted house resembles death.

The one straight ahead of Avery, Sunny and Ace looked scared.

Two long buildings enclosed a covered patio between them. It looked like southwest hacienda. Avery figured that if the house had legs, it would be running in that direction. Yard plants and trees had been planted with care . . . but were now dead.

Ace rubbed his dusty chin. "Someone must be home. There's smoke comin' out of the chimney."

"But it looks so abandoned." Sunny shaded her eyes with her hand. "The barn door is busted, the yard neglected. There's not one animal in the corral. What is this place?"

Avery slowed the team. "Someone's dream that didn't pan out. Let's see if they will let us camp in the barn a few days."

"Where are we?" Ace surveyed the country-side. "Are we still in the Missouri River Breaks? Could be Rinkman's men out here."

"I thought we might be too far north, but I'm not sure. Guess we'll find out soon enough." Avery parked the team at a busted gate, then slapped his hat off on his leg.

Two quick rifle blasts shattered the dirt in front of the horses. Avery fought to keep them in control.

"I reckon that answers your question." Ace's voice jumped as much as he did.

"I don't think they can tell who we are from that distance." Avery nudged the rig forward.

Sunny clutched his arm. "What are you doing?"

"Gettin' within shoutin' range."

"They can shoot us."

"Not until they know who we are."

Another blast splashed dirt next to the wagon. Avery stopped the rig and stood. "Ho, to the house. We need to talk. I won't come any further."

A tall, thin man sporting a Springfield trap-door rifle eased out to the covered patio between the buildings. "What do you want?"

"We need a place to camp," Avery shouted. "Can we fill our canteens in your well, and perhaps sleep the night in your barn?"

"Is it just you, your wife and your boy?"

Avery glanced at the back of the wagon where Clayton and Rinkman lay tied. "There are five of us. I'll pay you for the inconvenience."

"You got cash money?"

"A little."

"You want to buy this place?"

Avery, Sunny and Ace stared in surprise at each other. "I not lookin' to buy."

"I'll sell you a patent deed for three hundred and twenty acres . . . house, barn, furnishin's and all for $500 cash."

Avery's mouth was so dry, he had to speak slowly. "I don't have that kind of money. I'm not looking for a place to buy."

The man began to pace back and forth like a caged animal at the zoo. "Well then, go on. You can't stay here. I don't trust you."

"But you'd sell us the place?"

"Yep, just $250 cash. The wife and kids are with her mother in Bozeman. I'm giving up."

"Too harsh a winter?" Avery asked.

"Too much Rinkman. He and his gang stole my livestock, threatened the wife and kids, ripped up the yard, busted up my belongings and poured boulders in my well. The sheriff won't come out and do a thing about it. I've had it. I wouldn't be here now, but they stole my horse two nights ago. I thought you were them coming back for me. That's before I spied your wife and boy. This is good land, mister. Just some bad people around. Someday it will settle down. I just am not the one to wait it out anymore."

The wind drifted just enough to get a whiff of the smoke from the woodstove. "How much will it cost to let us spend a day or two here?"

"$250 . . . and I'll give you the patent deed."

"I told you I don't have that kind of money."

The man stepped out into the yard. "$100 and that saddled horse."

Avery tossed a quick look at Clayton's horse tied to the wagon. "Mister, you've got the potential for a nice little spread here. I don't want to take it from you."

"My wife and kids are too scared to stay . . .

my cows were stolen, wheat burned, and team shot. With a horse and $100 cash, I can collect my family and start over someplace that's never heard of Rinkman."

"Doesn't sound like a good investment for me either."

"You are new here. You ain't had an opportunity to make Rinkman mad. Maybe he'd leave you alone. I didn't have enough money to pay him off. You give him somethin' every month and he'll leave you alone. Besides, I heard there was a new sheriff at Ft. Benton that ain't afraid of him. So, you might be on the verge of a peaceful time. Me, I just want to get back to my family."

Avery sat down on the wagon seat. "And what if I don't want to buy it?"

"Then I'll have to shoot you and steal the horse. I could have shot you by now. I was in the army and I can tune this .45-70 to a thousand yards."

"Infantry?" Avery quizzed.

"Yep."

"I was in the cavalry, the 7th."

"With Custer?" the man asked.

"With Reno. And you?"

"At Rosebud, with General Crook."

Avery folded his arms across his chest. His shirt felt stiff and dirty. "What did you think of Crook?"

"Best man I ever met in my life."

"I'll buy the place." Avery reached into his pocket and fingered cold coins.

"You will?"

"$140 cash, and the saddled horse. You're right about General George Crook."

The man pushed his hat back. "I said you could have it for $100."

"And I said I'd pay $140."

The man's wide smile beamed. "I like the way you do business. I got the deed right here in the house. Come on up and sign it."

"I'll be right there. Ace, drive the wagon into the barn and park it. I want Rinkman and Clayton out of sight. I don't want this old boy telling others."

Ace slipped over to the driver's side of the wagon as Avery stepped down. "You want me to come over to the house, then?"

"Stay at the barn door. Keep your pistol handy. Could be more to this than we can see."

"Where do you want me?" Sunny asked.

"Come with me. The little missus needs to see her new house, doesn't she?" He offered her his hand.

"Don't tease me, Creede." She hopped to the ground.

"Sunny, I need you to pretend for just a few minutes. I don't want this man telling everyone that the sheriff's got Rinkman and they are holed up on his former homestead. Not only would that draw Rinkman's men, but also every saloon hanger-on that wants to make a name for himself by killing Jed Rinkman."

She raised her blonde eyebrows. "You think your darling Carla would approve of us pretending to be husband and wife?"

"I doubt it. She assumes my pal Sunny is a male."

"You never told her about me?"

"I never told her about lots of things . . . not yet, anyway."

Sunny clutched his arm. "When you do mention to her that Sunny is a fairly young blonde woman, what will you say?"

Avery tried to tug his arm back. "Can't we talk about this later?"

She grabbed as tight as a young child in a dark alley. "I want to know now, before I begin this pretense."

"I'll tell her that Miss Mary Jane Cutler is one of the two or three bravest women I've ever met."

"Who are the other two?"

"Eh . . . Pepper Andrews and Carolina Parke."

"Thank you for that compliment. And what will you tell her I look like?"

"This is really not the time . . ."

"I don't go one step closer until you finish the statement," Sunny snapped.

"I'd say you were as handsome as Isabel Leon Mandara, but with pale skin and yellow hair that shames the sunlight at noon."

"You'd say that?"

"I would . . . if pressed."

"That's beautiful."

"Thank you. Now can we go on?" Avery asked.

"Not until you admit one thing."

"What?"

"You would never describe me like that to another woman."

"Yes, I would."

"Admit it . . . you wouldn't describe me that way."

"Mary Jane . . . we need to . . ."

"Say it!"

"Okay, I probably wouldn't use that exact language."

"See . . . I knew it. But thank you for the compliment just the same."

"Now can we go buy ourselves a hiding place?"

She released his arm. "Is that what we are doing?"

"Yep."

The man with the trap-door rifle met them on the porch with a battered leather satchel and papers in hand. "Jist tie the horse to the post." He dropped the satchel and shoved out his hand. "I'm Chet Bishop."

"Nice to meet you, Mr. Bishop. I'm A.J., and this is my wife, Mary Jane."

He tipped his dirty felt hat. "Pleased to meet you, ma'am. This will be a nice place some day. My Maggie had it all planted with shrubs and flowers that we brought all the way from California. But between the harsh winter and Rinkman's wrath, everything got destroyed."

Sunny peered through the open front door of the building on the right. "We're sorry to take advantage of your misfortune."

"Don't be. I prayed to the Almighty this mornin' that he'd send me a way out of this. I reckon you're an answer to that prayer."

Avery pulled seven gold coins out of his pocket. "I think this is the price." He counted them into the man's dirty hand.

"You want me to show you around first?"

"Are you trying to rook me, Mr. Bishop?"

The man stiffened. "No, sir."

"Then I trust you."

Chet Bishop nodded to Sunny. "There's quite a bit of furniture that ain't broken."

"You take whatever you want," she replied.

"I got it all in that satchel." He reached into the bag and pulled out a pen and a bottle of black India ink. "Sign these papers. Fill your name in right there. You'll have to take it to the courthouse to get it filed."

"I'll do that next time I'm in town." Avery

printed in the name, then scrawled a signature across the page.

Mr. Bishop did the same. "The missus can sign as a witness."

Avery turned the yellowing deed over, then handed her the pen. "Just write that you witnessed these signatures on this date."

With a flourish, Sunny signed the paper.

"You got real artistic style. Just like my Maggie . . . only different."

Avery folded the papers. "Does that take care of everything?"

"I surmise it does." Bishop tied his satchel to the back of the cantle, then led Clayton's horse into the dry dirt yard.

Sunny sauntered into the building to the right of the roofed patio. Avery hiked out to Bishop.

"How come your boy is hanging out at the barn?"

"He got into a skunk. Can't you smell him?"

"I think the wind is blowin' the other way. Them kids can get rank, can't they?"

"That's for sure."

Bishop turned to gaze back at the house. "I think it's a mighty nice thing you did for your wife."

Avery nodded. "Sort of an insurance policy, I think."

"My Maggie will be pleased to hear that."

"She sounds like quite a woman."

"The kind that makes a man glad to be around, you know what I mean?"

Avery rubbed his chin. "I believe I do."

Bishop mounted the horse. "I do hope things settle down and you get to enjoy this place. Too many bad memories for me and my Maggie. See this little tree right here?"

"Looks like it got yanked out of the ground."

"That was Rinkman's doin'. You know what kind of tree it was?"

"Don't think I do."

Bishop tugged his floppy hat down in front. "A California almond tree. I told Maggie they wouldn't grow in Montana, but she insisted. So we dug it up at her sister's house in Marysville, then wagoned it all the way here. For two winters she draped a tarp over it at night, and stuck a bedwarmer full of coals under the tent to keep it from freezin'. This spring it blossomed out just as purdy as you can imagine. It was just settin' a few nuts when Rinkman's men hooked a chain to it one night and ripped it right out of the ground. That's when Maggie gave up. Said she couldn't take it anymore. Don't blame her. She said she'd be back when things settled down, but they only got worse."

"Perhaps the worst is past," Avery offered.

"Hope so for your sake. Goodbye, Mr. Cutler . . . may all your days be clear and calm."

"And may the Lord be with you and your family, Mr. Bishop."

When he rode away, Ace meandered over to the porch. "Why did he call you Mr. Cutler?"

Sunny stepped out of the house. "You told him your name was Cutler?"

"I didn't want to say I'm Avery John Creede. I wanted the appearance of a happy homestead family."

"Well, two of the family tied in the back of the wagon ain't very happy," Ace said.

"Unhitch the team and water them."

"The horses or the men?"

"Both."

"Where's the well?" Ace asked.

"We'll have to dig it out. Bishop said they filled it with rocks."

Ace swatted a mosquito on the back of his hand. "Sounds like a lot of work."

"No one said homesteadin' was easy."

"But we ain't homesteadin'. We're just hiding out."

"Yeah, and we still drink water."

Ace and Avery headed to the busted well next to the corral.

"Wait a minute," Sunny called out. "If you didn't want your name known, why did you put your Avery John Creede on that patent deed?"

He winked at her. "What makes you think I did?"

She unfolded the deed. "What is this?"

"It's a patent deed."

"In the name of Mary Jane Cutler? You bought this place in my name?"

"I told you I couldn't use mine, and Ace is too young to hold title."

She pranced across the porch. "Then, for now, this is my place?"

"Yep."

"It's kind of a strange design, like two cabins with a common roof."

"This one is the kitchen, dining room, living room and all that." The creases on Sunny's face disappeared as she gushed. "There's a cookstove, a china closet with the china gone and glass busted. There's a divan and a couple of side chairs, and towels, dishes. It's dusty, but furnished."

"What's in that other side?" Ace asked.

"The bedrooms. I think they ate out on the patio whenever the wind and weather would allow it."

"I've seen this style in California and New Mexico . . . but not up here," Avery remarked.

Sunny retrieved a busted broom from the yard. "She tried to fix it up like home."

Avery rubbed his chin. "Kind of sad, isn't it?"

"We can't turn Rinkman loose." Sunny waved the broom at the barn.

"We have to. But, we'll get Pete back and then nab Rinkman again."

She pointed the broken broom at him. "Did you hear me, Avery John Creede? We are not turning him loose."

"I heard you, Miss Cutler, but I'd rather have Pete alive than Rinkman dead."

"We need a different plan."

"I reckon we do, but right now we need water. Ace and I will be cleaning up the well."

She toted the broom over her shoulder like a rifle. "I'll straighten things up in the house."

With Rinkman and Clayton chained to a center post of the barn, Avery and Ace began to dig out boulders shoved into the well. At ten feet, they found the water line. Ace pulled off his shirt and Avery held his feet as he dipped down into the water to retrieve submerged boulders.

It was almost dark when they quit.

Avery studied the circular, brick-lined hole. "The silt should settle by morning and we'll get a cleaner drink."

Ace shook water off his arms and hands, then pulled on his shirt. "While you was dunkin' me like a cookie in coffee, I've been ponderin' on this place. It could be a nice little spread some day. You could have made up any old name you wanted to and he wouldn't know who you are."

"Yep."

"So why did you put it in Miss Sunny's name?"

"Don't know what's going to happen in this deal."

Ace perched on the boulders and tugged on his boots. "With Rinkman . . . or with Miss Carla?"

"Both. But it could be that my future is in California."

"I think mine might be in Ft. Benton," Ace asserted.

"The point is . . . we've got some future waitin' for us, but Mary Jane doesn't. Maybe this will be something for her someday."

Ace tugged up his britches. "She don't seem like a homesteader woman."

"You'd be surprised what a house can bring out in a lady."

"So you aim for her to have it as her own, no matter what happens?"

"Yep, but don't tell her that . . . yet."

"What do you think Miss Carla will think of you buying another purdy lady a ranch?"

"I'm trustin' that there is a lot about my past that she'll overlook."

"Do you miss your darlin' Carla?"

"I've been too hassled to miss anyone lately."

"I've been hankerin' for Miss Tabby. No matter how busy we've been, I miss her."

When the triangle rang, Avery grabbed for his gun.

"Supper time," Sunny shouted from the porch. Avery and Ace plodded toward the house.

"You look nice in that blue apron, Miss Sunny."

"Thank you, Ace."

"You cooked for us?" Avery asked.

"I do know how to cook. There was some food left in the kitchen. I assume it came with the house. You two wash up?"

"Yes, ma'am," Ace grinned. "I been in water most all afternoon."

"How about you, Mr. Cutler?"

"Would you like to inspect my hands, Mamma?"

"That's not necessary, but pull off your boots before you come in."

"Our boots?" Avery groaned.

"Avery Creede, you are not tracking mud into my clean house!"

CHAPTER TWENTY-FOUR

Daylight broke slowly. Visibility crept across the Breaks in a cadence most often reserved for the old or the injured. Avery had perched in the oak rocking chair, minus one rung, when the sky hung coal black. It was one of those mornings that the night sky dares you to count the stars. Once trapped, you get lost in its immensity and forget where you are. And who you are.

The broken chair sheltered Avery halfway between the two log buildings that made up the Bishop house. One pitched roof extended over both units, leaving the center like a huge, wide tunnel.

Behind the house, foothills swept up to sheer limestone cliffs of the rimrock, two-hundred feet above the buildings. Avery waited for the sun. And wisdom.

Neither appeared anxious to find him.

Avery Creede Emerson staggered out of the front bedroom onto the patio carrying boots in one hand, socks in the other. "Don't you ever sleep?"

"I slept."

"When? You were up checking on Rinkman and Clayton ever' fifteen minutes."

"I looked in on them every two hours."

"It seemed like fifteen minutes."

"Sorry. You can bunk in that back room tonight."

"I wasn't complainin'. You reckon Miss Sunny has some coffee ready?" Ace rubbed his jaw as if it were a pair of pliers locked tight.

Avery's ducking jeans felt frosty and stiff when he rubbed the cramp out of his thigh. "I'm not about to bother her, and either are you. When I told her that side of the house was hers, I meant it. We aren't going in there until she invites us."

Ace flopped down on an empty nail barrel and tugged on his socks. "I like this place. It's got a nice view of the rising sun."

Avery leaned back and stretched his arms. The bones in his shoulders snapped into place. "And the whole ranch. If a man's vision was good enough, he could almost see down to the river."

"Did you ever use one of them telescopes, the kind that opens up as long as a carbine?"

"In the army." Avery rubbed his eyes. For the first time in several days, his face felt clean.

"I think if I lived here, I'd have me one of them. That way I could tell who was comin' to visit."

"Not a bad idea." Avery peered out into the morning haze. The air tasted new-day fresh, full of potential. "If this were my place, I'd plow up about a hundred acres down by the river and plant hay. With a water wheel, or a steam engine, a man could irrigate that bottom land right out of the river."

"That's a long way to go farm."

"But not far to hunt. Deer, antelope and elk would go down to the river for a drink and stop at the hayfield for a snack. A man could almost sit on his porch and drop them."

"It would take a good shot, but it would be fun to try."

Avery bent over and drew in the dirt floor.

"Then I'd take the two hundred acres in the middle and divide it into two pastures. If there is water up here, I reckon I could dig a couple of wells, one in each pasture. That way there would be a waterin' trough in each, and the horses and cows could drink for themselves."

Ace buttoned up his cotton shirt. "You been ponderin' on this all night?"

"A little bit. Up here around the house, I'd repair that barn to hold the hay through the winter. I'd patch up that corral and extend it clean back to the bottom of the cliff . . . kind of a barrier as well as a pen. I'm thinkin' the wind blows most of the time from west to east, so I'd put a milkin' barn on the other side of this one."

"What about on the south side?"

"That's where the fruit trees and garden would be planted."

"You think you could grow fruit in this area?"

"Apples and cherries . . . maybe some plums. I do like plum jam."

"But no almonds?"

"No almonds. I don't know anything about growin' almonds."

Ace licked his fingers and swatted down his dark brown hair. "Do you know anything about growin' plums?"

Avery laughed. "No, but at least I like plums. Never cared much for almonds. Anyway, it's just a way to pass the time before daylight. Kind of things I think about, you know, if the place was mine."

Ace tucked in his shirt. "It is yours. You bought it, remember?"

"It most certainly is not his!"

Sunny loomed in the doorway, decked out in a light brown calico dress, the long sleeves pushed to her elbows. Her long blonde hair was pulled back and pinned up.

"Miss Sunny, you look," Ace stammered. "You look like . . . you know, like a ranch wife."

"Thank you, Mr. Emerson. I found a clean dress in the bottom of a busted trunk. I suppose Mrs. Bishop assumed it was damaged. Are you two ready for coffee?"

Avery stood slowly, stretching each muscle as he rose. "I didn't want to come into the kitchen until you invited us."

"Well, I'm not inviting you now. I'm still cleaning in there. I'll bring coffee out and we'll eat at that table."

"The table is busted, Miss Sunny."

"You two can repair it before the flapjacks are ready."

Ace nearly tripped over himself. "You cookin' flapjacks?"

"And molasses. But I'm afraid there is no plum jam."

Avery shoved his hands into his jeans pockets.

"How much of my meanderin' did you hear?"

"Enough to know that you think this is a nice location."

"Don't know how it winters. Might be frigid and lonely."

"All depends on who you wintered with," she replied.

They paused as if waiting for the roulette wheel to stop spinning.

Ace cleared the silence. "You want me to check on the horses?"

"I want you and your uncle to repair my table. I believe there are nails in that barrel you are sitting on, and probably a hammer in the barn. Then wash up."

"Wash up? I haven't been up long enough to get dirty," Ace griped.

"Look at you. Your hair is uncombed, your duckings covered with dirt, and your shirt looks like you slept in it."

"I did sleep in it."

"I want all your dirty clothes piled on the porch this morning, young man. I'm going to wash them."

"But, I don't think . . ."

"Don't argue with me."

Ace turned to Avery and mumbled, "I liked her better when she was an outlaw, wearing nothin' but her petticoats."

"I heard that!" Sunny marched over to Avery,

her hands slammed against her hips. "Are you going to let him talk to me that way?"

"Me?"

"Well, you are his . . his . . . ."

"I don't want to come between a lad and his mother."

"She ain't my mother."

Avery turned to Ace. "Do what she says."

"Are you playin' this game, too?"

"Did she tell you to do anything your mother wouldn't tell you?"

Ace glanced down at his boots. "I don't reckon so."

"When she tells you things your mother never would say, you can ignore her." Avery slung his arm around Ace's shoulder. "Up till then, mind your mother."

Sunny grabbed Avery's arm. "And you come over to the kitchen door. I'm going to wash and dress that knife wound. I found some Dr. Bull's Miracle Salve on the back shelf."

"My arm's okay."

"It most certainly is not."

"Mind your mamma," Ace hooted.

Four stout barn nails and a scrap two-by-four repaired the table.

Icy pan water flooded their hands clean.

Hot coffee from chipped porcelain mugs warmed their bellies.

The aroma of fried salt-pork and flapjacks tickled their noses.

Ace leaned across the table. "Why do you reckon Miss Sunny is behavin' like this?"

"She's an actress, playing a part."

Ace sat back. "You mean, it's all pretend?"

"No, I mean she's never been in this role before, and she's trying it on, sort of like trying on a new coat. You strut around the store to get the feel of it. That's what she's doing, trying to get the feel of this rancher's wife routine."

"She can sure be bossy."

"With your mamma gone, I'm about all the family you have, right?"

"Yep. All that I want to count."

"Next to me, who is it on the face of this earth that really cares about you?"

"Miss Tabby!"

"I mean, besides Miss Tabby."

"I surely miss her."

"You know that Sunny cares about you about as much as any person in Montana. Don't look at that lightly. You aren't goin' to get a lot of people in life that really care about you."

"You sound sad."

"Thoughtful." Avery studied the wooden table-top as if looking for a flaw. "My life has always been too hectic to acknowledge people who really cared about me. That's a tragedy you should try to avoid."

A string of curses flooded out of the middle bedroom and echoed across the patio like a hound dog who treed a cougar.

Ace glanced over his shoulder. "Sounds like Rinkman's awake."

Avery pushed himself out of the chair. "That's another practice you should try to avoid."

Sunny enlisted Ace's help to rearrange the kitchen. Avery fed the prisoners, then let them exercise by mucking out the barn, and corraled them back into the middle bedroom. He curried the horse team, repaired the barn door, greased the wagon axles, then sat cross-legged in the barn loft as September sun heated his face and shoulders.

At some point, he laid down on his back and watched a pair of doves fly in and out of the barn as if playing tag.

He was startled at the tone of the Captain's accusation.

"Sergeant, why did you cower and refuse to rescue your colleagues?"

"I neither cowered, nor refused an order."

"You decided that saving your own life was more important than protecting others?"

"Sir, if I might be allowed to present my case . . . I entered the battle leading eighteen men. At the first charge, six were killed, two severely wounded. Two others had their horses shot out from under them. I then had eight mounted men. Over nine hundred mounted Sioux and Cheyenne separated me and the Lt. Colonel. If I led the eight men through the enemy, it would mean instant, agonizing death to the two wounded men, and the two left horseless. The odds of any one of the eight making it across were so great, I deemed it not an intelligent or moral choice."

"You disobeyed orders out of 'moral' conviction?"

"No, sir. If I had done that, I would have not rode up that creek in the first place. Our original orders were to wait for General Gibbon. I believed that to be the wisest decision. But I followed direct orders and rode north."

"The truth is, you saved your life while watching others die."

"I believe our actions saved many lives. What would you prefer, that we all died in the battle?"

"It was a massacre, not a battle."

"We rode fully armed into combat with an unnumbered enemy. It was a battle."

"You could be court-marshaled for insubordination."

"Sir, with due respect for this inquest, at what point does a battle change from an offensive campaign to defensive? I gathered my men at a knoll by the cottonwood trees and determined that if we could continue the fight from there, we would distract some of the Indians, and also have a chance at saving lives. My hope was that would ease the number that pursued the Lt. Colonel."

"That's not much of a strategy."

"It was the best I could come up with at the moment."

"So you switched from offense to defense?"

Avery nodded. "Yes, sir."

The man in the starched uniform paced in front of him. "That was your own decision?"

The air in the barrack courtroom thickened with fine, yellow dust and the drain of tension. "I was cut off from command and felt the necessity to make an instant decision."

"You will testify to that during the court-marshal proceedings?"

"Yes, sir."

"In that case, I have someone for you to meet." The man faded into the shadows.

Avery rubbed his eyes. "What?"

"Someone wants to talk to you."

"Who?"

"Some German guy." The toe of a boot tapped against his shoulder. "Uncle Avery, a German wants to talk to you."

When Creede rose up in the barn loft, sweat rolled down his face and neck. Ace towered above him. "What are you talking about?"

"This German fellow with big black mustache and spiked hat rode in here and wants to speak to the 'papa.' "

Avery swatted his hat against his leg. "The papa?"

"Miss Sunny is still playing house. She thought that's what you wanted, so I'm the kid, and she sent me out to fetch Papa."

The sentry at the well stood at attention, hat in hand. Salt-and-pepper hair greased back above a waxed mustache. A long sword scabbarded at his left hip. A holstered revolver rode high on his right.

"Mr. Cutler, your wife has graciously watered my horse and offered me breakfast. I appreciate that. My name is Dolf Arnwolf, traveling clerk for Prince Rikard Berchtwald. I am in need of your assistance."

"What can I do for you?"

"We would like to bring our party onto your property and camp at your villa."

"My villa?"

The German marched back and forth at a precise cadence. "Prince Rikard is on a hunting trip in your country. We were going up to the Milk River, but he became quite ill at his stomach. His personal physician, Dr. Hunfried, insists on twenty-four hours rest with clean water and shade."

"Clean water?"

"We believe there was something spoiled in the Chinese banquet we feasted on yesterday in Ft. Benton. We will only use your water and the shade of your barn and pay you $20 in gold."

"That's a lot of money," Avery said.

"The prince's entourage includes twenty-three people."

Avery whistled. "That's a lot of folks."

"I know this is a great imposition, but we don't know of any other facility in the area." He brushed his mustache with his fingers as if standing in front of a mirror.

Avery glanced over at Sunny. "What do you think, darlin'? Are you up for company?"

Sunny slipped her arm in his. "We can use the money for a bolt of calico and to repair my sewing machine. Winter is coming on."

Avery gazed into her blue eyes.

"But they will not be allowed in my house."

"Of course not."

She turned toward the German. "Are there any women or children traveling with the prince?"

"The prince's son is accompanying him . . . as well as two lady guests he met here in the West."

Sunny raised her eyebrows. "We are a Christian family."

"I assure you, the women are very charming and proper."

"I do look forward to some feminine company. The life of a rancher's wife is quite solitary at times."

"I believe they will invite you to tea."

"Isn't that nice. I can't remember the last time someone invited me to tea."

Avery studied the man's starched white shirt and gold studs. "When will the prince arrive?"

"I would assume in about two hours. I will ride back and lead them here."

Arnwolf mounted the long legged black horse and trotted out of the yard toward the river.

Avery and Sunny stood arm-in-arm until he was almost out of sight.

"I'm surprised you let them stay," she said.

"Strength in numbers. With a European hunting party camped here, I don't think even Rinkman's men will approach the place."

"I was not joking about keeping them out of my house. Prince or no prince, I'm not having twenty-four pair of muddy boots tramping through my kitchen."

"Twenty-three," Avery corrected. Sunny's scowl muted his reply.

Four armed riders led the procession up from the river. Then followed three mahogany paneled wagons and a hansomesque black carriage with isinglass curtains. Behind that, four mounted men, with pointed hats, swords at their sides, carbines across their laps.

"Oohwee . . . would you look at that!" Ace called out. "It's like a parade in Charleston. Which one is the prince?"

"He and the ladies will wait in the wagons and carriage until the servants set up camp," Avery explained.

Sunny shaded her eyes. "You seem to know something about this sort of thing."

Avery listened to the constant whine of squeaking wagon axles. "I scouted for a French royal hunting party once."

Ace grinned. "Did you get to meet any French women?"

Avery rubbed his chin. "I suppose that's what you call it."

"Is that how you got that scar?" Sunny pressed.

Avery dropped his hand to his side. "No."

"Are you and Ace going to offer them any help?" she pressed.

"We'd just get in the way. Believe me, the Germans have a routine and it's best not to disturb it."

Ace stretched tall as if to appear more mature. "What are we suppose to do?"

"Act like a ranch family."

"What's a ranch family do?" Ace asked.

"I'll go gag Rinkman and Clayton."

Sunny turned toward the kitchen. "I'll bring out the scrubboard and wash some clothes."

"Am I supposed to amble down to the river barefoot with a cane pole to fish? I've read Tom Sawyer."

"I want you to make a wall between the well and that dead tree using the stones we pulled out of the well."

"A wall?"

"That will make it tough to ride up close to the house."

"You think the Germans will ride up here?"

"I think they'll be gone before noon tomorrow. I want us to be prepared if Rinkman's men ride in."

"You reckon they know we're up here?"

"They will, if they run across the Germans. We can't tell them to keep this a secret."

Tents were erected.

Awnings stretched.

A fine Persian rug was rolled across the dirt floor.

Gold inlaid oak chairs circled a table.

Asian silk room dividers were arranged.

Dolf Arnwolf strolled over to the well, where Avery and Ace constructed the rock wall. "Mr. Cutler, Prince Rikard and his son would like to meet you and personally thank you for your gracious hospitality. He would also like to meet your wife and son."

Avery buttoned up his shirt. "Ace, go get Mamma. It's time to say howdy to the new neighbors."

With Sunny on his arm, Ace at his side, Avery followed Arnwolf around the first room divider under the big white awning.

A small man with thick black hair and wild eyebrows slumped in a wide chair, his face pale, cheeks somewhat sunken. His silk jacket was unbuttoned at the top, and a wet white towel circled his neck.

Arnwolf offered introductions.

"Prince Rikard, this is Mr. and Mrs. Cutler and their son, Ace."

"Forgive me for not rising, madame. It was the meat," the prince muttered.

"What?"

"I normally enjoy Oriental food, but it was the meat that made me sick."

Sunny curtsied. "I'm sorry to hear that. A couple tablespoons of huckleberry wine with a spoonful of salts usually clears that right up."

The prince stared at Arnwolf.

"The doctor has the situation diagnosed," the spokesman explained.

The prince held up his hand. "I will try whatever works."

"I'm sorry, we don't have any huckleberry wine," Avery said.

"Yes, we do," Sunny insisted. "I hid some back,

saving it for company. Sometimes Mr. Cutler drinks a little too much."

"My wife told me the same thing."

"Is your wife with you?" she asked.

"No, my wife died last summer while we hunted tigers in India. Have you been to India, Mr. Cutler?"

"I've been to Indiana," Ace blurted out.

"Perhaps it is the same. Stay out of India, if you can. Now, you must meet my son." He waved his arm at the room divider. "Loritz!"

A young man about Ace's age appeared wearing duckings, polished black boots, a leather vest over a cotton shirt, and a holstered revolver. His wide brimmed, felt hat was turned up at the side.

"I am Loritz." He made a clumsy attempt to bow and remove his hat.

"He wants to be a cowboy," the prince offered.

"You look quite knobby, son." Avery suppressed a grin.

"Nobby?"

"Very well dressed."

"Thank you. And you look . . ."

"Modest," Avery interrupted. "That's the right word to use."

"Do you make your living with your gun?" the young man asked.

"At times."

Loritz yanked off his hat and dark hair sprang

out like dry weeds from under a wagon wheel. "Ah hah! Now I have met one of Mr. Buntline's gunslingers."

"Don't believe everything you read in the dime novels," Avery said.

The prince waved his hand. "That's what I have tried to tell him."

"Let me go get you some huckleberry wine and salts," Sunny offered.

"Wait . . . wait," the prince cautioned. "Dolf, will you please check with the ladies' wagon and see if they would like to meet the Cutlers?"

"Of course."

"I came across the daughter of a close family friend and invited her to travel with us a few days. She is quite a delightful lady and she brought along a young friend, not wanting to look improper."

Sunny grabbed Avery's arm and whispered, "Do I look alright? Do I have any smudges on my face? Should I roll my sleeves down?"

"I don't think it . . ."

Arnwolf re-entered. Avery heard the swish of silk dresses.

The first woman had dark black hair.

"Carla?" he stammered.

She stared at Sunny clutching his arm. "Avery?"

"Miss Tabby," Ace shouted.

Tabitha Leitner scrunched her nose. "Oh, Mr. Emerson, how could you do this to me?"

CHAPTER TWENTY-FIVE

Years back, while serving with General George Crook in Arizona, Avery had been sent to receive a report from friendly Yavapai scouts. His instructions had been simple . . . go north from Prescott to the Grand Canyon, camp in a white army tent with U.S. flag flying beside it, and wait for the scouts.

Twelve days later, Indians arrived with messages about Apache activity.

Twelve beautiful, quiet, peaceful days.

He sat at the canyon rim, his legs dangling over the edge, to marvel at the vast, ever-changing beauty. Soft oranges. Deep purples. The blue sky settled low and sweet like a muted lullaby.

Although the tent was pitched as a signal, he slept under the stars. The heavens skittered with movement and he hated to miss any of it. The crisp morning freshness and lung soothing air allowed him, for the only time he recalled, in his life, to stay in his bedroll until sunlight broke across the canyon rim.

The stillness of each day brought serenity to his heart and mind. No surprises. No threats. No hidden agendas. No expectations. He didn't have to say a word. He didn't have to settle a dispute. He fired one bullet to bring down a small antelope . . . and feasted the whole time.

Pure heaven.

Now, as he felt Sunny's grip tighten on his arm and stared at the fiery brown eyes of Carla Loganaire . . . he longed for the peaceful camp along the canyon rim.

Or, even the charge of a thousand Lakota Sioux braves.

Anywhere but here.

The tension magnified Carla's glare like the all knowing eye atop the unfinished pyramid of the Great Seal. "Avery . . . you are married?"

The burgundy silk dress with deep scooped neckline did nothing to relax his tight jaw, a natural reflex. "I am not."

Ace threw his hands in the air and stomped across the carpet. "I ruined everything? What are you doing here?"

Tabitha's mouth dropped open. "Mr. Creede is living in sin?"

The prince leaned back in his ornate chair. "What do you mean, Mr. Creede? You are Mr. and Mrs. Cutler, aren't you?"

Avery glared at the prince as if to silence an annoying dog. "No, we aren't."

Tabitha folded her arms across the flat chest of her green silk dress. "I'm taking a holiday with my dear Lor and his father."

"Where did you get that dress?" Ace demanded.

"None of your business."

"You look silly in it."

"Not all think so," Tabitha replied.

"Avery, I thought you were taking that madman to Great Falls. Where is Rinkman?" Carla said.

Avery waved his hat toward the house. "In the side room."

The prince tapped the arm of his chair. "I say, what happened to the Cutlers?"

Carla fully faced Avery, ignoring Sunny. "Avery, are you living with this woman or not?" Each word had the finality of a sharp knife slamming against a butcher's block.

"This is Pete's sister, Sunny, eh, Miss Mary Jane Cutler."

Carla held her chin high. "You didn't answer my question."

Sunny's eyes narrowed, her tone pinched tight. "We are not living as husband and wife."

"Then, would you please turn loose of my fiancé's arm?"

Sunny clutched his arm tighter. "Avery, are you engaged to Carla Loganaire?"

Avery felt like a pup trapped in the corner. "Eh, no . . . not yet."

"Then I will hang on."

The prince waved like a magician hoping the

rabbit would disappear. "Would someone tell me what is going on?"

Carla paced across the carpeted dirt. "As soon as I figure it out, I will let you know."

Ace leaned down eye-to-eye with Tabitha Leitner. "Your Lor? He is your Lor? Miss Tabby, I thought I was your Ave? What do you think you are doing?"

Loritz stepped between the pair. "Are you insulting my lady?"

Carla parked next to Avery's free arm. "You owe me an explanation. I want the truth."

To look at Carla, he had to turn away from Sunny. "I'm tryin' to find Pete."

"I assume you searched the bedrooms?" It was a low growl, like a lioness before she devoured her prey.

"Carla, that is uncalled for," Avery snapped.

Sunny shoved him to the side and leaned toward Carla. "I will forgive that offensive remark, knowing your rich-girl brain has never had much use."

Tabitha slipped her arm in Loritz's. "You see, as I mentioned to you, he's such an immature lad."

"Your lady?" Ace boomed. "That's a joke. I ought to . . ."

"You forgive me?" Carla strutted around Sunny like an eraser removing a smudge. "That would be like the Napoleon forgiving the Duke of

Wellington. Or is that illustration too complex for you?"

"June 15th, 1815, south of Brussels, in Belgium at a place called Waterloo." Sunny turned to the prince. "I believe Marshal Blücher led the Prussians on that day . . ."

"Quite so . . . actually, a distant cousin of my wife's. How did you know that?"

"I had a theater director who shouted 'ran wie Blücher' whenever anything went wrong. He said it meant 'on it like Blücher', that is, taking a very direct and aggressive action, in war or otherwise. Just like my Avery."

"This is insane!" Carla glowered at the prince. "Please keep out of this matter. It is no business of yours."

Avery tugged Carla back. She shoved his arm down.

"If you'll calm down, Carla, I'll explain."

"Calm down!" she yelled. "I find you living with that . . . that woman . . . and I am supposed to . . ."

Avery struggled to keep his voice low. "While you are out tenting with a man."

"A prince," she cracked.

"Royalty makes it virtuous?"

"I say . . . ," the prince began.

Avery held up his hand to silence the German.

"It's quite alright, Avery dear," Sunny cooed.

"I once played a young Queen Victoria in a melodrama in Silver City."

The prince stamped his foot. "This is getting nowhere. It's time we stepped back and . . ."

"Shut up," Avery snarled.

"No one talks to me like . . ."

"You may leave at any time," Carla added, then turned to Avery. "I can't imagine any explanation that will ease my emotional trauma."

"Then you may leave too," Sunny added.

"I am not talking to you."

"You should be. Because I can explain it all."

Ace shoved his hands on his hips. "Miss Tabby, are you sneaking around behind my back?"

Loritz rubbed his mustache that looked more like a smudge. "Are you impugning Miss Leitner's honor?"

The veins at Ace's temples bulged at the sides of his flushed face. "I'd like to impugn you at the end of my fist."

"Dolf, go get the guards," the prince shouted.

Avery grabbed Arnwolf's shoulder. "Don't escalate this."

"I must obey."

"You are not on German soil," Avery said.

"Wait!" the prince shouted. "Just whose ranch is this?"

"It is mine," Sunny boasted. "Avery bought it for me."

Carla licked her lips with a pink, pointed tongue. "You bought this . . . this wayward dove a ranch?"

"Sunny is a lady." Avery waved his hand like a conductor trying to settle the orchestra during warm-ups. "And I bought the place and put it in her name for a very good reason, but no one here is listening to reason."

Ace's finger jabbed inches from Tabitha's nose. "I'll listen to reason. Why did you dump me for some pasty fellow with pockmarks on his face and pretends to be something he's not?"

Loritz thrust Ace's arm back. "Sir, I take that for an insult!"

"Good," Ace sneered, "you aren't as dumb as you look."

Carla tugged a white linen handkerchief from her sleeve and dabbed her eyes. "I don't need an explanation of why this stringy haired hussy is hanging on your arm. I know what you two have been doing."

Avery shook his head. "You don't have a clue."

Sunny brushed her hair back out of her eyes. "Carla, you are pitiable. Your name calling is immature, and the hankie routine pathetic."

"Miss Cutler, and my dear Avery, may heaven forgive you for this horrible mess you have gotten yourselves into."

Loritz threw his shoulders back. "I demand satisfaction."

Ace held up his fists. "Come on, take a swing. I'll give you satisfaction."

Carla's glance eliminated every face except Avery's. "You told me Sunny was a man."

"I never said that. You assumed it."

The prince surveyed Sunny. "How could anyone not tell she was a woman?"

"I'd never seen her before." Carla circled the carpet, arms splayed across her chest. "Are you going to tell me that Pete, Tight and Dawson are women, too?"

Avery stormed after her. "Carla, let's talk this through."

Dolf Arnwolf leaned over to Ace. "I think the young prince challenged you to a duel."

"A duel? Guns? Good . . . go ahead . . . pull that Colt out, I'm ready." Ace fingered the walnut grip of his revolver.

The prince leapt to his feet. "Dolf, where are the guards?"

"I'll go get them." The clerk trotted back toward the wagons.

"No one is drawing guns," Avery boomed. "Sit down, princy."

The prince plopped back in his chair.

Avery yanked Ace's hand off his revolver. "And no one is going to have a duel."

"You think I'm a little upset?" Carla growled. "Compared to how I feel, a hurricane is a soft summer breeze."

"You aren't the only one upset. What would you have done, had I showed up in Ft. Benton looking for you?" Avery countered.

"I left word with Abraham Hermann."

"It will be interesting to hear what you told him to tell me."

Carla's voice raised with intensity. "Are you questioning my honor?"

"I'm questioning your wisdom."

Loritz addressed the prince. "Father, where are the dueling pistols?"

"I've got my own," Ace called out.

Shoulders pulled back, Loritz lectured, "We are following traditional rules."

"There's a different tradition out west. I'm just waiting for you to pull that pistol."

"Not from this distance . . . we should be . . ."

"You want me closer?" Ace lunged forward. Loritz backed into the Chinese silk room divider.

Carla paused behind the prince's chair. "You think I should have lingered for you in Ft. Benton, while you were out here with this . . ."

Avery's glare cut her off. "I am trying to save a good friend from being killed by Rinkman."

"I thought you said you had Rinkman."

"I do, but his men have Pete."

Tabitha clapped her hands and giggled. "Isn't it exciting? Imagine, a duel over me."

Ace frowned at Miss Leitner.

"This is the most thrilling day of my life.

Well, there was that time an entire infantry unit took off their hats and bowed to me, but this is even better. I'm sure it is."

"Miss Tabby, this isn't a game," Ace said.

"Oh, don't you two worry, whichever one loses I'll write a nice poem for your tombstone and strew rose petals on your grave."

Carla rubbed her neck. "And you are going to exchange Rinkman for Pete?"

Avery's voice lowered. "That's the plan."

Loritz stood shoulder to shoulder with Ace. "What did Miss Leitner say?"

Tabitha snuggled between them. She grabbed Loritz with one arm, Ace by the other, then towed them away from the awning. "Now, you two go on and do your duel thing. I can't wait to write this in my diary. Mindy and Karrine are not going to believe this. This is so romantic."

Ace jerked his arm away from Tabitha. "I changed my mind. Loritz, you can have her."

"Oh no, I insist, Mr. Emerson." Loritz pulled his arm from her grasp. "I will withdraw from the field."

The prince wiped sweat from his narrow, pale forehead. "Where's Dolf?"

"He went to get your guards," Avery said.

The prince picked a piece of lint from the sleeve of his white silk shirt. "I don't think they are needed."

"Don't be too sure," Sunny snarled.

Miss Tabitha cornered Loritz. "What are you saying? You can't withdraw. What about my honor?"

The German peered at Ace. "I don't think this matter is worth getting shot."

She reached for his arm, but he pulled back. "Lor, darling, you don't mean that."

Ace shoved his hat back. "Loritz, I take back my words. I shouldn't have said those things about you. You are smarter than you look."

Carla wiped her neck with her handkerchief. "Are you saying that nothing is going on between you and that woman?"

"You can call her Sunny or Mary Jane or Miss Cutler . . . but you do not describe her as 'that woman.' Don't use any name that you would not want to be labeled with yourself."

Tabitha entwined Ace's arm. "But Ave, honey . . . what about those promises you made me? You were going to love me forever and ever, remember?"

He shoved her arm down so hard she stumbled back. "I'm sure that was just the naïve lad talking, not a mature man."

"I can't believe this." Tabitha stomped around on the carpet "Carla, do something!"

"Grow up," Carla snipped. "Avery John Creede, let's go somewhere alone. I want to talk without interruption."

"Sunny needs to listen to this, too. It's her honor that has been questioned."

"She needs to ride off into the sunset, or the theater, or wherever she came from."

Sunny stormed up to Carla. "This is my property and you will be the one riding off."

Ace ambled over to Loritz. "Were you really going to shoot it out with me?"

The German youth pulled his gun from his holster and inspected it as if buying a ripe tomato at the market. "I hope not. I am a very bad shot with this. I am much better with a crossbow."

"We're losing a sense of purpose here," Avery insisted. "The important thing is that we find Pete."

"Who is this Pete fellow?" the prince asked.

"An army pal of mine. He was suppose to meet me and a couple other buddies in Ft. Benton."

"And some villain has him?"

"We have the madman . . . but his men have Pete."

Ace put his arm around Loritz's shoulder. "A crossbow? No foolin'? You shoot a crossbow? I've never even seen a crossbow, except in a book."

"I've got several with me."

Ace and Loritz sauntered toward the wagons.

"I'll teach you how to shoot a revolver if you teach me how to shoot a crossbow," Ace said.

The prince preened his waxed mustache. "Then what you are talking about is a prisoner exchange?"

Avery nodded. "That's about it."

Tabitha scooted around in front of the boys. "Wait a minute . . . I didn't mean it . . . I was joking. Look, you are both very nice young men, and I think . . . wait. Don't walk away. You can't do this. I am the mayor's daughter. You can't treat me this way."

"Why this horrible charade?" Carla quizzed.

Avery nodded toward the house. "We didn't want anyone to know we have Rinkman."

Sunny stared down at the gold swirls in the carpet. "That would jeopardize my brother's life."

Carla brushed a wayward strand of black hair back over her ear. "They really have your brother?"

"Yes," Sunny said. "And Avery has stayed out of my bed."

"I didn't ask that."

"You wanted to."

Tabitha twirled in front of them, like a final pirouette in a ballet. "I'm getting dizzy. Oh, what will I do? I think I'm going to faint."

"Stand still," Avery barked. "You are not going to faint. We don't have time for it right now."

"Maybe I should move to some other location," the prince offered. "This has been an intrusion in your plans."

"You can stay. We'll move back to the river tomorrow," Avery announced. "That's where we meet for the prisoner exchange."

"I'm not going to abandon my ranch to her," Sunny mumbled.

Carla tucked her hankie back into her sleeve. "He really bought you this place?"

"You want to know why?"

"I really mean it," Tabitha shouted. "I'm going to faint."

Carla grabbed the teenager by the shoulders and shook her. "Not now, you aren't. Straighten up."

"But . . . but . . . I thought you were on my side."

"You stepped over the line. There is no one on your side."

"I want to go home," Tabitha wailed.

Carla turned to Sunny. "Why did Avery buy you this place?"

Avery interrupted. "Because it was dirt cheap, we needed a place to hole up and I didn't want my name spread around."

"That's not the whole story," Sunny added.

"Sunny . . ." he cautioned.

"Look, Miss Loganaire, as much as you despise me . . ."

"And you, me."

"The truth is . . ."

"I think I'm going to vomit," Tabitha insisted.

The prince stood in alarm. "My word, this is an expensive carpet I bought in Baghdad. Go over in the dirt to vomit."

"I'm going to pass out," Tabitha sniffed.

"Not on my rug!" The prince nudged her toward the yard. "Where is Arnwolf?"

Carla took Sunny's arm. "What is the truth, Miss Cutler?"

"We are searching for my brother. Once found, Avery intends to leave me with my brother, and return to you so he can marry you in San Francisco and retire to be a gentleman farmer along the coast."

"I never said it like that," Avery replied.

"But that's what you were thinking. He bought me this place because, indeed, it was dirt cheap, and being the kindest and most considerate man I've ever known, he didn't know how to tell me that he chose you over me."

"Look at me, everyone," Tabitha hollered. "I am falling!"

"Tabitha, sit down and stick your head between your knees," Sunny advised. "This ranch is the consolation prize. You get the man. I get this little patch of Montana dirt. It wouldn't mean much to you, but it's more than I ever dreamed about. When you were a rich little girl in Chicago, you might have dreamed

393

of dining with royalty and marrying a prince . . . but all I ever dreamed about was having a place that was mine. Avery knows my heart. That's why he put this place in my name."

"Is that true, Avery?"

The prince strutted around the room dividers. "Dolf!"

"That thought crossed my mind, but I don't know how Sunny knew what I was thinking."

Carla tugged up the scoop neck of her dress. "Well, I certainly don't know what he is thinking."

Sunny lowered her eyes. "No, I don't suppose you do."

When Carla threw her shoulders back, she was several inches taller than Sunny. "What does that mean?"

"You are a busy lady, with many important matters on your mind. I'm an unemployed actress trying to find my brother, traveling with the bravest and most tender man I've ever met. I had much more time for reflection, to watch him up close, and from a distance."

"No one is paying any attention to me!" Tabitha fumed.

The prince marched back. "Have you seen Arnwolf?"

"He went to get your guards," Avery repeated.

"I hope he made it plain to them what I wanted. His English is not the best."

"English? Aren't your guards German?"

"My word, no. Just myself, Loritz, Arnwolf, my doctor, and Jakob, my valet. We employed the cooks and camp help in San Francisco. The guards were hired in Montana."

"But the uniforms . . . they looked quite German," Sunny said.

"I brought them over. That is what you might call our charade."

Avery left the awning and surveyed the dirt yard. "Where did you say you hired the guards?"

"Right outside of Ft. Benton, on our way in. I thought it would be safer, and more regal, so I costumed them . . ."

"Rinkman!" Avery shouted. "You hired Rinkman's men." He yanked his gun out of the holster as he sprinted to the house.

"I don't care what anyone says," Tabitha Leitner wailed. "I can faint if I want to."

CHAPTER TWENTY-SIX

Some ideas sneak into minds and hide in the corner for weeks . . . or months . . . or years. A slow realization dawns that they exist. A certainty grows of their truthfulness.

Other ideas seem to break down the door, demand immediate attention. The fact that

Rinkman's men had infiltrated the prince's guards, and now were in the process of liberating him, hit Avery like an unseen block and tackle that crashed into his stomach.

He wanted to shout "no," but the shock of reality muted his protest.

Avery Creede stalked back to the barn where the others waited.

Sunny stumbled toward him, blonde bangs drooped across her forehead. "Is Rinkman there?"

He shook his head. "They're both gone."

"It's good riddance, if you ask me," Tabitha said. "Now we can get back to important things."

"He'll come back, won't he?" Sunny pressed.

"Yeah, that's what I'm thinkin'. Ace, get the horses saddled. We're going after them."

Loritz scooted beside Avery. "I'll go with you."

Avery smoothed the saddle blanket down on the black horse. "I need you to stay here and help defend the ladies."

Carla bit her lip. "He won't need to protect me. I'm going back to Ft. Benton. I've been held hostage by Rinkman once. Never again."

"You can't go back yet." Avery set the saddle down lightly, then cinched it. "It's too dangerous."

Her hands and voice quivered. "You don't understand . . ."

"Carla, I don't have time to debate. If I don't get out there and stop him, Rinkman's goin' to come back here with guns blazin'. Sunny, get everyone into the house. Loritz, with your father and the others, set a defense in the building."

"A siege? My word." Prince Rikard seemed to come alive. "I haven't been in a siege since the Crimea."

"You and Ace can't take on all of them," Sunny cautioned as she tugged Tabitha out of the barn.

The girl moaned, "You are all so rude. You're just ignoring me."

"If we ride out after them, they will attack us first." Avery slipped the silver bit into the horse's mouth. "That might keep them from the house. Loritz, tonight, hitch up your team. Load everyone up and head back to Ft. Benton. But wait until it's good and dark."

Carla clutched his arm. "Avery, we have so much left unsaid."

"I know . . . I know." He patted her hand. "Wait for me at Ft. Benton. This is the last time I'm going after Rinkman. He's not interested in any of you, just me."

She released him, but didn't back away. "How do you know that?"

"He's so infuriated with me right now, he'll not rest until he empties his revolver into my head. He wants to kill me any way he can. It's an obsession with him. Now, get up to the house with Sunny."

"What are you going to do?" Carla asked.

"Kill him first."

"Why didn't you do that before?"

"I had other options then. Killin' someone is always the last choice. And that's what I'm down to."

"I insist on coming with you," Loritz's voice deepened somehow. "Father and Dolf can secure the cabin."

Ace slapped his horse's stomach, then yanked the cinch tight. "He's good with that crossbow."

Avery shook his head. "He and the prince need to be safe and . . ."

Prince Rikard rubbed the large gold ring on his left hand. "Dolf and I have secured ourselves many times. We will set up a proper defense. I am from the old country. Rest assured, we will defend each of the ladies with our lives. But, my son has not been in battle."

Avery slipped his Winchester 1873 saddle ring carbine into the scabbard. "This is not a good time to learn."

The prince stood at attention beside his son. They were the same height. "Is there ever a good time to learn? I am sure he will honor his family, and handle himself with bravery."

"Look, Rikard, this is not a military exercise

on the parade ground. There will be men who get shot and die."

"Mr. Creede, I am not naïve. I led troops into battle for over thirty years. All the while, my wife raised my boy the best she could. But it is left to me to make sure he becomes a man. This might be his best opportunity."

"I can't guarantee his safety."

"One does not become a man by staying safe. Besides, these men deceived me. I feel a personal stake in this. My son will represent my family well."

Avery pulled himself up into the saddle. "You're right." He waved at Loritz. "Saddle a horse."

Carla paused in front of his horse. "Avery, you know I can't live this way."

Sunny tugged at her arm. "No one can, Miss Loganaire. No one but Avery John Creede. Let's go to the house. I will tell you everything I can about your Avery."

"I know I don't understand him," Carla sighed.

"I do, but it scares me, too."

With military precision, Dolf Arnwolf hiked over next to Avery's horse. "Do we secure the right half of the house or the left?"

"It belongs to Mary Jane. Let her decide. She's a crack shot; position her near the door."

Sunny called from the barn's open doorway. "Avery, they will kill Pete now."

Avery rode out into the yard. "Not if we get to them first. If we can keep this bunch from joining up with those that have Pete, we might be able to save him."

"And if you don't?"

"Pete won't be the only one whose life is in peril. Get everyone into the house. Keep them there until dark."

"They will have to clean their boots first." Sunny's tight, troubled face managed a slight smile.

Tabitha rushed after Ace and Loritz. "You are going off and leaving me unprotected."

Ace faced forward. "Stick close to Miss Sunny, she'll protect you."

"Avery John Creede!"

He turned. Carla's brown eyes twitched with conflicting emotions.

"You know, don't you?" she murmured.

"Yeah, Carla," he rubbed his unshaven chin. "I know."

Sunny rubbed her arms hard. "And you know that Miss Loganaire isn't the only one who loves you."

Avery calmed down his prancing horse. "I reckon you both know how I feel."

Avery, Ace and Loritz studied the ground next to the busted window on the back side of the bedroom.

"What's that all about?" Ace asked.

Avery motioned toward the dirt. "Rinkman will be easy to follow. They plowed a road in the prairie just by their numbers."

"I was talkin' about that 'you both know how I feel' comment to Miss Carla and Miss Sunny."

"That was a private comment. Carry your guns across your lap, boys . . . we could run into trouble at any turn."

"You can't love 'em both, Uncle Avery."

"This is not the time or place for such a discussion."

"Yeah, and ever' time I bring up the subject you act like a cougar that's been treed."

"A cougar?" Loritz quizzed.

"Der <u>Berglöwe</u>," Avery explained.

"How did . . ."

"Your father isn't the only German to come out West to hunt."

Loritz cradled his crossbow on his lap. "How do we approach these men?"

Avery checked the lever on his carbine. "We'll ride straight at them. They'll shoot at us and reveal their position."

Loritz glanced over at Ace. "He is joking, right?"

"Nope. He don't know any other way."

They galloped east about three miles, then Avery reined up. "We need to pace the horses. We'll walk them a while."

Buckskin colored grass and a sprinkle of stubby gray and green sage covered the rolling hills.

Loritz unfolded a white silk handkerchief and wiped his neck. "Why didn't this man just turn and attack once he was free?"

Avery investigated the powdery yellow dirt. "I'm wondering the same thing."

Ace leaned his hand back on the rump of the horse. "I may be a kid and haven't been out west but a month . . . but if you have a pattern of always ridin' straight at the same enemy, ain't he goin' to figure that out sooner or later?"

Avery stood in the stirrups and stretched his legs. "What are you sayin'?"

"I got a feelin' there ain't many men who faced you more than once. So, ridin' at them is a surprise move. But Rinkman is smart. He might discern your pattern by now. What if he sets an ambush for you to barge into?"

Loritz wrapped the silk handkerchief around his neck like a bandanna. "What if he swings around and attacks the house?"

"He won't do that." Avery plopped down in the saddle. "This is personal. Rinkman wants me dead. He's going to track me down before he does anything else. But Ace has me thinkin'. He might be tryin' to lead me out here. But if I don't go after him, he will head back to the ranch to see what happened. I have to ride at him to keep the battle away from the others."

Ace trotted his horse to catch up. "They don't know how many will be following them. Maybe we should split up."

"You sayin' that one of us should swing wide to flank them?"

Ace shrugged. "It's an idea."

"It's a good idea. The problem is, Rinkman knows you and me real well. If we aren't following him, he'll be scouting for us."

Loritz pushed his hat back and rubbed the dirt line across his forehead. "He doesn't know I'll be following. No one will look for the rich German kid."

"You up to it?" Avery asked.

"I can do it."

"If we get pinned down, create a diversion. If we are beyond help, ride back to the ranch and help everyone retreat to Ft. Benton."

"Yes, sir, I'll do it. What is our objective?"

"Objective?"

"In military school, they say never go into battle without a clear objective."

"Our objective is to stop them from killing us first."

Avery and Ace waited for Loritz to disappear from view, then trotted the horses down the trail. The land felt empty, isolated. Late afternoon sun blazed away any hint of a breeze. No animals. No birds. No movement. They barely spoke for two hours before they pulled up a couple hundred yards short of a row of cottonwoods.

"Must be a creek up there, Uncle Avery."

"Yeah, but Rinkman's tracks head straight up that draw on the left. I can't figure why he'd go up there and avoid the obvious camp in the trees."

"He'd get boxed in if he tried to retreat from that draw. He has to be plannin' on an ambush there."

Avery nodded. "That one's too obvious."

"What do you mean?"

"I think he knows we won't fall for that, and has set up an ambush somewhere else."

"Which way? Right or left? There aren't any tracks either way."

"I'm ponderin' what I'd do if I were Rinkman."

"I've been thinkin' about what Loritz said. What is our objective here, Uncle Avery?"

"I told you . . ."

"Yeah, I know what you said, but I ain't buyin' it. Are we doin' this so we can kill Rinkman?"

"I told you, his goal is to kill me." Avery squinted at the cottonwood trees.

"If we ride in there and kill Rinkman, then what? Do we ride away? Do we kill them all?"

"You're askin' lots of questions."

"I learned that from my mamma. You once

told me I ought to behave like my mamma's watching me. Well, if she's watchin' now, I'm tryin' to figure what she would want."

"I don't think she knew much about men like Rinkman."

"She married one not a whole lot different."

"Okay, what would your mamma want?"

"She'd want us to save Miss Sunny's brother."

"I'm sure she wouldn't mind us protectin' ourselves in the mix."

"Yep, if they shoot at us, we have to shoot back. Uncle Avery, did you ever ask the Lord what He wanted you to do in a case like this?"

"I don't usually have much time to pray when I'm bein' shot at."

"But if you was to pray . . . what do you reckon He'd say?"

"Since there is no organized law and order down here, I think He'd want me to stop Rinkman from killin' others, destroying families, and ruinin' lives. There is no one else around to stop him."

"Yeah, that's what I was thinkin', too." Ace surveyed the rolling prairie. "You ever noticed that sometimes this land out West is so big a fella gets lost in it? It makes me feel like we are the only ones on the planet. It sets your mind to wanderin', don't it?"

A momentary glare, flickered like sunlight off a signal mirror . . . or a silvery rifle. Avery swung his boot up, kicked Ace off his horse, and dove to the ground.

Before he hit the dirt, rifle reports and puffs of smoke exploded from the cottonwood trees. The horses bolted west.

"Keep down!" Avery shouted.

"I'm eatin' dirt. I can't get any lower than this. He ambushed here in the clearing?"

"He must have figured we'd head to the creek, but he got tired of our ponderin'. Don't raise your head up."

"How can we shoot back?"

"Dig your chin in the dirt."

"What?"

"Do it. Scoop your gun up. Now, wait for them to stand or come closer."

Ace reached around to rub his eye. "They have a good position. They won't stand."

"They have to in order to get an angle on us. If they do, take a shot, but immediately roll away from me and dig your chin in. They will flinch when you fire and shoot at the gun smoke. So you have to roll every time you shoot." A brown hat appeared on the horizon. Avery squeezed the trigger. Then rolled.

A scream.

The hat disappeared.

Amost like a Gatling gun, six shots punctured the prairie where he had been. Another man lunged out of the trees.

Both Ace and Avery fired and rolled.

"We've got to get to those boulders. Once they surround us, we have no chance at all out here."

"How are we going to do that?" Ace fired another shot, then rolled. More shots blasted in his direction.

"Wait until I draw their fire. Sprint over there on a zigzag. Don't give 'em an easy target."

Avery rolled to his back, carbine across his chest. He yanked a handful of cartridges from his bullet belt and shoved them through the loading gate of his Winchester. "Lord, Ace is right, I don't pray much in a gunfight. But I just don't know any other way except to eliminate Rinkman. So, if You wanted to send down lightning from heaven right now and forward him to his eternal reward, that would be fine with me. But if not . . . I'm goin' to do it my way."

He blinked up at the deep blue Montana sky.

"I didn't mean that to test You, God. If this is where I die, then You are still Lord of all."

Avery rolled sharp left six times, firing a shot every time his chin jammed into the soil. A trail of bullets followed him.

Mashed flat into the dirt behind a sagebrush no more than a foot tall, Ace signaled him from behind the rocks. He jammed more cartridges into the loading gate of the carbine.

He gulped air, then tried to spit. *I'm tired,*

Lord. My whole life is like this chase. An evasive enemy, nebulous goals, shallow victories. I've been tryin' to stay alive until tomorrow for so long, I don't know anything else.

Grit burned his eyes. He blinked them closed.

Carla's right. This is no way to live.

Maybe I've just lived too long.

The bullet exploded from the right and shattered the buttstock of his carbine. Splinters showered his shirt and neck. He rolled left and yanked out his revolver. One of Rinkman's men stood up no more than fifty feet to the right. Avery's quick shot missed to the left, but through the smoke he heard a deep thud and a groan as the man tumbled forward.

Avery spied the arrow in the collapsed man's chest.

Only a crossbow can puncture that deep.

He heard a piercing Indian-like scream. A second arrow nailed the earth next to Avery. He yanked it from the ground and rolled left. He got his chin back in the dirt just as another of Rinkman's men peered out from the cottonwoods and fired at the sage. The man dropped with an arrow in his midsection.

Avery staggered to his feet, the arrow tucked under his armpit, then fell face down.

There was another war-whoop and Ace let out a cry.

Avery lay motionless, his face buried. *Loritz,*

this is either idiotic or brilliant. I don't have a clue which.

Two shots rang out from deep in the cottonwoods. Horses whinnied and hooves pounded. His right hand clutched his revolver. Avery relaxed his grip as the hoofbeats faded.

A whistle sounded from the rimrock. He waited for the second signal, then rose.

In the distance, Loritz stood in the stirrups and waved the crossbow. Avery struggled to his feet, tossed down the arrow, then pulled his bandanna to brush his mouth and eyes.

"Are you okay, Ace?"

"Yeah, wasn't that something?" He trotted out to his uncle. "Loritz can really shoot that thing."

Avery retrieved his hat and what remained of his carbine. "I'm impressed."

"You ain't shot?" Ace asked.

"My Winchester took the bullet for me."

Loritz galloped up next to them. "That was my first western battle. How did I do?"

"You did great," Ace called out.

"That was quite a scheme," Avery added. "It took me a minute to figure out why you shot at me."

"When I got to the rim, I couldn't tell if you were dead or alive. I didn't want to reveal my position if you were already dead."

Avery nodded. "Naturally."

"When I saw you roll and the man sneaking

up on the right, I just said to myself, 'what would Stuart Brannon do?' "

Avery tried to pick the splinters from his neck. "Brannon? What does he have to do with this?"

Loritz eased down from the saddle. "I've read all the books about him. They are very popular in Germany. I remembered 'Stuart Brannon and the Phantom Stagecoach.' I assumed you had read it and . . ."

"I know Brannon, but I've never read . . ."

"You actually know Stuart Brannon?"

"He scouted for General Crook one summer. But what's this . . ."

"Well, in the book, Brannon is surrounded by the Dastard Brothers gang, and it looks like he is about to die, but an arrow sails in out of nowhere and he pretends that it hits him. The others, thinking Indians are attacking and Brannon is dead, flee to the north. Of course, it was only Lord Fletcher and an English long bow."

"Things like that never really happened," Avery stated. "All of that is fiction."

"You mean, there is no Stuart Brannon?"

"Oh, he's real, but most all those adventures are made up."

"But it worked for us," Loritz added.

"Yes, well, I'm glad it did."

"So maybe it really did happen that way."

"Who's to say, Uncle Avery?" Ace grinned. "Maybe fact and fiction aren't that far apart."

"Today, I won't argue that. But the truth is, Rinkman is still out there."

"But he thinks you are dead," Ace replied.

"At least for a while. In the meantime, he'll set up camp to stay away from the Indians, but he won't worry about us pursuing him."

"So, what are we going to do?" Loritz asked.

"We'll trail him until he catches up with those who hold Pete. Meanwhile, we'll rest by the cottonwoods until dark. Then we will catch up with them."

"I'm feeling a bit peckish," Loritz said. "What do we do about a meal?"

Avery examined the early evening sky. "We left the ranch in such a hurry, we didn't grab any provisions. I guess we'll do without."

"Skip a meal? How far are we from a town?"

"Two days," Ace replied.

Loritz paced in front of his horse. "I just hadn't planned on anything like this. We are actually going without a meal?"

Avery slung the busted carbine over his shoulder. "Just say to yourself, 'what would Stuart Brannon do?' "

They made a supperless camp.

The sun set.

The horses got watered.

Saddles were pulled.

Avery stretched out on the grass next to a small creek that wandered through the cotton-woods.

Three rapid-fire gunshots in the distance, east of them, forced him to scramble to his feet.

Barefoot, shirtless, he grabbed for his revolver.

CHAPTER TWENTY-SEVEN

Danger and disasters hold a macabre attraction for men. People leave sod houses to watch a tornado. They hike up hills to witness an earthquake. Gawkers hurry to a dangerous fire. And perch on the beach to observe a tidal wave.

In a like manner, many who profess an aversion to blood seem drawn to the scene of an accident. Murders attract crowds. A massacre acts like a magnet for every newspaperman in a five-hundred mile radius.

No matter how foolhardy their response, each one claims he only intends to watch. Few want to get involved. None wants to be injured.

But gunfire along the Missouri River Breaks of Montana Territory in 1886 meant more than an accident.

For distant rifle reports, Avery developed a

three shot rule. He stayed away for three shots or fewer. He presumed that a hunter, whether pioneer or Indian . . . would either kill or scare off any game in three shots or less. Mule deer scamper down into the Breaks. Elk flee back to the trees. And cougars climb into rocky crevices.

In a like manner, if the distant rifle reports signal gunfight among men, and there are no more than three shots, the matter's been settled. Or one party is already dead. Or, as he knew could happen, both sides were dead.

But this time, the shots continued past three. Past ten. Past twenty.

He saddled his horse by firelight.

Ace held his hands over the flames. "You going to check out that gunfight?"

"Yep."

"You think it's Rinkman and that bunch?" Ace grabbed up his saddle.

Loritz stayed hunched at the fire. "Who could be shooting at them?"

Ace smoothed out the saddle blanket. "Could be the Blackfoot warriors we came across last week."

"Yeah, it could be." Avery jerked the cinch tighter. "But most times Indians don't start a face-to-face battle at night."

Loritz jammed his hands into his pockets. "I think I would like to go."

Avery jammed his hat on his head. "Saddle up.

We'll break camp. But we are only going to investigate. Stay behind me and out of the line of fire."

The shots provided a compass, pointing the way, but the evening shadows slowed them down like a forest of dwarf trees with a possible enemy lurking about. After thirty minutes of careful plodding, Avery slid to the ground and walked his horse to the top of a knoll. The other two followed.

"I can't see a dadgum thing but the fire flashes," Ace whispered.

Avery felt the dirt in the creases of his eyes. "They can't see anything either. It doesn't make sense."

"Do you think it's Rinkman and them?"

"Yep."

Loritz led his horse over to them. "Should we get closer?"

"Nope. We'll park right here. There's something strange about this. I expected them to regroup and head back to the ranch after me. It seems as if they got bushwhacked."

"Can you tell if it's Indians?" Loritz pressed. "I have never been in a battle with the noble savages."

"Some of 'em aren't any more noble than Rinkman. But it's not Indians. They wouldn't waste bullets fired random in the dark."

"Who else would attack Rinkman out here?" Ace quizzed.

"That's what I'm ponderin'."

"What do we do now?"

"Tie the horses off to a sage, but leave the cinches tight. We might have to leave in a hurry. We'll wait it out and see where this heads."

"Clouds are movin' in and it's gettin' colder," Ace added.

"No fires," Avery mumbled.

A volley of shots from one side of the draw, then the other, punctured the black night.

Ace squatted down. "You would think one side or the other would be sneakin' around to bush-whack the other."

Loritz fastened the top button on his coat. "Which side are we on?"

Avery massaged his stiff hands. "Neither."

"We just sit here and freeze?" Loritz folded his arms across his chest.

"Pull your blanket around you. We'll just wait until the next thing happens."

"The next thing?" Loritz quizzed.

Avery yanked his blanket from behind the cantle. "In a few days, you'll tell your father about this night. You will say, 'then we waited in the cold, dark night until . . .' I don't know what will complete the sentence, but that is the next thing. That's what we're waiting for. One thing I know for sure, boys, there always is a next thing."

Ace balanced his blanket on his shoulder, then jammed his hands into his coat pockets. "And you don't have any idea what that will be?"

Avery hunkered down on his haunches. "Makes life interestin', don't you think?"

Loritz's voice was high pitched. "Do you think it will rain?"

"That could be the next thing," Avery said.

Two blasts from the east were followed by two blasts from the west.

Avery sat in the dirt, his knees draw up in front of him. "This is a strange gunfight. One side is content with their position, the other afraid to finish the battle. And the shooters are bunched together. It's like neither want to be in a fight. That doesn't sound like Rinkman at all."

Ace scooted over until their shoulders touched. "What if this shootout doesn't have anything to do with him? What if old Rinkman has already killed Pete and is headed back to the ranch by now?"

"I've pondered that, too. But I think he spotted me out in the clearing by the cottonwoods. It's got to be him down there. Whether he thinks I'm dead or alive, he knows I'm not at the ranch. It's got to be him on one side of this. The Breaks are too deserted for it to be anyone else."

The sporadic gunfire kept Avery's eyes open, but there wasn't anything to watch. Just a flash of fire shooting out the muzzle of a gun, followed by a report that sounded muffled in the clouds that blocked the stars.

When it started to sprinkle, he pulled his blanket up around his shoulders. The drizzle turned to a downpour and he yanked it over his hat, leaving only his face uncovered.

This is crazy, Creede. What are you doin' *here? You ought to be doin' something to rescue* *Pete. Or, at least, you ought be in Ft. Benton,* *sortin' things out.*

Avery figured Ace and Loritz had stretched out under their blankets, but he couldn't see more than a few feet. One of them snored. His thoughts bounced from Rinkman to rain . . . cold to Carla . . . shivers to Sunny.

Ace said I had to choose. I can't love them *both. Lord, I'm not sure how to tell which one I* *love. I don't know if I ever learned how to love.* *I'm attracted to them. I respect them. I like* *bein' with them. But the same could be said for* *a good horse.*

His head drooped down until his chin rested on his chest.

That's not true. Horses can't kiss like that *and don't stir me up on the inside. But both of* *them seem to have marriage on their minds,* *and I don't know if I can be what either one of* *them needs me to be. How can I pledge that I* *will take care of any woman forever, if I don't have any idea what the next day will bring?*

A single gunshot caused his eyes to open again, but the fireflash had been swallowed by the storm and all he saw was thick blackness. And all he felt was cold rain. Very cold rain.

They seem to think I can be the man they need to spend their life with. But I reckon I'd be a huge disappointment if they had to be with me all the time. I'm impatient, stubborn, reckless and insensitive. Carla told me that years ago. She's countin' on me changin'. Shoot, I'm countin' on me changin'.

Can I change, Lord? The patterns of my life seem so ingrained. How can I make them different? I'll be down on that almond orchard along the ocean and some old boy like Rinkman will shoot my neighbor, and I'll head into the hills to bring him to justice. I'll come back with a bullet in the shoulder and a dead outlaw, and Carla will be hysterical.

She wants more than that. She needs more than that. But, I'm not sure I can spend my life drinking tea from tiny China cups and playing Whist with people who never had a callus on their hand or dirt under their fingernails.

Still, she is the most exciting woman I've ever met.

She walks into any room, any crowd, any scene, and takes over the focus, the conversa-

tion, the attention of everyone present. When I'm with Carla, I can stand to the side and watch. It's peaceful not to have to be the one in charge. I get to grin and nod and know that she will be on my arm when we finally leave the room. Every man in the room is scratchin' his head and wonderin' "what does she see in that old cowboy?"

I like how she makes me feel. I'd like to think she enjoys how I make her feel. I wonder how she would have turned out, had she been raised on a Nebraska homestead, instead of a Chicago mansion? Her weaknesses are learned and I reckon they can be unlearned.

I'm hopin' mine can be, too.

"Uncle Avery, are you awake?"

"Sort of."

"It's snowin'."

Avery blinked his eyes open to a dull glow on the ground. When he shook his head, snow tumbled from the blanket. "At least we can see a little more."

"It ain't even October. Does it usually snow this early in Montana?"

"It's one of those northerners blowin' down from the Athabaska Plains."

"Where?" Ace pressed.

"Canada . . . I guess they call them the Alberta Plains now. Those storms can drop the tempera-ture fifty degrees in just a couple hours. This time of the year, it won't last long, but they are sure cold when they hit."

"You ever been north to Canada?"

"Yep."

"What kind of war is it that they have going on now?"

"I think the Northwest Rebellion is over. Louis Real was executed for treason last November."

"Did you know him?"

"Yep. Up north, and when he lived in Montana."

"Which side were you on?"

"Both."

"Who won?"

"The way I see it . . . neither."

Ace clutched his snow-covered blanket over his head and around his chin. "It surely is cold."

"Yep."

"What will we do now?"

"Stay warm and wait."

"Are we waitin' because it's wise or waitin' 'cause you can't figure out what to do next?"

"Both."

"If you want to sleep, I'll watch for a while. I got myself a nap."

"Yeah, I heard you snore."

"That wasn't me, it was Loritz."

"He's not snorin' now, but let him sleep. I'll close my eyes. My head is too busy to get much rest."

• • •

One winter Avery got snowed into a cabin in the Sangre de Cristo mountains of New Mexico for six days. He had food, water, plenty of firewood, and a big feather bed. He slept until the fire died down, then puffed it up and slept some more. When he finally made it back to Albuquerque, he calculated he had slept over fifteen hours a day.

It was the last time he felt rested.

Thoughts of the cabin in New Mexico gave way to thoughts of the cabin on the ranch.

I like Montana, Lord, You know that. But all I want to do right now is find Pete and get out of here. The warmth of California sounds nice. But Pete's a pal, and that's about all I have left. A few pals. Sunny's a pal, too. She's easy to be with. I don't have to worry about what I say. She's tough. A lot tougher than she looks. And she's easy to read. That funny little smile gives away her heart.

I like that. I don't know if she ever had any- thing go right in her life, still there's that smile. Puttin' the ranch in her name was the smartest thing I've done in years. She deserves a break. She deserves someone a whole lot better than me.

That's the trouble, Lord. They both deserve someone better than me.

Three blasts through the storm opened his eyes.

All came from the same location.

Then a two shot reply.

"Uncle Avery, you awake?"

"Yep."

"That last blast looked like it was pointed straight up. You reckon that ol' boy got hit and was shootin' as he dropped?"

Avery leaned over toward Ace. "Either that or he wasn't tryin' to hit his target."

"Why would he waste bullets?"

When Avery jumped up, his blanket tumbled to the snow. "A diversion."

Ace struggled to his feet. "What?"

"No one fights a battle like this. It's stupid. Both sides sittin' in one place and shootin' into the dark."

"Who's divertin' whom? You think this is a show for us? But Rinkman thinks we're dead."

"Maybe. But he's coverin' tracks. He knows someone shot his men with arrows. It would be a good diversion for the Indians or us. It would slow down anyone who was chasin' him."

"It sure got us to camp and wait, but what kind of fool would stay back and do this for him? If we were Indians, wouldn't his men be dead by now?"

"I suppose you can pay enough to get someone to do most anything. I reckon money and whiskey have a lot to do with it."

"Are we going down after them?"

"Nope. I'm thinkin' the shooter is the bait, and there will be some waitin' in the background for us to sneak up."

"You mean, it's another trap?"

"It has to be. It's too dumb to be anything else."

"What do we do?"

"We ride wide of them and turn toward the river, then pick up Rinkman's trail."

"How do you know he'd go that way?"

"He knows someone is up here. And the river road can lead him back down in the Breaks."

"How we going to track them at night?"

"Night is no problem. Snow is the problem. Until this melts, all tracks will be covered. Maybe it didn't snow as much down there. We'll cut a wide circle. Wake up Loritz."

Avery shook out his blanket and began to roll it up.

"He ain't here. Loritz," Ace called out.

"Keep it quiet."

"He was complainin' about bein' hungry. Maybe he went huntin' for food. Maybe he went down to scout out their camp for grub."

Avery used the rolled up blanket to brush snow off Ace's saddle and his horse. "I tried to tell the prince it was too dangerous for him to come along."

"Loritz saved us down by the cottonwoods."

"Mount up. I'm stayin' here . . . you ride over to those boulders. I'll fire a few shots and see if

I can get them to come up this way. We'll pin them down. Don't fire until you have to, then . . ."

"Shoot fast and straight. Yeah, I know. So, we're goin' to ambush the ambushers? You think they'll fall for this?"

"They can't be the smartest of the bunch. Maybe it will divert them from discoverin' Loritz."

Ace pulled himself into the saddle.

For the first time, the gunfire sounded closer.

"We know you are up there, Creede. We've got the German kid."

Ace slid down to the ground. "What are we goin' to do?"

"Get them to bring him up here. The first rule of battle, choose the battlefield. Leave the horses here. Get to the boulders." He shoved Ace right.

"You heard us, Creede!" a voice shouted. "Come on in with your hands in the air or we'll kill the boy."

Avery yanked a tie-down string off his saddle and pulled seven bullets from his bullet belt.

Two more shots were fired, even closer.

Avery bunched the cartridges in a bundle, then tied them together with the leather string.

"We know you can hear us, Creede. We ain't bluffin'. We'll kill the boy."

He scrambled around the sage until he found a rock the size of a man's head. He rolled it over on Loritz's abandoned blanket.

"Creede!"

Avery propped the cartridge bundle on the rock, lead facing the voice in the draw.

"Creede!" The name boomed close in the light falling snow.

He grabbed his blanket and held it like a cape. He plopped down in the snow on his stomach, his backside covered. The snow soaked into Avery's coat and ducking trousers. He pulled the blanket over his head and peeked out. Only twenty feet away, he could see the rock in the storm, but not the bound bullets. He aimed at where he thought they were.

"Creede! Wake up!"

The second voice was younger. "*Vier Männer. Man ist auf dem Recht.*"

A shot was fired in the air, not more than one hundred feet below Avery, then a shout. "In English!"

"Mr. Creede, I am sorry to report I have been captured."

Four men, one is to the right? Whose right, Loritz, yours or mine?

"Creede, we'll let the boy go if you give yourself up."

Avery scooted back under the blanket until only the muzzle of the revolver was exposed.

"Mr. Creede, they have a gun pointed at my head."

"Wait," Avery shouted. "*Ergebnis zu drei. Fallen Sie dann zum Boden.*"

1 . . . 2 . . . 3 . . . Creede pulled the trigger. Several of the cartridges exploded, sending flailing gunfire and lead bullets in scattered directions.

A barrage of bullets stabbed the blanket next to the rock.

"We got him."

"Go make sure."

"Me?"

"Shove the German kid in front of you."

"Where is he?"

"I thought you had him."

Avery spotted movement to the left.

If that's Loritz, he got away. If that's the fourth man . . . this could be very stupid.

As soon as Avery opened fire on the direction of the voices, Ace did the same. A couple of shots were returned in retreat. Avery jumped up to pursue them. Ace sprinted out on his right.

"Watch for one more over there."

Before Avery took another step, gunfire punctured the storm. Ace fell down with a scream. Avery emptied four shots at the assailant before he reached Ace's side.

"Where are you hit?"

"My leg. It hurts bad . . . oh, man, it's on fire."

"Pack some snow on it. Fire is good. It just sliced you."

Ace struggled up on his elbow. "They're gettin' away."

"That's okay." Avery fumbled with cold hands to pull out his pocket knife.

Loritz ran to their side. "Is Ace dead?"

"He'll be alright. He got leg shot." Avery handed him his revolver. "Sneak over there and see if '*Man ist auf dem Recht*' is incapacitated. We don't want any more bullets flying this way."

"Who's over there?" Ace mumbled.

"The man on the right." Avery yanked off his belt and cinched it around Ace's leg.

A gunshot rang out. Then Loritz shouted, "He is incapacitated."

CHAPTER TWENTY-EIGHT

Avery learned in the army that on the battlefield an officer had to choose his words with care. Confusing commands cost more injuries and death than hundreds of enemy attacks.

Bugles, when played with clarity, give a distinct signal.

But buglers, like all soldiers, can get so scared of imminent death, the tune comes out blurred. The orders get befuddling.

In the midst of this present skirmish, he had a wounded nephew.

And no bugle.

"I didn't mean for you to kill him," he hollered. "I just meant to check and see if he was dead." Avery tucked a blanket around Ace's shoulders.

Loritz blew smoke out of the muzzle of his revolver as he meandered back to the clearing. "I didn't kill him. He was already dead."

Ace's eyes were pinched shut. "Then why the shot?"

Loritz shoved his gun back in his stiff leather holster. "The others were getting away, but they were too far off. I missed them. I missed their horse."

Ace grabbed Avery's arm. "You'd better go after them."

Avery tugged off Ace's boot. "Nah . . . I go chasin' after them, and it might slow them down."

Loritz rubbed his hairless chin. "I think I may have hit a tree."

Ace winced when his sock was pulled off. "Isn't that the point? Don't you want to stop them?"

"Nope." Avery sliced Ace's pantleg. "Looks like it tore through the muscles and went on out. If it doesn't get infected, it should heal up."

"What if it does get infected?" Ace quizzed.

"I thought we were suppose to chase them," Loritz asked.

"When they thought I was dead, we had to catch them before they killed Pete. But if they think I'm still around, they just might keep Pete alive, in order to get to me." Avery pressed his bandanna against Ace's wound, then he turned to Loritz. "Hold your hand on this."

"Me?"

Ace reached down and held the bandanna against his leg. "I said, 'What if it does get infected?' "

"You lose your leg . . . or you die."

"I don't like either option."

Avery left the bloody sock on the ground, but slipped Ace's boot on his foot. "That's why I'm getting you back to Ft. Benton to the doc."

"I thought you were going after them," Ace said.

"I am. You two are headed back."

Loritz threw his shoulders back. "I'll stay with you."

Avery wiped his bloody hands on his wet canvas trousers. "No, you'll see to it that Ace gets back to town. That will save a life. If you charge on down there with me, you might lose your life."

"I didn't come out here to be a coward."

"You already showed us what you can do in battle. I need my nephew alive. I'm going to trust him in your hands. Don't let me down."

Ace sat up and took a deep breath. "I think I can make it back on my own."

"I know a lot of brave young dead soldiers

that said the same thing. No argument, boys. You're going back."

"How can you attack them by yourself?" Loritz asked.

"I can't. I'll let them attack me."

"How will that be different?"

"I'll have position. And they won't know for sure how many are with me."

Loritz squatted next to Avery. "And you won't know how many they have . . . I overhead them talk."

"You snuck down there for food, right?" Avery said.

"A starving man chooses reckless measures."

"Starving? We've haven't gone twenty-four hours without eating."

"That's what I said."

Ace reached across the snow for his hat. "And what did you hear, before you were captured?"

"A couple of them thought Rinkman was crazy to go after you. They wanted to go back down into the Breaks. They urged him to turn Pete loose, so you'd go back to town."

Ace turned to his uncle. "Would you do that?"

Avery's response was deep, firm. "No."

"Then you and Rinkman are similar," Loritz declared.

"Except my motive is justice, his is revenge."

Loritz scratched his neck. "Is there a difference?"

"It's the gap between heaven and hell."

"You believe in heaven?" the German teen questioned.

"And hell."

Loritz stood and paced in the snow. "Back home, only the old people still believe in a real hell."

"It doesn't matter whether you believe in it." Avery helped Ace to his feet.

"It doesn't?" Loritz said.

"Nope, it's real either way . . . and you're going there if you haven't got things right with Jesus. It's as simple as that. It's like jumpin' off a cliff and saying you don't believe there's a rocky canyon below you. Doesn't matter what you say. If there's a canyon, you'll be crushed by boulders you didn't believe existed."

"Have you ever heard of Hegel?"

"Yeah, Georg Wilhelm Friedrich Hegel . . . and I've read Schleiermacher, too. I even read some of Ritschl, but it was in German and I must have not understood some of it. It seemed like a waste of time. They all sound like over-intelligent men trying to impress each other. They all deal in theory. Out here theory won't stop a bullet. And it won't get you to heaven."

Loritz looked Avery in the eye. "What do you mean, get things right with Jesus?"

"Ace is going to tell you all about it on your way back."

"I am?" Ace gulped.

Avery shoved Ace into the saddle, then handed him the reins. "Tell Loritz what your mamma would tell him if she were here with you."

Loritz swung up into the saddle. "Your mother is far away?"

"My mamma is in heaven, waitin' for me, I reckon." Ace leaned forward and patted his horse's neck. "Uncle Avery, are you sure about this?"

Avery's jaw tensed. "Tell him about Jesus, Ace."

"I meant, are you sure we should just ride away?"

"Yes, and don't stop until you get to the doc."

"Should we rest at the ranch?" Loritz asked.

"No, take the river road. It's shorter, and they might have someone watching the house. You're not out of action yet. If you run across Rinkman's men, you'll have to shoot your way out. Be alert."

"My leg's killin' me."

"No, not yet . . . but it can." Avery retied the bandanna around Ace's wound. "Leave the tourniquet on and don't stop until Ft. Benton. Loritz, if Ace passes out from loss of blood, don't slow down, keep going. His life might depend on it."

"What will I tell Miss Carla and Miss Sunny?" Ace said.

"Tell them I'll be back with Pete. Ask them to wait in town."

"Have you figured out what you are going to tell them?" Ace pressed.

"I think so."

"Are you going to tell me, now?"

"Nope."

The snow stopped before daylight. Dark, low clouds crouched in the Missouri River Breaks like a lost, frightened dog who didn't know which way to turn.

Avery knew it would warm up.

He just didn't know when.

With a bundle of snow coated firewood strapped to the back of his saddle, he plodded along, following the wide, easy tracks of Rinkman's men. As he suspected, they led to the river.

He rode for an hour, until the river came into view. It wound like a wide brown ribbon through the snow dusted hills. He stopped beside two dead cottonwoods, sentinels next to a rocky knoll.

Tying his horse to the tallest stump, Avery made several hikes up the rocks, each time toting more firewood. With three scattered piles tucked in the rocks, he hunched beside the first one until sparks from a flint struck against the checkering of the hammer of his revolver ignited the shavings.

When the first campfire crackled and smoked, he took a faggot and lit the other two. Then, making sure he was out of sight from the river, he retreated to the dead trees and his horse.

Avery watched the smoke curl to the clouds, then rode back down a draw and tied his horse to a sage. He tramped back to the clump of dead trees, but stopped short of it. Soaking wet and shivering as he lay flat in the snow, he concentrated on the knoll, the campfire smoke, and the trees.

About noon, a half-dozen men rode up to the trees. He could tell by the hand signals that Rinkman was with them. He ordered them to surround the hill and advance up toward the fires.

Avery kept aimed at one outlaw as he paced back and forth. He knew he was too far away for an effective shot. When Rinkman spotted something in the snow, Avery scrunched down even lower.

It's about time you studied those tracks. Now, come on . . . draw your gun . . . that's it . . . follow those hoofprints down into the draw . . . come on . . . a little more . . . my horse is way down there. You can get a little closer . . . be brave.

When Rinkman spotted Avery's horse, he threw his carbine to his shoulder and crept forward. Avery rose and prowled behind him.

At his fourth step, Creede shoved his revolver into the outlaw's ear.

"Drop it, Rinkman."

Instead of tossing the carbine, Rinkman dropped straight down. Avery shoved the gun away from him just in time to have it explode, sending the 200 grain bullet into the clouds. He clutched the hot barrel and yanked the gun from Rinkman's hand, tossing it into the snow. Then he reached for his ringing ears.

Tackled to the ground, Avery lost his grip on his revolver, which tumbled to the snow. The first punch landed at his kidney, and he staggered. When Rinkman lunged for his carbine, Avery caught him with a knee to the chin, followed by a bone cracking fist to the nose. Blood poured down Rinkman's face and splattered on white snow as the outlaw crumpled to his knees.

Avery snatched up his revolver and aimed it at the outlaw's head. His other hand clutched the outlaw's thick brown hair. He shielded himself from the hill, as Rinkman's men sprinted toward them.

"I want Pete, and I want him here right now or else Rinkman's dead. I'm not taking prisoners this time."

Five men, four with guns drawn, halted about fifty feet away.

"Go get Cutler," Rinkman shouted through the blood.

"Wait a minute," the tallest and thinnest of the men called back. "If we don't get Pete, you're going to shoot Rinkman?"

"That's what I said."

"Do you promise?" another shouted.

"What?"

"Shoot him," the tall one called out.

"Kirkley, I'll kill you!" Rinkman hollered.

"Not if you're dead."

"You boys saying Rinkman's life isn't worth anything?"

"It ain't a good bartering chip," Kirkley reported. "He already killed Pete."

"He what?"

"He gut shot Pete down at the river about an hour ago. Right before we got there to warn him that you was alive," the man with the shaking hand reported.

"Is Pete dead?" Avery demanded.

"He wasn't in good shape," the fifth man reported.

"Go ahead and shoot Rinkman. He's got too many of us killed just trying to get even with you," Kirkley said.

"I'll kill all of you!" Rinkman screamed.

"Mr. Rinkman," the short man, without a gun drawn, stepped forward. "I ain't goin' along with this, but there's nothin' I can do . . ."

"Shoot them," Rinkman's voice rang deep, gravelly . . . satanic.

"There are four of them, besides Creede, I cain't . . ."

Like a foghorn from a sinkhole, Rinkman growled, "Obey my words."

The man turned and drew his gun. It didn't clear his holster. One bullet pierced his neck, the other, his temple. He hit the snow, dead.

As Avery stared at the sight, Rinkman broke free from his grasp and dove for the carbine. Five bullets struck him at once. His body convulsed, his head whipped back, then forward. Then he fell into the shallow snow . . . his eyes open, his mouth distorted. The voice roared deep as an earthquake. "I'll see you all in the abyss."

Kirkley fired one more shot and Rinkman quit quivering.

Avery's gun was pointed at the four men . . . their guns pointed at him.

"What was that about the abyss?" Kirkley asked.

Avery kept his gun aimed at the men. "You boys know anything about demons?"

"You mean, like demon rum?" one asked.

"It's a lot deeper than that. Grab yourself a Bible and read about it. That is, if you live through today."

Kirkley, with gun pointed at Avery, took a step closer. "You figure you can take all four of us?"

"Not at this range. Two of you are dead. You and the guy with the dirty red shirt."

"Why me?" red shirt asked.

"Because you're an easy target to hit after I've been shot."

A third man shoved his gun in his holster. "You're right, two of us will die, and you. But why? Rinkman's dead. I don't have anything against you. I've got a wife and a little one on the way down in the Breaks. I'd like to ride down there, put 'em in a wagon and ride up to Canada. Why don't we let him ride off . . . and we ride off."

" 'Cause he'll come after us, just like he came after Rinkman. He won't stop until we're dead," Kirkley said.

"You are the first ones to make any sense in two weeks," Avery sighed. "Truth is, I'm tired of the chase. I don't want any of you. But, I'm sure when the other lawmen find out Rinkman's dead, they will be pushing down to the Breaks lookin' to arrest you all. You've got to face the wrath of the law and the judgment of God. So, ride off if you want to. Just tell me where Pete is."

Red shirt paced from one boot to the other. "How do we know you won't shoot us in the back?"

"He ain't that type," the one with the holstered gun insisted.

"How do we know for sure?"

"I was in the army. I know his sort."

"You said you spent most of your time in the stockade."

"That's why I know his type."

438

Avery kept his revolver steady. "If you don't trust me, walk backwards with your guns on me."

"Can we have Rinkman's body?" Kirkley asked. "Some down in the Breaks won't believe us."

"You can have it. I suppose you will blame me for his death."

"Yep, you shot him six times."

Avery glanced over at the dead outlaw. "From five different angles. Will your pals come after me to even the score?"

"You have no idea the delight his death will bring," Kirkley said.

"Why should I believe that you won't come after me?" Creede asked.

"Trust us, and you will have a chance to live. I was one of those pretending to guard the prince. I heard what Miss Loganaire said about her Avery. I think that might be worth taking a chance on."

"Where is Pete?"

"See where the river bends up to the west? Right at that bend there's a cave in the river-bank. You'll find him there. But I reckon he's dead by now. He was one tough hombre, but Rinkman went crazy."

"Go on," the one with the holstered gun insisted, ". . . ride on off. We'll take care of things here."

A slight grin creased Avery's dirty face. "How do I know you won't shoot me in the back?"

Kirkley's smile was wide. "Walk backwards with your gun on us."

Avery shoved his gun in his holster, then ambled down the draw to where he tied his horse. By the time he tightened the cinch, pulled himself up into the cold saddle, and rode back up to the men, they had Rinkman's body strapped down to his horse.

Avery tipped his hat. "Boys, no offense, but I don't want to ever see any of you again."

Red shirt crammed his foot in the stirrup and swung up in the saddle. "We meant what we said about goin' north of the border."

"I got a question for you, Creede," Kirkley said. "What made you turn your back on us just now? Any one of us could have killed you."

"Two things. First, I figured if that was your intent, you would have done it before now."

"And the other?"

"What's the worst that can happen? You shoot me and I waltz right into heaven. On the other hand, ever' one of you are still ponderin' Rinkman's comment about the abyss."

"My mamma's in heaven," the fourth man replied.

"So's mine," Avery added. "Shoot, they could be neighbors. Gives you something to ponder on a cold day."

Kirkley surveyed the clouds as if expecting a sign. "Sorry about Pete, Creede. We couldn't stop Rinkman. It always ends up with him killing someone. That won't happen again."

Avery pulled his hat low in the front. "Rinkman's dead alright. But the Evil One is still around."

The north wind whistled, so he turned up his collar as he rode away. His bones ached. His mind twisted with concern for Pete. But his soul seemed at rest. It was a sensation he hadn't felt in a long, long time.

Sunlight streamed through the clouds, a yellow sword that struck the ground to the west, just about where the Missouri River made a turn.

CHAPTER TWENTY-NINE

Like an advance man for a circus, early snows display what could be expected soon. Not the main event, just a handbill . . . a notice posted that wintry times were coming.

But, it wasn't winter yet. The snow-caked cottonwood leaves had just begun to yellow. A miserable cold, but not life-threatening. Beavers still worked their dams. Deer entered their rutting season. And somewhere, pioneers chopped wood for the long, gloomy days ahead.

Avery knew that sometime soon a warm southern breeze would usher in Indian Summer. Then he would bask in the sun's last fling. Those brief, pleasant hours would be the ones remembered during the frigid winter.

But now, Avery shivered.

Coldness is not based merely on temperature.

Rejection brings a shivering feeling.

As does failure.

And death.

A mile north of the river, he spied a horse with saddle hanging under its belly, wandering through the snow covered sage.

He patted Junior's neck. "Let's round him up, boy."

With Pete's horse in tow, Avery plodded along the Missouri until he reined up to the river-bend and tied both horses to the sage. He yanked a blanket from the cantle. He trotted over to a snow covered body, next to the mouth of a sandstone washout that served as a cave during low water.

The carpet of white made the body look as if it were fading back into the ground.

He dropped to his knees and cradled the head as he rolled the man toward him. The snow was stained a dark red, almost black in color.

"Pete!"

He unrolled the blanket over the downed man.

"Pete, it's me, Avery . . . I'm sorry I didn't get here sooner."

His cold, stiff, calloused fingers searched for a pulse on Pete's blood caked neck. "Hang on, now . . . I need you to keep fighting."

Avery pressed the blanket against the wounded man's stomach. "You got a pulse, partner. A weak one, but it's there. Keep fightin'."

He brushed the matted bangs off Pete's eyes, and pressed his hand against his forehead.

"Come on, Pete . . . this is Avery . . . we've been in lots of tough straights before. Remember when you and me hauled Dawson out of the line of fire on the Dakota Plains? He toted six bullets and two arrows. Remember? We both said Dawson wouldn't live through it, and that we'd likely be shot down trying to get him to the ambulance. But we did it. And Dawson's still alive, cussin' Yankees and chewin' his Carolina Blend."

Avery's eyes darted around as if hoping to spy an army medic and a stretcher.

"Pete, don't give up on me. We've got things to do. Remember how you always said we ought to ride down to Mexico in the winter and warm up along the beach? Let's get you patched up and go. What do you say? Warm sunshine, spicy food, and muy bonita senoritas. Let's round up Tight and Dawson and all head south."

He brushed back Pete's eyelids, but they blinked shut like those on a child's mechanical bank.

"I'll need to bring along my nephew, Ace. He's a good kid. Kinda like me at that age, but smarter. I think sometimes the next generation is always smarter than the past, but we can never let them know that. Pete? Soon as I get you conscious, I'll build us a fire and we'll both warm up."

Avery's shoulders shook. He clamped his jaw to keep his teeth from chattering. He noticed the front of his jacket covered with mud and blood.

"Did I tell you that Mary Jane is okay? Yeah, she's just fine and happy to have her own ranch. It kind of fell in my lap, and I gave it to her. She's a nice lady, Pete. Hang on for Sunny's sake. She loves you. I reckon you two are the only family you have left. Come on, Pete, fight it off. Let me get you to town. They have a good doc in Ft. Benton."

Avery scooted around so he could cradle Pete's head and shoulders on his lap.

"That's right, Pete. Did you hear me? Sunny needs you."

Avery tried to rub warmth into Pete's arms and neck. He glowered at the gray clouds that hung low above them.

"It's goin' to get warmer. The snow is startin' to

melt. Tomorrow will be better. You just wait and see."

One eye, then the other, blinked open. Pete glanced up, then both eyes shut like a strong-box lid. His lips moved. Avery bent closer.

"It's a cold day for dyin', Avery." The voice was raspy, halting, scared.

"Now, that's more like it. You're going to make it. I'm not letting you die out here along the Missouri Breaks. Not like this." Avery kept his left hand pressed against the bloody wool blanket that covered the gaping wound in Pete Cutler's stomach.

"I reckon it's always a cold day for dyin'." Pete twisted his back as if trying for a more comfortable position. When he coughed, blood trickled out.

The leather tough creases that framed Avery's brown eyes narrowed with each gust of frigid air off the river. "And the freezing can keep you alive a little longer. General Miles always said the wounded last longer in the cold." With his free hand, he wiped the blood off Pete's chin. "You need a drink?"

Pete closed his eyes and continued the long, slow gasps. "You got whiskey?"

"You know better than that. I'll make some coffee."

"You ever notice how right before he dies," Pete's sunken cheeks tightened with each

445

word, "every man complains of the cold?"

Avery scouted the barren riverbank. "I'll gather some sage and build a fire."

Pete's eyes blinked open. His hand twitched, but didn't lift. "Don't leave me, Avery. Don't leave me."

"I'm not goin' anywhere."

"Good." Pete stared through Avery as if he weren't there. "Death is a cold son-of-a-gun."

Avery pulled Pete's hand toward his mouth and blew into it.

"I can't move them any more."

With calloused, ungloved hand, he clamped Pete's fingers into a fist.

"I don't mean just your toes or your fingers get cold. It's more than that."

The snowmelt soaked Avery's trousers, numbing all that it clung to. "Don't be predictin' what's not going to happen. I'll figure out somethin'."

"Even my bones feel like river ice in January."

"If you'd just let me build a fire, I could . . ."

Pete's voice softened to a whisper. "And your heart gets cold . . . like all the feelin' is gone."

"Look, I'm not going to sit here in the snow and talk about you dyin'. I'll get you out of this. I'll get you to a doc, and he'll pull those bullets out and sew . . ."

"Is Mary Jane alright?"

"She's fine. She's safe. She's worried about you."

"I ain't been much of a brother."

"That's not what she says."

"You goin' to marry her?"

"One crisis at a time, Pete. Let's get you to town."

Pete coughed. Thick, black blood dribbled from his lips. "It's a hard two days ride to Ft. Benton. I ain't up to it. I can't bounce up and down on a pony."

Avery pointed toward the Missouri. "We'll go by river."

"Even Avery John Creede can't make a raft out of these granite boulders and paddle upstream."

"I'd try."

"I know you would, Avery. I can't think of anyone else I'd rather have with me right now, than you. I'm glad you came searchin' for me."

"Looks like I was one day late."

"I don't think it would have mattered. It's okay."

"It's not okay. Pete, This whole scene feels wrong. We stood side-by-side in four of the biggest battles of the Indian Wars. Twice I was wounded, and both times it was you who got me to safety and a doc."

"You would have done the same for me."

"But I didn't. You never got shot."

"That's because I didn't think I had to lead

every charge into the enemy, like some fool named Creede." Pete stared in the direction of the horses. "Is Rinkman dead?"

"Yep."

"Another bad guy killed by Creede of old Montana?"

"I had some help. Four of his own men added a bullet or two."

"They turned on him?"

"Some of them did."

"Kirkley?"

"Yeah, he was one of 'em."

"He wants to run the show, but won't get the others to follow."

"They talked about packin' up and goin' north to the Alberta plains."

"Most of 'em deserve to go to hell."

"We talked about that, too."

"Did you preach at them, Avery?"

"A little."

"You goin' to preach at me?"

"Do you need it?"

"Don't we all? I'm glad you came lookin' for me. The only thing worse than dyin', is dyin' alone."

Avery put his hand on Pete's neck. "Well, I'm not much, but I'm here."

"When I was young, I figured I'd die an old man, surrounded by my wife, kids, grandkids."

"We all have lots of plans when we're young."

Avery stared out at the silent, fast moving river.

"Dyin' is a lonely thing, Avery. Big, black, heavy . . . lonely. Like them big, black wool blankets we used to wrap the battlefield dead in, remember?"

"Yeah, I remember."

"You know what?" Pete's voice cracked. "I wish I had one of them blankets right now."

Avery released the pressure on the bloody blanket, wiped his hand on his jeans, then tugged off his wool lined, ducking coat. He spread it over Pete's shoulders.

Pete looked away, but nodded. Tears trickled from his eyes and melted into the smeared blood on his unshaven cheeks. "Do you believe in heaven, Avery?"

"You know I do."

"Yeah, me too. But these last few years ain't been too good. Ever since my Lilly died, I've struggled. You reckon there's still a tent or a cabin up there in heaven for me?"

"I think that's why Jesus died for us. We couldn't get there on our own. But I don't think there's a crummy one room line-shack waiting for you."

"You don't?"

"There's only big, fine houses, Pete. That's the only kind there are in heaven. You'll have to be satisfied with a mansion."

"I ain't never lived in a mansion."

"You will . . . you know, some day . . . when it's your turn."

"You don't need to play that game with me. We've both been on lots of battlefields. He pumped five bullets into my gut. I'm not goin' to live through it. It's okay to be honest."

Avery wiped tears from the corners of his eyes. "Pete, I wish there was something I could do."

"Tell me more about heaven."

"Well, there won't be any more pain, or sorrow, or cryin'. The Lord will walk with you ever' day. And there will be shady trees drippin' with juicy fruit."

"Will there be almond trees?"

"Why did you say that?"

"I like almonds."

"I'm sure there will be almond trees . . . and avocado trees."

"What's an avocado?"

"I'm not sure. But there will be all sorts of fine things we've never seen or tasted. It's a wonderful place, Pete. There will even be horses."

"In heaven?"

"Sure, the Lord's going to come back ridin' a big ol' horse. They must have a whole remuda in heaven."

"I know some that ought to be sent to the other place."

Avery let out a long, slow sigh and tried to smile. "All I know for sure is that it's Jesus'

450

home, and He's makin' it so it feels like home to us. Then He's comin' to take us there."

"You really believe that, don't you? I wish I had your faith."

"You'll have a lot more faith than me real soon." Avery rocked Pete back and forth in his lap.

Pete coughed twice, then turned away. "When I close my eyes, I don't see heaven."

"What do you see?"

Pete's voice rasped a faint whisper. "Nothing. Dark black nothin'."

Avery touched Pete's forehead. "That's the tunnel."

"What tunnel?"

"The one that connects this life to the next. All tunnels are black. Don't worry about it, just keep walkin'."

"I'm too tired to open my eyes." Blood pulsed between his lips with every word.

"Keep 'em closed, if that's comfortable." Avery tilted Pete's head higher. "Nothing to see out here but white snow and the rear end of a couple horses."

"You'll tell Mary Jane what happened?"

"We'll ride back together to Ft. Benton and you tell her yourself."

"You're a liar, Avery John Creede."

"You know I don't lie. I'm just lettin' my heart talk, instead of my head."

"I'm glad you found me. I ain't quite as terrified havin' you here."

"You'd do the same for me."

"I'd never get the chance. Avery John Creede is immortal, didn't you know that? I heard ol' Red Cloud tell you that you would never die."

"And I remember you, Tight, and Dawson rollin' on the ground and laughin' your heads off."

"Not until the old Indian left. Can you raise up my head a little more? I seem to have trouble catchin' a breath."

Avery propped Pete up on his chest. Wet snow soaked through the shoulders of his wool shirt, but he locked his jaw to keep from shivering.

"Is it night time?"

"Nope."

"All I can see is dark and black."

" 'Cause you're still in that dadgum tunnel."

"Tell me more . . . about . . . heaven . . ."

"It's always daylight, and it's never cold in heaven."

Pete's eyes were open, but as glazed as the snow filled horizon.

"I think . . . I can . . . see it . . ." Pete muttered.

"Isn't it a great vision?"

Pete's voice bellowed crystal clear. "It's no vision, it's real . . . I can see it."

Avery sat straight up. "Heaven? Can you see heaven, Pete?"

"No, but I can see the end of the tunnel. It's up there, and it ain't too far. You were right, Avery John Creede. You were right. Keep talkin' about heaven. You said it won't be cold."

Avery didn't bother wiping the tears that rolled down his cheeks. He clutched Pete's hand, and rested the other on the wounded man's forehead. "It won't be hot and sweaty up there, either. Every day is just right. Not windy like Wyomin'. The people there not only treat you like family . . . they are family. Oh, Pete, what a great day it will be. All the pain will go away. All that sense of failure. All those regrets in life when we should have done something different. Said somethin' more. The sleepless nights when we worried whether God would really forgive us. Think of the burdens that will be gone. We might be alone in death, but we aren't alone in heaven. Men like Colonel Wilson . . . Big Bog Sheffler . . . Jeremiah Greene . . . they will all be there. Shoot, Pete, your Lilly will be there. I bet she'll have a smile a mile wide and open arms to greet you . . ."

Avery slid his near numb fingers down and felt Pete's neck for a pulse. He shook his head then glanced straight up into the falling snow. His icy fingers closed the dead man's eyelids.

The clouds began to thin, but a snow flurry fell like the last curtain on the final day of a long running play.

It was ten minutes before he muttered, "Oh, Lamb of God who taketh away the sins of the world, have mercy upon us." And a good ten minutes after that before he stood.

He didn't pull his coat back on until he had Pete wrapped in his canvas bedroll. The numbness he felt gripped more than his fingers and toes as he lashed the body to his horse.

It was almost night when Avery pulled himself into the saddle. He rolled his coat collar up, and yanked his hat down into the wind. He weaved the lead line between his fingers, then jammed his hand into his coat pocket. He surveyed the barren landscape next to the wide bend in the river. The snow covered boulders looked like giant, soft pillows. Flocks of scraggly sage gave a festive, holiday appearance. Pristine whiteness now covered the blood and mud of the recent death.

"Just like nothin' happened," he mumbled. Then he glanced back at the blanket covered body draped across the horse's saddle like a long sack of potatoes.

"Let's go home, boys. At least three of us will be going home."

He kicked the heels of his boots and the black horse lurched forward.

"Come to think of it, I reckon Pete's already home."

CHAPTER THIRTY

Most of Avery's friends were dead.

Good friends.

Men he planned on knowing a lifetime.

But their lifetime turned out to be much shorter than his.

Weeks before, he rode into Ft. Benton, Montana, for a reunion with the last four men he could call pals.

Night after night around a small campfire in Colorado, and then Wyoming, he looked forward to the laughs, the memories, and the new adventures. Dawson Wickers would keep them laughing with stories of being run out of every town in the West. Tight Sheldon would fill their heads with rumors of gold mines and silver strikes. Pete Cutler could catch them up on every woman with a disarming smile they ever met. And all three would tease Avery about his latest gun battle, range war, or Indian raid.

In his mind, he could finally relax.

The second reunion remained on his mind for five years, the direct focus of his travels for five weeks.

But now, Pete was dead. Tight and Dawson hadn't come.

As he rode back to the ranch, he knew something besides Pete Cutler had died along the Missouri River. This ended an era for him.

This long journey lasted ten years. He could look back on his early days, his army stint, his post-army years.

In most ways, he was glad it was over.

But the thought that nagged him as he plodded through the muddy aftermath of the early snowstorm . . . he didn't know if the new chapter would be better . . . or worse.

It was quicker to reach Ft. Benton by the river road, but Avery swung north. Although it would be deserted, he felt compelled to check the status of the ranch.

The clouds drifted east at sunset, and stars lit the sky in a way that shouted "Montana." A slight breeze from the southwest melted the snow.

Several times he considered a stop to build a fire, try to sleep.

But his mind raced back over the twenty years he had known Pete Cutler. Then he branched off to army memories, and a few childhood days.

He rode a little further.

And further.

Until the stars faded.

The black night grayed.

And the air chilled.

Junior plodded in such a slow, methodical rhythm, Avery figured the horse was asleep.

It was still morning dark when he spied the silhouette of the barn, then the house. All signs of the prince and his entourage were gone.

No smoke curled from the house chimneys.

No lantern light from the windows.

No animals in the corrals.

He rode into the barn and watered the horses before laying out the wrapped body on straw near the anvil.

"Pete, I should have asked you where you wanted to be buried. Sunny will know. I don't have any idea where I'll be buried. Some lonely place, I reckon. All gravesites are solitary places."

With saddles balanced on the rails of the stalls and hay pulled down for the horses, Avery crawled back on the hay floor of a fairly clean stall and stretched out. He felt the mud and blood caked on his hands and face.

I'm not much cleaner than this barn. Old, used, and rank smellin'. Sunny would laugh if she knew I refused to dirty her house, even with no one at home. She has a nice laugh.

Shoot, she has a nice ever'thin', but I'm just too tired to think about it.

He pulled his hat down across his face, clutching his revolver in his right hand. The muscles in his neck, shoulders and eyes relaxed.

"Daddy, Daddy, Daddy!" The blonde headed girl with long dress and heavy, lace-up shoes sprinted toward him.

The sun was straight overhead but had the mild warmth of late spring. The horse he led stood tall, black, lathered. Behind the running girl, a large, two-story house peered through flowering shrubs and towering ash trees.

He glanced down, surprised to see he wore a clean white shirt, suit and tie.

The little girl looked familiar. She felt comfortable in his arms.

"I missed you, Daddy!"

She wrapped thin legs around his waist and he toted her with one arm as he tramped toward the house, leading the gelding.

Avery glanced at her blue eyes. "I missed you too, eh . . . darlin'."

She poked his chapped lips. "How many times do I have to tell you, Mamma is your 'darlin'. . . I'm your Deborah. You really mustn't call us both darlin'." She kissed his closely shaven cheek. "I can't wait until I am ten."

"Why is that, darlin'? I mean, Deborah."

"Because you promised to tell me how you got that scar when I am ten. That's just one year from August 11th. Mamma says she doesn't even know how you got it, but I think she just forgot."

"Are you only nine? I thought for sure you were sixteen."

"Oh, Daddy," she giggled.

Her long, straight hair, pulled behind her head, draped down across his arm. "Did I ever tell you that Deborah is a beautiful name?"

"Yes, quite often. But that's okay. Mamma says that older men often repeat themselves."

"I've heard that."

"I love you, Daddy."

"I love you, too . . . eh, Deborah."

"You can call me by my nickname, you know."

"I . . . eh . . . thought you wanted me to call you Deborah."

"I don't like anyone else calling me DeDe, except for you. Peter called me DeDe while you were gone and I punched him in the nose."

"You punched Peter? Eh, what did he do?"

"Nothin', 'cause you told him he couldn't hit girls."

"I did?"

"Yes, but Mother made me do his chores anyway. Little brothers can be such a bother." She hugged him tight.

He hugged her back. "I've heard that, too."

"How was Washington, D.C.? Did you ride in a carriage up to the Capitol building? Did you get to see the president like you said? Does he wear a revolver like you do? Is there a big privy behind the White House?"

"Privy? What kind of talk is that for a little girl?"

"I thought you said I was sixteen."

He leaned over to her ear and whispered, "No privies . . . they have indoor plumbing in the White House."

"Oh, yuck. Daddy, you are so funny. Put me down so I can go tell Mamma you're home."

He placed her on her feet, then examined the house. "Where is Mamma?"

"I think she's sipping tea on the veranda."

"Veranda?"

"She'll be very surprised to see you."

"Not nearly as surprised as I will be."

"Oh, Daddy, you've only been gone seven days."

"It seems like a lot longer than that."

"Wait right here, I'll go fetch her."

"I'll wait, DeDe. I'll wait as long as it takes."

At the check of a lever, Avery peered at the inside of his battered black hat.

"You two get saddled and ride on out of here. We don't need any bums sleepin' in our barn."

When he sat up, the hat tumbled, but the revolver remained in his hand.

With sunlight blazing behind her, the woman's face was a shadow.

"Are you Deborah's mamma?"

The voice softened. "Avery?"

He blinked. "Sunny?"

"You're a mess." She eased the hammer on the carbine and hiked over to him. "I've seen hardrock miners come out of a hole in the ground looking better than you."

"What are you doing here?"

"This is my ranch, remember?"

"But why aren't you in Ft. Benton?"

"Where's Ace?"

"He got shot. I had Loritz take him to town. Where's the German?"

"In Ft. Benton, with your Carla." She stared at his bloody coat. "Are you wounded?"

"Cold, hungry, tired, filthy and saddened, but not shot."

She took a deep breath, then bit her lip. "And Pete?"

Avery nodded at the canvas wrapped body. "Rinkman gut shot him before I could get there. I failed him, Sunny, and that's going to nag at me the rest of my life."

She dropped the carbine. Her head drooped to her chest. "I know you tried."

"All the way back to the ranch I kept wonderin', what would have happened if I'd just let you and the boys rob that bank."

"As I recall, I made you mad."

"Yeah, but if I'd taken a nap that afternoon, Pete would be alive . . . and you would . . ."

"Be hiding out in some crummy little hotel

wondering when Rinkman's men would find me." She wiped the tears away from her eyes. "And Rinkman?"

"Dead, too."

"Are you sure?"

"Positive."

She knelt beside Pete's body, and patted the wrapped canvas. "It was just me and Pete. We hadn't been too close for years, but he was always there. Just knowing in my mind that I had someone, somewhere . . . brought a sense of connection. I guess it's just me now . . . me and my ranch. I don't think I knew Pete very well. I suppose brothers and sisters never really understand each other."

Avery ambled over by her and placed his hand on her shoulder. "Mary Jane, look, I'm . . ."

She patted his hand. "Did you preach him into heaven, Avery?"

"I believe I did."

"Thanks."

For several moments the only sound heard was the wind drifting through the barn boards.

Her voice was so quiet Avery had to lean down to listen. "You know, you preached me into heaven, too."

"I did?"

"Yeah, I believe, Avery John Creede."

"I'm glad, Sunny."

When she stood up, Sunny surveyed him from

boot to hat. "I'll go warm up some bathwater for you."

"Maybe we should bury Pete first."

"I'll not have you read over my brother looking like that."

"No, ma'am."

She slipped her arm into his. "And you don't want your Carla seeing you like this. She'd faint."

"Look, Sunny, I don't want you to assume that I've made up my mind about my future."

"Avery . . . I don't want you."

"What?"

"In the weeks that I've known you, I've been chased, tied up, slapped around. Almost drowned. Shot at. Cussed out."

"I see your point."

"No, you don't. These have been some of the best days of my life. Because I've been respected, protected and kissed by the sweetest lips I've ever known. But I don't want you, Avery John Creede. Your heart belongs to Carla. I know that. I've always known that. But that doesn't mean a woman can't wish . . . and daydream . . . and pretend that it's different. Pete and I were a lot alike, I suppose. We both had dozens of dreams that never came true. Everything was up ahead. The best was just around the corner. But we both realized we only deceived ourselves. Because, if you believe the lie about tomorrow, you can make it through today."

"Mary Jane, I think . . ."

"Hush, let me finish. You have given me two wonderful presents . . . maybe three."

"Three presents?"

"You gave me this ranch. It's everything to me. I will spend my life making a go of it right here, or die trying. It's a right and noble venture, don't you think?"

"I believe you are right about that."

"And you eliminated Rinkman. He was a frightening black cloud, an evil storm that was so unpredictable, I haven't had one day's peace in years. But now he's gone."

"And the third?"

"You've made me feel good about myself. If it weren't for that dark haired queen of Chicago, I think I could have caught you. Second place isn't nearly as good as first place, but, at least, I'm not in last place. You know what, Avery? I like me. And I haven't been able to say that in years."

"Sunny, I never said you were in second place, it's just . . ."

"You didn't have to. I can live out here on this ranch all by myself, knowing I was in second place in your heart . . . what I can't do is live with you knowing that I'm second."

"One thing I'd like to know . . . why is it that you think you know my heart better than I do?"

"And there's one thing I'd like to know," she replied.

"Oh?"

"Why is it you sat up and asked me if I were Deborah's mamma?"

Sported out in a clean black suit too narrow in the shoulders, Avery led his horse over by the fresh, cross-marked grave. Sunny strolled beside him.

"You have my list?" she asked.

"In my pocket."

"I'll pay you back next year at this time. But you have to come here to collect."

Avery tipped his hat. "I'll come callin'."

"Is that a promise? Your Carla might not like that."

"I won't need her permission. Don't marry me off so quick."

"I've seen you drool over her."

"I've never drooled."

She laughed. "Maybe not, but you thought about drooling."

He squeezed her hand. "I've thought about lots of things."

"So have I, that's why we need to change the subject. Will you send back a bill of sale on the wagon and team? I don't want someone to accuse me of stealing them."

"I'll send the wagon and team back with the

papers, groceries and supplies. But it can be a long, hard winter."

"Avery, I've had lots of long, hard winters."

He stopped and turned toward her. "But this just doesn't seem right."

"I know, a lady in distress and all. But I'm not in distress. I've got a home. I've got a plan. I've got a future. And you aren't a part of it. Now go on."

"I feel like an unwanted dog."

"If I don't treat you this way, I'll break down and cry."

"Maybe I should stay another day and we can talk this out."

"Your Carla is waiting for her Avery in Ft. Benton. Besides, you stay a day and I might do something I'd have to seek the Lord's forgiveness for. Get out of here, Avery Creede."

"I can't go without hugging you, Mary Jane Cutler."

"I'm not sure I can turn loose."

"I'll risk that."

When his arms encircled her, she collapsed into his embrace. "Do you have any idea how good this feels?"

"I reckon I do."

"It feels like springtime. Avery, do you really know where your life is heading?"

"I've never known where I was headed."

"You going to marry Carla?"

"I honestly don't know."

"I'll be here."

"I do know that."

"You can come back and visit before next fall, if you want to."

"I'll keep that in mind."

"But you'll have to sleep in the barn."

"Fair enough."

"Do you remember the first day we met?" she asked. "I hated your arrogant guts that day."

"How sweet of you to remember."

She shoved him back. "Now get on your horse, cowboy, before I seduce you."

"I can't believe you said that."

"Then you don't know me very well. You heard me. Get on your horse."

He swung up in the saddle. "You think I'm an easy target?"

"No," she laughed, "but I'm good at it, Avery Creede."

He wove the reins between his fingers. "You are going to make it, Mary Jane Cutler. I know you are. You're smart and tough."

"You forgot pretty."

"That goes without saying."

"No, it doesn't."

"Okay, you are one beautiful lady, Miss Cutler."

"Thank you, Mr. Creede, and your scarred handsomeness make's a woman's heart flutter."

He turned Junior toward the distant river. "I've had chili in Laredo that could do the same thing."

She stuck out her tongue.

"You make me smile, Moose Lady."

"Mister, I'll shoot you dead the next time you bring that up."

"No, you won't. If you haven't killed me by now, I reckon it won't happen." He tipped his hat. "Goodbye, Miss Cutler. May the Lord bless you with your heart's desire."

"Goodbye, Mr. Creede. May the Lord help you discover what your heart's desire really is."

When he reached the pass, he turned back to wave, but she wasn't there.

He waved anyway.

CHAPTER THIRTY-ONE

Avery felt lazy.

The sun blazed autumn bright, the breeze brisk, but not biting. The snow had vanished. The cottonwoods still held their leaves.

But he was tired, sore. And in no hurry to reach Ft. Benton. He didn't want to arrive before he figured out what to say to Carla. The plodding rhythm and sway of his horse slowed his thoughts and he fought to stay awake.

Avery found it too melancholy to think about Sunny and the ranch and too confusing to think of Carla. He pushed himself to find a topic that didn't involve either woman.

On the big ranches of western Montana, they would be bringing the herds down off the mountains and into the valleys. Judge Reinhart gave him a standing invitation to run his Bitterroot Valley operation. But Avery figured he'd tire quickly of babysitting cows.

Miners in Colorado would be stacking cordwood for the long winter. The Big Snowy Gold and Silver Company offered top wages if he'd escort the ore wagons from the mine to the smelter. But the scenery would never change, and he'd likely get frostbit in those winters.

The Caribbean harbored tropical weather year round and Biggy Marton promised $5,000 if he'd lead a three-hundred-man company of mercenaries on an invasion of Cuba.

Finding work never troubled Avery. There was a U.S. marshall's opening in Wyoming, an army scout job in Utah, and a guard position at the Carson City Mint.

All of those options involved a gun on his hip, and someone willing to shoot back. For the first time in weeks, he was neither chasing anyone, nor being chased.

Right now, visions of a Spanish hacienda surrounded by almond trees settled peacefully in his mind. When the sun dropped behind the western hills, he yanked his hat down, shoved his collar up, pulled on his gloves . . . and kept riding.

Avery huddled by the campfire, blanket pulled around his shoulders, as daylight began to break. He heard the squeak of a wagon axle from a mile off and watched two dark brown mules lumber his way. The sign on the panel wagon was faded, and he couldn't read it until it rolled up next to his fire.

"Young man, do you mind if I join you for a little warmth? I'll boil the coffee." A round man with wide brimmed white straw hat bounded down from the wagon.

"Happy to have company, even though I'm not young."

"Yes, I can see that now." When the man hit the ground, his entire body jiggled. "Professor Alexander Houston." He held out his hand.

Avery shook his hand. "What's your area of discipline, Professor?"

"Eh . . . discipline?"

Avery pointed to the sign on the panel wagon. "It looks like you are a peddler now. What subjects did you used to teach?"

"I was the proud teacher at Carter Canyon Grammar School, near Scott's Bluff, Nebraska."

"What's a professor doing selling pots and pans?"

"Pots, pans, sewing supplies, cloth, some groceries, and the *Chicago Dictionary of Encyclopedic Knowledge*." The gray haired man filled a coffeepot from the water barrel on the side of his wagon. "Every Western homestead needs a set of these fine books. And besides, being a peddler allows me time to write my memoirs."

"I reckon writing memoirs is quite a chore."

"It can be quite tiresome. Have you ever tried it?"

"No, I surmise a man has to do something important in his life to be able to write a book about it. My life seems to be routine."

"Ah . . . in a rut? My Miracle Oil is tonic for manly achievement. You should read the many testimonials."

"I reckon those are as hard to write as memoirs."

A wide smile broke over the older man's clean shaven face. "Oh, no, the testimonials are quite easy to write." The professor chuckled, then nodded his head. "I like a man who is straightforward."

"And I like one that laughs at himself. How's the pots and pans business, Professor?"

"I did splendid in Ft. Benton, and look for even better days up ahead. I say, did you know you are only two miles from town?"

"Yep, but I got in late. Didn't want to show up at three in the morning. Where are you headed? Miles City?"

"Yes, indeed. But first I want to work the Missouri River Breaks. There are dozens of families down there, and now that it's safe to travel, I want to beat the competition." The professor handed him a tin cup of steaming coffee.

"So it's safe to go down in there?"

"Haven't you heard? That murderous scoundrel, Jed Rinkman, finally met his just desserts."

"So, Rinkman's dead. Did you hear how it happened?"

"The details are a little hazy, but for two-bits you can view his body at Billings."

"How did he meet his demise?"

The old man leaned closer. "People aren't saying, but I have it on very good authority that none other than Stuart Brannon came all the way up here from Arizona to take care of the matter."

"Brannon? Where did you hear that?"

"The clerk at the hotel in Ft. Benton. His cousin was painting the mayor's fence when he overhead a German prince's son tell the mayor's daughter that Stuart Brannon would never let this situation go on. Then the telegram arrived from Billings about Rinkman being on display. I just sort of put two and two together."

"Something a professor would be quite good at."

"Precisely. It's a discipline in deductive thinking. I'm afraid there's not a lot of that going around."

"How nice of the legendary Stuart Brannon to come up here and clean things up."

"So like him."

Avery stood up and began to fold his blanket. "You've met the man?"

"No, but I read all the books. Did you hear of his recent exploits in Guatemala? No wonder the senoritas all chase him."

"I don't suppose he needs any of your Miracle Oil?" Avery grinned.

"He might be the only man in America who doesn't. Say, what kind of work are you in? I mean, if you don't mind me asking. I've been wanting to hire an assistant."

Avery tied the dirty tan blanket to the back of his saddle. "Not lookin' for a job, but thanks for the offer. I'm an almond farmer from California."

"You don't say?" The professor sipped his coffee and studied Avery. "No offense, but I had you pegged for a man who lived a harder life."

When Avery yanked out his gun and inspected it, the man flinched. "Almond farming can be a dangerous business."

"That so?"

Avery pointed the gun south toward the river. "Gangs of thieves often bust into an orchard."

"To steal almonds?"

"The whole almond tree."

"What? How can anyone steal a tree?"

"When they are little fellas, they steal them and sell them up and down the coast for two dollars a tree."

"Why, I never heard of such a thing. The depravity of it all. By the way, what's an almond farmer from California doing in Montana?"

Avery shoved his hat back. "Visiting a lady friend."

"Oh . . . well, excuse me for being nosy."

"That's quite alright." Avery nodded at the panel wagon. "Say, how much is a set of those books?"

"Four beautifully bound volumes for only six dollars."

"I'll give you four dollars for a set."

"I couldn't possibly . . ." The professor sat his tin coffee cup down and rubbed his chin. "Well, for a friend, I could forfeit my profit and sell them for five dollars."

"You and I both know you'd take four dollars and double your money. But I'll pay five."

"You will? Splendid, I'll fetch them . . ."

Avery held up his hand. "You'll have to deliver them for me."

"Deliver? Where?"

"You ride on this trail toward the Breaks and about five hours from now, you'll spy a big barn and house a mile north of the road. The lady's name is Miss Mary Jane Cutler."

"You'll pay now, I presume?"

Avery tossed him a gold coin.

"Twenty dollars? I'll get your change."

"No, keep it. Tell Mary Jane she has fifteen dollars credit. Let her select anything she wants."

"Oh, yes . . . very fine, indeed."

"Give her your best prices."

"Of course."

Avery yanked the cinch tight on his horse. "I'm headed on into town now. The fire is yours."

"Mister, thank you for the business, and the trust. Most people think traveling salesmen are . . . eh, rather unreliable."

"I know you will treat Mary Jane fair . . . and tell her of the credit. If you don't, I'll come after you."

"The Breaks is a mighty big place."

"You plan on cheating me?"

"No, but I'm just saying that a less scrupulous man than myself might just ride on and pocket the money."

"Professor, I figure a man is honest until he proves himself otherwise. And if I find you dishonest, I will track you down and hold you accountable."

"You are saying wherever I go in the Breaks, you will find me?"

"I found Jed Rinkman and shot him; I reckon I can find you."

"You shot Rinkman? Are you Stuart Brannon?"

"No, I'm Avery John Creede."

"Never heard of you. Why do you suppose they said Brannon killed Rinkman?"

"Maybe your two and two didn't add up to four. Besides, no one wants to give credit for bringing Rinkman to justice to an almond farmer from California. What kind of story would that make?"

"Quite right. Eh, I suppose there are men all over the West who will claim to have been the one who killed Rinkman."

"I figure people will forget the whole matter by Christmas. Remember what I told you to do for Miss Cutler."

"I certainly will . . . I'm curious about a woman who has captured the attention of a . . . California almond farmer."

A dozen columns of chimney smoke pointed the way to Ft. Benton, even before he crossed the knoll and descended down Main Street. Several freight wagons were backed up to shops. Workmen grunted and groaned to unload them. Avery had just rode past the Elim Dover's Hotel, when he heard a shout from the raised boardwalk.

"I say, Mr. Creede." A short balding man with thick mustache approached.

"Abe, how are you?"

"I am feeling much better, seeing you. We heard of Rinkman's death, but we didn't hear whether you had survived. I believe the Almighty was looking after you."

"I reckon you are right."

"Is it true? I read the telegram from Billings."

"Rinkman's dead."

Abraham Hermann clutched his hands together. "I will sleep better at night."

"Me, too. Abe, I need to check on Ace. Do you know where he's at? He got leg shot and I'm worried."

"He's staying at the mayor's house. I heard he is doing quite well."

"The mayor's house?"

"Yes, the mayor's wife insisted."

Avery was surprised to see the charred remains of the house next to the mayor's had been cleaned up and all signs of the devastating fire removed. The recent cold snap left the flower garden in a permanent wilt. He tied off his horse to the iron lamppost in front of the white clapboard home, then pushed open the wooden gate.

A lady's voice rolled down from the porch. "Mr. Creede, I'm glad to see you. Young Mr. Emerson is in the parlor. I need to go visit Mrs. Shamolsky. She gave Chop-Chop a trim and a shampoo."

"You found your dog?"

"It seems he inadvertently got on a steamboat and ended up in St. Louis. At least, I believe it was inadvertent. He was a filthy mess, but happy. He reminded me of cowboys after the fall gather."

"I'm surely glad you found him."

"Divine Providence led him home. Now, if the mayor returns, tell him I'll be home shortly. I will expect you to stay for supper. I baked one of my famous lima bean pies." The sturdy woman in the high collared mauve dress swooshed by him.

Avery tipped his hat, then muttered, "Is Ace alright?"

"Don't dawdle in the yard. Go see for yourself."

Hat in hand, Avery entered the silent home. The entry was cream painted paneling with imposing portraits of the mayor, his wife, and daughter, Tabitha. The door to the left was closed, but the one on the right led to an oak paneled room with bookcases, sitting desk, huge fire-place, brown leather sofa, and a sleeping Avery Creede Emerson.

Avery studied his nephew's linen wrapped lower leg, then slid up a black wooden side chair and plopped down, hat still in hand.

He cleared his throat.

Ace blinked his eyes open and sat straight up.

"Uncle Avery! We heard Rinkman was dead, but no word about you."

"A few new cuts and bruises, but I'm fine. How's the leg?"

Ace flopped back down. "Doc said this morning that it's healing very nicely. Said I can walk around if I use a crutch for a couple of weeks. It still hurts like the devil, but I reckon you know about gunshot wounds."

"Never pleasant."

"You got him, huh?"

"Me and three of his own men, but I'll tell you that story later. Nice looking suit you're wearing."

"Miss Carla bought it for me." Ace tugged his tie loose. "I told her I didn't have much use for one, but she seemed to think I'd need one for the wedding."

"Wedding? Are you getting married?"

"Not me, Uncle Avery, you."

"Oh . . . she's making wedding plans, is she?"

"Not that I know of. Did you hear that the prince, Loritz, and all of them headed off for New York City? They went down river to catch the train yesterday."

"So, the hunting days are over?"

"He said they are coming back. There's some important government meeting in New York that he needed to attend."

"What are you doing at the mayor's house? I thought you and Miss Tabitha had cooled things."

"Yes, sir, I reckon that's over. The mayor's wife was determined I stay here until you got back."

"Isn't that a little awkward, having Miss Tabby hanging around?"

"She's not here. I told you, they went to New York City."

"Miss Leitner went with the prince and Loritz?"

"Mainly she's the traveling companion of Miss Carla."

Avery felt his neck tense. "Are you saying Carla went to New York with the prince?"

"Yep. She got a telegram from her daddy to meet her in New York, that she was needed to be hostess of this German-American meeting. I couldn't figure it out. But Miss Carla said she had to go and offered to take Miss Tabby along."

"Now I'm getting really confused. Carla couldn't wait a few days for me?"

"Why, no, this meeting is of great importance, Uncle Avery. Loritz told me the future of Africa hangs in the balance."

"Africa? What does Africa have to do with two people in Ft. Benton, Montana Territory?"

"Shoot, I don't know anything about Africa, except Mamma said Egypt was in Africa and Moses led the Hebrew children out of there."

Avery leaned back in the chair and ran his fingers through his hair. "Why is it that when I get close to Carla, the entire world spins out of control?"

"You reckon that's what love is like?"

"I hope it's more peaceful than this."

"Anyway, the doc said I could ride a horse by tomorrow, if I took it easy and kept the bandages clean."

"You planning on going somewhere?"

"I figured you'd want me to be part of the wedding."

"How can there be a wedding with Carla on her way to New York?"

"Miss Carla? You ain't going to marry her."

"I'm not?"

"She said she explained it all in the letter."

"What letter?"

Ace reached into his suit coat and tugged out a white envelope. He shoved it across to Avery.

"If I'm not going to marry Carla . . ." Avery took the letter. "What is all this talk about a wedding?"

"She said you were going to marry Miss Sunny."

"Sunny? I'm not going to marry Sunny."

"You ain't? What's wrong with her?"

"Nothing's wrong with her. It's just that . . . well, I'm not sure I should marry any woman, and besides, she made it quite clear she didn't want me."

"Miss Sunny don't want you?"

"She said she wouldn't marry me."

"You asked Miss Sunny to marry you while Miss Carla waited here in town?"

"Waited? She's in New York. Besides, I didn't ask Miss Sunny, she just told me not to think about it, because she didn't want me."

"Ain't women something? I, for one, am relieved to know you ain't getting married. Now we are both free to go find your pals Dawson and Tight."

"I don't know where they are."

"I don't reckon that stopped you before."

"Carla's gone, Sunny kicked me out, and a lame nephew wants us to go off on a wild goose chase? What kind of life is that?"

"Sounds like your life story, Uncle Avery. Could you hand me that hickory crutch?"

"You going somewhere?"

"To the privy." Ace hobbled across the room.

"Eh, you need . . any help?" Avery mumbled.

Ace turned and grinned. "Read your letter. It's been burning a hole in my pocket for two days."

Avery unfolded the paper as he ambled to the window. He bent toward the daylight that filtered through the white gauze curtains and recognized the swirling penmanship of Carla Loganaire.

My Dearest Avery . . . I am not sure when you will read this, but I know you will return to Ft. Benton. You promised you would and Avery John Creede keeps his word, even if his timing is delayed. When we heard Rinkman was dead, some wondered if you had survived the ordeal. I had no doubt. My Avery is the bravest and most noble man I have ever met.

Yes, I'm on my way to New York. Father pleaded. There seems to be a place for me . . . a sort of social diplomat . . . soothing international feathers in the parlor, instead of the halls of government. I plan to stay through October for the dedication of our glorious Statue of Liberty.

I would have liked to have been there and tell you of all this face-to-face, but as we both know, that is dangerous. You are hard to resist, my sweet Avery. I was thinking this morning, that I will probably never marry . . . since no man can live up to the level of my Avery. You are the only man who refused to let me change him. And I love you for that. Of course, I love you for the way you make my heart feel when your arms are around me, but I mustn't dwell on that.

I've tried very hard the past couple of weeks to understand you and life out on the frontier. To be honest, I've been scared most of the time. Scared for my life when held captive by Rinkman . . . and scared for your life most every day. You have lived on the edge of a cliff for so long, I imagine you fail to even consider the danger. But such a life frightens me. I realized that I would spend day and night exhorting you to move away from the dangerous precipice. We would both be miserable. And if my darling Avery changed his ways just for me, he would no longer be the man of my dreams.

It takes a different type of woman to live with Avery John Creede, one who can clutch on to the present moment, without worries about the future. It takes a woman whose heart doesn't drop at the sound of gunfire, one who doesn't need her dress starched and ironed, and perfume sent from Paris.

I probably shouldn't have come to Ft. Benton, but my heart made me. Oh, how I wanted this to work. Every time I dreamed about that hacienda along the coast of California . . . I envisioned a restless Avery on the front porch, cleaning his guns and waiting for some old pal to ride up and say his services were needed.

That's who you are, dear Avery . . . and I have no business changing that. This great western wilderness needs you, at least for a few more years.

Rest assured my heart hasn't changed.

I do believe Miss Cutler has a better chance at meeting your present needs. I *trust you will marry her and have many delights. But, I must say, you will cause her much anxiety also. You just can't stop being Avery John Creede.*

Rest assured you will remain in my heart forever.

I must close before the tears smudge my ink.

always your Carla

P.S. Ace tried to get me to tell him about your scar. I didn't, of course. Thank you for not repeating that most embarrassing story.

CHAPTER THIRTY-TWO

Henry David Thoreau once said, "I have a great deal of company in the house, especially in the morning when nobody calls."

He enjoyed his solitude.

Not all do. Robinson Crusoe exclaimed, "O Solitude, where are the charms that the sages have seen in thy face?"

Solitude can bring peace . . . or fear. Contentment . . . or loneliness.

Stillness gripped the early morning and froze everything in place like a fine portrait . . . everything except the sun, which forced the sky into shades of black to charcoal gray, light gray to off-white, then to pale blue.

The morning air felt mellow around her shoulders as Sunny huddled on the front porch of the ranch house. She sipped a golden porcelain cup of steaming coffee. A four stripe Hudson's Bay blanket draped her shoulders and covered the new flannel nightgown she had purchased from the traveling salesman. Her feet were tucked into an old pair of knee-high moccasins, a legacy from the ranch's previous owners.

The horse team stood side-by-side in the corral, each with left rear hoof tilted in a comfortable sleep position. She expected a rooster to crow. Sunny had already put chickens on her list of items to purchase when she had the funds.

No neighbors to call on.

No travelers to intrude.

She shivered and wrapped her arms around her shoulders.

And no one to hold her tight.

Sunny downed the last gulp of coffee, then shuffled into the house. In the shadows of a kerosene lantern, she examined the contents of her world: table, chairs, cupboard. Kitchen counter, cookstove, fireplace. Old sofa, desk, leather chair, pictures on the wall of people she did not know. Old travel trunks. A busted pump organ. Sewing machine. And a brand new set of the *Chicago Dictionary of Encyclopedic Knowledge.*

She plucked up the first volume and carried it over to the table. Plopping down in the chair, she flipped the pages until she found "Creed." Her right index finger traced the words: "A statement of essential beliefs of a religious faith." Sunny surveyed the spread of Solitaire cards, plucked up the queen of hearts, and jammed it into the page for a bookmark.

She sighed with her eyes closed.

Lord, I have never talked to You much. Never sought Your wisdom. Never felt like I needed You as I do this morning. My heart tells me one thing, my mind another . . . and my poor soul doesn't know which way to turn. I am trying very hard not to make a fool out of myself. But I don't know what's wrong with being a fool. If it's only pride that keeps me sitting on this porch, gazing in the direction of Ft. Benton, then I must overcome such arrogance. But if it's Your leading that keeps me here, I dare not do anything else.

Lead me . . . in paths of righteousness.

The mirror was cracked, but the image clear. Sunny ogled the blonde looking back at her, as she fastened the high collar button on her purple gingham dress. Narrow face. Pointed chin. Faint eyebrows. Hair pulled back in what she considered "neat messiness." She brushed down the cuffs of the dress, and turned for a sideways glance.

"You aren't Carla Loganaire, sweetie. Your shape is more like a thirteen-year-old than a thirty-year-old. You realize you're only going to embarrass yourself, don't you?"

Yeah, I know. But I also know I will regret not going. I will regret it every day of my life.

"Well, Mr. Avery John Creede . . . I don't have fancy perfume to win you over. You'll just have to smell Mary Jane Cutler." She gulped in a deep whiff of air. *I have no idea what Mary Jane Cutler smells like.*

She strolled across the room, plucked up her wool shawl, her heavy coat and handbag, then shut off the lantern. The bright morning sun cast long westward shadows as she marched from the house to the barn. When she glanced back to the front door, she had to shade her eyes with her hand.

"Lord, take care of my place. It would break my heart to lose it."

The team stood in place, familiar with the routine, waiting for her to strap on the rigging.

Mr. Creede, you didn't know that I can rig a team, did you? Well, mister, there are lots of things I can do you don't know about. Hah! There are many surprises awaiting you. That is, if you aren't already married and moved to California.

She chewed her lip as she harnessed the team.

After a final inspection, she tossed her coat, shawl and handbag on the seat, then pulled up into the wagon.

"You boys might as well get used to it. Mamma's driving and there's nothing you can do about it."

She drove past the barn and through the front gate. Then she swung the team around and drove back to the house. Tying the lead lines to the footbrake, she swung down off the wagon and headed to the house.

She exited toting the double-barrel shotgun and three extra shells.

"I am my own protection, boys. I better get used to that."

As Sunny drove out of the ranch, she broke open the shotgun, checked the chambers, then closed the gun and stuck it under the wagon seat. The extra shells she dropped in her handbag.

If it weren't for Annie Oakley, I might be the one who toured with Buffalo Bill. Of course, then I would never have met Avery. But . . . maybe I'd be happier not knowing what I'd missed.

The farm wagon bounced and shuddered along the rough road. Sunny spied only rolling hills, brown grass and gray-green sage in every direction. At the ranch, she felt alone . . . but secure, protected . . . a sense of belonging. Out on the prairie, she just felt alone.

Soon, the jiggle and rattle of the wagon formed a routine pattern. Her eyelids sagged.

Lord, I don't think I know the real Mary Jane Cutler. I seem to be shaped by the people I'm around. In Denver, I was a brash and not too successful actress. When I first met Jed Rinkman, I was a woman of interest and mystery. Down in the Missouri River Breaks, I became an outlaw, fighting for every advantage I could find, and using any means to accomplish it. With Avery, I became a lady, a woman who was important in this world, one who captured the interest, if not the heart, of a fine man. And now . . .

She let out a deep, long breath and opened her eyes.

And now . . . oh, my . . .

Over the rise, a band of horses fogged the fine dust and trotted toward her. Behind them, a half-dozen buckskin clad Indians.

Most of the horses flashed paint colors, one was solid black.

The Indians all carried carbines across their laps and stern expressions.

Sunny pulled up, stopped, and yanked the shotgun to her lap.

The loose horses and Indians surrounded her.

The one with a sleeveless buckskin vest and massive muscular arms rode up to the wagon. He leaned forward, stared at her face, then signaled the others.

She gripped the shotgun so tight, her fingers ached.

Finally, the man sat up straight and leaned back on his saddleless horse. "You the Moose Woman?"

"I most certainly am not."

"You're the Creede's woman, aren't you?"

Sunny cleared her throat. "Yes, I am."

"I thought so. My name is Creede also! Last time you hid under a blanket."

Sunny fingered the trigger, but left the shotgun on her lap. "A safety precaution."

"Where's the Creede?"

"He's in Ft. Benton . . . I'm on my way to . . . fetch him."

He grinned, then turned and spoke in Blackfoot to the others. "I know what you mean. My wife has to go to town to fetch me from time to time. Is anyone watching after the Creede's ranch?"

Sunny bit her lip and stared at the dark eyes, brown skin and square jaw of the Blackfoot warrior. "Just the Lord."

He spoke rapidly to his compadres, pointing to the sky.

They all nodded.

"We hear that he killed Rinkman."

"Yes, he did."

With flourish, he spat on the ground. "He deserved to die. He was a bad man for both whites and Blackfeet."

"He will no longer bring harm to either."

"We were going to visit the Creede."

"I will tell him you came to call."

"We will put these ponies in his corral."

"Why?"

"They are our gift to him. He is a brave man."

"You are giving him the horses?"

"We stole them from the man who used to live there. Now, we give them to the Creede. One stallion and his women."

"I thank you very much for the fine gift." She glanced around at the empty wagon. "I, eh . . . wasn't expecting to visit with anyone and I'm afraid I don't have any gift for you."

"Having Rinkman dead is gift enough. Next time you may give us a gift. Tell the Creede we will not raid his ranch and we will make sure none others do."

"Thank you. He will appreciate that."

"And tell him to boil sage leaves and stir in wild honey . . . it will hasten recovery from too much whiskey."

"I will tell him."

He started to turn away, then paused. "Don't cover your head with a blanket so often. You are so pale white that you look sick."

"I will remember that."

With a whoop and a gallop, six Indians and ten gift horses thundered east.

When the dust settled, Sunny slapped the lead

lines and rattled on over the knoll.

A stallion and his women? I can sell a couple of the mares for some income, and perhaps breed the others. I don't know how to breed horses . . . well, horses know how to breed on their own, but I know nothing about breaking them for sale.

What am I saying? Avery will come back with me, and he'll know exactly what to do.

Lord, why am I so hesitant to believe that?

Horses, wagons, buggies and busy people crowded the streets of Ft. Benton when Sunny rolled into town. Few noticed her driving slowly up Front Street. She was just another farm wife coming to town for supplies.

She looked over each face, searching for a square jaw, scar, dark hat, and piercing sea-green eyes.

No Avery. No Ace. No Carla. No Tabitha. No Mayor.

She couldn't spot anyone she recognized.

Sunny parked the wagon in the shade of the cottonwood tree, near the bench by the river. She stepped down, retrieved her handbag, then followed the foot trail east along the river.

It seems like years ago when I tried to lure Avery down that trail away from the bank. I wonder the result had he followed me? Ah, but Avery John Creede would never do that.

As she strolled over to the hotel, she gazed at the "New Owner" sign on the front of the brick bank. Sunny started up the stairs to the hotel when she heard a noise on the second story balcony. A small, dark haired girl with starched white dress peered down at her.

Sweetie, you would never believe that I stripped to my undergarments and climbed down out of that balcony. I don't know if I believe it. Maybe that wasn't really me.

She sauntered through the open door of the hotel lobby. The clerk perched behind the counter.

"Yes, ma'am," he grinned, "we do have some extra rooms. You look familiar, have you stayed with us before?"

"I'm not looking for a room. Could you tell me if Mr. Avery Creede is here?"

"You're her."

"I'm who?"

"The woman who caused all the trouble with Creede."

"I am sorry for my previous behavior. I don't intend to repeat it, provided you answer my question. Is Mr. Creede staying here?"

"He's gone."

"Out of his room?"

"Gone. Left town. And if you ask me, good riddance."

Sunny clutched her aching stomach and sucked in a deep breath. "He's already gone?"

"That's what I said."

"Did he . . . go to California?"

"Don't know and don't care, lady. Creede's gone and maybe things will calm down."

"Did he leave with a lady?"

"I don't care if he left with a lady, a donkey or a jackrabbit . . . he left, and I'm glad of it."

Sunny's neck locked up. "I said, 'did he leave with a lady?' "

"All I know is that he and his nephew . . . the one with the crutch . . . left town. He didn't say who else he's traveling with. Didn't tell me what direction he was headed. Didn't tell me if he wore clean socks. And he didn't tip me."

She rubbed her temples. "I am amazed that with your temperament and arrogance that anyone stays at this hotel. It is a mystery to me why you haven't been shot."

"What?"

She gritted her teeth, spun on her heels, then muttered, "Don't press it. I have a shotgun in the wagon."

Sunny stomped out of the hotel and into the dirt street.

Mary Jane, that went well . . . Lord, You still have a lot of work to do.

With hands on her thin hips, she surveyed the street. A block away, she noticed Abraham Hermann's jewelry shop. She glanced at her team and wagon, then hiked down the dusty street.

If I leave soon, I can make it back to the ranch around dark. I shouldn't have come . . . but Abe will know. I need to find out if he seemed happy when he left with her.

She almost reached the jewelry store when a woman's voice stabbed her in the back. "Miss Cutler?"

Sunny spun around. Her eyes widened. "Carla? What are you doing here?"

The deep burgundy silk dress showcased Loganaire's wavy dark hair and the glittering gold necklace that draped her smooth, tan skin. "I was going to ask you the same thing."

"Where is he?"

"Avery? I assumed you knew that."

"Why on earth would I know?"

"When I left, I assumed he wanted to be with you on the ranch."

"You left?"

"Father wants me in New York by month's end. I went down river to catch the train, but I changed my mind. Look, I know you despise me. Sometimes I despise me. But I do care about Avery. I found I just couldn't leave. My heart forced me to turn around."

Sunny rubbed the back of her neck, trying to ease the aching stiffness. "Yes, I know. I chased him off the ranch and told him his heart belonged to you."

"Then you came to find him anyway?"

496

"I guess I decided that even second place in Avery John Creede's heart was better than any other option I had. I don't really know. Where is he, Carla?"

"I left before he returned. I just dropped Tabitha at her parents' house. They said he came to town, gathered up Ace, but didn't have any idea where he headed. Perhaps they went out to the ranch to find you."

"They weren't on the road. I don't think they headed east."

"Miss Cutler . . ."

"Call me Sunny."

"Sunny, do you hate me?"

"Not as much as I used to. It's time for me to be real honest. I do love Avery. I know I'm not much. I know I'm way beneath what he deserves. But I love him . . . and I can't help doing what my heart aches to do."

"I know how you feel, but I need Avery. Most of my life swirls with insane people making crazy demands. Being with him gives me hope for a different kind of life. I need that man. I need him badly."

Sunny glanced at the jewelry store. "I thought Mr. Hermann might know where he went."

"My thoughts too."

A balding man with thick mustache and a wide smile burst out of the back room when the bell above the front door rang.

The smile melted when he spied the women. "My word, both of you."

Carla marched to the counter. "Abraham, we're looking for Avery."

"At the same time?"

Sunny's voice was soft. "Yes, both of us. Have you seen him?"

"He stopped by yesterday morning."

"What did he want?" Carla pressed.

"To say goodbye."

Sunny licked her narrow lips. "Did he mention either of us?"

"He just said, 'she didn't want me.'"

"Didn't want him?" Sunny sighed. "Which one of us didn't want him?"

Carla drew her gloved finger across the dust on the glass case. "It sounds to me like neither of us wanted him."

"Where did he go?" Sunny asked.

"To Lander."

"Where's Lander?" Carla inquired.

"Somewhere down in Wyoming. I think it's by the Wind Mountains, but I'm not sure where they are. He said it was a long journey, and he needed to travel fast."

"Why did he go to Lander?" Sunny asked.

"The story I heard was that a man name Bitey Travers came through Ft. Benton on his way to Camp Whoop-Up . . . that's over in the British

Possessions . . . and told Mr. Creede that a friend needed him in Lander."

Sunny leaned across the counter. "What friend?"

"A friend named Dawson Wickers."

Carla tapped her fingers on the glass jeweler's case. "He's one of Avery's closest army pals."

"I think the matter was most urgent. Mr. Creede said that Wickers was to be hung in Lander, Wyoming, for the murder of a woman of questionable reputation. This man, Travers, reported that Wickers claimed innocence, but was scheduled to be hung in two weeks." Hermann hiked around the counter. "He and Ace left town yesterday morning, each leading an extra horse so they could ride night and day."

The ladies strolled out to the raised wooden sidewalk; side-by-side they surveyed the noisy, busy street.

"They don't know, do they?" Sunny offered more of a grimace than a smile.

"That the finest man on the face of this planet rode off to Wyoming?"

"Yes, and that my future has turned from vibrant colors to a dull gray."

Carla slipped her arm in Sunny's. "Well said, Mary Jane Cutler. We have both lost him, haven't we?"

"I'm not sure either of us ever had him."

"Quite right, but we came close enough to know what we are missing."

Sunny held Carla's hand. "Will you go to New York, now?"

"Yes, trying to keep up with Avery would be like traipsing across quicksand. Two steps more into the journey would swallow me up. Are you going back to the ranch?"

"I think so . . . I was so confident driving to town, but now . . . it seems more lonely going home."

"Sweet Sunny, you have to promise me one thing. If Avery shows up at your door, write to me and tell me how he is doing."

"I will, but you must do the same. If you hear from him, please let me know." Sunny kept clutching Carla's arm, her eyes burning. "I just want to know . . . that he's safe . . . and he's happy. That's all."

Carla gave Sunny a hug. "I believe under different circumstances, we could have been best friends."

Sunny grinned. "You mean, if Avery had married me, and you stopped by the ranch some day?"

Carla laughed. "No, that wouldn't work. I was thinking that if I married Avery and you came out to California some time."

"If that happened, I would show up at that almond ranch with a .44 pistol stashed under my sweet smile."

"So, you are saying, it's better for our friendship that it ends this way?"

Sunny hugged Carla. "We will both have some long, lonely nights. We waited too long, didn't we?"

Carla nodded. Tears cut a path through the make-up on her cheeks.

CHAPTER THIRTY-THREE

The clerk at the Emporium followed Sunny's every move as she trudged through the door with boots and worn shawl. "May I help you?" The middle aged lady's salt and pepper hair was pulled so tight to the back of her head, her eyes slanted.

"I want to buy a new dress."

"The ready made ginghams are over on the far wall. Or were you looking for used clothing? We do have a rack with 50¢ dresses."

"I want your best bright yellow dress." Sunny marched over to a glass door on a large oak wardrobe closet. "I believe you have one in here."

"That is our special Paris collection. I'm afraid . . ."

"Are they for sale?"

"Yes, but quite expensive, as you can imagine. Most are in the $12 to $20 range."

"Let me try on the yellow one."

"I really don't have time to dawdle."

"I am seriously considering buying that dress. Please take it out of the case."

"Those are for our select customers."

"Are you refusing to let me try it on?"

"I repeat, those dresses cost . . ."

"I heard what you said. I know what they cost. I can add. I have the money. Now, have you always been this demeaning, or has it just been years of living alone that has shriveled you up and made you this way?"

"I beg your pardon!"

"Now we have both insulted each other. Why don't we get down to business and you sell me a dress?" Sunny pulled a $20 gold coin from her purse. "I own a ranch east of town, and have money for the dress."

The woman rubbed her temples. "It was a rather bad start, wasn't it? I suppose I'm tired, but that's no excuse. The yellow one is quite lovely. Would you be interested in a matching parasol?"

"By all means."

"Shoes?"

"Whatever I can get for $20. I intend to look my best."

The clerk opened the glass door then pulled out the yellow silk dress with subdued bustle and black velvet trim. "You must be meeting a special man."

"No, I lost a special man. These clothes represent part of his memory."

Sunny felt as though she glided out of the store. Men's heads turned her way, to view the lovely lady in yellow. She spun the parasol slowly over her shoulder as she ambled down past the hotel.

It's been a long time since I've felt this dressed up. I should enjoy it. But I thought it would make me feel better than this.

She promenaded down to the Missouri and watched the current carry deep, muddy-green water east. When she closed her eyes, the past several weeks flowed across her mind, much like the river.

He came out of the hotel . . . and sat on the bench by the tree . . . I strutted down the riverbank, with the best sway and wiggle I had.

Sunny sauntered along the bank, still spinning her parasol.

Oh, Lord, what I would give to turn around and see that man sitting on the bench. That would be the last request I would ever need to make of You. I would storm over there, throw my arms around his neck, and never, ever, turn loose.

She heard some commotion in the street behind her, but refused to turn around.

I remember as a child hearing my aunt talk about how the Lord led her, but I never knew how that worked. I suppose I thought You actu-

ally showed up in person and led her by the hand. Or, I thought perhaps she heard voices no one else heard. But maybe it was just a divine idea placed in her mind.

The rustle of the silk dress caused her to take longer steps, then she stopped.

Like right now. What if You were telling me to turn around? What if it was You that prompted my heart to buy this dress, take this stroll, and now Mr. Avery John Creede is sitting on that bench by the cottonwood, waiting for the lady in yellow to turn around once again?

Is that the prompting of Your Holy Spirit? Is that what it means to be led by the Lord? This could be a total spiritual awakening for me, Lord. Maybe I'm really starting to figure this out.

She brushed down the front of her billowing silk dress and played with the black velvet covered buttons.

I'm ready now, Lord. Thank You for leading me. Thy will be done.

Sunny spun around and stared . . . at the empty bench by the cottonwood. She searched up and down the dusty street and observed horses, rigs, women, children, dogs, and men . . . but not the right man.

And now, Lord, I feel absolutely stupid. Why did I even think You were in this? Why did I think some miracle would happen? Mary Jane Cutler, you are pathetic. You are trying to be something you are not.

Go back to Denver. Go back to what you do know. Go get a job as a clerk in a store. Find a tiny room and live by yourself until your hair turns gray and you pull it tight in a bun to hide the crows' feet around your eyes.

She marched toward the dock, holding the parasol more like a shield from the cruel world and her own foolishness.

I have enough money left to make it back to Denver. I'll see if the mayor will sell the ranch for me. He can send me the money. But how can I sell something that Avery gave to me? But he did give it to me. And then abandoned me there.

Well, not really abandoned. He never said he would stay.

A sternwheeler named "Missouri Belle," waited at the dock.

I've got to leave now. I can't go back to that empty ranch. I can't. He'll have to understand that. I can run the ranch by myself, but I just don't have the heart for it.

Sunny paused outside the shipping office and dug in her handbag. The flash of burgundy inside the building caught her eye.

Carla? Of course, Carla is taking this same boat. I told her I was going back to the ranch.

Sunny pivoted on her heel, then hiked back to town. "This is absolutely crazy. Even when I make a decision about my future, I can't do it. I can't follow Your will, Lord, because I don't know what it is. I can't follow my own will, because Carla's on that same boat."

"What did you say?"

He wore a three piece, charcoal gray suit that emphasized his square jaw, sandy blond hair and two dimples when he smiled. But he had no scar.

"Excuse me, I'm afraid I was mumbling to myself."

He tipped his wide brimmed, felt hat. "I often do the same thing. It comes from spending too much time alone. I suppose we both have that same problem. I'm Linc Crowly, just arrived in town."

She shook his hand.

He seemed reluctant to turn loose. He blushed and pulled off his hat. His eyes shone a brighter blue. "I'm very sorry if I seem rude. You might think this a bit bizarre. But last night on the boat, after supper, I felt tired and turned in early." He took a deep breath. "Please hear me out . . . this is very strange. I had a dream about a yellow haired lady in a yellow dress meeting me when I arrived at Ft. Benton. And here you are. I . . . I can't explain it."

"Perhaps it was a touch of food poisoning. That sometimes accounts for strange dreams."

"But . . . here you are . . ."

"Yes . . . here I am."

"Don't you think it could be Divine Providence?"

Sunny hesitated. "I don't think so, Mr. Crowly. You see, I've been speaking to the Lord quite intensely over the past hour and He didn't mention you at all."

He slipped his arm into hers. "I have a splendid idea. Why don't you let me buy you dinner? We'll get to know each other better and sort out the mystery of this most amazing coincidence."

"I assure you, we have nothing to discuss. And I do not choose to have dinner with you."

"Good for you. Don't let yourself get pushed around by some fool who finds himself smitten with your charms, Miss . . . eh, I don't even know your name."

"Mary Jane . . . Creede."

"Well, Miss Creede . . ."

"Mrs. Creede."

He dropped her arm. "You are married?"

"Isn't that what Mrs. usually means?"

"But I didn't see a ring."

"Would you like to see the pocket revolver I carry in my purse?"

He stepped back. "My word, I've never met a woman like you."

"That's strange. I've met hundreds of men just like you, Mr. Crowly. Good day."

He jammed his hat on and meandered across the street, with a peek back at her every few steps.

Sunny turned west toward the hotel and the cottonwood tree next to the team and wagon. *Nice work, Mary Jane . . . you lied your way out of that. He was pleasant enough and certainly nice looking. And you treated him like dirt. Not your finest hour. Lord, I just didn't want to talk to him. Is there a pleasant, honest way to tell a man to get lost?*

She shoved the parasol up on the wagon seat, then circled the team and checked the rigging.

"Boys, we are going home. I've failed at finding my will . . . and the Lord's will . . . so I think I'll just sit on the porch and wait until something makes sense. Of course, that will take an act of God."

She pulled up into the wagon. "It's not a complete loss, boys. I have this beautiful new yellow dress that I'll lock in a trunk and save for my wedding day. Hah! Now, let's buy some groceries before we head home."

Two miles east of Ft. Benton, Sunny steered the team south. *Okay, I know . . . the river road is longer. But there is no hurry. Memories hide down here . . . some bad, but mostly good.*

The sun paused straight above when she reached the river. She drove the team down to a small eddy. Holding the parasol across her shoulder, she watched the river's steady flow as the horses drank.

"You two will have to get used to me talking to you. I'm a very social person and have no business living alone. You see that river? It's just like my life. I've spent my years bobbing along with my head barely above the water, going wherever the current pushed me. And now I'm being pressed back to the ranch. How long will I stay there? I don't know."

The sound of the steam whistle on the stern-wheeler turned her head. *Here comes the Missouri Belle. I might have been on it, going to Denver. I'd rather be here than in Denver. I think.*

Chugging downstream, the riverboat glided within a hundred feet of the shore. At the railing, several men tipped their hats. She nodded. A group of tall men clustered near the rear. In the middle, she spotted a woman in burgundy.

Carla! I've never known anyone who could attract men like you do.

None of the men turned to view the lady in the farm wagon and bright yellow dress. Not even the blond headed, blue eyed Mr. Linc Crowly.

Sunny leaned back and laughed out loud. "Mr. Crowly, you have no idea what you got yourself into. Whatever happens, I'm sure you deserve it. He's all yours, Miss Loganaire."

She turned the team back to the road. *That scene made my day . . . well, almost.*

The sun slid low on the western horizon when she spied the ranch barn. She surveyed the horses that milled in the corral.

"You've got friends, boys. I didn't know the Indians brought that many. I guess I didn't count this morning. I think I'm horse rich."

I might be able to move back to Denver in style. If, of course, that's where the current leads me.

She parked the wagon behind the barn, then turned the team out with the others. She trekked to the house, but tensed when she heard a commotion in the barn. She stopped at the doorway as her eyes adjusted to the shadows. A gray haired man, stripped to the waist, hovered over a buck of water.

"What's going on?" she called out. "This is my barn."

The man grabbed a suit coat to cover his bare chest. "Oh, my . . . excuse me. I just wanted to clean up a little first."

Sunny felt her neck relax. "No, no . . . that's fine. I've been gone all day. I'm just not used to people stopping by."

"Thank you so much . . ." He waved his hand at her.

She turned around toward the house. "My, you are a modest man."

"I come from a family of modest people."

"Are you alone, or did you bring your family?"

"Just my wife, Emaline."

"Where is she?"

"I'm afraid she got a little too much sun, and I sent her in the house . . . your house. I didn't know who . . . I'm sure she's alright by now. I'll have her come out."

"No, no, that's fine. Frontier hospitality takes a little getting used to."

"That's what my Emaline says. She's from Baltimore."

"I spent most of my life in Denver, which isn't like eastern cities, but quite different than here, I can assure you."

"Yes, the challenges are quite diverse out here, aren't they, Miss . . . ?"

"Miss Mary Jane . . . eh, Mary Jane Cutler."

"You may turn around now. I'm looking decent again . . . I'm . . ."

Sunny gaped at the man's clerical collar.

"I'm Reverend Jeremiah Clithe."

"A . . . a preacher?" Sunny choked out the words.

"At the moment, I'm a circuit preacher for several rural Methodist churches."

"I can't believe this."

"I trust you have nothing against Methodists."

"Oh, no . . . in fact, you are a godsend."

"That's nice to hear."

"I struggled just this morning with how to

know what God wants me to do. I'm so new at this. I wanted so very much for someone to help me understand, and here you are."

"Yes, here I am . . . actually . . ."

"You must spend the night with me. You and your wife, of course."

"I don't think that will be practical, you see, after . . ."

"Reverend, I need some spiritual counsel. You must stay."

"I'm sure we'll be able to stop back by at a future date and . . ."

"Whatever business you have will wait until we've had a chance to visit. Don't you see? The Lord led you here. I'm not letting you go until you accomplish what He has led you here to do."

"Yes, well, I suppose . . ."

"Good. Now, would you please grab that box of groceries out of the back of the wagon? I'll get supper started. This is so wonderful. The Lord did answer my prayer."

Sunny hiked up to the house, the parasol over her shoulder. A thin lady in a long, dark gray dress, hair stacked on her head, scooted out on the uncovered porch.

Sunny held out her hand. "You must be Emaline, the reverend's wife. I'm Mary Jane Cutler."

Emaline clutched Sunny's arm with both hands.

"I was such a mess after the ride out here. I must confess I used your combs to straighten up a bit."

"Use anything you want. I am so excited to have you and the reverend here."

"I imagine you are."

"Are people always this happy to see you?"

"On occasions like this, it is common."

"Please come in and visit while I fix some supper. I've been in anguish over finding the Lord's will, and you and the reverend can . . ."

"Honey, you don't need to fix supper. And now might not be the time for a theological discussion."

They both turned to watch Reverend Clithe struggle with a large box of groceries.

"Jeremiah, set those inside. We'll get started with the service before dark." She turned toward Sunny. "I think we should have it right here, don't you?"

A church service on my front porch? "I suppose so. I didn't realize how these visits worked."

"Mary Jane, don't worry, everyone gets nervous."

"Do I need to get some chairs? A hymnbook or anything?"

"Oh my, no. It's quite simple, nothing formal needed when you're out on a ranch."

"Do we stand the whole time?"

"Yes, but it won't take long."

"Like I said . . ."

"Honey . . . relax, there's nothing to it. Just follow Jeremiah's lead."

The reverend emerged from the house, white linen stole drooped down like a scarf, black book in hand. He turned to his wife. "Call the other witness."

Sunny gazed around, then looked up at the empty evening sky. *She's going to call who? What? This is very strange. Lord, are You sure You led the right people to me?*

Emaline traipsed across the dirt patio to the other portion of the house and rapped on the door. "Mr. Emerson, we need you out here now."

Sunny twirled around, yellow dress and hair flying.

In a new suit and tie, a mop haired young man hobbled out on the porch.

"Ace!" she choked.

"Howdy, Miss Sunny . . . beautiful dress."

"What are you doing here?"

"Me and the reverend's wife are supposed to be the witnesses."

"Witnesses?"

"Don't worry, I'm riding back to Ft. Benton with the Clithes after the service."

"I thought you were on your way to Lander."

"That's what we wanted others to think, if you catch my drift. We figure ever'one lookin' for us will tramp off to Wyomin'." Ace turned to the minister. "Where do you want me to stand?"

"Right here will be fine. Emaline, if you stand over there, and Miss Cutler, if you would hand your parasol to my wife, then turn your back to the barn."

"But . . . what? Wait. I . . ."

Reverend Clithe took her shoulders and turned her around. "Now, Mr. Creede, if you would just take Miss Cutler's arm and . . ."

Sunny spun back.

Scrubbed face.

Piercing eyes.

Clean shaven

Hair slicked down.

A big beautiful, wonderful scar.

A new suit and tie.

And a silly grin.

"Avery!" Sunny threw her arms around his neck and bawled. "I thought I lost you. I almost died when you weren't in Ft. Benton. I can't believe this. I can't believe you're here. Thank You, Jesus."

She mashed her mouth onto Avery's and could taste her salty tears trickle down their lips.

Ace pulled back with a sillier grin. "I don't think the reverend said it was time to kiss the bride yet."

Reverend Clithe stepped closer. "We really should proceed while we still have some day-light."

Avery turned them both to face the minister.

515

"Mr. Creede, do you have the ring?"

Avery pulled out a purple velvet bag. "I've had it for a long time. I hope you like diamonds and rubies."

Sunny nodded as she dabbed her eyes on the sleeve of her dress.

"Are you ready to proceed, Mr. Creede?"

"Yes, sir, I am."

"Are you ready to proceed, Miss Cutler?"

Sunny felt a lump in her throat. "Yes, I believe . . . NO!"

"No?" Reverend Clithe repeated.

"NO?" Avery boomed.

"You don't want to marry Uncle Avery?" Ace asked.

"I didn't say that. I said, I was not ready to proceed. I am not going to marry a man until after he asks me to marry him. I have not been asked."

"Would you like a few moments alone?" Emaline asked.

"He can say it right here with witnesses."

She clutched his hand while he dropped on one knee.

"Eh, Miss Mary Jane Cutler, will you marry me?"

"Do you love me and me alone, Avery John Creede?"

"You are suppose to say, 'yes' or 'no.' "

"You didn't answer my question."

"Mary Jane, I love you more than my words can express. More than any other woman in the world. I reckon it will take me a lifetime to prove to you the extent of that love. Now, do you love me?"

Tears rolled down her cheeks. She licked her lips, then sobbed, "More than life itself."

"Will you marry me?"

Sunny threw her shoulders back. "Yes, I will."

Reverend Clithe nodded. "Good. Good. Now let's proceed. Miss Cutler, you may release his hand for the time being."

"I'm not turning loose of this man until we are completely married."

The next few moments tumbled by in a blur. The vows, a prayer, some scripture and a ring placed on her left hand, while Sunny clutched Avery with her right.

"By the authority committed unto me as a minister of the Gospel of Jesus Christ, I now pronounce Avery John Creede and Mary Jane Cutler Creede, husband and wife, in the name of the Father, Son and Holy Ghost. What God has joined together, let no man separate. Amen."

"Congratulations, Miss Sunny." Ace's attempt at a kiss slid off her cheek and landed on her ear. "I reckon I can call you Auntie now."

"You may not call me Auntie until my hair turns gray. I don't intend for that to happen for a long, long time."

Avery tried to shake the clergyman's hand, but she wouldn't turn him loose. "Thanks for coming clear out here, Reverend Clithe. I will never forget your graciousness."

He patted their clinched hands. "It was a delight for us as well. By the way, Mrs. Creede, you are officially married now. You may release his hand."

"I didn't say I would turn loose when we were officially married." Sunny raised her eyebrows. "I said, I would not turn loose until we are completely married."

Mrs. Clithe grabbed the reverend's arm. "Get your things, Jeremiah. It's time to leave."

Center Point Publishing

600 Brooks Road ● PO Box 1
Thorndike ME 04986-0001 USA

(207) 568-3717

US & Canada:
1 800 929-9108
www.centerpointlargeprint.com